e. marie robertson

beyond this dark horizon

iona duology, book 2

Book cover by New Moon Media

First edition: 2026

For my Hearties. You know who you are.

1

WE ONLY GET A handful of days to process our disastrous mission to Bardazel before things go from bad to worse.

The renegade flight to recover the Planetary Equity Alliance members was supposed to be a key to Iona's independence, a core component in our escape from the Company's grasp forever. Instead, it's a colossal failure. We find no PEA members, no clues to who hired Kerrit Arduval—in fact, we find nothing at all. The infrastructure, the buildings, and even the sand is gone.

Within days of our return, Iona's petition for Independent Core World status is rejected by the Governing Council. Wenda's disappointed, but not surprised. Without the rescued Planetary Equity Alliance members on-planet, Iona falls well short of the required minimum population. We next learn that the Company's application for Transactional Jurisdiction over Iona has been approved. We'd held out hope that there was still a chance a decision would at least be delayed after Arden, Graham, Dr. Heron, Lt. Nam, Fallon, Karloa, and Tommas all submitted statements to the Governing Council countering the Company's narrative of risk and lawlessness on Iona. But these eyewitness accounts were apparently meaningless in the face of the Company's influence and cash.

The proctor satellite arrives only an hour or so after the Governing Council's announcement. It must have been sitting in near space, waiting for the decision to be finalized—more proof the Company never had any doubt of the outcome.

The ugly thing hangs above Iona in synchronous low orbit, a blood-red blemish in our sky. During the day, it looks relatively benign; sometimes obscured by our gritty atmosphere. At twilight, it takes on a sinister appearance, menacing our little moons with its glow and painting the horizon with a pulsing scarlet light.

As I cross Iona Town on my way to visit Karloa, I'm struck by how still and silent it's become. The pads are empty, there's no rushing to and fro, people aren't laughing and congregating in the square. The few Ionians I encounter simply nod solemnly in my direction and hurry on their way. I used to like walking at this hour, but that thing in our sky makes me feel like I'm being watched. Clearly other Ionians have the same reaction.

"What is that thing?" Karloa asks, peering at the satellite from the window of the room she shares with Tommas in Clinical. In the fading twilight, its beacon tints her face red with each flash.

"It's a proctor satellite," I explain. "The Company uses them to keep track of inventory whenever something happens that concerns them. It'll be here at least until their Success Team arrives."

I can't say the term without cringing. Karloa notices and snickers a little. She takes one last look, then resolutely taps the windowpane, activating the window's privacy mode and blocking the view. "There. Better."

A small table stands near the window, along with two chairs scrounged from a meeting room down the hall. Karloa, a cup of hot tea in her hand, settles into one of these and curls her legs under her. I sit down across from her.

"How are you doing? Is your memory coming back?" I ask.

I'm coming to like Karloa very much and I enjoy visiting her, but this is the real reason I'm here. She's the last link we have left to Kerrit Arduval. If she can remember something, anything, about who he might have been working for, it could turn this whole Transactional Jurisdiction ploy on its head and keep the Company off Iona for a long while.

"I'm remembering things every day, but it's the oddest, most useless garbage—almost nothing about my brother or the incident on Bardazel. I'm disappointed in myself," she says, her face crumpling in disappointment. "I recall Kerrit talking plenty about how important he was and how rich his 'mission' was going to make him, but I'm either blocking the details or he never mentioned them."

Karloa huddles in her chair. I remember the ache of not being able to right a wrong you believe you're at least partially responsible for, and I empathize with her more than she can imagine.

"I wish I could do more to help," she says with a sigh.

I rub my forehead reflexively, fighting off despair. I keep reminding myself that it's early yet; Karloa and Tommas have been out of stasis for less than two weeks. She could still remember something that could help us home in on who hired Kerrit Arduval to wipe out Iona's population and leave our planet up for grabs. But every minute that ticks by without a new clue feels like an eternity, especially with that red blinking blister in our sky.

"Don't worry about it, Karloa. Please. You were as much his victim as anyone else—possibly more so. Focus on getting stronger and healthier. You and Tommas have a wonderful life ahead of you. Keep thinking about that."

A sudden flash of realization crosses her features, her eyes widening and her eyebrows arching upward.

"You should ask Tommas," she says. "He'd heard of Kerrit before he came to Bardazel, and we talked about what an odd coincidence that was back then. Something about knowing Kerrit by reputation? Maybe from when Tommas worked for Darwin-Cross; I'm not sure of the context."

I can tell by her phrasing and the casual way she tosses out the company name that Karloa has no idea how infamous Darwin-Cross is and doesn't understand the significance of Tommas'—and her brother's—connection to it. I rein in my astonishment and sound nearly normal when I respond, "That would be great. Is he around?"

"He's in a rehab session with Macha right now, but if you can wait, he should be finished soon," Karloa says. Her face is etched with relief; she's delighted to have contributed something that might help us. She can't imagine how big a storm she may have set in motion.

"Sure," I tell her. "I'll make a couple of hails and be right back."

I hurry down to the lobby and ping Arden. I'm so excited I can barely breathe.

His response is a mirror-image of my own.

"*That's* unanticipated." he says, the pitch of his voice escalating in surprise. "Last I heard, Yeva Darwin was cooling her heels on some reclaimed asteroid paradise and atomizing anyone who dropped by for a visit. It fits that she could be involved, though. Somebody could have made her an offer she couldn't refuse."

"Weren't her business assets frozen after she was censured by the Governing Council?" I ask. "I thought she'd been on house arrest for the last ten years."

"There are lots of ways around those rules for people as rich, connected, and driven as Yeva Darwin. If she's already made a move on Bardazel, that could explain what happened to the terrain."

I'd had the same thought myself. Darwin's controversial business practice of 'reclaiming' barren asteroids, moons, and mini-planets always began with a thorough scrub of the surface. The contention that she was actually eradicating native biology in order to replace it with genetically modified flora and fauna tailored to the preferences of her wealthy clients was what got her in trouble with the Council to begin with, although they were never able to prove that she did any real harm. Plus, the fiercely reclusive scientist never hired more than a handful of people to work with her directly. That Tommas was one of them adds to a potential link between Arduval and Darwin-Cross and feels like too much to be a coincidence.

"This could be the connection we've been looking for," I say, the excitement bubbling up into my chest. "I'm going to talk to Tommas in a little while, so I'll be late getting home. We'll talk more when I get there."

By the time I make my way back upstairs, Tommas has returned. He's more than happy to chat, and we settle into a conference room with a window overlooking the scrappy little scrub garden in the courtyard below.

He already looks stronger, verging on healthy—not like a man who was awakened a few weeks ago from a months-long stasis. The only tip-off that he's still an inpatient is the glowing yellow admit chip embedded in the back of his hand.

I'm comfortable sitting with the *real* Tommas. His personality is easy-going, relaxed, and open; essentially the exact opposite of the imposter I initially got to know as 'Tommas Berinbart.'

"I thought it would be better to talk in here," he says, gesturing around at the pool-blue walls of the conference room. "It's a little more pleasant than a patient room. Plus, Karloa ... I'm not sure how much more she can stand to hear about her brother. It's all still very upsetting for her."

"I know. I hate to keep asking her about him, but we're desperate for any potential leads."

"We both remember new things every day, so keep asking." He smiles a little, his expression becoming contemplative. "It's an odd process, this re-entry. She's a little discombobulated by it. I'm grateful it's happening at all."

We sit in silence for a moment, looking out at the scrubby little plants in the courtyard, surviving despite their surroundings. I wonder if he sees a reflection of himself in those tough little succulents and vines.

"So. Kerrit." He says the name with a certain finality. I don't think Tommas has many enemies, but it's clear from this one word alone that he and Kerrit Arduval were not friends.

"Karloa said you'd heard of him before you met on Bardazel. Is that right?"

A chuckle escapes him, more ironic than amused.

"To be specific, I heard my former boss call him a liar and a cretin and threaten to kill him if he ever contacted her again. That's another thing I didn't want Karloa to overhear."

This is already not going the way I expected. I'm simultaneously disappointed and intrigued.

"Was that while you were working for Darwin-Cross?"

He stares out at the little courtyard garden wistfully. "Yeah. I worked for Yeva for several years. This happened a few months before I went to Bardazel."

"That recently? How did she get around the Governing Council shutdown?"

"They only shuttered the corporate entity that was Darwin-Cross. Yeva has plenty of customers that come to her directly. She figured out how to run everything from that punky little asteroid of hers, so she doesn't have to leave. The whole 'house arrest' thing didn't even put a dent in her profit margins; it just changed the business model."

"Was Arduval working for her?"

"No. He kept pestering her about some 'great opportunity' and how he'd cut her in if she'd fund him until this thing came through. He was incredibly persistent about it. And also annoying as hell."

"She wasn't interested?"

"Yeva doesn't do profit-sharing, and she doesn't fund anyone else's interests. She doesn't have to."

I remember Arduval's overinflated sense of his own importance and his grasping, preening personality. Mix in the fact that the Governing Council's decree did nothing to shut down Darwin's business, and it's starting to look like the clear motive-and-opportunity Arden and I speculated about.

I decide to be blunt.

"Be totally honest with me," I say. "Did Yeva Darwin send you to Bardazel? Was that where Kerrit's 'opportunity' was?"

Not only is Tommas is completely unphased by my question, he seems pleased by it somehow. "Yeva would like you," he says. "You're right, she's the reason I was on Bardazel. She sent me there to track Arduval and learn whether this opportunity was real."

"Was it?"

He looks down and contemplates his hands, rubbing them together slowly. "You already know the answer to that," he says. "The sand did exactly what he said it did, and someone was already moving to clear Bardazel of its population, one way or another. Yeva was never going to partner with Kerrit Arduval. She had nothing to do with what happened to me, or on Bardazel, or here on Iona. That was all his doing, maybe entirely on his own."

"He wasn't working for Darwin-Cross at all?"

"No. Part of his 'business proposition' involved double-crossing whoever had hired him if Yeva made him a better offer. He obviously had no idea who he was dealing with. Yeva's opportunistic, but she has a strong sense of fairness. She wanted no part of this dirty business."

"Then who was he working for?"

I hold my breath. The spark in Tommas' eyes goes flat, and he shakes his head. My spirit sinks before he speaks.

"I don't know. Yeva might have found out at some point, but if she did, she never told me. My charge was to go to Bardazel, find out if Arduval was telling the truth about the sand, and get a sample to her. Of course, my assignment kind of went out the window once I met Karloa. Yeva understood and let me off the hook when I told her how crazy things were getting. All I could think about was getting Karloa out of there and away from him. It was obvious he was unhinged and dangerous, and I was terrified something was going to happen to her ..."

His voice falters and he stares out at the garden again, his face crumpling as he fights back a wave of emotion.

I let him take a moment, then try to sound as reassuring as I can.

"You did get her away from him," I say. "Now you're both okay and you have a new home here with us, and a chance to have happy lives. You did good."

His turns to me again. "Thank you for that," he says. "It means a lot to hear it. I'm sorry I can't give you the answers you want. I know this is plaguing you—all of you. If I remember anything else, I'll ping you right away."

I try not to let my disappointment show as we part. He's doing the best he can, but we're still no closer to learning who unleashed Arduval to wreak havoc on Bardazel and then Iona. More alarming still, Tommas raises the possibility that

Arduval was making decisions entirely on his own. If that's the case, we might never find out who offered up the money he was so happy to kill for.

I walk out of Clinical and look east, where the proctor sits heavy in the sky, beyond our vacant landing pads. The Company has throttled its business here in the wake of Arduval's attack, and prohibited any other entity's ships from landing, yet it sends a device to "monitor ship traffic" and "track inbound materials."

Ship traffic that they've made certain isn't coming. Materials they know won't be inbound.

No, I'm sure the satellite is there to track us, so no one can leave undetected and spread word of their false narrative. They want us stuck here, waiting for whatever they want to do to us.

They won't simply show up one day and take over—that's not the Company's style. It's too controversial and attention-grabbing a gesture, and the Company cares about optics almost more than it cares about profit. But they can imprison us on our own planet and get away with it for who knows how long.

We have to learn who Arduval was working for and find a way to make it public in spectacular fashion. We then have to convince the Governing Council of the truth. I have no idea how can we do either of those things with no reliable communications, no connections, no money, and no plan.

My teeth clench and my chest tightens as I think about it. The last time my home was threatened this way, the Company took everything from me, and I let them. Then, I did nothing about it for almost a decade.

I won't let that happen again, no matter what it costs me.

By the time I walk into our Common Room, the evening meal is done and most of my podmates have headed to their quarters. Fallon still sits at the far end of the big communal table, glued to a holotablet. I drop into place next to her. She doesn't look up from her holo.

"That damn satellite is jamming our communications," she mutters. "Nothing is going out over normal channels. Plenty coming in, but nothing going out."

"Do I want to hear what kind of stuff is coming in?"

"Probably not." Fallon tosses the holo unceremoniously onto the table, where it continues to scroll. "More trash about lawless troublemakers causing problems for the good and gentle people of Iona. We get mentioned a lot. So does Arden. Graham is conspicuously absent."

"That's probably his family influence at work," Arden says, coming in from the kitchen carrying two plates of Hinn's delicious hash. "He may be the odd man out, but he's still a Thorn."

"Odd man out?" I ask. "Wasn't he planning to send all Fallon's research materials back to his family business?"

"Sure, but he didn't do that, he returned everything to her so she could use it to develop the antidotes and immunity serum. My outside sources say the elder Thorns were not delighted by his impulse to do the right thing."

He sets one plate down in front of me with a flourish, then sits beside me with the other for himself. His eyes search my face for clues, and after I shake my head no, he sighs and drops his head. We both begin to eat in silence. After a few bites, he pulls out his own holo and begins to flip through the floating imagery. I see one picture of a much younger Arden armed to the teeth, shouting and brandishing a fist at the camera, then one of Fallon from her most recent Company promotion stream, looking precise and perfect in her favorite burgundy jumpsuit. Finally, there's a singularly unimpressive image of me—a wildly unflattering shot from my old Company employee file, nearly ten years old. My eyes are hollowed with dark circles under them, and I'm showing no emotion of any kind. That must have been right after my promotion, a few months after Arden disappeared.

Even though it's the distant past, it still cuts at me like a rusty knife sometimes, dragging at the remaining loose ends and fraying tensions between us. Before I get stuck in my own angsty feedback loop, Fallon's voice pulls me back to the present.

"Are you kidding me?" she shrieks, her volume soaring up half-a-dozen decibels as she grabs the holo and scrolls back to an announcement that flashed by. She thrusts the holo into Arden's face. "Good luck convincing me you didn't know about this in advance, Mr. Oh-Let's-Give-the-Company-a-Chance."

Arden looks truly perplexed as he squints at the holo screen. “What?”

Fallon thumbs the display into the air in front of us. It’s an internal Company communique entitled ‘Changes in Governance on Iona.’ She proceeds to read aloud.

“Effective immediately and in accordance with the granting of Transactional Jurisdiction on Iona are the following changes in governance. Medical Lead Macha Timin is demoted to assistant medical lead, replaced by Dr. Janelle Heron. Task Coordinator Graham Thorn is relieved of duty with a replacement to be determined after a process evaluation. Security Lead Maybree Zaitsev is relieved of duty and replaced by Commander Arden Wilson.”

“Arden, what the hell?” I ask. He’s already shaking his head.

“I know nothing about this,” he says, waving one hand in the air as if to ward off the accusations coming his way. “This is the first I’ve heard of it, I swear.”

Fallon isn’t swayed and kicks off a loud argument with Arden. “That’s a real stretch to believe,” she snaps. “We knew you were still on the Company payroll, but this is abhorrent. Come on now, tell us all about how this is a sign of all the great things the Company is going to do for Iona.”

“First, Transactional Jurisdiction means we’re all on the Company payroll for as long as it might last. Second, it might not be a bad thing for us. If I’m in a position of power, I could ...”

“Seriously, Arden, don’t come at me with that garbage. I’m not ignorant of how you continue to work the system to your advantage.”

“I’m not working the system, I’m thinking practically. If you consider how we can position ...”

“What about Maybree?” I interrupt. “What does this mean for her? She’s our friend, our podmate. She’s had her position snatched away from her. What’s she going to do?”

Fallon and Arden both fall silent and have the decency to look vaguely ashamed of themselves. They’re still quiet and ignoring each other when Maybree comes into the pod. Her face is pale and her eyes are red-rimmed; her expression is somewhere between shock and misery. She takes us all in with a glassy gaze, then drops into one of the chairs at the hearth.

"Maybree," I say softly. "We just found out. I'm so sorry."

"I had no idea this was happening," Arden says. "I'm going to reject the appointment and demand you be reinstated."

She favors Arden with a wan half-smile and responds haltingly.

"That's kind of you, but no. I don't need you to do that."

"But I want to. They have no case for replacing you."

"True," she says, her voice still shaky. "There's more to it than what you saw in the announcement. You see, the Company didn't dismiss me. I resigned."

I can tell by the way she delivers the news that this wasn't *exactly* a choice. My guess is that she never had a chance against the Company's expertise in psychological warfare, but I let her tell her story anyway.

"I got a private hail from some Company boss this morning. I figured they would be about changing stuff, since the takeover was approved," Maybree begins.

Arden opens his mouth to correct her, but I drive my foot sharply into his ankle under the table. His mouth closes again quickly.

"It was one of the Tactical guys. He might be your boss, Arden. A guy named Shimauy?"

"That's the Tactical Security Chief," Arden confirms. "He's a couple of bosses up from my boss."

"Oh." A flash of anxiety crosses Maybree's face. "He said a lot about my performance here and how well I was handling *the situation*. I tried to tell him there wasn't a situation, but he seemed convinced. He kept at it for the whole conversation."

Of course he would. No highly placed Company official is going to admit any deviation from the chosen narrative.

"You resigned?" I prompt.

"Well, I did, but not right then." Maybree gets her thoughts back on track and continues. "He said I had talent and a real gift for security and was doing such an amazing job and all this other stuff that's nice to hear."

"Let me guess, he started asking why you were wasting your talent on this crappy little planet with no opportunities for you," I interject. The way they work is so obvious when you've been through it.

"Yeah. When I didn't fall for that, he made me an offer."

"An offer?" Arden's anxious, and I hope he's remembering when the Company made *him* an offer, nearly ten years ago.

"Some classified job doing some security thing he kept saying I was perfect for. That's the thing, though, he wouldn't tell me what the job was or where. He was only specific about the pay. He said he couldn't tell me more until I'd accepted it. Then he said I'd be doing Iona a favor to move on and all this other not-so-nice stuff ..." Her voice falters and I hear the stress come in behind her words. I remember this part too; the way they make you feel like you're an incredible prize one second and selfish trash the next.

"So you took the offer," I say, my heart bursting with sympathy.

Maybree shakes her head. "No. I told him I only wanted to do what was right for Iona, so I resigned, period. I told him I thought you should take over, Arden. I'm sorry I didn't get a chance to talk to you about it. I didn't realize they'd announce it right away."

Now we're all in shock, for more reasons than one.

"Does this mean Arden's not a dangerous insurrectionist anymore?" Fallon asks, tapping the table with one long fingernail. "I can't wait to see what the stream thinks about that."

"It's weird," Maybree says. "He didn't miss a beat when I said Arden's name. I thought I'd have to make a case for it, but he said he admired me for trying to do the right thing for Iona and accepted my resignation."

It's too easy, too simple. I look from Arden to Maybree and have a bad feeling about the way this has been handled.

Meanwhile, Maybree's on the verge of breaking down.

"Is there anything else you need to tell us?" I ask, as gently as possible. The question alone makes her tears flow.

"I kind of got ahead of myself, I guess, and I forgot that the Company is controlling our money now," she says. "After he accepted my resignation, Shimauy told me I have 48 hours to leave. If I'm not on the payroll or not supported by someone who is, I can't be on Iona. So they'll be sending a skiff for me tomorrow. I'm going back to Caleighn. I'm going home."

Before any of us can react, Fallon is barking into her comm. "Mom, get over here right away. Bring everybody with you. Yes, even him."

WITHIN A FEW MINUTES, the group from the Preservation Theater pod arrives, and ten people settle into our Common Room. Fallon's mother looks sleek and statuesque though she's wearing the same dowdy serviceable clothing as the rest of us. Fanny sits arm-in-arm with Wenda, who's taking the news of Maybree's impending departure hard. Bringing up the rear is Graham, looking stressed and exhausted. Rather than sit, he stands at the side of the room, leaning against the hearth.

"What can we do about this?" Fallon asks her mother pointedly. "Maybree and Graham can't leave; we need them here. We can't let the Company start flinging people off the planet."

"I'm not sure what we can do," she replies. "No one asked me if I was willing to become Medical Lead; one of Chairman Fine's henchmen merely sent me a communique announcing I'd been appointed. I took it upon myself to draw up a contract with Macha that makes it clear I hold *the title* of Medical Lead, but otherwise everything else is precisely as it's always been. Although I did write in a fat salary for her, since we're playing with Company money now."

"Graham, have you received a 48-hour ultimatum also?" I ask.

Graham's posture straightens and rubs his hands together, a habit I've noticed that signals he's fighting anxiety.

"I have. They won't even let my family send a ship to pick me up. They insist on loading me onto an automated skiff and dropping me at Meridian Station. Assumably someone from Thorn Industries will show up to collect me. If not, I'll spend some time enjoying myself in the Personal Evolution Annex until someone figures out I'm spending family money on sex toys and personal Attendants."

Fallon rolls her eyes aggressively at Graham, then turns to her mother.

"Can you put them on the staff in Clinical?" asks Fallon. "Maybe come up with some kind of contract the way you did with Macha?"

"I'm afraid not. We squeezed through a loophole to create that contract—since Macha was demoted and not dismissed, she still had an officially recognized position. Our contract significantly expands that position, but it's classified as a change to an existing assignment, which the dunderheads in Personnel haven't thought yet to ban. Maybree and Graham have been relieved of duty altogether, so we'd have to create all-new positions for them. New positions must go through the Company's assigned Success Team. We don't know who they are yet, so it's obvious they won't be here before that 48-hour window expires."

"Can you just not go?" I ask. "Ignore the skiff when it arrives?"

"There would definitely be, uh, negative consequences for them and for Iona," Arden says. He looks dubious.

"I'm game to try that if you like," Graham says with a shrug. "How much worse for me do they think they can make it?"

Maybree isn't having it.

"I appreciate what you're all trying to do, but I don't want your help, not like this," she says, her face reddening and her voice shaking with emotion. "I did what I did; it was my choice. It's fine; I want to go home. I haven't seen my mom in like six years, and my little sister is almost grown up and I hardly know her. The last few months have been a lot, okay? It will be good to have some time to get my head together. I won't be gone forever. You guys will get through this, and Iona will become an Independent Core World, and then I'll come back. I will, Wenda, I promise. You can visit me on Caleighn, my mom and sister would love you. I'll be okay, I swear. We'll all be okay."

Wenda begins sobbing inconsolably. Maybree, shattered and fighting back tears of her own, hurries to her side. They wrap their arms around each other and weep into one another's shoulders.

Watching them, I've never been more certain that we absolutely will *not* be okay. At least Maybree has a home and family waiting for her. Graham has a fortune to fall back on, even if his family relationships are strained. Fallon and her mother have each other, and at least for now, Dr. Heron is still held in high regard by the Company hierarchy. When I look at Arden, I see a man I love who is supportive of me, but not without the shadow of the person who left me, the secret-keeper who made decisions for me that dramatically affected the course of my life. I wonder if when he looks at me, he sees me as I am, or the girl he 'protected' by destroying her spirit and leaving her behind.

Maybree excuses herself to start packing; Wenda goes with her. The rest of us talk far into the night, trying to think of solutions to problems that haven't yet occurred. A news item comes over the stream describing the "situation" on Iona as "rapidly stabilizing" thanks to the work and guidance of "undercover operative Tactical Commander Arden Wilson." I have to snatch the holo out of Fallon's hand to keep her from throwing it across the room.

"They had to say something, or his appointment would seem weird," I say.

"His appointment *is* weird," she responds, carefully making sure Arden is out of earshot. "I know Maybree thinks it's her doing, but the Company doesn't give a rip what we think, and they didn't have to accept her suggestion. It's some kind of set-up. We just haven't figured out yet how they're going to use it against us."

Later that night as we climb into our hammock, Arden promises he'll use his new role to find a way through for Iona. "I'm going to play along with the Company to get as much out of them as I can," he says. "I hope you can remember that while I'm playing along with them, it's an act and my heart is with you." His tone is warm; he's trying to be reassuring, but the effect of his words is the exact opposite.

"And you remember that if I'm not able to see the line between your 'play acting' and your true thoughts and feelings, you might have played along too far," I respond. He blanches and looks away from me for one moment too long to make me comfortable.

"You can't keep secrets from me anymore, Arden," I say. "If there's anything circulating in your networks or between your alliance members, you have to tell me. If you're put on a special assignment, I need to know. No more secrets, not even little ones, not even for my own good. Especially not for my own good."

He takes my chin in his hand and tilts it up toward his face, looking hard into my eyes. "What if something could take you away from me if you knew it?" he asks. "Or endanger your life? How can I ever make that choice?"

"You *don't*," I say. "You tell me everything, and then you trust me to be capable of managing myself and making my own decisions based on facts. You have to be humble enough to admit you might not know what's best for me, or what's right, or what's destined to happen—and if you do, that doesn't mean I have to accept your view over my own." He's never heard words this strong from me before, but really—it's past time. His eyebrows knit together in a worried V briefly, then he lets out a long breath.

"You're right," he says. "I promise, no more secrets. No more withholding. No more assumptions."

"Thank you," I say. He presses his lips to mine and we share a long kiss. When we turn out the light, Arden falls asleep, but my brain keeps working. The tenderness of his fingers caressing my cheek and the sincerity in his eyes makes me believe, at least, that *he* believes he'll keep to his promise, but I'm not completely reassured. Part of me remains wary of letting my guard down. I'm not sure whether it's our past or our future keeping me on edge.

I've barely slept by the time Holly rings the rising chimes, and the Common Room begins to echo with the sounds of our pod coming to life—although it's a different kind of life than we've known previously. No ships coming in means no landers to unload, no business to process, no tasks piling up, no warehouse goods to catalog, no hustle and bustle on the General Channel with assignments and complaints and banter. Arden receives an early ping about a meeting with Company higher-ups, no doubt to receive his marching orders as the new Security Lead. Maybree escorts him to what used to be her workspace, now cleared of her personal items and projects, to get him up to speed on her activities and processes.

I walk over to the Theater to see how Wenda's feeling. Thc vibe in their pod is similar to my own; lackluster, frozen. Wenda sits at their communal table with Fanny and Graham; all three look dejected and tired. After greetings and a hug, Wenda heads into the kitchen to make more coffee.

"Any ETA on the skiffs?" I ask. Graham shakes his head.

"Not yet. I'm guessing tomorrow."

"Any other news?"

"The stream is delighted with sneaky hero Arden Wilson, who apparently single-handedly quelled a violent planetwide uprising using only his sparkling personality and radical hair care products," he quips. Fanny snickers behind her hand.

"That's the first joke I've heard you make in eight months," I say. Graham shifts in his chair and props his elbows on the table in front of him. Despite the lightness in his words, it doesn't extend to his face or demeanor.

"I can afford to make jokes because the individual stakes for me are low," he says. "My family is so worried about the illustrious Thorn reputation that they'll make sure I don't suffer a day of consequences, no matter what happens here. In fact, I wouldn't be surprised if it turns out they're behind my dismissal. I don't want to leave. I want to be here, fighting for Iona."

"Maybe you can do more from the outside," Fanny offers, half-seriously. "Weasel your way back into your family's good graces and then use your fortune for nefarious purposes backing Iona's push for Independent Core World status."

Graham grins at her. "I've always liked the way you think, Fanny. That would be a much better use of my family money than sex toys and Annex Attendants."

"You don't really think they'd abandon you on Meridian Station, do you?" I ask. "They can't be *that* put out with you."

His mouth quirks dismissively.

"I'm sure they're trying to figure out how to pressure me back into the fold right now. If they dump me on Meridian, it's only because they have some odious task for me to perform that will make rejoining the family feel like a better option."

I wince. "That's ... appalling."

"Yes, yes, it is. Now you know why I stayed on Bardazel and let my family go back to Home World without me all those years ago."

I remember the first chat we had about Home World and family, and those walks we used to take up into the hills around Iona; how he let me see things through his eyes in those extended conversations, whether good or ill. I hear him again tell me he was more Bardazelian than Home Worlder, and how he might one day be tempted to go back to Home World only for the right person or situation. I wonder if the right person might be *himself*, if perhaps the situation is something like Arden's "playing along."

I catch Graham looking at me. From the warmth of his smile, I can guess he's remembering too. We had a pleasant connection then and were truly friends. We may still be friends, but our connection has been overlaid by so much trauma and difficulty, it's hard to tell.

Things were so much simpler then. I can't imagine they'll ever be that simple again.

Then Wenda comes in with coffee, and Graham's headset goes off and he steps into another room, and the moment between us is broken and gone, much like everything else on Iona these days.

Twenty-four hours later, two automated Company skiffs settle on our landing pads. One is designated to fly Graham and Maybree to Meridian Station, where they'll await connections for the next leg of their journeys. The other contains basic supplies we're happy to receive but also includes an automated message demanding Fallon March come aboard to fly to a Company holding vessel for "disciplinary action."

Fallon waits for the cargo to be unloaded, then pulls out the monstrous firearm she reclaimed after Kerit Arduval's death. With a deeply satisfied smile, she takes aim and proceeds to blow the skiff into unrecognizable fragments.

"Oh boo," she says, kicking at a smoldering pile of plexi remnants with the toe of her boot. "Technical difficulties. Guess I won't be able to comply."

She eyes the second skiff and waves the weapon over her head. "Happy to cause technical difficulties for you also, friends. Just say the word and stand back."

Graham laughs and envelopes her in a hug, weapon and all.

"We'd be so tight in different circumstances," he says, smirking as she squirms out of the embrace.

"I don't know what you're talking about," Fallon mutters. "Maybree? Sure you want to go?"

Maybree, who is clinging to Wenda as long as possible, shakes her head. "I don't want to go, but I need to go. I love you for offering, though. Don't worry, I'm not going to hug you."

Others are arriving at the pads now; Arden and Lt. Nam, Dr. Heron, Fanny, Hinn and Holly, Bennid, Quimby. There's an impromptu send-off party as autoflats load Graham and Maybree's small collection of belongings onto the remaining functional skiff.

"We'll miss you, Governor Thorn," says Bennid, shaking Graham's hand. "Thank you for everything you did for us."

"We love you, Maybree!" Hinn and Holly call out in unison. After an extended time of hugging and more than a little weeping, Graham and Maybree ascend the ramp and board the skiff. Graham pauses in the hatchway, and looking squarely at me, mouths the words, "You can do this."

The ramp retracts, the door seals shut, and the skiff lifts off the ground, pointing itself toward the stars.

IN THE WEEKS AFTER Graham and Maybree's departure, the mood on Iona sours further. The proctor satellite continues to plague our sky and jam our communications, and people start to feel the toll of isolation. Simple pod management tasks, like maintaining food and water stores, become herculean planning efforts, since all our supplies come from the Company now and have to be requested through their warehouses. Every activity requires a new set of forms, a new set of authorizations, and a new set of bureaucrats who don't understand anything other than a command economy.

When the Company at last starts sending us work orders, most Ionians are relieved to have something to do. They don't care that the jobs have nothing to do with our official purpose as a service and maintenance planet, but instead are a laundry list of "improvement projects." Soon Company skiffs cluster on our landing pads full of building materials and supplies, and before long I'm leading a work team burning up 3D printers making struts, joists, and framing. The damage to Fanny's pod from her final assault on Kerrit Arduval is repaired, the inside shell of the Preservation Theater is reconfigured, and the Warehouse structure is finally reinforced, making the building usable again. We're even tasked with rebuilding the Star Parlor. Despite lingering skepticism about the long-term intentions of the Company, Ionians are pleased to be working again instead of sitting around waiting for the axe to fall. It looks, at least from a distance, like the Company is investing in Iona for Ionians.

This isn't the red flag to most people that it is to me.

Meanwhile, Arden is putting in long hours and participating in an endless spate of holo meetings with Company officials. For the most part, he's been directed to work on an elaborate "threat assessment," which is interesting given the lack of any actual threat, accompanied by a minutely detailed description of all of Iona's security practices. He always answers specific questions I ask about his work, but almost never volunteers anything, and I get the feeling he's not being as forthcoming as I want him to be. I shrug it off until the night I bring up the buildings we've been ordered to construct near our landing pads on the eastern edge of town.

The blueprints themselves are unremarkable—three basic boxes built to a not-terribly-impressive two-story height. They're small structures—all of them together would probably fit inside Clinical's footprint. Their floor plans are open, with hardly any interior separation. They seem too small to be mechanical workshops, too large to be offices, and too unfinished to be housing. The second floor features only high transom windows near its ceiling; the first floor offers no windows at all, and only a single door, oriented toward the path that leads to the pads.

What really draws my curiosity is the construction material we've been sent for them. It's unusual—some kind of polycarbonate-metal alloy, lightweight but strong with highly conductive properties. The pieces arrive pre-formed to size; all we'll have to do is print the joins and supports, then hang and seal the panels at the corners. They're tinted the same beige as Iona's sand. The few window segments are clear but made of the same material.

I do some research and learn the stuff is state-of-the-art in blast, pressure, and fire resistance, with integrated corrosion protection. It will hold up much better to Iona's blowing sand than our normal materials, which are coated with an anti-corrosive on the outside as a final step. This material is a hundred times stronger than the plexi we normally use for skiffs, a thousand times stronger than the shells of our other buildings. Its level of conductivity makes it a natural electromagnetic interference shield, which could be used to hide anything inside from tracking, as well as disrupt communication signals both inbound and outbound.

Alarmed, I ask Arden if he knows what they're supposed to be. He says their purpose isn't designated on any Company communiques he's seen. But I hear the hesitation in his voice, the sound of his mental wheels turning, and I know he's not telling me everything ... again.

"What do you *think* they're supposed to be?" I ask. "What's your hunch?"

We sit side by side at the communal table. It's just the two of us; Arden's had another late night and is eating dinner, although evening mealtime is well past and most of our podmates are already asleep.

"I don't have a hunch," he says carefully, between bites. I know this behavior all too well, and I fight my irritation to keep my voice calm and unemotional.

"Arden. What are you hiding?"

He puts his fork down on the table, thoroughly chews and swallows, then takes a long drink of water.

"I've answered every question you've asked me," he says. "That was our deal."

"That was *not* our deal. Our deal was honesty and transparency. You're not being transparent. You know something about this construction—something you're making excuses not to tell me."

"I don't *know* anything," he persists.

"Fine," I snap, losing the battle with my frustration. "I'll tell you what *I* know. Whatever the Company is planning on doing inside these structures, it's inherently dangerous and they don't want it tracked from outside. That sounds like a weapons laboratory to me. The Company got Maybree and Graham off Iona because they'd recognize a weapons lab under construction the instant they saw it and had no Company loyalty that would keep them from alerting everyone. Now please tell me how wrong I am. I hope you can convince me, because I don't want to be right about this."

I can see the conflict written on his face; his forehead creases and his jaw tightens. He pushes his half-eaten meal aside.

"Let's go for a walk and look for meteors," he says. "It will help us stop fretting and get to sleep."

Meteors. He removes his headset and places it on the table in front of him. I nod to show that I understand, and remove my own headset, placing it next to his. I follow him through the kitchen into the courtyard, and he takes my hand as we stroll out into the night, along a Company-ordered, freshly installed lighted pathway at the base of the ridge that runs behind Residential. We walk past the end of the pathway for a few minutes before he speaks again.

"I can't say that you're right about them, because the data I have are inconclusive," he says, "but I think it's more likely true than not. There are other possibilities, though."

A kernel of anxiety blooms in the pit of my stomach.

"What other possibilities?" I ask, my mouth dry.

"They've ordered top-level security features for the whole complex, in addition to the unusual materials, and that's not something we need ... unless they're thinking Iona needs someplace to house dangerous insurrectionists."

"So, it might be some kind of maximum-security holding area."

"Yeah. Or if you want to leap off into the void, it could be both. Three buildings, one for insurrectionists, one for unsanctioned weapons development, one for something else we don't want to think about yet."

"Sands." My throat tightens in a way it hasn't in years. "What can we do?"

"They can't start any Company enterprise here under Transactional Jurisdiction, so it can't use those facilities for its own purposes unless Iona gives them permission," Arden explains. "If we're going strictly by the Governing Council's regulations, anything the Company might want to do with those structures would have to be approved by the residents of Iona."

"We'd never okay a weapons lab or a prison here, not even temporarily."

"Right. That makes me worry there's something else going on, but I'm not sure what. Despite being the alleged hero of Iona, the Company hierarchy doesn't exactly trust me. I get left out of almost as many meetings as I'm pulled into."

Arden sighs, rubbing the back of his neck with one hand. "This is one time I wish I *was* keeping something from you. I'm not sure what options we have other than waiting to see what develops."

This isn't the news I want to hear, but the way it's delivered is so open and without artifice that it feels like the beginning of a bridge across the distance that's been growing between us.

"I'm a little relieved to hear they don't trust you," I say, looking into his eyes. "I trust you, though."

It's more of a hope spoken aloud than a fact; as I say it, I'm not certain it's true. He's frequently distant and preoccupied, and he never volunteers information. But the warmth between us is palpable now. He smiles softly and pulls me into a gentle embrace, rocking me against him.

"That's all I need," he says. "I'll do anything to make sure that never changes."

We stand under the stars for a while longer, wrapped around one another, not speaking or plotting or hatching intrigues, simply being in the moment together. Eventually, though, we turn around and head home. I may find a new reason to question him tomorrow—knowing me, I'll find more than one—but right now, I'm content, wrapped in the strength of his love and support, and I'm happy to immerse myself in it, even if it feels like it's destined not to last.

The little buildings continue to take shape, sprouting from Iona's sands like determined scrub. Arden's efforts to learn more about what they are yield nothing. More busywork "enhancement" projects come in from the Company, but none eclipse my focus on those beige boxes. Self-de-sanding lighted pathways are nice, but they won't make up for what could go on in those nondescript structures.

After what seems like an eternity in limbo, the Company at last announces Iona's Success Team. Of the three members, one is a name I've heard recently: Jarek Shimauy. Of the others, Gemma Laurel is vaguely familiar; according to the bio on the stream, she was part of the corporate hierarchy during my time working for the Company, so it makes sense that I'd have heard of her. One name, though, stands out to me. I'm certain he worked on Home World, and although I don't recall meeting him in person, I remember seeing his name on dozens of documents related to my compensation, my promotion, and my eventual transfer to Iona. His biographical information suggests he's spent most of his career off-planet as an embedded Company Incident Manager with the Governing Council.

"Who is Breton Cabot-Klaar?" I ask Arden. He's been frustratingly reluctant to discuss the visiting dignitaries. "Why is that name so familiar?"

Arden puffs out his cheeks and peers at me, his eyebrows arched. "You never met him?"

"His name was all over my professional stats, but I don't think so. It's peculiar that we wouldn't have met at some point."

"Not that peculiar, if the terms of our agreement were held to."

"What does that mean?"

Arden takes a deep breath and holds both of my hands hard in his.

"My agreement with the Company, after our 'accident'. Cabot-Klaar is the person I made that agreement with, the one who ensured I left Home World and promised to guarantee your safety. He was my official handler for a few years afterwards. When he left Home World to join the Governing Council, no one replaced him. I suppose because I was so firmly entrenched with them and you'd moved on to Iona. I haven't had any contact with him in years, but his assignment to this team doesn't feel incidental and it worries me. I don't know what his plans might be."

As soon as he says the words, my peripheral vision starts to flutter, and I have the powerful sensation of slipping underwater and leaving my body. If not for Arden's strong grip anchoring me in the present, the panic might have pulled me down in a way that hasn't happened for almost a decade. I manage to come back to myself quickly, although when I become fully aware of my surroundings again, I'm hyperventilating and sweaty.

"I'm okay, I'm okay," I say, trying to reassure myself more than him. I've stayed on my meds and learned techniques to quiet my mind over the last eight years, but sometimes the terror still seeps through.

I try to force a smile, but Arden's eyes are wide, his face frozen in alarm.

"Are you sure?" he asks, squeezing my hands before pulling me into his arms. "I've never seen you like that. Is that what I did to you?"

I'm still a bit rigid physically; it takes conscious effort for me to relax my body and let him hold me. "You didn't do it," I say. "It's okay, I'm better now. I didn't go all the way under. I've learned to control it over time."

"That was controlled? Dear gods, Faith, I had no idea ..."

There's misery in his voice, and I fight a powerful urge to soothe him, to tell him everything is fine. Realistically, everything is *not* fine. Just as he spent a substantial portion of our time apart shooting up everything in sight, I spent a substantial part of it walling off the emotions that threatened to overwhelm me at nearly every turn. Just as he, over time, came to grips with his refusal to process his sensations of terror and loss, I came to grips with mine. We are each as damaged as the other, in the same way, with sharp edges that still sometimes grate against each other despite our best efforts.

We don't need platitudes or sympathy. We need truth and the healing it can bring.

I reach up to stroke his face and cup his cheek tenderly. "We're both broken," I say, "and we may be even more broken by the time this is all over. But hear me out, my darling. I have a plan."

4

As the Success Team's arrival draws closer, the tensions between Arden and myself become palpable; most of our friends aren't shocked when we split up a few weeks later. Once our break is official, the news travels fast. Wenda pings me before he manages to move his things down to his new quarters in Fanny's refurbished pod. My guess is Fanny let her know the instant he inquired about available space several days ago. Wenda's done well waiting this long to grill me.

Her arrival at my pod is carefully timed. She finds me in the kitchen, sorting out the latest change in our supply requirements.

"I was wondering about you two," she says, gesturing between me and the ghost of Arden's presence with the coffee she holds in her right hand. She's working hard to be a supportive friend while getting every detail out of me. "Arden's been preoccupied the last few weeks. What's going on?"

"That's the problem," I explain, shifting my focus to her with a sigh. "He won't tell me anything. The deeper he gets into the Company's plans, the less he has to say about it. Every time I ask him a question, he shuts down and won't discuss it. I tried to make him understand how unsettling it is to be constantly in the dark, but he doesn't get it. It's heartbreaking, but this is best for now."

"You're doing the right thing," she says. "You nearly got killed because he wouldn't keep you in the loop before. Who knows what these Company creeps are up to? They aren't even here yet and already things are going crazy."

Crazy is an understatement. The Success Team's arrival is still pending, but they've made a raft of demands regarding their comfort and safety that Iona is not prepared to accommodate. Most egregious is their insistence that the Preservation Theater be given over to them for their use alone, including the storerooms, the theater itself, and Wenda's new pod. Efforts to explain how problematic a demand this is yielded nothing from the dignitaries' handlers.

With our last attempt at compromise rejected yesterday, the shuffle began in earnest this morning. At least the Success Team agreed to permit Dr. Heron to continue living at the Theater. Wenda will return to my pod—making those arrangements is ostensibly the reason for her visit. Fanny and the other former residents of the pod beneath the Star Parlor get to move back "home" ahead of schedule. Lt. Nam, and now Arden, will join Bennid in the space that would have housed Bennid and Graham, if Graham had been allowed to stay.

It's a time to change the subject. I ask Wenda if she's heard from Maybree.

"I got a short communique from her; she's a little sad but overall, all right," she says, her voice taking on a tint of wistfulness. "She tried to send pictures, but that damn satellite is still jamming up our personal communications and they wouldn't come through."

I end our chat by promising to help her move back in. Once she departs for the Preservation Theater to see to her belongings, I walk down the hall and open the door to the empty room that Maybree first occupied with Karloa, then later shared with Wenda. How will she feel, moving back into this room alone without the vibrant quirky Maybree at her side? If there's pain to be had, I'd like to spare her from it, but we don't have any options; space is again at a premium thanks to the demands of the Company. They never understand that what's easy to accomplish on a planet like Home World can be an order of magnitude more difficult—or impossible—in a place like Iona.

I complete the adjustment to our supply requests and finish some pod administration tasks, just in time for Wenda's personal possessions to arrive on an autoflat. I unload them into her old room, and as I hang up her hammock, I find myself smiling. I'm not happy about the circumstances surrounding it, but I am looking forward to having my best friend down the hall again.

My reverie is interrupted by Fallon exploding through the doorway, supreme irritation on her face. "Get out here," she says, jerking her head toward the Common Room. "You won't believe it."

I follow her to see what's got her so flustered. She has the stream up, floating in the air above the communal table. It's a dry business journal that I usually have no interest in, but this time the daily headline leaps out at me.

Thorn Industries Family Dynasty Expands with Key Buy and Director of New Enterprises Appointment

It's accompanied by an image of the six family members who make up the Thorn Industries team, all smiling stiffly at the camera. In the center, looking simultaneously droll and deadpan, is Graham.

"Wow," I say. "I guess they didn't leave him on Meridian Station after all."

"Director Cedric Thorn says son Graham's experience with back-sector planets Bardazel and Iona, where he held crucial leadership roles, gives him valuable expertise in both crisis management and understanding how to best leverage low-use distant installations," Fallon reads aloud, her words dripping with sarcasm. "Crucial leadership roles my ass," she snarls. "What an obnoxious thing to say. He wasn't leadership here. He almost got us all turned turquoise and shipped off to god-knows-where."

"It's PR," I tell Fallon. "You know he doesn't think that. And we knew his family was going to pressure him to join the business. Really, what did you expect him to do?"

"I don't know. Just ... not this." A thousand emotions flit across her face, tinges of irritation and sadness and even something like betrayal flash in her eyes before she sets her mouth resolutely.

She's already worked herself into a thunderous mood, but as she continues reading, the next paragraph almost makes her head explode.

"The younger Thorn played a key role in negotiating Thorn Industries' recent purchase of Bardazel from the Company last week," she reads, her voice reaching a shriek in tone. "The planet, unused since a past contamination scare, is an unusual purchase for Thorn Industries and may represent a new direction driven by Graham."

I'm almost never speechless, but this is a stunning and bizarre development. Fallon and I both sit in silence for a few beats. "I don't know how I feel about that," I say at last.

"It doesn't matter," Fallon responds, scowling. "He's gone. Good riddance. And now the family has scooped up the scene of his past crimes, so that will never come back to haunt him. I can't imagine what ..."

The rest of her sentence is lost in a deafening roar passing overhead. Only a full-sized Company lander makes that much noise. It's obvious our dignitaries have arrived without so much as an hour's warning.

I'm already hurrying toward the pads by the time Arden's voice rings through my headset on the General Channel asking for Incoming support.

"Feathergrass responding to Pad Arrivals in three," I say.

"Feathergrass, hold," Arden responds. "There's a different task for you."

What?

"Can you be more descriptive?" I say into my mic, struggling to keep the irritation out of my voice.

"Dr. Heron has details," he replies crisply. "Report to Preservation instead."

I bite back a frustrated response and instead settle for muttering, "Heard. Rerouting to Preservation Theatre." He acknowledges my response, then leaves the channel without saying more. I hail Dr. Heron to tell her I'm on the way.

What decision has Arden made for me without my knowledge this time?

I'm still trying to keep my annoyance in check when I reach the Theater. Dr. Heron is waiting for me outside. She greets me with a cool smile.

"Good, you're here," she says, wrapping one arm around my shoulders as we walk inside. "We can start."

"Start what?" I ask, following her through the maze of the Theater toward the room that was formerly Wenda's common room. "I thought Wenda was handling the accommodations."

"She is, she's done a beautiful job."

"Then why do you need me?"

"You're part of the official welcoming committee."

I physically flinch.

"That's something Wenda's more suited to," I object. "My social skills are not up to par."

"Nonsense. Don't worry, you don't have to play hostess or anything that involved. We did have the sense to assign that task to Wenda also."

"Are you sure it's a good idea to have a dangerous insurrectionist on the welcoming committee?" I ask as I step across the threshold. I'm surprised to find Arden sitting at the long communal table. He's intently studying his holo, carefully not looking in my direction as we walk in.

"Absolutely," Dr. Heron says, coming in behind me. "What better way to demonstrate you're not some hot-headed rabblerouser than by making you part of the welcoming committee? You're our citizen liaison."

"Our *what*?"

"Citizen liaison," Dr. Heron repeats. "Our representative of Iona's rank-and-file citizens. Which, technically, is everyone, since this planet doesn't buy into the whole idea of levels of leadership, but these Company buffoons won't know that." Arden's gaze is still directed downward toward his device, but his mouth tilts up at the corners in either a guarded smile or a smirk; he must have been behind this idea to look so pleased with himself.

For an instant, my stomach knots and anxiety clambers up my throat, but I breathe deeply and work hard to steady myself.

"Whose idea was this? Yours, Arden? Is this aa plot to make sure I'm as uncomfortable as I can possibly be? I'm no actress. How will I pull this off?"

Arden at last looks up at me; he's definitely smirking now. "It was a group decision," he says, "and you know perfectly well that you'll do fine. You're not getting out of this."

Great.

I fidget with my holo anxiously for the next twenty minutes while the lander clears protocol. When Arden gets the all-clear, he stands and gestures to the doorway. "Let's go meet the Success Team and find out what they've got up their sleeves," he says, standing back to let me go first. Dr. Heron fixes me with an expectant smile, and I reluctantly lead our little group through the darkened hallways. Wenda joins us as a we step out onto the theater's portico.

I'm trepidatious as we make our way to the landing pads and can't stop pulling at the edge of my jacket. Arden, Dr. Heron, Wenda and I line up as the dignitaries disembark. It's a simple handshake greeting for them at this point; having endured the fourteen-hour trip from Meridian Station, they'll need some time to decompress. Not even the extra room of a full lander makes that kind of trip easy. There's a momentary flicker of recognition in Breton Cabot-Klaar's black-brown eyes when we're introduced, and his face takes on a sneer when he shakes hands with Arden. He's younger than I expected, about my age. He's tall and extremely pale with thick pillowy lips and narrow nose, which he tends to look down given his height. A rash of buzz-cut blond stubble crowns the top of his head. I'm certain we never met on Home World; he's distinctive enough that I would have remembered.

Jarek Shimauy is a shorter stocky man. His hair, pulled back into a tight short ponytail, is streaked with white and gray; his clothing is a nondescript gray tunic and pants. By contrast, Gemma Laurel's golden skin and eyes glow in Iona's pale light. Her glossy jet-black hair is bound up in a hefty braid that hangs halfway down her back. The brightly colored long tunic and soft flowy pants she wears makes her seem like an entirely different species from the men who accompany her.

Both she and Shimauy are senior executives, a bit older than Dr. Heron. They're most likely lifelong Company employees. Laurel proffers a smile, at least, but neither she nor Shimauy seem impressed with anything in their immediate field of view. They are, however, polite, and no one asks any difficult questions. In short order, Dr. Heron herds them all off in the direction of the Preservation Theater to settle them into their quarters, and Wenda makes for Fanny's pod, where she's putting the final touches on the official reception happening later this evening in the newly restored Star Parlor.

That leaves me with Arden. We stand awkwardly on the sands beside the pad like shipwreck survivors on an island, watching everyone hurry away from us. His eyes stay focused on the dignitaries trailing Dr. Heron across the sand.

"Well," he says. "They're here."

"That they are. Cabot-Klaar clearly remembers you."

"Yes," Arden's voice trails off and his eyes narrow, "and he recognized your name when you were introduced. I don't suppose it makes sense that he'd have forgotten, but I was still hoping he might have."

"It's all right, Arden. He can't do anything to me now. Not here, out in the open, with two other Company types to answer to."

I can tell from the set of his mouth and the way he tips his head he's not convinced. But he lets the matter drop. Silence fills the air between us.

"This is harder than I thought it would be," he eventually says. The wind dances his hair across his face; he pushes it away with one hand, impatient, irritated. His eyes are intense. He's not talking about dealing with Company officials now.

"It will get easier. It's only been a few days."

"How can you be so calm? It's like nothing's changed for you."

"I have more practice disguising my emotions."

The statement doesn't shake him; I'm not sure he understands what I mean. He nods wordlessly, and his gaze wanders back over the sands, after the disappearing figures of the dignitaries.

There are a few more beats of disjointed silence. Arden clears his throat.

"You'll be at the reception, right?" he asks.

"That's the plan." I've hated the idea of an official reception from the instant Wenda came up with it; making small talk with strangers and trying not to spill things on myself for ten minutes feels daunting. And now I have this additional role to play, *citizen liaison*. Just thinking about it makes me uncomfortable; even more uncomfortable than standing here with Arden.

"So I'll see you tonight," I say with what I hope is finality.

"Yes, see you tonight," he murmurs. He's distracted, but it's not my place anymore to beg him to tell me what's on his mind, so I remain quiet. He hesitates for a few beats and seems on the verge of saying something but apparently thinks better of it and instead strides out across the sand toward Fanny's pod—his pod—without looking back. I watch him walk away, then return to the pod that used to be ours, taking a different path.

"You can't wear that," Fallon barks, inspecting the clean basic Ionawear I've laid out on my hammock. "That does not say 'I am the citizen liaison, and I speak for the people'."

I roll my eyes. "It's not an official title, for crying out loud. How many people did your mother tell about this scheme? Everybody?"

Fallon smirks, crossing her arms and leaning against my desk in the corner. "A few," she says. "Thank fire she told me, though, so I could keep you from walking out of here looking like Backwater Betty."

"I don't have anything else. It's this or naked."

"Naked would at least make a statement."

I give Fallon my sternest side-eye, to no effect. She lifts her head and studies me; I'm standing in my underwear in the middle of my room and it's making me supremely self-conscious.

"This isn't helping. I'm already anxious enough as it is," I complain, hoping she'll leave the room or at least stop inspecting me. But something about the comment energizes her.

"I have a solution to your problem," she says, then darts out before I can reiterate that I'm not the one who thinks there's a problem. In a few moments she returns, carrying a large rectangular opaque box. "Mom brought this from Home World for me. I haven't had a reason to wear it, but it's the perfect thing for this."

The sarcastic words "What is it, a burgundy jump suit?" leave my mouth just as she opens the box and unfurls a burgundy jump suit, the twin of the one she lost when the Star Parlor was attacked months ago.

I have to admit it's beautiful. It's a perfect balance between elegant and pragmatic, showy and serious. The pants have discreet pockets and a slight bit of flare at the bottom; the bodice and sleeves are tailored like an expensive suit jacket, except for a dramatic cut-out over the right shoulder. A wide self-belt at the natural waist completes the piece. The stitching on it is incredibly fine and as I finger the edge of one sleeve, I'm surprised to find the fabric sturdy and soft at the same time.

Fallon holds it up in front of me and pushes me over to the mirror.

"That color makes all the difference," she says. "You have to wear it."

"I'll feel weird. I'll stand out."

"You'll get over it, and standing out is the point."

"Everyone else will be wearing normal clothes, though."

"No, they won't. My mother won't. I'm certain the Success Team won't—those people don't know what normal clothes *are*. Arden and Lt. Nam are both wearing their Tactical dress uniforms. And I helped Wenda pull something together just for this event and she's going to be stunning. So, you can wear this and look official, or wear that,"—she stabs a finger at the clothes in my hammock— "and look like you dropped by to tighten up the elevator fittings."

Fallon crosses her arms over her chest. As far as she's concerned, the decision's been made and it's a matter of wearing me down until I accept it. I take another look at my reflection holding the jumpsuit against me. I do like its vibrant color, and there's something about its brightness that makes my eyes sparkle.

"We put that hair up and no-one is going to deny you anything," Fallon says.

"All right, all right. You win. It's remarkably generous of you, and I'll be honored to wear it. What are you going to wear?"

Fallon makes a hideous face. "I'm not going," she says, "in case the Success Team has ideas about capturing me. I emphatically don't want to be shipped off to some creaky Company Adjudication vessel without forewarning."

"Surely you don't think they would ..." I begin, but her face tells me she's not kidding. Her eyes are narrowed and her jaw clenched; she's balled her hands into tight white-knuckled fists at her side.

"We won't let that happen, ever," I say, as reassuringly as I can. "You're an Ionian and I'm the citizen liaison, so nobody gets to you except through me."

Fallon snorts derisively, but her posture becomes less rigid and her forehead less tense. We get back to talking about the jumpsuit; whether it makes sense to cinch the waist more and add sparkly accessories (Fallon votes yes, I vote no) or if a scarf draped across the shoulder peekaboo would make it more subtle (I vote yes, Fallon votes no). In the end, it's a compromise on both sides. I wind up with the scarf—a gauzy black sheaf of nearly-transparent feather-light material—and Fallon pins it in place with a shiny silver brooch made up of an abstract pattern of a dozen fine intertwined lines. The design is extraordinary, like nothing I've ever seen, and I'm struck by it.

"It's stunning," I say. "What does it represent?"

Fallon tugs at the scarf, making infinitesimally small adjustments until she's satisfied with its placement, then pats the brooch for good measure.

"I'm not sure; I've had it for years," she says. "Maybe it means something about the beauty of interconnection and interdependence."

We look at each other for a significant moment, feeling the weight of what I'm about to do. I understand why it's so important to Fallon to contribute to this moment in any way she can, and gratitude washes over me. I whisper, "Thanks," to her; she rolls her eyes in mock annoyance and flashes a quick smile.

Then we start arguing about shoes.

I'm able to assuage her concern about footwear faux pas when I pull out the pair of elegant black flats I bought almost ten years ago, when my transport to Iona stopped at Meridian Station. After a final appraisal, she's satisfied.

"You look grand," she says, stepping back and clapping her hands in approval.

I feel grand. There's something about this outfit that's given rise to a sense of confidence I didn't have before. I feel strong and capable, and like I'm about to claim my due from the Company at last. Fallon leaves me alone to finish my preparations. On a whim, I pull out my box of treasures and slip the battered dog-eared Congratulations card into the jumpsuit's pocket, as Fallon shouts, "Hurry! Wenda's leaving!"

Wenda and I walk to Fanny's pod together. Her outfit is a beautiful long tunic made of bright multicolored woven cloth, with a matching head wrap and delicate sandals. Even in Fallon's spectacular burgundy jumpsuit, I'm a touch frumpy next to her.

"Are you ready for this?" she asks as we walk. "It might be a lot."

I'd rather talk about fashion, and for me that's really saying something. My stomach knots again and I take a few deep breaths to calm down.

"I'm as ready as I can be," I say. "The real work starts tomorrow, after all the social niceties are done."

"Social niceties are never done with Company officials, you know that. The whole social game is as important as the political one."

She's right, of course. We've had a number of conversations in the last few weeks about how to gain social advantage with the team members. It's not lost on any of us how much of a chess match managing their presence is going to be.

"Tonight, I want to get a sense of who they are," I say, hoping I sound convincing. "I want to learn more than I reveal."

We reach Fanny's pod, and Wenda pauses to shake the sand out of her shoes at the doorway. We continue through the Common Room and down the little side hallway that terminates in the refurbished lift tube to the Star Parlor. I shiver a little, remembering being trapped here with Fallon as Karloa's insane brother menaced us from the open end of the hallway. I thought my life was ending that day, and worse still, that I was going to have to watch everyone I loved die before my eyes. But with everyone's help and a lot of luck, I got through it. Spending a few hours making small talk with Company officials who may be in a position to decide Iona's fate forever ... by comparison, this should be easy.

We step into the Star Parlor, and I survey the thirty or so people crammed inside. I begrudgingly admit that Fallon was right to insist I dress as a person of some importance rather than as a neatened-up version of myself. It doesn't matter that our structure doesn't employ the duality of leaders versus followers. The Success Team members are presenting themselves as occupants of a rarified place in a hierarchy that supersedes Ionian standards. If it's a game they're playing only with themselves, if they're convinced they've won, they've won.

Dr. Heron glides over. The glittering pantsuit she wears is a blinding white and made from some sort of reflective material that makes it challenging to look at, despite the soft atmospheric lighting of the party.

"You're perfect," she whispers as she leans in to give my cheek an impromptu air kiss. "Ready to hop into the fray?"

I laugh a little, in part because I think she might expect me to, and also to give the impression of being relaxed to the other people in the room—I'm simultaneously grateful for and cursing the time I spent with the Company that made me so conscious of optics—and put my arm through hers. "Lead on," I say.

I don't need to tell her where I'd like to start. She steers me to Breton Cabot-Klaar.

He's wearing all-black: a short tunic constructed in sharp lines and angles over fitted pants tucked into shiny military-style boots. Heavy black eyeliner demarcates his upper lids and a brilliant slash of red spreads across his lips. I feel like I'm about to have a conversation with a heavily stylized carnivorous bird.

He takes my hand and bows over it, his eyes boring squarely into my own.

"Ah, Madame Citizen Liaison," he says in a syrupy tone that hovers just at the edge of sarcasm. "A pleasure."

My anxiety crumbles in the face of nearly overwhelming resentment.

"It's not a formal title," I say in a lighthearted breezy voice. "We should call each other by name, I think."

I pointedly remove my hand from his grip. A ripple of chills run up my spine as his lips spread in a flat, insincere smile. His eyes remain cold and unamused.

"Of course," he says, straightening to his full height. "Ms. Feathergrass, was it? Faith Feathergrass?"

My teeth clench at the way he says my name—familiar, insidious, with a heavy dose of smarminess, like he knows all my secrets.

"Why yes," I say smoothly, still riding a high of rancor. "Impressive, since our meeting this morning was so brief. You must have done your research. Or perhaps you recall me from somewhere else?"

His expression becomes pinched, startled. He appears taken aback that I'm not cowering in front of him, and I've caught him out with the reference to my past. He could easily dig his way out of this hole I've dropped him into—after all, I've been a constant feature on the stream for the last few months—but I decide not to give him that opportunity.

"At any rate, I look forward to working with you, Mr. Cabot-Klaar," I continue. "Or shall I call you Breton?"

His eyes dart to and fro for a moment before he chooses his next move.

"Cabot-Klaar will do for now," he says, then dropping his voice to a conspiratorial low, he leans forward and says into my ear in an intimate tone, "Breton after we become close friends."

I'd like to scream, run back to my pod, and scrub myself until I bleed. Instead, I throw my head back and emit a practiced tinkly laugh loud enough for everyone in the room to hear, followed by, "Aren't you *charming*." I follow up by placing my lips close to his ear and snarl, "Count on this, Cabot-Klaar—we will *never* be close friends."

I excuse myself and walk away, towing Dr. Heron along behind me. His face shows an instant of shock and disquietude before he regains control of his features, and I have the heady sense of having won a sparring match—immediately followed by the prickly sensation that I've lit a fuse without knowing what it's connected to.

"Well done," murmurs Dr. Heron. "I'm sure you won't think of this as a compliment, but you'd make an excellent Company officer."

"You're right, I don't."

"Of course not, dear. At any rate, I think you can relax for the rest of the party, the difficult part's been achieved. Here's your next victim."

Dr. Heron goes into full hostess mode as we approach Gemma Laurel, who is chatting amiably with Fanny. Sweeping me toward the older woman with a flourish, she kicks off a conversation between us and then detaches from me and makes her way toward another small conversational grouping. Laurel appears to be the opposite of her fellow team member, interested in the people and things around her. She asks me specific questions about life on Iona, what shortcomings it might have, how it could be made better for the residents, and when I mention the proctor satellite and the difficulties it's caused, she pops out a holo and sends a request that it be removed.

"I appreciate that," I say. "I admit I was concerned after we greeted you this morning. Everyone seemed so detached and uninterested."

Laurel laughs, a lovely musical sound. "Oh, I'm sure," she says. "I know I wasn't myself. But I'd just spent fourteen hours crammed into a lander with Shimauy and Cabot-Klaar. That would make anyone sour."

She glances around, then gestures for me to lean in.

"Iona is not what I was led to believe. I'm quite surprised," she says. Her tone is casual and factual, as if she's confiding in a friend. If she's engaged in gameplay, she's so proficient that it's practically seamless. Or maybe it's her voice; with its pleasant lilt, she could be calling my planet an utter hellhole and I might still think of it as positive feedback.

"We should take this up right away," she continues. "Transactional Jurisdiction may not be the correct course of action here. We may have to adjust our charter."

"Please let me know if there's anything you need for your review," I say. "I'll be most interested in your recommendations."

I *hope* I present as calm, pleasant, and helpful. On the inside, I've turned to soup.

This is precisely what we were hoping to achieve. Persuading the Company to abandon Transactional Jurisdiction was our ultimate never-going-to-happen supernova stretch goal. We were sure it would take weeks of experience and hours of convincing. Could it go down before the Success Team completes its first full day on Iona?

Macha joins our conversation and Laurel proceeds to quiz her on how Iona's health system functions. I'm only half-listening, adding in an exclamation or clarification now and again. When an appropriate amount of time has passed, I offer some additional pleasantries and then excuse myself from our conversation. I drift over to where Wenda stands with Jarek Shimauy at the edge of the Parlor looking out over Iona Town; they're taking turns pointing at different features and chatting energetically. I greet Shimauy then watch them for a few minutes—Wenda in social scientist mode is always a beautiful thing to behold. Eventually, I make my excuses and edge my way through the crowd looking for someone—anyone—to tell about Laurel's comments. Lt. Nam is talking to Cabot-Klaar, whose expression suggests he's perilously near death-by-boredom. Dr. Heron has joined the discussion between Gemma Laurel and Macha. I decide to drift over to the refreshments table and help myself to a drink, and hopefully someone will be free by the time I finish.

I turn and walk directly into Arden.

I take him in as we both apologize and untangle ourselves from one another. He's wearing his formal dress uniform, as Fallon said. It's modeled after a long-sleeved cargo suit, but crafted in a luxurious dark blue material, shot through with occasional surprising threads of gold. The single piece fits him so closely I can see the muscles in his abdomen flex with his breath. Golden rank insignia are pinned to the suit's shoulders, and a wide black sash full of commendations and medals sits diagonally across his torso. His hair is tied back at the nape of his neck and there are several heavy gold rings, also bearing rank insignia, on his fingers.

Looking at him, I almost forget to breathe.

I'm still trying to get a grip on my sudden wave of emotion when he reaches up, captures a strand of my wild brown hair that has escaped from the careful updo Fallon helped me construct, and tucks it behind my ear.

"You shouldn't do that," I whisper, on the verge of tears.

He looks lost.

"I know," he says. "I'm sorry."

"Don't be sorry. Just ... don't do that."

He grimaces. "I'm trying, but some habits are hard to break, and ... you look beautiful."

"Don't say things like that. Please. I mean, you look wonderful too, but we can't ... I can't ..."

"I didn't mean to make you uncomfortable. I'm sorry, this is still new to me, and I'm not doing a very good job of repressing ..." His voice drifts off as he thinks better of what he's about to say. "I'll do better. I promise." He sounds sincere, at least, but the expression in his eyes is so pained it sucks the air out of my lungs.

A wave of anxiety sweeps over me, and I feel the weight of every set of eyes in the room grinding against me, evaluating, judging. My peripheral vision dances, and my brain screams for me to run, run away, run anywhere, just run.

"I think I've had enough reception for tonight," I say, pushing past him and heading for the exit. From the doorway, I take one last scan of the room. Contrary to my fears, no one is looking at me at all.

Except, that is, for Breton Cabot-Klaar, who's eyeing me over Lt. Nam's head with a self-satisfied smirk on his face. He's wearing the expression of a fighter who believes he's discovered a major chink in his opponent's armor.

If I'm being honest, he has.

INSTEAD OF FOLLOWING MY first instincts, I make myself slow down. I glide my eyes over Cabot-Klaar and pretend I'm scanning the room for Dr. Heron. I find her, wave casually, and stroll to her side to bid her goodnight. Then I manage to walk calmly to the exit, making certain my face is relaxed and wearing a slight smile.

I step into the elevator. As it begins its descent, I let a few tears squeeze out. I'll have a good cry later, but this is not the time. I wipe my face before the lift reaches the ground, hoping I'll appear normal by the time the doors open. When they do, I take a deep breath and pause a moment, centering myself, then step out into the little hallway.

For an instant, it seems the lights flicker and the shadowy form of Kerrit Arduval hovers near the hallway's end. My breath catches in my chest, but then my eyes adjust to the pod's lighting and the hallucination disappears.

I need to get home *now*.

I find a sand scooter in the courtyard and mount it with a profound sense of relief. As I navigate across Iona Town toward Residential, I realize the proctor satellite is no longer splashing Iona's sands with its hostile crimson light. Gemma Laurel's been true to her word; it's either gone dark or is gone altogether.

As much of a relief as that is, it's nothing compared to my pure elation when I reach my pod. I drop the sand scooter in the courtyard and head inside. The kitchen and Common Room are dark, although there are a few lights on in sleeping quarters. It's later than I thought.

I fill a cup with water and stand in the dark kitchen for a moment, breathing deeply and drinking until I start to feel solid again. There's so much to process about tonight, and though I had a rough dismount, things went reasonably well. I survived my first extended encounter with Cabot-Klaar, although thinking about him makes me grind my teeth and sends a wave of distaste through my veins. I was expecting the entire Success Team to be like him, honestly—the Company certainly employs plenty of people like him—but Gemma Laurel was a surprise. And despite the fact that we barely exchanged ten words altogether, Jarek Shimauy is pleasant if somewhat preoccupied. At least he was openly curious about Iona.

I really want to talk to Wenda about her experience with him when she gets in, so I decide to wait up for her.

I take a seat at our big communal table in the Common Room. The newly installed automated lighting system detects my presence and shifts the darkness to a soft ambient glow. All pods have these now and they're very popular; the Company earned some points with the living quarter upgrades. It's created relief, too; surely, they wouldn't put money into improving where we live if they plan to drag us all off-planet and take over Iona for themselves. But this is the Company we're talking about, so my skepticism is still strong—the Company isn't altruistic, and I'm certain there will be a cost of some kind down the road. Here, though, only Arden understands as well as I do the games the Company plays, and what they're capable of.

Arden.

An ache creeps up inside me as I see him again in my mind's eye, the struggle written on his face. I thought I had things in hand, at least a bit—I set this in motion, after all, and even though he came up with a million objections, I thought we would work through it and everything would be fine over time. It's hurting us both, and my response to him tonight is proof that it's not fine.

I'm not fine.

But I also wasn't fine living with obfuscation and partially answered questions either, so here we are.

"Oh, here you are!"

I jump as Wenda's voice echoes through the room. I was so lost in my thoughts I didn't hear her come through the kitchen.

"What did you think of the party? You left a little early," she says, sitting down beside me and beginning to unwrap her colorful headpiece.

"It was a nice event, but I didn't want to overextend myself," I lie. "Better to leave some mystery for these Company people to figure out."

Wenda chuckles, her eyes sparkling, and I smile despite myself. It's good to have her in my pod again.

"You're much better at that than me," she says, dropping the headwrap on the table and using both hands to fluff out her hair. "I've no taste for mystery. The Company is mysterious enough on its own."

"Did you learn anything about their plans?"

Wenda lets out a long breath, pondering.

"I might have, but I'm not sure," she says. "I spent most of the night talking to Jarek. He was relatively pleasant and had lots of questions. He's particularly interested in our social structure. As pleasant as our conversation was on the surface, I kept thinking there was something else going on—that it wasn't a conversation at all, but a subtle interrogation."

I think back on my chat with Gemma Laurel and begin to see a pattern there too. Pointed questions covered over in smiles and lilting laughter, focused on what makes Ionians tick. I thought I'd found a potential friend and supporter in her, but now I'm wondering if what I found was the best actress in the room.

"We should all compare notes tomorrow," I say. I send holo messages to Fanny, Dr. Heron, and Lt. Nam. I hesitate for a moment, then add Arden to the list. He's so tied to the Company at this point that I'm not certain which side he's on, although his favorite argument of late is that there are no 'sides'. If he's willing to add any insights, I'm happy to hear them. Something's about to drop, and we may have missed all the signs.

Wenda stifles a yawn. "Hopefully it won't drop before morning. I'm beat." She stands and kisses the top of my head. "I will have sweet dreams tonight. I hope you do too."

With that, she strolls out of the Common Room, disappearing down the dark hallway to her quarters. I sit where I am a few moments more, trying to override the adrenaline rush from earlier this evening. Tonight, in the space of a few hours, I felt every feeling a human being can feel, from revulsion to joy, from hope to panic. Now I'm backtracking over every sensation, wondering if it was somehow choreographed by the Company to learn exactly how far they could push us all.

I'm awake well before Holly rings the rising chimes, uncertain whether I actually slept at all. By the time I lay down in my hammock last night, I was exhausted, but my brain wouldn't stop turning over every second of the Success Team reception, every decision I've made in the past three months, and every assumption we've had about what the Company's goals might be.

The chimes start to sing, and the pod stirs to life. I heave myself out of my hammock and get dressed. I wrangle my hair into its usual messy bun and do a quick check in the mirror. It's not a stunning burgundy jumpsuit, but it'll do—I look like me. Before I leave the room, I push open my window and crane my neck to see the eastern sky. A ripple of self-satisfaction runs through me. The proctor satellite is gone.

In the Common Room, Wenda is the center of attention this morning; the communal table is packed with our podmates jockeying to sit next to or across from her. It's her first breakfast with us in quite some time, and everyone is delighted to have her back. I accept a cup of coffee from Holly and take a seat beside the fireplace, happy to watch my friend bask in the love directed her way.

A spot at the table will open shortly, so I decline when Holly offers to bring me breakfast in my room. I stretch my legs across the hearth and open my holo to pass the time.

The first thing I see are messages from Fanny, Dr. Heron, and Lt. Nam, agreeing to my proposed meeting. They all have thoughts on what Wenda and I spoke about last night, although in some cases they're diametrically opposed.

There's also a message from Arden. It's short and to the point, and not what I expected.

You're already familiar with my opinions; they haven't changed. We should avoid these sessions in the future.

I reread the message, both my original one and his response. I send him a quick reply: *Let's talk, hail me when you have time.* Within seconds, he answers: *We're done playing games.*

I draw in my breath, a sharp inhale that makes the people sitting closest to me look around. I catch Wenda's eye and gesture for her to follow me to the courtyard. It takes a moment to extricate herself from all the adoration; I pace back and forth across the small sandy enclosure until at last, she comes through the door.

"What's going on with you?" she asks, visibly concerned. "Why the panic?"

"We have less time than we thought. I don't know exactly what's going down, but it's something that could affect the entire planet, and it's happening soon." I stumble over my words, trying to get them all out of my mouth at once.

"How do you know this?"

I hold out the holo. Wenda reads the message from Arden, and the confusion etched on her face deepens.

"Is he saying he's siding with the Company?" she asks.

"No, no ... I mean, he might be, I don't know, but that's not what this is about. Look at the last line. That's a code we devised ages ago as a compromise. Whenever he learned something was about to happen and he couldn't tell me outright, he'd send me a message referencing gameplay. This ... *we're done playing games* ... means *we* have to focus fast, or we're going to lose Iona."

"Why wouldn't he say that?"

"He thinks his internal communications are being monitored. That's the *opinion* he's referring to."

"Is the part about avoiding each other code too?"

"That part he means literally. We have to be careful around the Company about casting suspicion on one another somehow, or creating the impression of a relationship that could be leveraged ..."

"... just like last time on Home World." Wenda finishes for me, her tone soft. I blink in surprise and stare as her eyebrows go up in sympathy.

She comes to my side. I don't realize my hands are shaking until she takes them into her own.

"That's what all this is about, isn't it?" she says, squeezing my hands hard. "You're terrified the past is going to repeat itself. That's why you two broke up; you and Arden are desperately trying to protect each other. You're making the same mistakes you did then. Can't you see that?"

I shake my head. "No. We broke up for specific reasons that have everything to do with how we function in the world as people. I won't go into it now because it's not important. We need to focus on what's happening before we lose Iona altogether. I don't think we have much time."

Wenda isn't convinced but doesn't pursue it. Fanny and Lt. Nam arrive for our gathering; a few minutes later Dr. Heron comes in. Wenda and I are already sitting at the communal table. As we describe our conversations at the reception the night before, the clear pattern emerges. Wenda spent most of the evening monopolized by Jarek Shimauy, talking primarily about Iona's social structure and typical work-and-reward patterns. Gemma Laurel chatted up both Fanny and me about what makes Ionians tick, what we as a group tend to like about life here and what we tend to find challenging. Lt. Nam spent a large part of the evening in conversation with Breton Cabot-Klaar, who pressed him consistently for an "outsider's view" about individual Ionians' leadership styles and potential, anyone who seemed to have potential or seemed threatening or who behaved suspiciously.

"And by 'behaving suspiciously,' he made it clear he didn't mean psychopaths trying to take over Iona; he meant anyone who seemed to have a problem with the Company," Nam explained. "I told him most of Iona's population was here because they have a problem with the Company—that's what drives independent planets. But he was working hard to get me to name names."

Dr. Heron found herself being questioned by both Gemma Laurel and Breton Cabot-Klaar. "They were pressing me for names of more 'prospective leaders,' people who have the respect of Ionians in general," she confirms. "I suppose because they didn't like the names I'd already given them. Cabot-Klaar had a list of questions about Ionians' health status, both physical and mental. I could tell he wanted to push me into saying something he could use, but I wasn't quite clear on what that might be."

"What did you tell him?" I ask.

Dr. Heron raises an eyebrow and cocks her head in the same way her daughter does, one half of her mouth curling up into a self-satisfied smile.

"Nothing. I don't have to answer to him; I'm *far* above him on the Company org chart."

I love this woman.

Fanny reports she was also pressured to give names of prospective leadership, and things start connecting in my head. The Success Team is digging for very specific information, while simultaneously demonstrating an interest in changing the Company's existing narrative.

"What would it mean to change the Success Team's charter?" I ask Dr. Heron. "Do you know?"

"Any change to the charter has to be approved by the Governing Council," she explains. "That could happen very quickly or take a long time, depending on what they ask for."

"Could they just take over Iona somehow?"

"Only Permanent Jurisdiction would let them stay here and meddle in things forever, but that would require a new petition with supporting documentation, demonstrating a need and desire for the Company's longer-term involvement by the residents, and couldn't be finalized without 70% of Iona's adult population voting in its favor."

"What are some of the quicker changes?"

"The fastest one is Industrial Partnership Status. That requires only a request by the team, sign-off by the Governing Council's Economic Development Director, and approval by the target world's Chief Designate. It's usually granted in cases where the Company is already working with a planet and has some kind of business or industry in development that they want to speed along."

My mind goes to the set of buildings out by the pads, constructed to the Company's specifications, waiting for a purpose. With sufficient control over Iona's resources and workforce, the Company can churn out whatever they want in those little labs, and with the tacit blessing of the Governing Council. Met with the reality that Iona has no actual single "leader" per se, they've been asking specifically about leadership roles and people who might fill them.

That has to be it. They're going to appoint a 'leader' for Iona, someone who will sign off on their plans.

"Has anyone mentioned how they plan to proceed?" I ask. Dr. Heron shakes her head.

"No, they're very tight-lipped around me. You might ask Arden, though. They appear to have had him on speed-dial since the instant they arrived. He's been in several hours of meetings with them at the Theater this morning alone."

My heart rate jumps uncomfortably. I think about what Wenda said to me in the courtyard; a bubble of anxiety rises into my throat.

At that moment, every holo messaging system in the room goes off. The five of us trade nervous looks. I open my messaging and pop the notification up into the air in front of us.

Wenda reads the text. "Mandatory all-hands meeting tomorrow morning in the Preservation Theater to discuss the future of Iona and lucrative new partnership opportunities identified by the Success Team."

"That can't be good," Fanny mutters.

"We don't know for sure," Dr. Heron interjects, always the devil's advocate. "I've always said that Iona could make tremendous use of the Company's resources and ..."

I tune her—and everyone else—out. I see it now, clear as starlight from orbit. The Success Team's going to appoint Arden as Iona's 'leader' and use our connection to compel him to sign off on anything they want—again. It doesn't matter that we're not together anymore. They know we still care about one another, and they'll use it against us.

That means the only person who can do anything to head this off is me.

We finish the meeting, and my friends go on their way. Wenda's noticed the change in my demeanor, and she shadows me for a while at the pod, checking in, waiting for me to tell her what's going on. As much as I would like to, I'm not going to do that. I putter about working on pod administration tasks until she's distracted by something else, then slip out the door.

I'd like to run across the sands as fast as I can, but this is not the time for impulsive behavior. I eschew the sand scooter still lying in our courtyard and instead walk to Clinical at a leisurely pace. For good measure, I stop and chat with a few of my fellow Ionians on the way, mostly about how wonderful it is to look up and see our pink-beige sky without the hovering proctor satellite. I'm fully in control when I step into Clinical's lobby and wave cheerfully to Pepper, who is staffing the reception desk. She waves back and says, "They're expecting you, go on up."

On the outside, everything is normal.

On the inside, not so much.

My heart won't stop pounding.

It thuds, drumlike, as I congratulate Karloa and Tommas on their impending discharge from medical supervision. It flutters like a wounded bird as I invite them to move into my pod together in a few days' time. It batters at my ribs as a delighted Karloa hugs me, thrilled to be forgiven for transgressions she's perceived as her fault. And it's in my throat when I say quietly to Tommas, "I need a favor from you, if you can."

A few hours later, the message I'm waiting for comes through. It's long and wildly specific; some things I'm being asked to do feel almost random, like I'm being made to jump through hoops to prove my intentions are pure. There's assurance, however, that it will be well worth my time, and ultimately *important*. It's an odd choice of words, but I let it go. Frankly, anything will be worth it if it means I can save Iona from becoming the next home for a Company illegal weapons development program.

I craft a careful response, following the advice Tommas provided. My breath catches in my throat when it's time to send. This arrangement could change everything, including some things I'd rather stay the same, and it might turn out to be an entirely futile effort. I still don't have a clear plan and wish I could sleep on it, but we're out of time. The wheels have been set in motion. I take a deep breath and steady myself, tap into my resolve, then say the single word that sends the message is on its way.

7

THE ALL-HANDS TAKES PLACE before the afternoon meal. I file with all the rest of Iona into the cool darkness of the Preservation Theater's main auditorium. The Success Team is already seated on the stage; Fanny stands ready to help with presentation tech. Dr. Heron, standing in the aisle, spots me and waves me over.

"They've asked for some of us to sit here," she says, pointing out seven seats reserved by name in the front row. Fanny, Dr. Heron, and I are three of them. The last four are Macha, Arden, Wenda, and Fallon.

"What do they want with Fallon?" I whisper. "Is this some kind of disciplinary action?"

"Not at all. It's required an enormous amount of negotiation, and calling in more than a few favors, but ..." Dr. Heron's voice trails off as she sees her daughter in the crowd and hurries to intercept her.

It takes the better part of an hour to get everyone into the theater and seated, but the Success Team doesn't care. Gemma Laurel shoots me large, overly friendly smiles I attempt to return; Shimauy and Cabot-Klaar discuss something on a holo. Finally, Cabot-Klaar looks up and gestures to Fanny to kill the lights. His expression is the same as it always is: irritated and sour.

Arden slides into the seat next to mine. "Are we okay?" he whispers. He must be trying to figure out if I understood his message.

"We are."

"Did they talk to you?"

"About what's going on here today? No, no one said anything. I figured it out on my own, though."

"And you're good with it?"

"I have to be. We don't have a choice. Yet."

"I'm worried this is going to make things far more difficult. I don't know how we'll manage to ..."

He's interrupted by a burst of loud music and a series of dramatic—or annoying, depending on your point of view—lights circling and flashing across the Success Team.

Arden stops talking but can't stop moving. His fingers fidget in his lap as Gemma Laurel stands and steps to the front. The music fades away and Laurel begins her speech.

"Hello, Iona!" she calls out in her cheerful lilting way, throwing her arms wide as though she's welcoming the crowd to some kind of festival. A smattering of voices return the greeting, although the predominant response is skeptical silence.

She spends a few minutes pattering on about who she is and her role in the Company and introduces the other members of the team, both of whom merely nod when their names are mentioned.

"As you might know, we came here as part of a petition granted by the Governing Council to provide Iona with guidance and support during what we were told was a troubling time," she says, and my ears perk up. Surely she's not about to say they no longer believe the story they invented and circulated about the events on this planet?

"We understood within a few hours of landing on your delightful home that the reports had gotten it all wrong," she continues. "In the place of unrest and dissatisfaction, we've found calm, along with serious hard-working people. Instead of anarchy, we've found a social structure so innately natural to the people here that law enforcement as we understand it elsewhere is unnecessary."

Laurel's voice builds to a crescendo. "Instead of insurrectionists and threats to Iona's safety, we found heroes dedicated to the cause of this planet's preservation.

We want to take this moment to recognize these individuals who played a crucial role in saving your home from wanton destruction by a madman!"

Spotlights turn on the front row and a blast of recorded triumphant music plays. I shade my eyes, in part to protect them from the intense light but also to hide my shock. Equally surprised, the audience begins tentative clapping, which, egged on by Laurel, soon becomes energetic applause.

"What is this bullshit?" Fallon hisses, earning an elbow in the ribs from her mother.

Laurel pauses dramatically while the applause dies down, then calls out, "We have surprises for them all! Let's hear from them!"

She's gesturing toward the front row, at Fallon and Dr. Heron. Fallon's face is ashen, and she digs her nails into her mother's arm. "Are you serious?" she says, but her mother gives her an icy side-eye, links arms with her, and drags her up onto the stage.

The other members of the Success Team come forward and join her, looking a bit bored as Laurel continues to talk at length about how the two women were involved both in the development of Blue and its antidote. At last, Shimauy takes over.

"Ms. March, we're all well aware that certain allegations were filed against you. They were ill-informed, and I'm happy to tell you they've been dismissed. Additionally, I'm pleased to offer you the opportunity to rejoin the Company as our embedded trade director here on Iona."

Fallon's mouth drops open. For once, she appears to have nothing to say.

"If you choose to take on those duties, I'm also authorized to present you with an expansive bonus and perks reserved for our best employees. You'll find the details in your official messages now, but take your time in considering this opportunity; we don't intend to rush you."

She moves like an automaton as all three members of the team shake her hand, and as Laurel ushers her and Dr. Heron off the stage. When Fallon drops back into her seat next to me, she looks stunned.

"What just happened?" she whispers.

"I could be wrong, but I think you got pardoned and offered a lot of money."

"Do they expect me to keep my mouth shut because I'd be a Company officer again?" she growls, brows knitted together in a scowl.

"It certainly didn't have that effect the last time," Dr. Heron interjects. "Let's try to enjoy the moment and see what they have to say about everyone else."

Fanny, Macha, and Wenda are called to the stage individually. They're each praised for their roles in defeating the always-unnamed threat that was Kerrit Arduval and his so-far-undiscovered employer. Fanny tears up when Pauly is recognized, and she's assured his full revival and recovery is now a priority for the Company's best medical team.

Then, Macha is named leader of a new clinical research institute, which Shimauy claims the Company will establish on Iona, for Iona. Wenda learns she's now leading a fully staffed project to pursue the requirements necessary for Iona to become a Core World, which Cabot-Klaar unenthusiastically says the Company will fund. She manages to look appreciative, skeptical, and excited simultaneously.

I expect to be called up next to learn what kind of carrot they're going to dangle in front of me, since Arden's elevation to Grand Fancy or whatever stupid thing they plan to call it will be the dramatic finale. But Laurel calls us to the stage together. I glance at Arden; his face is blank. At this point he appears to be going through the motions.

Laurel heaps on accolade after accolade, so much so I've lost the plot by the time she launches into her description of how the charter will change to "reflect the real Iona." She says something about strong leadership with Company experience, trustworthy decision-makers, guiding the planet through the next phase of its development, blah-blah-blah. I'm painfully aware of Arden's fidgeting, and Cabot-Klaar's sneer, and how tired I am of standing here listening to Laurel talk.

I'm shaken back to the present as the theater erupts in cheers and applause, lights flash, triumphant music fills the air, and it takes me a moment to process what I've just heard. I can't swallow, I can't breathe, and Laurel is shoving a tiny microphone toward my face.

The inversion of the narrative is complete.

Iona's new Chief Designate is me.

I manage to murmur "thank you" into the mic, but can't mask my shock. The members of the Success Team surround me to shake my hand. Cabot-Klaar in particular holds it a beat longer than necessary and throws in an extra sneer at my obvious discomfort when he says, "We'll be working closely together from now on. What a delight."

Gemma Laurel beams at me like a proud mother and gushes her congratulations in a familiar tone. Shimauy mutters a vacant, "Well done; my assistant will have a meeting schedule to you this afternoon," before drifting away, distracted.

As we step off the stage, Ionians gather around. Most want to congratulate me, but others want to know what this appointment means for Iona. I have to tell them I don't know for sure. That's true, but only partly—thanks to Dr. Heron's explanation yesterday, I have an idea, and I don't like it at all.

We file out of the theater into Iona's weak sunlight, and I turn to Arden. "Let's walk," I suggest, struggling to keep the irritation out of my voice, and he nods. We head toward the northern ridge. His mouth is taut and his eyes narrowed and unfocused; I can almost hear the wheels turning in his head. He must have known this was coming, and he's probably already hard at work rationalizing why it was the right choice to leave me in the dark about it.

We stop, as soon as we're away from the bulk of people filing out of the theater. "You knew about this," I say, facing him. I'm trying to be calm, but it's next to impossible.

He crosses his arms over his chest defensively and looks squarely into my face. "I did. I assumed you did also. You said as much."

"I thought they were going to name *you* Chief Designate."

His expression turns to complete surprise.

"That was never going to happen."

"Why not?"

Arden blinks. I can tell he's trying to come up with an answer that doesn't give everything away, yet again. I grind my teeth in frustration.

"It just wasn't," he says. He can't look at me.

"But you knew they were announcing this today. You could have at least given me a warning."

His face goes red, the muscles in his jaw tighten.

"And you could have given me some warning before you started buddying up to disreputable criminals who've been sanctioned by the Governing Council," he says, anger building in his voice. "Security picked up that message almost as soon as you sent it. If it hadn't been me working the comms last night, you would have been in more trouble than you can imagine. I don't know how I'd have covered for you."

"Okay, there's our first issue. How about if you don't worry about covering for me because I don't need you to? I can speak for myself, including answering any questions raised by anyone here," I say flatly. Part of me wants to shake him. "But even that's not the point. Iona needs help. The Company is trying to take over this planet, and we know when they do, they'll be pursuing the development of the kind of offensive weapons that have been illegal for a thousand years. Plus, there's the potential relationship with Kerrit Arduval, and whether they ordered and paid for what he did here and on Bardazel. Don't you care about finding those lost members of the Equity Alliance? Don't you want to preserve Iona?"

Arden's eyes spark. "Obviously, yes. But your assumptions aren't supported by evidence. And I can't imagine anything you might be cooking up with Yeva

Darwin will have a positive impact. It's impulsive and rash and it won't end well. She's not interested in anyone but herself."

"She was one of the last people Arduval spoke to off-world, and if Tommas' recollections are right, he told her quite a bit about his plans," I retort, my voice sinking to the level of a furious whisper. "If she can help us prove he was working for the Company, we can get the Governing Council involved. We can get out from under Company control and make Iona free from them forever. It will be worth the cost."

Arden makes a short, exasperated sound, his hands flailing in the air. His eyes are narrowed and brows drawn in hard; even his posture is screaming he's had enough.

"Company oversight doesn't mean Iona's in danger," he growls. "Arduval is dead, and the Company has the security and medical personnel to make sure it's never threatened that way again ..."

My entire body goes cold as I let what he's said sink in. I fix him with a steely glare.

"You're already planning for them to be here forever," I say. "You know they intend to apply for Permanent Jurisdiction or something like it, and you're on board with it."

"I don't know what they're going to do; they haven't told me anything beyond what all of Iona heard this afternoon. But I do know they have the ability to give this planet a new life, to reinvigorate it in ways we could never ..."

I'm so angry I'm shaking.

"The Company never gives anything away without expecting twice as much in return, and no one knows that more than you," I say. "There's nothing the Company can do for us that we aren't better off doing for ourselves. If we're any kind of line item in the Company portfolio, no matter what they say, they'll use us any way they want, and we'll be stuck with whatever they choose for us."

"I'm not having this conversation with you now," Arden says in a low, terse tone as he turns away from me. "The Company is here, period. We have to deal with them and stop wasting time concocting wild plans and indulging conspiracies. I have to get back now, and you should as well. We've both got work to do." He stalks away over the sand.

He has no idea the effect his words have on me.

They reverberate in my head through the rest of the day. As I move through half-a-dozen boring meetings and a substantial stack of paperwork certifying my new "position," his voice is constantly in my mind. I return the greetings and congratulations of Ionians with a smile on my face. I graciously accept the enthusiastic hug Gemma Laurel wraps me in when I meet her to get "up to speed" on her thoughts for Iona's ongoing improvement. I even manage to copy Breton Cabot-Klaar's smirk with a raised eyebrow that leaves him staring after me in puzzlement.

Always, I hear Arden saying: *We've both got work to do.*

Yes. Yes, we do.

After the evening meal in our pod, I corner Wenda in the kitchen and explain my plans to her. She's surprised but supportive. I wait in my quarters until the wee hours when the pod is still, then slip out into the chilly night. I pull out my holo and fire off a single communication saying *on my way*, and head for the natural cavern where the *Gabriella* waits for me.

My little skiff is worn and a bit slap-dash, to be sure. I built her across eight years of fear and paranoia, from a wild collection of scavenged parts I transformed into something to be proud of, just as I rebuilt my battered spirit after the trauma of my life on Home World. The friends I cherish so much here would never make sense anywhere else. Yet we're a solid group who have each other's backs.

I'm not going to let them down now.

I stride up the ramp into *Gabriella* certain of one thing: it's time to go, to sort out a plan, to save this place and the people I love.

My little plexi bird is as quiet as death when I power her up, and I experience a rush of pride as she lifts off the surface like a feather finding wind. I hover over the ridge, then guide her north toward the landing pads, I hang there in low altitude, trying to memorize the way our little moons paint Iona Town in pale periwinkle and dusty dark pink. A voice in the back of my mind says I'm taking too long to get going; I have a timeline to meet. But I indulge myself a moment longer.

I imagine I can see my pod, nestled at the base of the ridgeline behind Residential. Inside, my friends sleep, most unaware of what I'm doing. I wonder what their reactions will be, if they'll feel abandoned or if they'll understand. I wonder too about Arden. When he finds my message on his holo, will he feel the way I did when I discovered he was gone all those years ago? Will he feel angry and betrayed? Will he accept it and move on?

I remember how I felt typing out *I have to do this for Iona and for myself* and the way my heart twisted as I hit "send." Maybe that's why he didn't leave me a message when he left Home World. Maybe it was too hard for him. Or maybe he simply couldn't admit defeat.

The last few months have been challenging for us all. When the Company came and things went very differently from how we'd expected, we let down our guard and let them take control of the narrative *again*. But we can take it back.

I can take it back.

I set the skiff's nose skyward and climb. The cliffs roll out from under the ship, their surfaces painted in tones of beige and rust and periwinkle, and my heart squeezes at their beauty. At altitude, I circle the planet—Iona's so small, it doesn't take long. I'm not ready, but I'm not sure I would ever be, so I prepare to break through atmo anyway. When my comm goes off, my pulse skips before I answer.

It's Wenda. I sigh, with both relief and the old familiar ache of disappointment. I didn't want to debate Arden about my choices at this moment, but still ...

"I felt like someone should thank you for what you're doing, so ... thank you, for all of us. Good luck." she says. Her voice trembles.

"Thanks, dear friend. Keep everyone together," I say, trying to sound bold. So much is riding on this, on me.

"You take care. Come back to us if you can."

She logs off, leaving the channel silent.

That's my cue. *Come on, little bird, let's fly.*

I engage *Gabriella's* primary thrusters and burn through Iona's atmosphere, leaping out into the sparkling vastness of open space. I plot out the course to Meridian Station and try not to think of the little beige ball behind me, becoming smaller with each passing second.

THE FOURTEEN-HOUR FLIGHT TO the station goes by without issue. I'm anxious approaching the docking port when Station Control hails me to finalize the process. My benefactor can't possibly be as thorough as she claims; someone is bound to be curious about this little unmarked bird and her undocumented pilot. But once I input my anticipated length of stay and pass the initial health and safety scans, Control issues permission to dock and drops out of my channel without a single question. I guide my skiff through the primary bay door and let the tugbot pull me to the proper location. Only a few minutes later, we're in the pressurized docking area. I slip her into her assigned berth, then listen for the chime indicating I may safely disembark. I look around for a moment as I step out onto the gangway, attempting to settle my nerves, and follow the lighted pathway into the heart of the Station.

I was last at Meridian ten years ago, on my way to Iona, for barely a day. It seemed unremarkable to me at the time, coming from Home World. But now it's nervy and bustling and busy in a way I forgot places could be, and a little overwhelming.

There are travelers from every sector here, doing every kind of business. The mix of shapes and sizes and colors and accents is both riveting and wildly overstimulating. My heart flutters a bit and my mouth is getting drier by the second, so I hurry along the outer rim corridor until I reach the Overnights—an electronic banner over the escalator to the section entrance reads *affordable temporary accommodations for the discreet traveler.*

I pass under the banner and go by several different Overnights before I find the one I've been assigned. Its vestibule is decorated in garish gold and red, and is meant to be ... sexy? Clandestine? I can't figure it out. After a quick ocular scan at the entry, the door purrs open. Inside, the dimly lit lobby is devoid of other guests. Though there are some amenities available, like a comm port and free holostreaming, travelers at these little budget operations don't hang out in the lobby to chat up others—another reason it was a smart choice.

A bell sounds, and haptics vibrate under my feet. I look down to see the square of plexiglass I'm standing on is now glowing green. After a few seconds, a series of tiles leading away from it also turn the same color, forming a path that guides me through the maze of hallways to my assigned room. Another ocular scan lets me inside. The room itself is clean, small and basic, with a nod toward Home Worlder taste—a bed with a mattress, a heavily cushioned chair, a little table with a holostreamer built into it. One wall is taken up by some kind of gigantic screen. I'm studying it when the holostreamer unexpectedly comes to life behind me and I nearly jump out of my skin.

"Welcome to Meridian Station, traveler Diana Beach!" shouts the holographic projection, a quirky androgynous young person at one-quarter scale, now floating above the table. I startle at the use of my alias. It flashes a brilliant smile, continuing to look this way and that, shoving a strand of shimmering silvery hair out of its eyes. I remain silent, but it begins its standard monologue anyway. It must detect my presence in the room, though I'm not engaging with it.

"I'm your personal AI concierge. Thank you for choosing this property as your home away from home. We are delighted to have you with us for ..." The hologram freezes and flickers for a moment while it accesses my file.

"... four wonderful nights!" it finishes, losing none of its enthusiasm for the delay. "Your visit package includes general stream access from your room. Specialized topic streams may be purchased through me. Lights, locks, and temperature are all voice-command ready. We hope you will enjoy your stay, Traveler Beach! Do you have any questions?"

The hologram pauses and I understand it's waiting for me to move or speak, to give it some clue about where I am in the room. I clear my throat softly, and it immediately turns and directs its gaze toward me. That answers one question. I'm still not sure how intelligent this artificial intelligence might be.

"What's this thing?" I ask, tapping my knuckle against the wall-screen.

The virtual concierge looks a bit blank and the image flickers again. This is definitely not the latest and best tech around; I've seen far faster and much more seamless holo projections, even on Iona. But I suppose it's what one gets with a basic Overnight.

In a few seconds, the dazzling smile returns, and the concierge begins another energetic narrative in answer.

"We're excited to offer you a room equipped with a ViewPort Wall by MassAppeal Incorporated," it shouts. "Customize your view to fit your mood! We provide 150 natural planetary and real-time feeds, plus a variety of exciting immersive fantasy scenarios, designed to enhance your every ..."

I wince. "That's fine, thanks," I say. "How does it work?"

"Say 'control' to access the menu. If you prefer me to make a selection for you, you can say 'select random' ..."

It soon launches into a detailed description of how to purchase my very own ViewPort Wall, but I interrupt it, saying, "That's enough, thanks. How do I get you to leave?"

"Oh, that's easy!" says the hologram, still irritatingly cheerful. "To dismiss me, say 'I'm done.' To get my attention anytime, say 'assist me'."

"Okay. I'm done."

It smiles at me again and winks. "Enjoy your stay, and if I can be of any assistance, don't hesitate to ask. I provide many personal services and may have the perfect one for you. I'm Virtual Concierge Agent 224, or if you're more comfortable with a given name, you can reference Xeric. Have a great night!"

The projection dispels, leaving me in exquisite peaceful silence. A sudden ache behind my eyeballs suggests it's later than I thought, and it dawns on me I'm both hungry and exhausted. For now, exhausted is winning. I drop onto the bed, wincing at its squishy softness. Tentatively, I lean back and tuck one of the plump pillows under my head. It's a bit unfamiliar after nine years sleeping in a hammock, but not necessarily unpleasant. It reminds me of the bed Arden and I shared on Home World so long ago.

The weight of memory descends on me, the gravity of what I've taken on, the risk but also the rightness. Along with that, my heart turns to what I could be giving up in the process. That's dramatic and hard, no matter how imperative this mission has become. I sit with those thoughts for what feels like a long time, devoured by uncertainty, conviction, passion, anxiety, fear, and resignation.

I call up the ViewPort Wall menu, and after a brief search through the options, say, "Iona evening stream" and turn out the room lights. Wrapped in the sounds and colors of Iona's night, I fall asleep.

I wake up after a full shift of solid sleep. It's time to tackle the Carnival, Meridian's main drag.

I leave the Overnights, pausing on the mezzanine above the market floor to take in the enormous hallway that runs like a vast indoor boulevard through the station. I've not been around this many people all at once in a long time, and my heart rate is spiking. As I deep-breathe to calm myself, the scents of people mixed with incense and a multitude of unidentifiable foods is an almost unbearable assault on my senses.

In addition to its collection of aromas, the Carnival presents visual and auditory challenges. I have to squint for a few minutes as my eyes adjust to the dramatic increase in illumination. Massive holo ads flicker and leap down the length of the Carnival, enticing passersby with things to buy or do or be. Near the displays, vendors stand close at hand shouting enthusiastically to anyone who makes eye contact with them. They're ready to escort prospective customers to what the holos promise, or at least to some version of it.

Less savory types hover in the shadows, looking for opportunities to direct the unaware to back rooms or isolated hallways where they can be more forcibly parted from their credits.

I edge down to the Carnival floor and begin weaving my way through the crowd. I need to be careful and keep my wits about me, but fortunately I look like what I am—a tired bare-bones space traveler picking up some basics to further her journey to its end. Most of the vendors don't even look at me, since I'm obviously not here for kinks or luxury items or fancy food. But after about ten minutes of working my way through the main hall, I see a vendor peer at me curiously and track me as I walk past. I look away for an instant and he appears at my elbow, as if unbound by the laws of physics.

"Hey polay-ah," he shouts, trying to be heard above the din of the Carnival and reestablish eye contact with me. He's a full head shorter than me and his face is marked by the signs of advanced middle age. His accent is dense though somewhat familiar, maybe Gordonian or Sharjeet. There's an "ah" sound both cultures use to denote exclamatory sentences, making his entreaty sound more like an energetic "Hey playah!" If we're going by the Intergalactic Lexicon, this man has called me a distinguished person of refinement.

I struggle to keep my smirk on the inside; I can't wait to see what he's selling.

"You come with me," he says, hurrying his steps to get in front of me. "I got what you looking for."

"Not interested, thanks. I'm here for something in particular."

"Okay, so what you looking for then?"

The question takes me by surprise. For the most part these vendors focus on convincing you that you're looking for whatever it is they have. But it also brings to mind the fact that I don't actually *know* what I'm looking for.

"Information. I'm looking for information," I say, trying to push past him. Surely that will make him back off. But instead, his eyes widen and he hops from foot to foot, keeping up with me.

"You're a special one. Eidor is my name. You come with me."

"Eidor," I stop near a burbling water feature that's also advertising anti-nausea pills with a jarringly bright ad floating over it. "I don't want to ..."

He interrupts energetically. "You're looking for information, but you're looking for *somebody*. It's me. I'm who you're looking for."

I laugh and gesture at the circus happening all around us. "All these guys say they're who I'm looking for."

Eidor laughs, his lips parting over slightly gray-stained teeth. "No, not them. You're looking for that." He jerks his thumb over his shoulder toward another floating ad several paces behind him. This one shows an elegant home surrounded by vast fields of flowers and a star-splashed night sky above. I'm about to shove him out of my way and walk on when a familiar logo appears in the air in front of it and I do a startled double-take.

Darwin-Cross Development Partners Inc.

Eidor sees my reaction and smiles more broadly.

"I'm right-ah," he says jubilantly.

I mutter, "Let's go."

Eidor leads me through the Carnival to an area where six smaller hallways spread away from the main drag. He treats me to an energetic monologue as we take one of the small branches, follow it for a while, then take a still smaller branch off from that. I learn he's originally from Sharj but has lived on the station for sixteen years. He has a wife who is a saint for putting up with him and runs their business with the skill of a general, along with a pre-teen son who only wants to play video games and listen to terrible music. He worries about his parents because they're so far away. He worries about his daughter, currently on Home World studying to be a bioengineer. He asks me numerous questions about my own life, but he keeps right on talking so I don't ever have to answer.

By the time the monologue slows, we're deep into the station, well out of the hustle and bustle of the Carnival. The shops here are small with more space between them, and much less extravagant. No vendors or agents lurk along the walls, and the crowd has thinned to station residents picking up necessities and chatting up their neighbors. The annoying holo ads are long left behind.

Eidor stops in front of an open shopfront, decorated with a blue and bronze awning over the doorway and a signboard proclaiming "TEA – HOT, FRESH, BEST ON-STATION OR OFF."

"Here we are," he says. I raise my eyebrows, but he shakes his head vigorously before I can say anything and grabs my hand, pulling me forward. "You're in the right place. I see your concern, but this is correct. Trust me, please."

He sounds sincere, although he wouldn't be the first sincere-sounding outright liar I've ever met. But as I'm trying to decide, a woman inside catches sight of us and shouts over the counter for Eidor to introduce her to his new friend. This turns out to be Eidor's wife, Lipop. Eidor shouts to her I'm not just anybody, and she should wait. He starts the monologue again as he pulls me into his shop, and I find between him yelling to me and yelling to her and her yelling back to both of us, I'm beginning to lose track of what's actually being said. After five solid minutes of everyone yelling and no one addressing me, I can't understand anything at all, so I clap my hands. Eidor and Lipop startle and fall silent.

"Quiet-ah," I say, worried I've managed to insult them. But Eidor and his wife turn wide smiles on me and laugh.

More importantly, they stop yelling.

"You're funny," Lipop says. "Here, have some tea."

The shop sells tea leaves and serves tea—or at least what is considered tea on Meridian Station. The cup handed to me is full of a grayish thick liquid with an aroma somewhat reminiscent of unwashed socks. But it's hot and I feel the need to be polite, so I brace myself and take a sip. I'm surprised when the flavor is quite pleasant.

"It's good, thank you," I say.

"I'll get some for you to take with you," Lipop says, disappearing into the back.

As his wife bustles around in back, Eidor offers me a seat at one of the little tables inside, then sits next to me. "Here is what you want," he says without fanfare, taking a small piece of acrylic out of a pocket in his sleeve and pushing it across the table to me. It's embedded with a series of numbers in gold, with a familiar logo etched at the top.

"This is what I want?" I ask. I'm not sure what I was expecting.

Eidor nods. "Yes, yes. This sequence," he says, emphatically tapping the tab with his index finger, "is what will keep everything from going boom-ah."

Oh.

My face must reflect the sudden sinking feeling in my gut. Lipop, emerging from the storeroom with a small container in her hand, begins to yell at him in Sharjeet, switching seamlessly between sympathetic, almost motherly looks at me and furious glares at her spouse. Still yelling, she sets the canister down on the table, on top of the engraved piece of acrylic. She pats me on the shoulder, lifts the canister to show me the acrylic tab has magnetically attached to the cannister's bottom, pats me again, and favors Eidor with one more annoyed look. She then utters a sharp expletive before sitting down beside me. I don't have to know Sharjeet to understand what she said.

Eidor takes it all in stride, sighing and favoring his wife with a fond smile.

"A general," he says to me. "I told you."

Lipop looks significantly at the tea canister then into my eyes. "You may be wondering about your benefactor," she says, her voice soft and serious. "She has been good to us. I do not believe she is good to everyone, but she looks after those who mean something to her. She will be an ally to you." I take this in as I tuck the canister of tea with its small secret into my bag.

"I hope that's true," I say, and Eidor makes a gesture that is the physical equivalent of "what choice do you have?"

Lipop reaches out to clasp my hand tightly, her face earnest. "Come to dinner," she says. "We will have more privacy and can tell you everything we know about her. I don't know anything about your mission, but I do know you're far from home. Here, a person needs friends."

I'm touched by her unexpected concern, and her offer. I have a lot ahead of me over the next few days, and both friends and additional information would be welcome, but I'm anxious about exposing myself too much. I don't know these people—but in my mind I hear Eidor's voice saying *keeps everything from going boom-ah*, and decide they've demonstrated well enough they're on my side. And in a less public setting, they might be able to answer some more sensitive questions.

"I'll come," I say. "When?"

"Tomorrow?" Lipop proposes. Eidor nods in enthusiastic agreement.

"Come to the shop," he adds. "We'll go from here."

Both of them walk me to the doorway. When I look back over my shoulder, they stand under the awning arm in arm, watching me walk away. But Eidor's brow is creased with worry, and Lipop is no longer trying to hide the anxious expression she's had on her face since she yelled at her spouse over his cavalier presentation of the little acrylic tab.

I'd rather not focus on my uncertain future at the moment, however, so I take advantage of this less raucous section of the station to do some basic shopping. I purchase a few items that will make the long journey easier on me—some sleeper tablets and some concentrated nutrition, along with some emergency supplies to be onboarded over the next couple of days. I also order a custom pressure suit and a set of ocular enhancers—things that require a few days. They're standard issue for distant space travel, and also provide an unremarkable reason to be on the station for the full four days I've planned. When I run the gauntlet of the Carnival again on my way back to my Overnight, the floating real estate ad with its shocking logo has disappeared.

I breathe a sigh of relief when I see the luridly colored entryway to my lodging. When the ident system approves my ocular scan and greets me by my alias, there's a little rush of adrenaline followed by an almost crushing sadness. I walk into my room to find the ViewPort Wall showing Iona at dusk. The display of golden pink and lavender across the whispering sandy surface makes me ache, and for a fleeting instant, I wish I was playing any other role in this story, that I was the old me, a regular grunt doing menial work on a tiny planet without any care for anybody or anything.

But that's not me anymore. Really—it never was.

After a last long look, I turn off the Viewport Wall and sit down with my holo to check my stream. I find an encrypted private message, from myself to myself, that says, *enjoy the tea*.

10

THE NEXT MORNING STARTS with an energetic, offensively loud greeting from Virtual Concierge Agent 224, who appears in my room to "congratulate" me on yesterday's purchases and to let me know some have already been onboarded while others are proceeding "on schedule." I'm not sure how it knows what I bought or where I went, although I supposed all merchants on the station would be networked together in some way. Noticeably absent from the rundown is anything from Eidor's shop.

I'm about to dismiss the AI when an entry on the list catches my attention. It's from a seller I didn't visit yesterday, for something I didn't purchase, simply called "special inventory."

"Can you give me details about purchase number eight?" I ask, working hard to keep my inquiry casual.

"Absolutely!" chirps Xeric. I wait while the AI freezes and flickers as the file is accessed. It takes a little longer than I expect, and I'm getting antsy. When the AI moves again, it unfurls a lengthy virtual scroll in my direction, which deploys the contents to my personal holo. My internal musings about the professionalism of Xeric's programming team (*A scroll? Really?*) are interrupted when it says in a somewhat abashed voice, "I'm sorry I can't read it aloud for you. That would be our normal practice, but this invoice is marked for your eyes only. You have to read it privately and it can't be expressed by a virtual concierge."

The change in the AI's style of expression is so dramatic I wonder for a moment if it's concerned I'm going to be angry with it or ask to speak to its manager. It's no longer the chirpy artificial salesman that greeted me on my arrival here, or even the one that shouted me into consciousness a few minutes ago; its behavior is calmer, more direct, more mature. It's definitely smarter, and when I glance up, its appearance has also changed. Instead of a generic hyper-enthusiastic young person, I'm looking at a calm capable adult.

I decide to be obvious.

"Are you different?" I ask. "You seem different."

"I'm still Virtual Concierge Agent 224, or Xeric, he/him, if you prefer," Xeric confirms. "You're probably noticing some of the enhancements that are part of the upgrade you purchased yesterday."

I'm so caught by the sudden designation of pronouns I almost miss the most confusing word in his speech.

Upgrade?

"Oh, right," I say, hoping I sound convincing, then wondering why I'm worried about sounding convincing to an AI.

"Would you like to review your purchased enhancements?" Xeric asks. "We appreciate how discerning our patrons at this level can be. You now have access to a number of bonus services. I would be delighted to help you take advantage of any of them."

My skin crawls as the AI's lips curve up and his expression drifts a little more toward lasciviousness. He runs a hand through his glowing hair, and lifts an eyebrow in my direction. It's still unnerving, but at least this time he didn't wink.

"I'd like to read about what's included, but you don't need to explain it to me or ... help me ... with anything."

"Of course," Xeric says calmly, now displaying a reassuring professional smile. "You'll find a file entitled Golden Key Upgrade among your Overnight notices. Be advised that it contains sensitive information, so please review it in a secure space, as this Overnight's rooms are only moderately secure and could be subject to data leakage. I'd suggest one of our excellent protected reading pods, such as those in the library in the Personal Evolution Annex. Might I assist you with anything else?"

"No, I'm done. Thank you."

"You're very welcome, Dr. Beach. Have a pleasant day."

Doctor Beach? *Doctor?*

"That was some upgrade," I mutter as the projection dissipates into the air. Grabbing my personal holo, I pause for a moment at the Golden Key Upgrade file but think about Xeric's warning and stanch my curiosity for now. I open the mysterious document from the invoice instead.

The invoice itself is not unusual. It lists the shop name, its location on the Station, and the goods purchased. The items I bought are there, but there's also a lengthy list of things I didn't buy. They range from obscure (what in sun's name are PanMallow Gel Treats?) to vaguely practical: a large backpack, a Home World Primitive Hunting kit, a box of spare holo parts, a variety of electronics, an entire barrel of adamantine flour). Aside from the flour, most of the objects are not large, and none of them are things I needed or wanted. They were all acquired via holotablet under my alias, paid for from a redacted account, and are scheduled to be loaded to my skiff over the next few days.

According to the time stamp, the purchases were made while I was having tea with Eidor and Lipop. I ponder this for a moment, unsure of my next move, but decide again that obviousness will again be the best course of action.

"Xeric, assist me," I say, and the holograph jumps to life in front of me.

"How can I help?" he asks, casting around until he pinpoints my position, and swiveling to face me. I've comfortably used AI tech for decades, but there's something about Xeric that leaves me feeling a little unnerved. Every time I call on him, he's become smarter, more competent, more ... *real*.

"The payment account on this invoice is redacted. I need to verify which account it came from," I say, watching for a reaction.

The virtual concierge looks dour. "I'm very sorry, Dr. Beach, but I'm unable to provide that particular information. I do apologize."

"Can I get it another way? Perhaps sent to my holo? I forgot to note down this expense, you see, and I may have to move some credits around to cover these purchases. You understand, yes?" I again wonder why I'm making up a story to explain myself to an AI.

"I do," Xeric says, looking perfectly sympathetic, "but I'm sorry to say I can't send you the account information at all—it's been made inaccessible to me. However, it may be reassuring to note that your Golden Key Upgrade includes an open-ended overage guarantee. There will be no problem if your account credits are temporarily exhausted."

"Oh right." I try to sound casual, but my heart is thundering in my chest so hard I wonder if Xeric can hear it. An overage guarantee of this magnitude means almost limitless funds have been put at my disposal. I'm terrified by what I might be asked to do with them before I leave Meridian Station.

Xeric continues to look at me levelly until I remember to dismiss the AI. This time, the hologram departs without any carnally tinged offers of assistance.

It's time to find out what this Golden Key Upgrade is really about. The tradeoff of security for anonymity is the clear downside of Overnights like this one. I decide to take Xeric's advice and review it somewhere it won't be scanned by nefarious data scammers or tracked by any overzealous salesbots. Half an hour later, I depart the Overnight and join the throng of people crossing the Carnival, heading for the Personal Evolution Annex.

11

The Personal Evolution Annex is self-contained and private, isolated from the core systems that keep Meridian Station running day-to-day, and separate from Meridian's networked vendors, security, arrivals and departures, hospitality, and AI. The idea is to provide complete privacy for those using the Annex, and that disconnect is one reason for my interest in going there. Looking around me, I wonder what the hundreds of others moving toward its entry portal hope to find. In our current linguistic paradox, "personal evolution" can and does mean anything, from sexual services to massage to spiritual experiences to more straightforward learning and education. The ordinary 50-ish woman on my left might be lining up for an extreme tantric encounter, while the fresh-faced young man on my right may be searching for tips on how to manage chronic disease. That's the problem with all of us. None of us look like what's on the inside. We perfected the veneer long before we found ways to solve the problems it hides.

At the entrance, there's no ocular scan and no personal data collection. A notification floating in front of the entryway lets us know that holo recording functions are disabled in the public areas but may be restored in private spaces at the discretion of the owner. I walk through the shimmering light of the digital banner, hear my holo whine in my pocket as its recording function shuts down, and step into the strangest, most extraordinary place I've ever seen.

Soft, spacey music rolls over the crowd, driving gentle displays of muted color in patterns across the floor and walls. Above us, the roof is crystal clear, the breathtaking display of blackness, stars, and planets stretches out overhead.

There's something strange and evocative at work. I'm standing in an enormous open vestibule that is so full of people I almost can't move, and yet there's a feeling of intimacy. The environment seems to be speaking directly to me, reaching into the core of my being, tugging at a part of me that longs for something I can't define. I'm in a trance, floating in this space.

The woman on my left begins to cry softly.

But I'm not here to have a mystical moment. I refocus and force myself to separate from the bulk of the crowd, moving purposefully. Glowing signage hovers over the half a dozen openings leading out of the vestibule: EXPERIENCE, HEAL, EXCITE, RESTORE. I thread my way toward the one marked by blue letters that spell out 'LEARN.'

The LEARN passageway soon widens out into another light-splashed atrium. Here, four floors of "private spaces" and commercial enterprises encircle the open center. Water features burble peacefully, and the walls are punctuated by flowering plants and vines climbing sleek silver trellises. I scan the range of doorways until I see the one I want, on the third floor: LIBRARY.

It's strange to me that they call it a library. From the station info packet description, it sounds more like a sex shop with documentation. It also offers a secure, anonymous, and un-com-linked place to review messages and data. Hopefully no one working at the "library" will be interested in selling me anything else.

I find the tube up to the third floor and wend my way around fountains and planters until I reach the entry. I'm a little surprised to be met by a person standing beside a reception desk. As I enter, he bows respectfully, waiting for me to speak. He's quite tall and his eyes are an unusual light amber, made even more dramatic by his dark skin. He's dressed in the same flowing orange robe worn by all the Annex attendants with an elaborate turban covering his hair.

"You're startled to see someone here to greet you," he observes, puncturing the awkward silence. "Please don't be concerned. We are utterly discreet."

"I'm sure you are," I say. "I'm just surprised you're not an AI. They run everything else on this station."

"Counterintuitive as it might seem, people are a better fit for situations that require prudence," he explains, his voice mellifluous and deep. "Artificial Intelligence Units give the impression of anonymity, but in truth provide the opposite, collecting data on every interaction that can then be preserved indefinitely and distributed at will. A live being, on the other hand, can look away and in time will simply forget. And we're much less susceptible to hacking."

He offers up a comforting smile, which I find irrationally unnerving. I fight back a shudder and instead attempt to smile back. From the expression that flickers across his face, I gather I'm only partly successful.

"Fine," I say in a voice harsher than my natural tone. "I'd like a reading room, please."

He bows his head, the soul of discretion, as he hands me an entry card and a set of crystalline eyeglasses. "Do you already have your materials? Or do you require help selecting from our offerings?"

"I'm good," I say, instinctively patting my holo through my jacket pocket.

Maintaining his deferential posture, the attendant gestures toward the hallway leading to the library's maze of rooms. The sleeves of his robe fall back as he does so, revealing well-muscled arms decorated by half a dozen geometric tattoos.

"Activate the glasses and follow the lighted path that appears. Please resist straying from the path as it's designed to ensure your privacy and that of our other patrons. Once you reach your reading room, use the entry card to open the door. Touch the call beacon in the room if you need anything." He lifts his eyes to mine. "We attendants are highly skilled in interpretation of the library's holdings, so should you read something you don't understand or would like demonstrated, I am at your service. A price list is available on your room's holostream."

"I'll be fine, thanks," I mutter through clenched teeth. What is it with Meridian Station and all the damn demonstrations? Sucking in a steadying breath, I don the glasses and tap the frames to bring them to life. In a few seconds, they reveal a glowing path along the crisp white floor tiles that leads into the depths of the library, and a blinking message that reads *enjoy your visit*. I leave the vestibule without bidding the attendant goodbye, certain I can feel his eyes on me as I walk away.

The library itself is a combination of digital file access points bracketed by paper items of almost incalculable value. I follow my directions past high shelves groaning with data and written work from every culture we know. The glasses have the added benefit of making the titles appear in midair when my eyes focus on a shelf. Some are in languages I can't understand, and some are in scripts I've never seen before. A few of the ones I can read are terrifying to consider. The overall effect of so many words and symbols dancing in front of me is hypnotic. I slow my pace to take in all in, but my glasses begin to chirp and the path they reveal flashes yellow with the message *please continue toward your reading room or hail an attendant to assist you.*

So much for actual anonymity. Clearly something is monitoring my progress.

I take one last look at the titles tumbling over one another, then go on my way with more deliberate steps.

The reading rooms are placed in a variety of little nooks and angled spaces scattered almost haphazardly throughout the library. The one assigned to me is nestled behind a tall panel of digital access points. I place the card the attendant gave me against the door frame and after a few seconds, the glasses splash the message, "tap to enter" in front of me. I tap it again, the door slides open, and I step inside.

The room itself is simple without feeling stark. Soft white light trickles down from the low ceiling. A series of small abstract paintings decorate the windowless walls, and a thick carpet muffles my footfalls as I walk into the room. It's so quiet the whoosh of the door closing behind me makes me jump.

A niche in the far wall contains a beverage-maker. A side table, comfortable-looking chair and plush footstool sit in one corner, and a pile of pillows occupies another. In the center is a holostreamer, not unlike the one in my Overnight. The glasses float a description above it that explains it is not linked to the stream nor the rest of the station and can only be used to examine data brought in by the user. Next to it is the call beacon the attendant mentioned.

I take off the glasses and drop them onto the side table, then make myself a cup of tea to help calm my nerves. Finally, I settle into the chair and pull out my holo. Its recording functions remain disabled. I wonder if the only way to get them turned back on is by asking for a demonstration.

Pushing that thought from my mind, I open the Golden Key Upgrade file. I'm shocked to see that the only thing it contains is a short sequence of numbers and letters that mean absolutely nothing to me.

I close the file, check the name, open it again. I search my downloads, my incoming, and everything that doesn't require a comm connection to see. There's nothing else. I'm looking at the right thing.

I huff in frustration and toss my holo onto the table. *What am I supposed to do with this?*

I stand and start pacing the room, reviewing my conversation with Xeric in my memory. Is there a companion file I need? Is this file corrupted in some way? Is it encrypted and I'm missing the key? They did say it included sensitive information. Did I misunderstand what he was telling me?

Wait.

Xeric said the file contained the information I'm seeking. *Xeric* suggested I come here to read it. Have I walked into a trap? Does my very expensive upgrade also include an upgraded version of Virtual Concierge 224 designed to be specifically malicious?

I'm being manipulated. I have an idea by whom, but I'm not sure why.

"Damn it," I mutter aloud, picking up my holo. "Now what?"

The glasses lying abandoned on the side table emit an insistent chirp and startle me. The light on the edge of the frame blinks blue, and when I put them on, I see the closed reading room door illuminated by a glowing yellow banner that reads *This Way.*

It has to be some kind of generic message. I must have used up my room time, or there's a malfunction, or ....

Before I can finish my list of excuses, the glasses chirp again, and the message changes. Cold shock runs through my whole body.

This way Faith now blinks across the door.

Part of me is panicking and wants to get the hell out of this creepy place and go home to Iona. Another part is profoundly curious—to what am I being led, and what possible role could it play in my work here? A third part is resolute. I came here for a reason. This might be an attempt to dissuade me, but it might also be a key—another link in the daisy chain toward my ultimate goal—a symbol of a bargain kept.

In my head, I hear Xeric's voice: *it includes the information you're seeking.*

I tap the doorframe and the door slides open. A new illuminated path glows before me, leading even deeper into the library. My glasses cycling the path's colors from gold to blue. *This way Faith* appears in front of me.

My mouth is dry and my heart is slamming inside my chest so hard I'm concerned about cracking a rib.

I take a deep breath and square my shoulders. I look left, then right, and see no one. I pat my pocket to make sure I've retrieved my holo and the entry card. Anxious chills run up my spine, but I set my jaw and, rubbing my palms together, start down the highlighted path.

This time, I'm guided though the data stacks in a complex, twisting pattern. The floating titles leap out in front of me and crowd my vision—at one point I have to stop and take the glasses off to get my bearings. I'm still in the primary holdings, but I'm now on the other side of the library from my assigned reading room. I'm so far away from the entrance, I can't even see the rectangle of light that marks the vestibule.

The material in this section is ancient, almost entirely objects made of paper. Although I'm sure these books were sterilized before being brought aboard the station, there's still a particular smell here—dusty, earthy, oddly comforting. I run my finger down the lush blue spine of a tome in the shelf on my right, and my heart squeezes. If only things were different and I was here for a vacation. I could pull this volume down and sit here with it, open it, absorb the script on its pages and breathe in that scent for a minute or an hour or however long I wanted, with nothing dramatic or difficult or deadly ahead of me ...

In my hand, the glasses issue a gentle chirp. I put them on again, and the path reappears, this time with the legend *keep going.*

I take a last look at the blue book. Its title, *Confessions of a Moral Skeptic*, flickers in front of me. I bid it goodbye in my head and continue.

Maybe one day I'll come back and read that book.

Maybe one day I'll sprout wings and fly on my own.

I take a deep breath and begin walking again. After several more minutes of twists and turns through the towering stacks, the path angles me toward an unadorned archway and into a small side room.

This room is barely lit, in contrast with the pleasant soft glow that fills the rest of the library. Even the material under my feet has changed. It's older, and definitely not the shiny stone-replica plexi of the main building. Titles no longer float in the air in front of the shelves.

The pathway stops in front of a wall of both paper objects and data ports. I come to the end of the route, and my glasses flash *please wait.* After a few seconds, they display the words *ready to download.*

I inspect the shelves in front of me. Although everything here is free of dust, I get the feeling the things here are seldom accessed. Given the prurient nature of most of this library's holdings, I'm a little concerned that they might describe kinks and practices I'd prefer not to be acquainted with. But the titles printed on the spines are innocuous enough—collections of love poetry, artwork, and reflections on the social aspects of gender constructs and sexual orientation. It feels more like one individual's personal study than a massive sex library on a space station that hosts hundreds of thousands of people at any given time.

As interesting as this is intellectually, I'm still not sure why I'm here. Although my panic has abated somewhat, as I'm becoming more certain who is behind this elaborate bit of theater, I'm still unclear on what I'm supposed to download. I reach out and run my fingertips along the volumes and ports in front of me, willing them to help me somehow.

That's when I notice the labeling.

Under each section, affixed to the shelf is a physical label—a sequence of numbers and letters in a configuration that looks suddenly familiar.

My pulse jumps with anticipation as I pull out my holo and open the Golden Key Upgrade file.

The organization is the same.

I examine the designations more closely. Shelves marked with ascending lettering combined with descending numbering from left to right and top to bottom form a repeating pattern. I creep along the wall, checking each label until I find the section bearing the sequence in my Upgrade file. Although there are at least forty holdings there, with only a single data port, I set my holo to receive and tap the indicated screen. Instantly, volumes of information begin to transfer to it.

The download completes, and the glasses chirp quietly. The path comes alight again and the legend says *return to your reading room*.

I drop my holo into my pocket, take one last look around this extraordinary room, then proceed out into the library. My curiosity about what I've obtained is intense, but I make it a point to move at a relaxed pace. Although I've not seen anyone other than the attendant since arriving here, that doesn't mean I'm alone. In fact, given some of the muffled sounds coming from other private rooms I've passed, not only are there other patrons here, it appears a fair number of them are heavily involved in "demonstrations."

Suddenly, the lighted path changes course. The legend *please leave the library* flashes in front of my eyes. I hesitate for a moment, confused. I need the privacy of the secure reading room to explore the material I've downloaded. It's counterproductive to go now. Are the glasses malfunctioning?

I tap them once, twice. Nothing changes. Perplexed, I begin to follow the path. It's not the complex twist-and-turn designed to keep me out of other people's way. Instead, it's an almost direct route to the exit. I move warily, until it suddenly turns red and begins to flash. The glasses chirp loudly, making my ears ring.

The message changes to *RUN.*

I run.

I make it to the vestibule as a loud jarring bang comes from behind me. I turn and see flames sputtering from one of the shelves. A phalanx of service bots drop from the ceiling and quickly extinguish the fire, protecting most of the volumes and data ports, but an intense black swath along the central pathway marks where the explosion occurred. Anyone near that spot would have been injured, and anyone inside the blast zone would have sustained injuries serious enough to be life-threatening. It's no more than three meters from where I was walking.

I stumble out of the Library vestibule onto the balcony overlooking the LEARN atrium. Drawn by the commotion, a small crowd is beginning to form. An electronic barrier drops over the entrance, announcing in glowing golden light that the library is closed. Other patrons hurry out, confused expressions on their faces. The obsequious attendant is nowhere to be seen.

I rush away, stopping behind a tall burbling water feature to try to calm down.

I'm bending over with my hands on my thighs attempting to regulate my breathing when I hear a chirp and realize I'm still wearing the glasses. A message superimposes over my line of sight: *time for tea.*

12

I'M STILL RATTLED AND shaking as I leave the Personal Evolution Annex and rejoin the throngs of people coursing down Meridian's raucous Carnival. The holo ads and vendors are particularly loud and obnoxious and I want to get away from everyone while I collect myself. The thought of going back to my Overnight right now doesn't fill me with comfort. After all, my Virtual Concierge did send me to what could have turned out to be my death—or more accurately, the person directing my Virtual Concierge did so.

But assuming the same person was also directing my movements in the library, they may have saved me as well. And they may still be guiding my movements—to what end, I'm not sure. It might be a mistake to presume benevolence, but at the moment I'm inclined to agree with the last message I received. There's one place on Meridian Station where I might have the emotional support to help me get myself together.

I continue down the Carnival until I find the right set of branching hallways, then follow the winding path we took yesterday. It's almost an hour before I stand in front of Eidor's shop. Lipop smiles and waves me in from behind the counter. Eidor has tea on the table by the time I sit down.

I sit quietly inside for a long time, watching the flow of Stationers in and out, listening to Eidor banter with passersby as Lipop bustles around serving customers, stocking shelves and generally doing all of the work. She looks at me from time to time with a reassuring smile. Eidor eventually abandons his public relations in the hallway. He brings me another cup of tea, along with one for himself, and sits down beside me.

"You had a difficult day," he says. It's not a question.

"You heard about what happened in the Annex library."

"Yes, there was a disturbance. You were there. That must have been terrible. You're okay and that's what's important." He takes a long sip of tea as if this settles the matter altogether.

Wait. How did he know I was at the library?

I open my mouth to ask, but he reaches across the table and pats my arm in a way that is part comfort, part warning.

"We will talk more about this later."

Lipop is closing up now, and she gestures for us to move out into the hallway. We stand in front of the tea shop as the awning withdraws and the electronic barrier descends. A holographic sign reading "We Are Closed" appears across the door, and Lipop exits through it and joins us.

"We're ready to go," she says. We walk to one of the station's Local Travel tubes, which will take us to Meridian's residential districts.

We get off at Residential 16. It's pretty, as space station living areas go. Lighting mimics sunrise and sunset, day and night, although the timing is more random than a replica of any planet's actual day/night cycle. At the moment, it's early evening in Residential 16, with gentle silver and purple tones shading the "sky" overhead. Alongside the travel tube platform are blocks of multistory residences, each with a slightly different façade. The extra splashes of color and design keep the structures—likely all the same on the inside—from looking like the personality-free metal and plexi boxes that they really are. I assume this would be where people of Eidor and Lipop's standing as reasonably successful Station merchants would live. To my surprise, we walk past half a dozen of these buildings before turning down a narrow passageway that runs between two dwellings and opens into a space that looks for all the world like a fancy planetside courtyard, complete with small trees, blooming flowers, and hedges surrounding its perimeter. There's even a seating area beside a water feature.

Eidor grins at my expression, shrugs, and says, "Lipop missed her plants from Sharj."

At the courtyard's center stands Eidor and Lipop's building. It has a lower profile than the other residences we've passed, only four stories high. The exterior isn't decorated, maintaining its original gray plexi and opaque square windows in front. I'm guessing it's older than the massive structures that surround it. It's still not small. It could be large enough for five or six typical residences depending on their size.

Then we step inside.

The vestibule, painted an improbable electric blue, presents only two doors and a lift tube. We get into the lift, Eidor punches in a code, and we ride up to the third floor. At this level, only one door is accessible, marked with Eidor and Lipop's names.

The residence is substantial even by Home World standards, filled with cozy rooms and narrow nooks. Each room I pass through is decorated in a beautiful array of colors and textures, with soft comfortable furniture and elaborate wallpaper patterned with traditional Sharj motifs. There are pictures of children and extended family members everywhere. I'm taken by one that includes not only Eidor and Lipop but also their parents, frolicking unselfconsciously under a waterfall.

"You miss your family," Eidor says, coming up behind me.

"I don't have any family, but I do miss my friends."

His lips arc up in a small smile, his eyes sparking with warmth. "They *are* your family. You'll be with them again," he says, inclining his head. It's not a question but a statement of surety. I don't know if he has some kind of inside information I'm missing, or if he's talking about some spiritual alternate reality. I decide not to ask, and instead say, "I hope so."

Dinner preparation is a group activity. I meet young Hamiit, their son, and find him exactly like every other teen I've ever known; Eidor probably shouldn't be worried about him. Lipop puts me on side-dish duty, preparing two simple vegetable dishes while she and Eidor work on the main course, a meat-equivalent steeped in a rich spicy-smelling sauce. We manage to all work together in the small kitchen without tripping over each other's feet. After an hour, dinner is ready. Based on the spread covering their countertops, I'm comfortable estimating that there's enough food to feed most of the neighborhood should they decide to drop in.

Eidor catches my eye and says, "We invited a friend. I hope you are not offended."

I'm startled. My intention has always been to fly under the radar here on Meridian, and even becoming this friendly with Eidor and Lipop feels a little dangerous to me.

Eidor notices my hesitation. "No worries," he says. "He's trustworthy, I know him now for many years."

He is looking at me with such a sincere almost pleading expression on his face that I give in. "It will be an honor to meet your friend," I say.

I'm still concerned, because I do want to ask Eidor about a safe place to look at what I downloaded in the library. Having one more person for dinner will delay that by only an hour or so, and there's no reason for them to have any idea of who I am or what I'm doing on Meridian Station. As Hamiit and I set out plates along the dining table that extends and retracts from the wall in one of the elaborately decorated rooms near the kitchen, I hear the door open, and Lipop call out a greeting. I can't make out the words of the response, but the guest says something in low deep tones, followed by relaxed laughter.

"Look who is here," Eidor says, coming into the dining room smiling. Behind him, outside my field of view, the guest follows. Hamiit shouts "Uncle Nico!" and races to bear-hug the guest, who comes into the room with Hamiit wrapped around him like a vine. Eidor beams fondly at both of them, then turns to me. "Faith, this is Nicodemus, our oldest friend on Meridian Station."

I'm surprised enough to hear Eidor introduce me by my real name, but that's nothing compared to when I find myself staring into the face of the library attendant.

I'm not sure if that's a spark of recognition or something else in his amber eyes as he disentangles himself from Hamiit to come forward and bow to me, his fingers tented at his chest. "Well met, Faith. A friend to Eidor is a friend to me as well. Please call me Nico," he says. If I'd had any thoughts that I was mistaken, his distinctive mellifluous voice immediately dispels them.

"Thank you ... Nico," I say, then turn away to hide my confusion. He makes no reference to the library, or to having seen me there.

"As usual, you are just in time to eat," laughs Lipop, appearing from the kitchen. "Come, everyone, let's set out the chairs and fill our plates."

Dinner is convivial and relaxed, although an edge of anxiety still hovers in my consciousness. I spend most of the meal listening rather than talking. I'm still not sure what to make of Nico's presence and no one has gone further in explaining his connection to Lipop and Eidor except the continued reference to a long-standing friendship. That part is not in dispute. They banter and fuss among themselves in the way that old friends do, a way that can't be faked on the spur of the moment. Nico even teases Hamiit about a game the two of them shared recently—one of the only times the ravenous teen looks up from his plate. I do later catch Nico eyeing me with a curious expression. Despite his speech at the library earlier, he hasn't forgotten me after all.

Once the meal concludes, Hamiit escapes to his room and Lipop settles us in their comfortable family room. One entire wall is covered by a ViewPort screen, which Eidor sets to early evening on Sharj. "It's not everyone's taste but Lipop likes to be reminded of home," he says with a shrug.

I don't mind the bright undulating aurorae that dominate the Sharj night sky; in fact, the display is entrancing. I say as much, and Eidor smiles at me, then retreats to the kitchen with Lipop to load the sterilizer and pack away the leftovers. This leaves me sitting with Nico in awkward silence for the second time today. Given how he tracked me over dinner, I'm not surprised when he asks, "Did you find what you needed in the library?"

"I thought humans look away and forget," I say, smiling to show him that I'm making a joke rather than criticizing his job performance.

He looks at me levelly, his amber eyes dancing and mouth-corners tugging up as if he's fighting back laughter.

"We generally forget," he says smoothly, "but some people we cannot help but remember."

I smirk. "That sounds like a demonstration proposal."

He laughs aloud now, a rich baritone. The smile takes over his face, transforming it from a carefully held mask to something more genuine.

"I was speaking outside my official capacity," he says, "although I'd gladly offer you anything you might require."

"I'm sure I'm the first person you've ever said that to," I say, in as dismissive a tone as I can muster. "Are there pay bonuses for off-hour demonstrations? Will this conversation show up on my final invoice?"

He seems undeterred and studies me frankly.

"You didn't answer my original question," he says. His expression is still light, but no longer quite so playful.

"You're right. I didn't."

At this, his expression becomes thoughtful. "I understand your mistrust. I believe I can help you in another way, all of my other areas of expertise aside."

I'm confused until Lipop clears her throat from the doorway. "He can help you with your mission," she explains. "It's why we invited him."

Eidor appears behind her, and nods to underscore her point.

"Then you all know who I am and why I'm here," I say, looking around the room at each one. I'm simultaneously comforted and alarmed. My mouth has gone distinctly dry and my palms are starting to itch.

It's Nico who responds.

"A picture was painted for us in broad strokes," he says. "We know no details of your plan, nor any of your personal information aside from your given name. We don't need to, and really, it wouldn't be safe for us to know. We were asked to keep an eye out for you and to assist you as necessary. We can be conduits of information, or provide skills you might not have. If you can't consider us friends, at least consider us resources."

I think of Eidor's worried face as he slipped the plastic triangle to me in the tea shop yesterday, Lipop's concern with his lack of subtlety, Eidor introducing me to Nico by my real name rather than my alias despite my never having told him either. I look from one face to the other, weighing my options. I'm not sure if I should feel grateful or manipulated or both—a sensation I'm guessing I need to get used to.

I turn to Nico again. "What happened in the library ... was that you?"

Nico's face shadows for a moment and his eyes narrow, a flash of anger quickly covered over. "I have no knowledge of what happened in the library from your perspective, either before or after the disturbance. I only know that some of our unique volumes were damaged beyond repair and promises of reimbursement will not cover their loss."

His dismay over the damage and contempt for the notion that mere money can make up for it makes me feel much better about him.

All right then. Decision made. I turn to Eidor.

"Can I use your secure stream?" I ask. "I won't know what I'm looking at, and some help would be most appreciated."

13

A SEPARATE ROOM HOUSES the secure stream, at the rear of the flat, separated from the common living areas by a short narrow hallway. Still, it's decorated like the rest of the house, and the vibe is like some great-aunt's fussy reception room—if that great-aunt were Sharj and had a strong affection for floral prints. High impact plexi tables, rendered in bright colors rather than the more ordinary white or clear, are positioned around the room, their tops decorated with pretty fabric covers. The remaining furniture is a mix of comfortable and functional. Fat print-covered pillows are tucked into ergonomic chairs, wall-mounted holostreamers are encircled with lively patterned borders that make them look like pieces of art. One full wall is dedicated to a ViewPort playing a scene of a neatly edged flower garden against a backdrop of stars, where butterflies serenely flitter. In an instant, I realize where the inspiration for this residence's courtyard came from.

Eidor ushers us into the room and closes the door. He sits in one of the chairs, unceremoniously tossing its decorative pillow onto the carpet at his feet, while Nico and I settle on a pretty carved bench under one of the holostreamers.

"Lipop," Eidor says, "likes her decorations." Lipop, who has perched herself on the edge of a flowery hassock near the garden Viewport wall, makes a defensive harumphing sound and rescues the pillow from the floor, hugging it to her chest like an injured child.

"It's fine," Nico and I say in unison.

"Now. How can we help you?" Eidor asks. I pull out my personal holo and connect it to the streamer with a few taps, then pop the Golden Key Upgrade file up into the air where everyone can see it.

"This is what I came to the library to read," I explain.

Nico leans forward as I open and enlarge the file.

"These are catalog numbers," he says. "They're quite old. I'm not certain I know where this volume would be."

"Well, someone knew, because my glasses sent me there."

Nico's face shows complete surprise.

"They can't, they don't have ..." He pauses. "Are you sure?"

"I'm sure. After I opened this file, the glasses directed me out of the reading room, through the library to a small holding room, and to the data port for the volume listed here. They instructed me to download to my holo and then shooed me out before the explosion."

"Those messages and the pathways are generated by the library's primary central processing unit," Nico says. "The process is almost entirely automated. Even attendants can only submit rudimentary commands in an emergency."

"Could the signal have come from outside?" asks Eidor. "From a satellite relay or an off-world comm center?"

Nico shakes his head. "No. There are no receptors for that kind of communication built into the glasses, or into the library itself."

"What about AI support, like the Overnights? Does the library utilize upgradable intelligence?" I ask.

"There's nothing like that," Nico explains. "It's basic 'if this, then that' programming. Hamiit could write it. It's that simple."

"That means it's also easy to modify."

"That's theoretically correct, but it would require direct access to the Library's CPU. Only a few people with administrative oversight have any access at all, and no single person has the necessary permissions to create such a modification without approval from the others."

"If I examine the code, I'll be able to figure out how it was accessed and modified," I say, excited to encounter, at last, something on this Station I might understand. "There might also be clues as to who performed those modifications, signatures and identifying characteristics in the way it was written."

Nico is already shaking his head. "The system undergoes a wipe and a full re-install every night," he says. "We're too late. The reset had begun by the time I left this afternoon, since we closed early."

"Maybe that was the real reason for it," I say. "I thought at first it was directed at me, to stop me from leaving the library with this information, but the glasses were parsing messages that got me out of harm's way instead. With the library closing early, the process would start sooner than normal, covering the tracks of whomever is responsible."

Lipop sighs and hugs the fancy pillow she's been holding. "We are wasting time here," she says. "We all know who is behind this. It could not have been anyone else."

"I agree," Nico says. "We may never understand how she did it, but she's the only person I can imagine who could have orchestrated this. Somehow, this is all Yeva's doing."

"All right," I say. "Let's assume for now that particular question is answered. Let's look at the file."

I send the library file to the holostreamers, and the document begins to unspool into the air between us, so data-heavy the stream momentarily obscures Eidor from my view. Floating in front of me are a sequence of line drawings with all their parts jumbled, with captions and what might be a series of ordered instructions written in a script I can't decipher. All of these elements continue to move rapidly, swimming around and through each other, never quite resolving or becoming stationary. We can only get a general impression of what it contains. This is encryption of the highest order; sorting it out will not be easy.

"This isn't from our library," Nico says with certainty. "It's not the kind of material we have. This had to be inserted into the system for you to find."

"And because the digital holdings are wiped and rebuilt from a master file daily, chances are good that it's no longer there," I say, and Nico nods.

"What could this be?" I ask, enhancing the documents as much as possible. The text and imagery moves faster the more I try to adjust them. "This line drawing ... the parts appear regularized ..."

"They are architectural," Eidor says, his voice heavy with certainty. "I believe it may be a 3D schematic of some part of the station."

Nico starts. "If you're right, old friend, we must be very careful indeed," he says, his eyes widening. "This is tightly controlled information. Anyone discovered with it would face a harsh sentence."

We look at one another silently for a moment, considering each other through the blur of the file's contents. I speak first.

"I understand why that's so," I say. "Something like this in the wrong hands could lead to the destruction of the entire station. It's been given to me for a reason, and I don't think it's to set us up for dire consequences." In my head, the careful cynical part of me wonders if I believe myself, but I again hear Tommas saying *she has a strong sense of fairness*. There would be no point to bringing me this far to simply knock me down.

Eidor squints at the dancing holograph, poking at it with one finger. The file doesn't appear to like this and begins taking evasive maneuvers whenever he reaches toward it. "It's marked," he says, jabbing one finger at the holograph, which ripples and avoids his touch. "There."

There's a single small golden squiggle amid all the other blue and black squiggles tumbling over one another in mid-air.

"It won't stop moving long enough for me to see it," I sigh, "and the resolution is starting to degrade. We need the decryption key, and some top-line computing power."

"I can provide one of those things," Nico says. "How do we get the key? Do you have it?"

Key. Golden key. Golden Key Upgrade.

"I don't have it now, but I think I know where I can get it," I say.

After a quick negotiation, we leave Eidor and Lipop's home. Nico will accompany me back to my Overnight. If I'm able to obtain the key, that will place us closer to the Library with its secure reading rooms, and he'll get me inside. As a bonus, his position as an attendant makes it unremarkable for him to escort me through the station and even into my room.

We walk to the transport in silence and take our seats on the next Local back to the Carnival. I'm preoccupied and don't even notice the stations as we pass them. After a few minutes, Nico leans close and whispers, "We've constructed this ruse to convince anyone who might spot us that there is a perfectly obvious reason for you to be returning to your Overnight accompanied by me."

I can't help myself. "A demonstration, naturally," I say with a smirk.

His eyes dance, and he chuckles. "Of course. To be convincing, however, you should look happy about it. Anticipatory. Here, demonstrations are by definition something pleasurable. Your demeanor suggests something altogether different."

"Is that so? How do you know what I look like when I'm anticipating pleasure? This might be my exact response."

He pulls back from me and studies my face, then leans in again and whispers playfully into my ear.

"You look as though you're anticipating dental surgery."

Oh.

"Sorry," I mutter. "I'm ... out of practice."

He takes my hand and pats it gently. "The nervous client, then. A first experience with a demonstration, easing back into things. So be it."

He inclines his head, eyes sparkling, and the corners of his mouth tip up as he murmurs with great sincerity, "Don't worry. I will be gentle."

I feel a dam open a bit inside me and my tension moves aside for now. I laugh and shoulder into him. He laughs also and laces his fingers through mine. He then proceeds to keep me distracted by pointing out features of the local stops we pass, telling me stories about life on the station, and cracking ridiculous sexually tinged jokes. He holds my hand until we arrive at the Carnival stop and keeps one hand on the small of my back as we exit. It feels both protective and sensual. All a ruse, I remind myself. It's an act, a "demonstration" of our own for whomever might be watching, because I'm quite sure someone *is* watching. Still, Nico is good at what I assume is a significant part of his job. I feel particularly attended-to. My heart rate jumps when his hand travels down to my hip to guide me in the right direction, and I have literal chills when his fingertips trail lightly across my shoulder blades as I walk beside him through the still-clamorous Carnival.

We are only steps away from the garish entryway of my Overnight when I'm brought up short. I stop and turn to face him.

"I'll pass an ocular scan to get in, but what about you?"

"The Station has a master list of attendants," he explains. "The system will recognize me and I'll be permitted entry."

"The Station tracks your movements?" My lip curls in disgust, but he's nonchalant.

"It does. It may seem invasive, but it's an important part of maintaining the integrity of our services. It's difficult to become an attendant. Not only does it require years of training, but one must also pass a battery of psychological and physical tests and maintain good standing with our professional guild. We're very serious about this."

"Was there some kind of problem in the past that caused all this caution?"

"No. The Annex developers began with a particular vision, and this level of confidentiality and safety was part of it. It's a safety mechanism for us, too. Visitors can be ... complicated. And sometimes travelers have specific interests that we will not support."

I cringe. He seems chagrined and strokes my hair, then enfolds me in his arms and pulls me to him. His body seems exceptionally warm, and I can hear his heart beating as I rest my head against his chest. He smells wonderful, like incense and spice.

"This might become dangerous for you," I whisper. "There are forces at play here that may go beyond what you've been told."

He looks into my eyes, serious now.

"Do *not* worry about me," he says softly.

I stay in his arms several counts longer than I absolutely need to. When we separate, I take his hand and lead him to the vestibule of the Overnight. He steps up to the ocular scan first, then I do, and the door whirs open and admits us both. When the plexiglass pathway appears, it contains a green line for me, twinned with a gold line for him.

"You see?" he murmurs in a reassuring tone. "It's all as it should be."

We enter my room to find the lights set to a dim glow that mimics candlelight. The Viewport Wall has activated and shows a feed of a Home World beach at night, gentle waves lapping rhythmically against the shore in the moonlight. Soft tinkly music fills the room. The whole scene makes me grit my teeth.

"Your accommodations anticipate me," Nico chuckles. "I'm a bit surprised by the theme, however. Are you such a fluffy romantic? I'd have thought a more frank, lusty eroticism would be your taste."

I'm not sure whether I'm more taken aback by his words or the idea that my room is trying to set a mood. He notices the discomfort on my face and says, "Tell it to reset to default."

Increasingly irked, I growl, "Reset to default."

The lights come up to full and the ViewPort scene and music disappear.

"Better," he says matter-of-factly. "We have work to do."

I walk to the center of the room to stand close to the table that contains the holostreamers, while Nico stands a respectable distance behind me.

"Xeric, assist me," I say. The Personal Concierge pops into the room, turning until it finds us.

"Oh, I see you have a guest, one of our most esteemed attendants!" he says in a tone just short of applause. "Good evening to you both. How can I be of assistance?"

"I need a full copy of the Golden Key Upgrade file—one with the detailed information," I say, making sure to accentuate the words *golden key*. "I'd also appreciate any additional data related to Golden Key Upgrades, delivered to my personal holo."

"Of course. Please be advised that some of the information is sensitive, and this room can be subject to data leakage."

"I understand."

My holo chirps almost immediately, indicating it's has received the information.

"Do you require anything else?" Xeric asks.

"No, thank you. I'm done."

"Have a wonderful experience, Dr. Beach." Xeric delivers a courteous bow to me and then peers over my shoulder and nods to my "guest" before disappearing. I turn to Nico and gesture toward the door.

"Time for step two," I say, "but first, do we need to make some noises to convince the AI that I'm having a wonderful experience?"

"They don't listen unless you call them by name," he says, then pauses. "Why do I feel like I've missed an opportunity?"

"Possibly because you've missed an opportunity. Come on, let's go." I take a moment to pull on my jacket, then on a whim release my hair from my standard messy bun and use both hands to shake it out, hopefully in a way that is consistent with having had a wonderful experience. Nico extends his arm and I take it, pressing in close to him. We leave the Overnight and head for the Annex.

It's late by Stationer standards, but the throng in the Annex is no smaller than it was this morning. The primary difference appears to be that a significant number of visitors are now drunk or in other forms of altered consciousness. One couple in particular is especially incoherent, having collapsed on the floor near a water feature. They're shouting unintelligible phrases to one another that could be love poetry or threats of violence depending on what language they're speaking. Fortunately, there's no immediate threat to anyone, since they're too discombobulated to even stand up.

I try not to stare at them as we move through the entryway with the rest of the crowd, but they're impossible not to notice.

"They'll be all right," Nico says, marking my gaze. "If they're truly in some kind of difficulty, someone will come. The Personal Evolution Annex is not aptly named. Many of the services provided here create a great deal of devolution for our visitors before any progress is attained. Inner demons aren't as easy to defeat as outer ones. Not everyone has the courage to come here without a little help."

It's the first time I've seen the Annex through anyone's eyes but my own, and it's a startling revelation. I've been thinking of it as a place of ridiculous self-indulgence, when its actual purpose is healing of a very specific kind. It's not about the material, physical comfort I associate with carnal "demonstrations" and perfumed spa treatments, although that's part of it. There's also an opportunity for deeper healing that only comes from seeing oneself clearly.

"I should come back here one day when all of this is behind me," I say, only half-aware of speaking aloud.

"So, you shall," Nico says. He sounds quite sure of himself, and squeezes me a little closer to steer me by a couple that has fallen into passionate kissing in the middle of the crowd.

Once we reach the LEARN atrium, I'm surprised to see the yellow "Closed" banner still glowing across the library entrance. I stretch up and place my lips close to Nico's ear in what I hope looks like a playful sensual moment to the people thronging around us, and whisper "How are we going to unobtrusively barge into a closed library?"

He bends down and whispers in my ear, "We're not going there; as a most esteemed attendant, I have other alternatives at my disposal."

I laugh at his appropriation of Xeric's elaborate descriptive language. He drapes his arm around me as though soothing a nervous child and walks me to an almost unnoticeable door built into the back of the atrium, well past the ascent tubes used to reach the upper floors. The door responds to the touch of his hand and slides open, and we step into a low-ceilinged, softly lit hallway. When the door closes behind us, the noise of the atrium is reduced to a mere background hum.

"What is this place?" I ask, feeling a bit anxious, compounded by a little claustrophobia. "I'm not about to find out you're one of the bad guys, am I?"

Nico tosses me disdainful look. "What do you think?"

"I think ... I don't know what I think," I say, disentangling myself from him. Instead of questioning me further, he walks a few feet down the hallway and taps on the wall. Only after it responds to his touch do I realize it's another door. He looks back at me.

"Are you coming?" he asks.

I ignore the closed door behind me, and the solid walls on either side of me, and walk toward him slowly, trying to push my misgivings aside. When I reach him, he takes my hands and guides me through this new doorway. The panel whispers shut, closing us up together in the dark. I can hear his breathing, slow and even, and feel the gentle pressure of his hands on mine, strangely intimate and warm.

"Lights, please," he says.

The lights come up. We're standing in an elegant sitting room with a faux fireplace and a real viewport that looks out on the strange cold beauty of space. The Governing Council's expansive enviro sparkles in the distance. The small cadres of ships arriving and departing look like bees dancing around a silver flower, and the scene is so mesmerizing I have to tear my attention away to take in the rest of the room. In stark contrast, it's elegantly furnished and rich with color and artwork. There are fresh flowers and fine ceramics placed here and there. A piano stands in the corner.

I can only imagine the expression on my face. Nico gestures toward a pair of exquisitely upholstered armchairs facing the fireplace and I drop into one.

"Welcome to my home," he says. "The sex dungeon is across the hall."

It takes me a full five seconds to realize he's joking.

"You *live* in the Personal Evolution Annex," I manage to say, shaking my head.

"Technically, this section isn't part of the Annex," he explains. "It's a special residential unit for those of us who have a certain standing in the community." He takes a decanter and a pair of small tumblers from a tray on the piano and then sprawls comfortably in the chair next to mine. Everything about him has changed; even the cadence of his speech is different. It's as though he's stripped off an entire personality to reveal another. He's clearly no longer playing the role of "library attendant." This is who he really is.

"Are you telling me you're important?"

"Important isn't the right word." He fills the glasses with the golden liquid, hands one to me, then takes the second for himself and sets the decanter down on the table between us. "I have certain responsibilities here that merit compensation. This lovely apartment, full access to every part of the Library including its processors, and the most secure unmonitored stream connection available on Meridian Station are all part of that compensation."

Ah. So that's why we're here.

I take a sip of the drink and find my mouth graced with an exquisite brandy.

"Is this also part of the compensation package?" I ask, swirling the liquid in my glass and watching it sparkle in the firelight. "How about that piano?"

He chuckles. "I admit the piano is a personal indulgence."

"Do you play?"

He looks insulted. "Of course I play."

I take another deep drink then set the brandy down, feeling my tongue already becoming a touch unwieldy in my mouth. I'm a solid drinker on Iona, but that means nothing in the face of high-quality alcohol.

"Let's see if we can sort out that schematic," I say. "Maybe another day I'll ask you to play the piano for me."

He drains his glass and sets it down next to mine, and I imagine I see a hint of wistfulness in his eyes. But he pulls himself upright in his chair and says, "Another day, then. Let's get you to work."

He calls out a short string of commands, and a sleek streamer descends from the ceiling. We connect my personal holo to it, and in a few seconds, we're looking at the familiar tumbling text and line-drawings from the library. I pull up the information Xeric passed to me at the Overnight; there are more than a hundred files. I begin opening them, and soon the room is full of floating symbols and letter sequences of varying lengths. At least the contents of these files sit still, and I'm delighted that the format is something I recognize.

"Any of these could be the decryption key," Nico mutters. "What's the point of all this?"

"They're all the decryption key," I explain, enjoying the opportunity to show someone my area of expertise. "Specifically, we're looking at decryption logic, broken down into tiny chunks. I'll need to structure it correctly first, but after that it should be fairly straightforward to deploy."

"How long will that take?"

"The initial set-up won't take long, but I don't have a lot of experience with this level of multidimensional encryption, so I don't know about that particular process. If Eidor is right about what this is, there will probably be some surprises that pop up during the process. I might have to get creative to work around them, but it shouldn't be anything I can't handle."

Nico rises from the chair and carries the brandy decanter back to the piano. "Carry on, then," he says. "Let me know if you need something." Then he disappears to another part of the apartment, leaving me swimming in the floating files.

I reach for the code bites and start manipulating them, feeling a pleasant, powerful rush that I haven't enjoyed for a long while. What was I doing for the last eight years, buried under sand and grease and machine parts, when I could have been doing this? Why did I become what I became? I thought I had my reasons then, but as I pull the pieces of the puzzle together the pain of the past seems far away, leaving me energized and alive. I work steadily for the next two hours, not even noticing time passing, until the program that will decrypt the library files is ready to run. I take a deep breath and set the process in motion.

I stare at the display for as long as I can tolerate the silence. Nico has stayed out of the room so I could remain undisturbed, which I appreciate. However, now I'm anxious for company.

"Where are you, Nico?" I call out. "I'm done. It's running."

He comes in through a door next to the piano and crosses the room to stand behind me. He takes a long studious look at the files as they blink and slowly re-assemble themselves in the air.

"Excellent. What can I contribute?"

He's changed out of his attendant robes into loose-fitting casual pants and a black tee that shows off the chain of tattoos on his arms. His braids are uncovered and cascade down his back like a ropy waterfall. He's also kicked off the simple sandals he wore and is cruising around barefoot.

"More brandy?" I hold out my empty glass. "I'll need your knowledge of the station layout once this is done, but that won't be for a while yet."

He retrieves the decanter and refills my glass, then drops to the floor next to my chair and stretches out on his back on the thick carpet. I slide out of my own chair to sit beside him.

"Tell me about Yeva," I say. "You've known her a long time. What is she like?"

Nico makes a face and lets out a sigh. "We've met in person less than ten times, although we communicate much more frequently. She's direct and doesn't tolerate bullshit. I can say she's fair and honest—at least, her version of fair and honest. She's always one step ahead of anyone who tries to get to her, so nobody ever gets to her. And she chooses her friends carefully. It would seem you've been chosen, so I hope you appreciate the rarity of that."

"I've been *chosen*. Is that so?" I want to laugh, but the expression on Nico's face kills the urge in an instant.

"She wouldn't do this for a random stranger, no matter how valuable a thing they might be bringing her."

I start. "What do you know about our arrangement?" I ask.

"Again, not much. That there's an exchange of some sort, as there always is with her. She doesn't do favors. She does seem to be going out of her way for you, to keep you safe and make sure you get whatever it is you're supposed to find. She's on your side."

Whatever it is you're supposed to find. The words echo in my head, and I wonder how different her idea of what I'm *supposed to find* might be from my own.

"I don't know how I feel about that," I say, "but then, I don't know how I feel about a lot of things."

I drain the brandy from my glass and stretch out on the soft fluffy carpet next to him. It feels good not to be lurching forward squinting at the holo display, but now that I'm no longer absorbed by programming, my tension is creeping back to the forefront.

He pushes up on one elbow and considers me, his expression droll. "You sound as if you might benefit from a demonstration."

"And here I thought you were off the clock." I feel the corners of my mouth pull into a sardonic half-smile. He really is a lovely man.

His eyes sparkle and his face shifts, his full lips curving up seductively. He reaches out and strokes my face with a featherlight touch, sending shivers down my spine. I hold his gaze, and my breathing quickens as he leans toward me until his face is nearly touching mine.

"This," he whispers, his breath warm against my cheek, "would be another entirely personal indulgence, but perhaps you and I might consider ..."

I don't get to hear the rest of what he has to say. At that moment, a short sharp chirp that signals the completion of the decryption sequence echoes through the apartment. I bolt upright and crawl across the rug to the streamer. The library files have stilled and snapped into position.

Eidor was right. A detailed three-dimensional schematic of the station now floats in the center of the room.

14

I CROUCH IN FRONT of the streamer, trying to make sense of what I see. Only a fraction of the station's hundreds of sectors and thousands of corridors and pass-throughs are represented. A blue line runs through the schematic, starting so far away from parts of the station that are familiar to me that I have no idea what I'm looking at. There's no sign of the Carnival, the Overnights, or even the Local Tube. I have to spin the 3D model through half a dozen views of the schematic to find the endpoint. It's labeled with the icon of a gold key.

Nico crouches next to me, studying the schematic with a worried expression on his face.

"Where is this?" I ask, pointing at the key. "Do you recognize the location?"

He leans forward, examining the floating diagram.

"That's the Long-Flight Bay," he says.

"What's there?"

"Cargo transports, mostly. Things queued up waiting for clearance to ship off to distant destinations, like Home World or Gordonia Network or the Outer Rim Collective. Any goods being shipped far away."

"Any passengers?"

"Not there, no. Skiffs and transports carrying people dock on the other side of the station where they can disembark and move around freely. Long Flight is almost completely automated, and it's heavily secured."

"Yet she expects me to get in," I murmur, more to myself than to him.

Nico scowls. "That's going to be incredibly difficult," he says. "I don't like it."

"It must be important. She went to a lot of effort to get this schematic to me."

"Yes. But I still don't like it."

"I don't suppose you have a way to get in touch with her?"

He shakes his head. "No. Contact is always on her terms. Everything is always on her terms."

I stare at the schematic again.

"What's the best way to get there?"

Nico's eyebrows arc in surprise. "You can't be serious. You're going? Without having any idea what's waiting for you?"

"Of course I'm going. I'm going now, in fact. This is part of my deal with Yeva." I start downloading a 2D version of the schematic onto my holo; while it loads, I find and put on my shoes.

"At least speak with Eidor first. He might have some sense of what this is about, or know a way to reach her ..."

"Even if he does, I still have to get there. My departure window is coming up, and I'm running out of time. There's something there she wants me to handle, and I'm going to handle it. I'm not going to risk losing her trust. I can't afford it."

He takes a deep breath. I can almost see the words collecting in the front of his brain, the arguments surfacing and making their way to his lips. His calm, cheerful manner has been replaced by concern bordering on anxiety.

"All right," he says, exhaling with finality. "I'm coming with you."

"I don't need you to ..."

"I'm coming with you," he insists. "You can agree and I'll walk next to you. Or you can resist and I'll track you in a way that you'll never see me, but I'm not letting you go into this alone."

"Fine, then. Put on some decent shoes. We have some walking ahead of us." I'm one hundred percent sure I'll figure out how to evade him at some point, and arguing with him now is taking up valuable time. He pulls on shoes and a jacket, and we leave the apartment without discussion.

We move through the Personal Evolution Annex quickly—the crowd has thinned out and only a few stragglers remain in the hallways. When we reach the section of the Carnival that branches off toward the Overnights, I pull out my holo and activate the wayfinder. The start of the schematic is further away than the wayfinder can actually 'see,' and if I take its directions now, I'll be winging it. I don't have time for that.

"I'm going to need some shortcuts," I say. "Do you have any suggestions?"

He hesitates.

"It's not the length of the trip you should be worried about. There are two checkpoints in that sector that are monitored by robots whose only job is to make sure no one gets past them."

"Robots but no people? Are they mobile?"

"Technically, yes, but they're programmed to prioritize remaining at their posts. They're heavily armored, so disarming them with standard weaponry is impossible without blowing yourself up."

"Technology is susceptible to trickery that people might see through," I say, reversing the sentiment he expressed when we first met at the library. He doesn't miss the reference, and I catch the brief curve of the corner of his mouth. "I can bluff my way past them somehow."

"These robots are significantly more dangerous than people. It's kill first and ask questions ... well, never. They're protecting the core business interests of the station, and that's paramount here. Any unauthorized persons are in violation of their protocol and that's all they need to know."

A smile creeps across my face.

"Then I'll need some ideas for getting around that, along with better directions. Let's drop into my Overnight," I say. "I'd like to chat with Xeric."

The room is calm and silent when we walk in. I'm relieved that no schmaltzy "theme" has been activated by Nico's ocular scan, although the lights have been adjusted to a pleasant softness. Nico is uncharacteristically quiet as he comes in behind me. I point him toward the chair, then move to the opposite side of the streamer once he sits down.

"Xeric, assist me," I say, and within seconds the concierge has popped into the room.

"Good evening, Dr. Beach," Xeric says, in a voice two octaves deeper and several dozen decibels softer than the one it used on my first night here.

Nico stays quiet, and the AI either doesn't register his presence or doesn't care. "How can I help you?" they ask.

"I have some questions for you. I hope you can answer them. They're important."

"Of course. Anything you need."

"Let me show you something." I toss a clip of the decrypted schematic to the AI, which freezes for a moment while receiving and reviewing the data. Nico almost jumps out of his chair, but I give him a cautioning look, and he settles down again. Still his body remains tense and his face is creased with concern.

"Do you recognize what I gave you?" I ask.

"It's a section of the Station schematic," Xeric replies.

"You knew I had this, correct?"

Xeric smirks. "Of course. One of my priority tasks was to make certain you received and decrypted it."

"I thought so. Here's my question. Can you communicate with other AI or networked robotics on the Station? Anything that's not part of the Overnight network?"

"I can, in some circumstances."

"What about the robots at the checkpoints on that segment of the Station?"

Xeric frowns slightly. "Not from here, but perhaps if our physical proximity is improved ..."

"Interesting. You mean if we find a way to get you closer to them, you could communicate with them?"

"Possibly. I don't know if they would listen to me. That particular model is ... obstinate."

It spits out the word dismissively. Nico grunts.

"You do speak a common language, correct? Working from the same basic source code?"

"Yes. A core language protocol is shared across all networked entities on the Station."

I'm trying to sort out how to leverage this information when Nico, talking more to himself than to me, murmurs, "I should say something."

This triggers me, and for an instant, all I think of is Arden telling me nothing *for my own good*.

"Say what? That it's risky?" I snap, struggling to regulate my irritation. "That I don't know what I'm getting into? I know those things already. You don't know my history. Just because I was a generalist on Iona doesn't mean I don't have any training, and my expertise ..."

Nico, surprised by my outburst, stares at me. He waves one hand in the air as if physically wiping away my objections.

"I have no doubts about you; I've seen your programming chops firsthand," he says, hesitating for a moment before completing his thought. "I should tell you I built them."

I blink in the face of this new information. So many words pile up in my throat they almost choke me. None will come out and most of them are contradictory anyway, all variations of *what a stroke of luck* combined with permutations of *you utter asshole*.

Nico watches me, his posture tense.

"You built them," I repeat. "You built these killer robots that I have to get around."

"Not every part of them, and it was a long time ago, but yes. The 'intelligence' aspect of their artificial intelligence—the core language and behavior protocol—is my design."

My exasperation overtakes me.

"Who the hell *are* you?" I blurt. "Honestly, the 'sex worker' thing and the 'well-off guy with a piano' thing and the 'I program killer robots' thing aren't all lining up for me right now."

Nico looks miffed. "Attendants are not sex workers," he mutters.

"Fine. You designed these things. Can you disable them?"

"No. Which is why I didn't mention it immediately."

"Is there anything you can do to get me past the checkpoints without getting vaporized?"

"It might be possible, if you're planning what I think you're planning."

"And what exactly is that?"

"To use Xeric to inject some malicious code into the DefenderBots that will ... I don't know, make them attack each other, or make them shoot me instead of you, something like that."

I laugh. Nico remains somber, however. He's not joking.

"I'm not interested in murdering you," I say. "My plan's a little more straightforward. I want Xeric to serve as a distraction. Get the ... what did you call them? DefenderBots? ... to focus on him and whatever bogus information he might be able to pass to them to hold their attention and create a diversion that buys me enough time to get past them. See? No shooting. Nobody dies."

Nico sits back in his chair, and an odd mix of worry and relief overtakes his features.

"Oh," he says, blinking. "That would be simpler, and I do like the part where I don't die. Except it won't work because of the way they process input."

"Is that something you can help me change?"

"Not really. Maybe we should go back to malware injection."

"Malware, ugh, what an unsophisticated approach," a third voice says, dropping confidently into the discussion. "I have a better idea."

I forgot we left Xeric processing data behind us. Finished with that task, he's now decided to become a full participant in planning this assault.

I look over at Nico, who shrugs. "Why not?"

"Okay, Xeric. Let's hear it," I say.

"The DefenderBots are charged with destroying anything trying to get onto the cargo bay ramps that is not authorized. So we get you authorized."

"That's so obvious, it's brilliant," I murmur. "It can't be that easy, can it?"

"I don't have the permissions to do that," Nico mutters, looking at the AI skeptically. "Are you suggesting *you* can do that?"

Xeric's face turns smug. "Of course I can do that. You're late to the party. I've been upgraded significantly since the last time you looked into my code."

15

IT TAKES LESS TIME for Xeric to create my authorization than it did for us to walk to the Overnight from the Personal Evolution Annex. The hitch comes when he tries to obtain authorization for Nico, whose credentials have been embedded in a block list.

Nico frowns. "That isn't right," he says. "I should have open access to the entire station."

"A date-based restriction has been applied to your profile. Your permissions will resume after it expires," Xeric explains.

"And when is that?"

"Ten solar days."

"Well after my departure," I murmur.

Xeric nods, silver hair bouncing. "Correct. As it stands now, he won't be able to go beyond the DefenderBots; he cannot be authorized. Given his status here, however, it's unlikely they would shoot him without cause."

"*Unlikely*? This just gets better and better." Nico spits out the words in a frustrated tone. He's not happy about this development, but I'm less bothered. I don't know what I'm going to be expected to do once I'm past those bots. I'm not sure I want any witnesses. It sounds like Yeva might not want any either, which is simultaneously useful and disturbing.

Xeric calculates the round trip to the location marked on the schematic will take five and a half hours, by the shortest route—and that's assuming nothing goes wrong. My thirty-minute departure window opens in six hours. It's not a lot of time, but it will have to do.

"How far will I have to go once I'm past the DefenderBots?" I ask

"Walking at a normal speed, the destination is less than three minutes beyond the second checkpoint."

Nico twists in his chair. He clearly has an opinion, but I'm not going to entertain it now.

"Thanks. Send the information to my holo."

"It's not that simple," Nico interjects, unable to remain silent any longer. "You can't just use the shortest route. It's heavily patrolled by Station Security, and rare for anyone who's not an employee to be in most of those sections. You don't need authorization to move around on the floors leading up to Long Flight *per se*, but you'll be out of place and attract attention, and someone's going to notice and ask questions you can't answer."

"Is that true, Xeric?" I ask. Nico's exasperation with me writes itself across his face.

"There are ongoing patrols on twelve of the seventeen levels. Ten of those are not used by the civilian population," Xeric confirms. "You would without doubt be questioned as to your intent by security forces and removed. The top floors are protected by the DefenderBots and accessible only to authorized personnel."

Before I can react, Nico joins me in the center of the room, addressing both me and Xeric. "I have a suggestion," he says. "I know an alternate path between Levels Six and Sixteen. It will be easy enough for us to blend in with the pedestrian traffic through Level Three. Levels Four and Five are less utilized but aren't under scheduled patrol. We can access it at Level Five. The last DefenderBot is on Level Sixteen."

"What's the catch?" I ask, already certain I know.

"It's not an easy route," he says cautiously.

"Define 'not easy.'"

"A physically demanding climb, low light conditions, extreme temperature shifts, some very tight passageways ..."

"That's a normal workday on Iona. Still waiting for the 'not easy' part."

"It's also not documented. I'll have to take you myself."

There it is. The perfect excuse for him to come along.

"You can't zap the directions to my holo?"

"No," he says, the irritation rising in his voice. "Another consideration is that with a guide, it will be faster. You'll be less likely to get off track, and you'll have help if something goes wrong."

"Faster and help is good, but if you can only go so far and can't send me documentation of this super-secret route, how am I supposed to get back? Are you going to camp out next to the killer robots, waiting for me?"

"Getting back is easier," Nico says. "The down elevator is separate from the general use elevators, and unsecured. All you have to do is take it to Level Three and merge with the pedestrian traffic."

"I can confirm timing if you describe it to me," Xeric says. "I have access to a full station schematic, as well as the 3D partial you uploaded."

"You two work on that, I'll be over here," I say, dropping into the chair Nico just vacated. It's still warm from his body heat and smells delightfully of spice. Nico and Xeric confer. I pull out my holo to distract myself from the uncertainty of our upcoming adventure, and find a message, from me, to me, that reads *Exchange complete. Ready for your arrival.*

It doesn't take long for Xeric to calculate the timing on the new route; as Nico guessed, it *is* faster. Unfortunately, the virtual concierge isn't able to create a wayfinder file for me to take along, since portions of the path we intend to follow are outside "general pedestrian access" and I'd need special permission from the Stationmaster. I have no choice but to agree to Nico's guide services. I'm worried about the danger he'll be putting himself in, while also miffed that I can't complete this task, whatever it is, on my own.

"Can I be of further assistance?" Xeric asks, looking to me. It gives me an idea.

"I have a bizarre request for you. I hope you don't mind."

"Glad to help," the AI says. "What do you need?"

I pull my high density mini-drive out of my pocket. "Can you copy yourself onto this so I can carry you with me?"

Nico laughs aloud. "Xeric on a stick," he says. "Genius."

Xeric shoots him a disdainful look before addressing me.

"I can copy part of myself onto your drive," he says. "Not my graphical presentation, but a version that will at least have voice capabilities. I may not be able to access all Station systems, however."

"I understand," I say. "Let's think of it as a failsafe. Can you do that now? Afterwards, you can go."

He nods. I insert the drive into the streamer, and the copying process begins. In less than five minutes, the job is complete. I drop the little square of plexi back into my pocket and dismiss him.

"I'm happy to have helped you, Dr. Beach," the virtual concierge says. "Good luck and I hope to see you off on a positive note in a few hours' time." With that, the AI vanishes.

My anxiety level ramps up to 1000. Even if what's waiting for me on the other side of the checkpoint is as easy as saying my own name, the timing is going to be tight. I can't miss my departure window. Meridian Station's schedule is so notoriously crowded, missing it could mean that I'll be stuck here much longer than I can afford to be.

Nico is scrolling through something on his own holo, scowling and muttering to himself. I clear my throat to get his attention, and he looks up.

"We have to go," I say.

"We do," he says, slamming the device into his jacket pocket as he rises from the chair.

"You're okay with this? Even though you only *probably* won't get shot?"

"I'm coming with you as far as I can go," he says, eyeing me levelly. "I have to say again that I don't like any of this. Our friend has gone to a lot of trouble to put you alone in a very isolated spot, and you have no idea what the point might be. There's a real risk something could go wrong."

"Right now, the biggest risk is that I'll pass out from exhaustion before we get out of the Overnight," I say as we step out into the hallway. "I need some low-anx stimulants. Can you suggest a vendor who won't sell me dirt in a capsule and claim it's top-grade pharma?"

"Sure. We'll grab them on the way. Some nutritabs too, for good measure. We're going to expend a lot of energy."

I look over my shoulder at him, and although his voice is calm, his face is lined with worry. He's trying to keep me from seeing how concerned he is about this mission; that makes me more worried than I already am.

I have no choice, though. Whatever this is, I have to do it. Yeva set this task for me, and they've all told me she doesn't do anything without reason.

We leave the Overnights section, taking the escalator down, and soon, we're in the thick of the noise and disruption of the Carnival. True to his word, Nico comes through with stimulant capsules. I pop one in my mouth, and the world around me becomes brighter and louder. My pulse quickens in an invigorating way. A couple of nutritabs round out the effect and my mental strength and agility come roaring back to form.

I'll need to plan for side effects, though. Although I love the burst of confidence that comes with consuming them, I remember all too well the dramatic reversal at the end of the high. Coming down can feel like being thrown off a cliff into a pit of despair. The low-anx variety should limit the effect to something milder like simple distress, but either way I'm anticipating a crying jag in my future.

We continue along the main artery for a short distance before Nico directs us through a sequence of side passages and hallways that lead away from the crowd of vendors and their marks and into a part of the station most of those who pass through here can't imagine. It's populated by people hauling maintenance gear and humming service robots, and is as minimalist and calm as the Carnival is excessive and loud. We reach Level Five and slip through a service door that takes us into the guts of the structure, riveted struts and welded panels and tight tiny passageways in between. We creep forward, single file—they weren't designed for people, especially of Nico's height, and even I have to walk slightly hunched to keep my head from bumping support beams overhead. The temperature starts out blistering hot, but becomes increasingly cold as we move farther away from inhabited areas. I'm glad I have my jacket, but my fingers are getting stiff, despite being stuffed inside my jacket pockets.

"I hope this task doesn't require any manual dexterity," I say, looking back at Nico, who has been keeping pace behind me.

"You okay?" he asks. "Want to rest?"

"I want to be warm, mostly, but stopping is a terrible idea on a tight deadline."

"We can stop. It's not much farther, and we have a tough climb ahead of us—we'll have to go up several levels to the access point, so you'll need your strength. After that, the conditions will be more habitable. Sit down for a minute. I'll keep us on schedule."

The head clearance is so low here he's almost bent double. I slide down to the floor and lean against a cold steel bulkhead with my eyes closed. I'm suddenly aware how much my upper body hurts from the strain of maintaining such a tight compact posture for so long. I pull my freezing hands out of my pockets and rub the back of my neck, grimacing.

He folds his large frame with some difficulty and squeezes into a sitting position behind me. "Let me get that," he says. He begins to massage my shoulders and aching neck.

"You were right," I murmur, my eyes still closed. The aches dissipate as he chases them with his fingers.

"Of course I was. Remind me what I was right about this time?"

"This is a really challenging route. You warned me. I thought you were exaggerating to put me off going through with it, but you weren't. You were serious."

He's quiet for a moment, the only sound our breathing and the soft rustle of his hands kneading my shoulders.

"You do that a lot," he says. His voice has changed from flippant to thoughtful.

"Do what?"

"Assume everyone is trying to game you, instead of believing someone might have your best interest at heart." He keeps working on my upper back as he talks.

"Maybe it's a programmer thing. Need for verification, and all that."

"It's not a programmer thing. It's a 'you' thing." His fingers keep up their rhythm, and the kinks and knots in my shoulders loosen, the tension in them draining away. When he speaks again, his tone is intimate and considered, as though he's been thinking about this for a long time.

"I'm sorry your personal history included people who wanted you to believe that all the important things were about them," he says. "I imagine you've missed some growth and beautiful connections because of this habit of mistrust you learned from people who kept telling you they were shutting you out because they cared about you."

In an instant I see every episode of lying, secrecy, pantomime, and political theater I've been subjected to since Arden Wilson appeared on Iona, and I feel the weight of opportunities lost and friendships put on hold in the wake of his machinations. Yet part of me continues to insist none of it was his fault, that he had very good reasons for what he did.

If only he'd shared those reasons with me.

I let the emotion well up for a second, then push it down again. My back is still to Nico, and I hope he can't tell from my voice the effect his words have had on me. He finishes his ministrations to my aching neck and shoulders, and gives me a little squeeze from behind, as if trying to hold me together for one more moment. He releases me, and I shift my posture so we're facing one another. I stretch out my arms for a real hug.

"Thank you," I say. I'm grateful for far more than the massage.

"Feeling better? Need another tab?"

"Yes, much. I don't need another tab, I'll make it."

We get back to our feet and resume our slow trek through the cold unyielding passageway. When we reach what Nico's been referring to as "the climb," I'm glad we stopped to regroup.

The access point is a tight tube built into the side of the wall. We have to crawl through on hands and knees. It opens onto a small metal landing affixed to the inside of a massive open vertical cylinder. After so much time in such compressed spaces, the sheer size of it is particularly shocking.

The expanse of space inside the cylinder is enormous. It must be the central core of the station. It's hundreds of meters in diameter, and stretches out so far above and below us, I can't see where it begins or ends. The faint greenish-blue glow of service lights placed at wide intervals along the inside creates a sinister atmosphere. Sound bounces and echoes in a way that makes the smallest noise seem thunderous and distorts it into monstrous wails.

I feel like a sand gnat stuck on the inside of a cup.

"At least we can stand up now," I say, hoping my voice isn't shaky.

Nico is already standing. He's keeping his back pressed against the wall, one hand on the metal round-rung ladder that runs through the cylinder next to the landing. It's reachable from our position, but requires enough of a stretch over the gaping emptiness below that it makes my heart skip several beats.

"Ready for this?" he asks. He's gripping the rail so tightly his hand is shaking, and there's a fine sheen of sweat collecting on his forehead.

"How far do we go?"

He points up. "See that white space up there? That's the access point. That's where we're headed."

Squinting, I can barely make out the pinprick of light punching into the darkness overhead. It's a very long climb, straight up, hand over hand.

"All right. Let's go," I say, getting to my feet.

"You first," he says, stepping out of my way, but keeping his hand wrapped tight around the ladder. He helps me reach out and securely grasp the railing. I position one foot solidly on one rung, then lift myself out over the gut-wrenching open space to settle my second foot beside it.

Nico checks my handholds and gives me a thumbs-up.

"Go," he says. "I'm here behind you."

It's a significant effort to make my right hand release its hold on the rung and reach up for the next one, straightening my legs to propel my body up. The vastness of the cylinder pulls at me and for a moment I feel like I'm dangling over a precipice. I manage, though, and the next step is psychologically easier. After five or six shaky steps upward, I get into a rhythm of grab, step and lift, grab, step, and lift. I keep my eyes focused on the next rung above me, never stopping and never looking down. I hear Nico several rungs below me, breathing hard, but we don't speak. We just climb.

And climb. And climb.

My grip stays strong—thank the suns for that—but my calves cramp and my arms tremble a little more with each rung. Nico asks if I want to rest a couple of times during the ascent, but to me "resting" means more time I'll have to hang on to this damn ladder. So I decline and we keep climbing until I see the glint of pale light on the metal struts, and the area around me takes on a less gloomy cast. I lift up one last time and find my gaze even with a landing accessed by another tight tunnel, marked by a sparkle of white. I almost forget my concentration and my right foot slips off its rung. Nico gasps aloud, and his hand glances off my ankle as he reaches for me. But I catch myself and maintain my balance.

"I'm okay," I call out. "I think we're here."

I edge my way over to the side of the ladder closest to the landing and reach out with one leg. Finding purchase, I manage to swing my body onto the surface and collapse in a heap as soon as I land. In a few moments, Nico joins me, and we both burst into relieved, exhausted laughter.

"Oh, dear cosmos, what were we thinking?" Nico spits out between heaves. "I have never been so terrified."

"My company is that scary?"

"I'm deathly afraid of heights. I just surrendered twenty years of my life out there."

I blink, incredulous. "I can't even process that. How did you manage?"

He shakes his head. "I suppose I tried not to think about it," he says, wiping away the tears that ran down his face as we laughed. "Let's go face some killer robots. That will be so much more pleasant."

We crawl through the tunnel that leads away from the central tube and through the wall of the station. After a few tight steps, we're in a dimly lit hallway, made with large automated hoverflats of cargo in mind—wide and high-ceilinged and blissfully easy to navigate. As expected, it's also deserted and quiet. We walk in silence until we reach an intersection with another corridor.

"We'll turn there," Nico says, pointing the way. "The first checkpoint will be visible as soon as we round the corner, but the AI won't engage unless we're within its kill range."

I wince involuntarily at the language.

"Here's hoping Xeric got everything right," I say.

We move into the new hallway with caution. It has more light; a series of pathway illuminators like those in my Overnight shine beneath its plexi floor. Each features a sequence of information, some readable, some not. The color-coded pathways extend as far as I can see.

"Those are cargo designations," Nico explains. "The bay numbers, the name of the entity, and the intake data are there. That's followed by shipping encoding—the scheduled departure date and time, destination, status. The contents are classified according to Interstellar norms. Sometimes there's a ship schematic as well."

Why has Yeva brought me here?

The text stretches along the ribbons of light in one long repeating spool, and I try to decipher it as we walk. At least some of the content classifications are the same ones we use on Iona. The destinations are all abbreviations: HWLD, GDNA, OUTC. I'm so engrossed in the data stream that I don't realize we're approaching the checkpoint until I hear something stir and come toward us, making a clatter that echoes and reverberates in the empty corridor.

I don't know what I was expecting the DefenderBot to be; maybe a tougher, metallic version of Xeric? When I finally see it, my guts clench and it's all I can do not to shriek and fall back.

The robot is not humanoid. It stands at least eight feet tall, crafted of some kind of jet-black matte material that reflects almost no light. It moves on many multi-jointed legs that propel it forward using the walls and ceiling, if need be, like a room-sized mutant spider. It has six articulated "arms," each terminating in a different weapon. In the middle of all the limbs and firearms, I spot a single laser placed above a sensor, and a speaker below that.

It doesn't have a face—or even a head—of any kind.

The thing rattles toward us, threatening enough from its sheer size and horrifying spiderlike locomotion alone. It stops short of where we stand and uses its laser 'eye' to trigger a blue horizontal band across the corridor in front of us.

"Access beyond this point is restricted and requires authorization," it says in a hollow mechanical voice.

I take a step forward into the wavering blue light. "I have authorization," I say, much bolder than I feel.

"Authorization," says the DefenderBot.

"I'm authorized," I say again.

"Authorization," it says again. Its tone has changed. It's not a comment, it's a demand.

I suddenly realize I have no idea how to interact with it. I turn to Nico, who is staying well clear of the blue band of light.

"Give it your name," he says.

I freeze. "Which one?" I ask. "Did Xeric say? The alias or my real name?" Nico shakes his head. He doesn't know.

"Authorization," the thing barks, rattling one of its weapons into ready position. Its laser target makes a bright red bead in the center of my chest. "Authorization ... authorization ... authorization ..."

"Faith Feathergrass!" I shout, my voice a high-pitched squeak. I squeeze my eyes shut, waiting for the sound of weapons fire.

"Verified," it says, its address now calm. "Please stay within the marked boundaries to avoid injury or death."

With that, it rattles back to the checkpoint station against the corridor wall and folds up its many limbs and deadly bits until it's transformed from a fearsome killing machine to a neat black rectangle about four feet tall. One limb remains extended beneath it to hold it up off the floor, like a single leg.

"The next one should be the same," Nico calls out to me. "Hail me if you need help and I'll ... I'll try to do something and not die."

The DefenderBot, apparently reacting to Nico's voice, extends its leg, lifting itself up a meter or so, turning its sensor toward him. It scans the corridor again.

"You'd better go," I say. "I don't think it wants you talking to me."

Nico waves acknowledgement and takes several large steps backward, away from the boundary. The DefenderBot stops scanning but remains lifted, turned in Nico's direction. Still backing away, he shoos me onward and mouths the words "good luck."

I pull out my holo and call up the file I made from the schematic in Nico's apartment. It guides me through the next sequence of hallways until I reach the next checkpoint. The Defender guarding this one is built in the same way as the first but is silver instead of black. For some reason that feels significantly less threatening. As I approach, it lifts itself up to my eye-height and bleats, "Authorization." I give my name, and it drops back down into its rectangular form without further interaction.

Beyond the second checkpoint is a darkened maze of docking ports, access ramps, and air locks, spread across multiple levels. The rainbow-effect of the floor pathways becomes dimmed and muted as lines branch away and disappear down the various hallways. Every few minutes the violent shaking of the structure underfoot signals the arrival or departure of another spacecraft. I reach a small viewport that looks out into the open center of the circular bay, and when I peer through it, I'm overwhelmed.

Thousands of driverless cargo ships are docked here, possibly tens of thousands—I can't begin to see them all. Each ship locks into a massive rack system, with smaller automated service vehicles shuffling them from one location to another like a deck of cards. From this vantage point I can see that they tend to depart in groups rather than one at a time as passenger-occupied craft do, which explains the intense vibrational effect. I watch a collection of thirty ships docked above my head release their hold on their airlocks and are towed up to their launch positions by service drones. Together, they fire thrusters and scream away in formation. Almost instantly, more service drones appear, preparing the open slots for a new set of ships.

Following the schematic, I locate the stairs and go up one more level. Time is ticking by—the trip here took longer than we'd planned, so I have to make every minute count. I'm still unclear on what I'm going to find when I arrive at my destination, or what I'm expected to do once I get there. But I can't spend time thinking about it now. I follow the directions through another peopleless corridor to a section labeled *atmosphere-stable access*.

It turns out to be another multi-level collection of ships pinned against short telescoping airlocks built into the walls, in a way that makes their interiors accessible without venturing out into the oxygenless open bay. There are fewer spacecraft docked here, perhaps only 100 or so, and some of them appear to have been here a long time. No service vehicles hover here, and the contrast between the silence here and the noise of the rest of Long Flight is distinct.

I look around. Not so much as an autoflat or a killer robot populates this level.

I check my holo. I'm close to the point marked on the schematic, and I'm being directed to a specific airlocked bay, just ahead.

When I at last stand in front of Bay 7B, one thing separates it from the hundreds of others clustered in this section. Below the access display, marked with a green + indicating a ship waits on the other side of the airlock, is an active countdown timer. This ship will begin an automated departure cycle in a little more than 30 minutes. I touch the information panel beside the door, and the ship's details appear.

I read the origination data and gasp aloud. This ship, called the *Heretic*, arrived here almost a year ago, from planet-of-origin code BDZL.

Bardazel.

16

THERE'S SOMETHING ABOUT THIS ship that Yeva wants me to see or needs me to manage—she wouldn't have brought me here otherwise. Part of me is trepidatious, but so far she hasn't steered me wrong, despite her peculiar methods and secretive nature. I examine the ship's data. No owner is listed, and no end recipient. Its destination is a series of intergalactic coordinates instead of a recognizable location code. Based on my knowledge of our system, this ship is scheduled to fly to empty space, light years away from the nearest inhabited planet or space station, far outside the routes traced by cargo and passenger lines.

My eyebrows knit together in consternation. It doesn't make sense. I need to see what's inside.

I try pressing the control panel, but the airlocked door tells me in a pleasant voice that I require authorization to perform that function. It similarly informs me that it doesn't recognize the name that got me past the DefenderBots, nor my alias, nor anything else I attempt. I try to hail Nico, but the communications shielding on this level makes that problematic—I'm not sure my hail pinged his holo at all.

I examine the access panel closely and find a universal terminal slot that will fit the native port in my holo. After some jostling around, I get a connection and hack my way into the code behind it. I'm not surprised when I encounter a built-in kill switch, designed specifically to prevent this kind of manipulation. Working quickly, I manage to disable it, but not before it gets the best of my holo, which winds up in an unbreakable spin. I disconnect the device; it emits a single, pathetic chirp and dies in my hand.

Now what?

I pace in front of the airlock door, watching the inexorable movement of the countdown timer. So much effort went into bringing me to this spot, and I only have twenty-one minutes and thirty-nine seconds to figure out why.

Frustrated, I stuff my dead holo into my pocket. My fingertips encounter something small and hard, and I remember my fallback plan. I hold my breath when I insert my mini into the terminal slot, then say, "Xeric, assist me."

Thirty seconds later, a tinny strained voice comes through the panel and acknowledges me.

"Xeric, it's Faith ... er, Dr. Beach. Do you know me?" I ask.

The copy is faithful enough to sound disdainful when it says, "Of course. What might I do for you?"

"I'm trying to get into a ship in long-flight cargo. I have you plugged into the access panel. Can you help?"

Silence. I hope this means it's thinking about it.

Eventually, Xeric's voice floats out of the speaker. "I can open the airlock for you, but please understand it's dangerous to enter the ship this close to its scheduled departure. It will take me several minutes to rewrite the protocol."

"Can you delay the departure?"

"No. After the countdown reaches twenty minutes, it can only be delayed by the originator or the Stationmaster."

Given that I'm here illegally to begin with, chatting up the Stationmaster to ask for a favor seems like a bad idea.

"Who's the originator?"

"Benta Sarsen."

"Benta Sarsen? Chair of the Governing Council, Benta Sarsen?"

"The title listed is Senior Incident Manager."

Why would the Chair of the Governing Council be managing a long-flight cargo ship from Bardazel to the middle of nowhere?

"Get me in," I say. "Go fast."

Every second feels like an eternity as I wait. The countdown timer in my field of view makes it worse. I'm both impressed and horrified that it takes Xeric two minutes to complete the work; I only have eighteen minutes now. When I finally hear the words, "You may enter," I slap the access panel and the door opens.

I step into the narrow airlock. A larger control panel is built into the wall on my right; emergency gear including fire retardant, a handlight, and breathing apparatus hang on the left. The secondary door linking the airlock to the spacecraft slides open with a touch.

The ship's interior is dark, lit only by floor bars set to their dimmest glow. I can't see what's inside from this vantage point—I'll need to work my way up to the front of the ship to access its lighting controls. The fresh cool air of a working enviro floats out to greet me, so it seems reasonably safe to go inside. I pull the emergency handlight from the wall of the airlock and turn it on, shining it inside.

The width of the cabin is taken up by a hefty cargo rack system leaving only a narrow central aisle, just wide enough for two people to pass through, if they turn sideways. I slowly step onto the ship, shine the light to my left, and nearly scream aloud.

The ship is full of bodies.

The racks hold people, deck after deck of them, running the length of the ship. There are probably 200 silent bodies onboard.

I turn the handlight onto the form lying in the rack closest to me, and my heart accelerates to a new level: her skin is turquoise blue.

I move from one rack to the next, checking each face, finding the same result over and over again. These aren't bodies at all. These are live people locked in stasis after exposure to Blue. They have to be Equity Alliance operatives that Kerrit Arduval dosed at the Bardazel compound.

Questions erupt in my mind. Have they been here all this time? Why are they being moved now? Their destination designation isn't to Home World or any GC system location. I don't know what's going on here, but none of it feels right. These people shouldn't be heading off into the unknown. They should be going somewhere safe.

I hurry down the aisle and locate the ship's core controls and bring the lights up to full. The stark brightness contrasted against the still, blue human cargo makes the effect even more horrifying. I run back to the airlock.

"Xeric," I say, "can you change this ship's destination?"

There's an almost painfully long pause.

"I believe that's possible," the AI says at last. It doesn't sound confident, but it's the only shot I have.

"Please replace with coordinates for Iona's landing pads. Do you have time?"

"Difficult to say. Estimated work duration is approximately ten minutes. You'll need to manually confirm the override on the control panel in the airlock once it's completed."

That's going to cut it close.

"Do it," I say. "Go as fast as you can."

I walk reverently through the ship as Xeric works, shivering as I take in each still blue face. I've never met these people, but I feel like I owe them. I can't send them to their real homes, so I'm going to send them to the next best place. On Iona, they can be revived. They'll find friends there, and before long it will be like home to them. They'll get to start over. In a way, I'm profoundly jealous of them.

I'm so wrapped up in my vision for them that I don't realize I'm no longer alone until a familiar voice behind me shakily says, "Put your hands up over your head and turn around slowly. I don't want to hurt you, but I can't let you mess this up."

A mixture of shock, disappointment, and sorrow bubbles up in me as I comply, raising my arms and turning to face Maybree. She's standing at the airlock entry with a stun stick in her hand. Her eyes are wide and she's visibly shaking. A sheen of sweat sparkles on her forehead.

"What are you doing here, Maybree? What do you have to do with all this?" I gesture around me.

"This is my job, looking after this ship and this launch. It's important. I don't know why you're here, but I have to make sure you don't screw this up." She takes a few cautious steps toward me, holding the stun stick out in front of her.

"Is this the job Shimauy offered you? You told us you turned him down."

Her lips pinch together, as though she's trying to push down a powerful wave of nausea.

"I did turn him down. Then some guy from the GC pinged me and he ... he ...I needed to take care of my family, and he said ..." Tears pool in her eyes and for a moment she looks utterly lost, staring down at the ship's textured composite deck. But she recovers, straightening up and trying to make her expression stern. "Things changed," she says. "I need you to step toward me really slow and let me put some restraints on you and get you off this ship."

I make a calculated guess.

"Breton Cabot-Klaar," I say. Maybree's involuntary flinch lets me know I'm right.

"What?"

"Breton Cabot-Klaar is who contacted you, right? Who hired you for this job? He's the guy who forced Arden into a deal under the pretense of keeping me safe ten years ago. He's on Iona now, trying to take everything away from all of us who worked so hard for it. That's the guy you're trusting. He doesn't deserve your loyalty, Maybree. He doesn't care about you or your family. He doesn't deserve anything from you, no matter what he promised you."

Maybree stares at the floor, shaking her head as if trying to shake my words and her conflicting feelings out of it. She's weakening emotionally; if I'm going to talk my way out of this, this may be my only chance.

I gesture at the silent cargo all around us.

"You know these people," I say, in a voice I hope is calmer than I feel. "You used to see them every day on Bardazel. You know they aren't what the Company said they were."

Maybree nods, and tears fill her eyes. "I know."

"Are you going to kill me *and* them?" I ask softly. "You're a security pro. You're supposed to keep people safe, not hurt them."

"I'm going to take you into custody," she says, moving toward me again. Her breathing has become ragged; bright pink patches spread across her face. "Station Security knows you're here; they're on the way to pick you up." She sniffs, keeping her eyes on me but stopping her advance long enough to wipe her nose on her sleeve. The stun stick now hangs limply at her side. "This ship has to launch and get where it's supposed to go. It has to."

"It's headed for empty coordinates in deep space, with all these people on it," I say, fighting back fury. "They're going somewhere they'll never be found. They'll be lost forever, and no one will have to take the blame for what happened to them." I shake my head in exasperation. "Maybree, Hinn and Holly's parents are on this ship."

This brings her up short, and she looks guiltily around her at the silent prone blue bodies, almost as if waiting for them to speak. Her expression is pure misery. "I'm so sorry ... I have to stop you; I don't have a choice. I have to turn you over to them. The launch has to go as planned or they'll ... they'll ..."

"They'll what? Hurt your family, the way they hurt these people? Destroy your home, like they did theirs? Physically injure you and wreck your life for a decade or more, the way they did me and Arden? I should apologize to you. I could have called them out back then, but I put my head down and ran instead. That's how they win, they count on us to be scared, to run away, to be quiet. Maybe if I'd said something, they wouldn't be doing this to you now. Just like I had a choice back then, you have a choice now. You can leave, Maybree, and pretend you never saw me. I'll pretend I never saw you, and it can all stop right here."

She hesitates, as if considering it, and for an instant I'm hopeful I've gotten through to her. But then she lets out an anguished wail and runs at me, swinging the stun stick at my head. I throw myself to the floor, diving beneath the stick's arc, and catch one of her ankles with both hands. I wrench her foot out from under her, sending her tumbling over me. She cries out and goes down but keeps her grip on the stun stick. I regain my feet and whirl to face her as she gets up again.

Now I'm positioned the way I want to be, with my back to the airlock. She's blocked into the ship's interior.

She runs at me a second time, swinging the stun stick over her head. I back up as she advances, letting her draw as close as I dare, then kick out hard. My boot smashes into her side with a crunch. She shrieks and her fingers lose their grasp on the stun stick, although the lanyard wrapped around her wrist keeps it from flying away. Still gasping from the hit, she piledrives her full weight into me. We both crash to the floor, and something pops in my shoulder. Now on top of me, Maybree slams her fist hard into the side of my head. She fumbles with the stun stick on its lanyard, trying to get a grip on it. I claw at her face with both hands, and manage to grab her short, cropped hair at the roots and yank her to the side, smacking her head against one of the racks. She yelps and a thin stream of red begins to run from her scalp. I shove her off me and go into a defensive crouch. She recovers enough to sling the stun stick at me wildly. It connects with my ankle. The jolt that runs through me is so powerful I see stars.

I collapse back against the racks, clinging to them in an effort to keep my feet. She gets up and begins to hobble toward me. I hear the whine of the stun stick powering up to full.

"This is gonna hurt," she says, her words slurring. "I'm sorry, Faith. I really am."

She takes a deep breath, whimpers with the effort, and reaches toward me.

Suddenly the cabin is filled with flashing red light and a mechanical voice says, "Launch countdown beginning, three minutes. Airlock will secure in ninety seconds."

Maybree looks up, startled, and it's the break I need. I grab her shirt and pull her off balance, then knee her injured ribs. As she shrieks and falls back, I yank the stun stick from her hand, breaking the lanyard at her wrist, and throw it into the depths of the ship behind her. She tries to get off one more punch, but I block the blow and elbow her in the face. She drops to the floor.

I stagger to the airlock as fast as I can. Something is wrong with my left eye, and my right shoulder and upper back feel like they're on fire. I'm finally able to stumble through the ship's hatch and into the air lock. The control panel is flashing the message *confirm new coordinates to set course.*

The mechanical voice drones, "Airlock will secure in thirty seconds."

Before I can touch the screen, I'm slammed from behind by Maybree. She anchors her hands in my hair, my clothing, struggling to drag me back inside the ship and away from the panel. I use my legs to wedge my body inside the airlock as firmly as I can, while Maybree continues pulling at me from behind. I stretch my left arm out, reaching toward the control panel. My fingers flail at the edge of the touchscreen before Maybree digs both hands into my hair to slam my head against the wall behind me.

I release my hold and grab one of her extended arms with both hands. Before she can react, I spin out of the airlock and under her arm, shoving it upward and twisting until I hear a nauseating crack. She shrieks in pain and releases her grip. I brace myself in the entryway and use the last of my strength to slam my foot into her stomach.

She collapses backward into the ship and falls with a hard thud onto the deck, moaning.

"Airlock securing in ten seconds ... nine ... eight ..."

I spin into the airlock and slam my hand against the control panel. The message changes to *new coordinates confirmed* and I hurl myself into the station corridor with less than two seconds to spare. I land sprawled on the floor as the ship hatch slides shut and both airlock portals seal at zero. Then the launch begins in earnest. I try to sit up, but I'm no longer in control of my body; instead, I collapse, eyes closed, and listen to the angry rumble of the *Heretic*'s engines powering up. Seconds later the walls and floor shake violently as it disengages and the tugs pull it up into the safe zone. There's another intense vibration as it powers out of the bay on its way to Iona.

A feeling of satisfaction washes over me. I know I've done a good thing. The Equity Alliance crew and even Maybree will be safe now, in a place where healing can begin. As for me, I'm not going to be safe anywhere. A Security Force is on the way to intercept me, several Company officials want me dead, I'm deep in the guts of this station with a fried holo and no way to contact anyone for help. The metallic taste in my mouth means I'm bleeding, every part of me hurts like hell, and I'm drifting in and out of consciousness. It is what it is. I'm ready to be done with the struggle.

I don't know how much time passes as I float between levels of awareness. Eventually, I hear footsteps hurrying toward me. A soft familiar voice says, "I've got her. Bring the ship around. She's injured, but it's nothing we can't fix."

Someone rubs a medicinal-smelling balm on my lips, then gently turns me onto my back and lifts my head. The pain is so intense lights flash behind my closed eyes. A warm flowery-tasting liquid pours into my mouth and over my tongue. It's soothing and sweet, and I swallow it gingerly.

Tea.

The pain starts to ebb away, bit by bit, and my eyes flutter open. Lipop sits beside me holding a warming flask. My head is propped up on her pack.

She looks into my eyes thoughtfully, then smiles at me. "You will feel better soon."

I can't quite find my voice, so I attempt to smile back.

"There's a sedative in that tea so you can relax," she says. "Don't worry. We'll take care of everything."

The rest is a blur of soft sounds and gentle touches and whispered instructions, hands lifting me gently to my feet and helping me stumble through an airlock onto a ship on the other side. Someone helps me lie down and tucks a blanket around me. Part of my brain registers the sounds of Eidor and Lipop talking quietly, the purr of this smaller ship powering up and departing the long-flight bay with barely a rumble. A warm strong hand cradles mine. My flight-or-fight response fades, and as the adrenaline leaves me, I fall asleep.

When I come back to consciousness, it's just enough to note Lipop administering medicines and rubs and patches, and to swallow the innumerable different tea concoctions she pours for me. I start to feel like myself again—a sore, hurt, exhausted version of myself, but myself, nonetheless.

I'm finally able to open my eyes and look around. I'm in a small delivery ship with a plain, serviceable interior. I'm lying on a soft, thick pad made of a stack of colorful blankets and printed Sharj throws, sandwiched between several dozen large crates of tea. Eidor and Lipop sit in the forecabin chatting, perfectly relaxed. Nico sits beside me, holding my hand in an impossibly gentle grip.

"You're awake," Nico says, in a tone that suggests he had his doubts. "Lipop, she's awake."

"Oh good," says Lipop, unsurprised. She smiles at me. "You feel terrible, yes? But you'll be okay. A few days and you'll be back to normal."

"How did you find me?" I ask. Eidor chuckles.

"My wife," he says. "She's a genius-ah." Lipop rolls her eyes but also proffers her spouse a warm smile.

"We heard you might need some help," she says, lifting her shoulders.

"How?" I look among all three. "I tried to hail out, but I couldn't reach anyone. And then my holo got scorched by the airlock kill switch."

"Something flashed my holo, and I thought it was you," Nico says. "It wasn't, though."

"What was it?"

Nico holds up my jacket and pulls a small black square from its pocket. "This guy."

"Xeric?"

"The copy working the airlock was able to send a message to its other self at the Overnight, and that version of Xeric contacted me."

"And these two got involved how?"

"I was relaxing at the tea shop when his call came in."

Eidor snorts. "He was at the tea shop having a meltdown. He doesn't like to be excluded from anything, especially if it's something dangerous where he could maybe die."

I raise one eye at Nico. Yet another odd character trait to file away with all his other unmatching character traits.

"How did you get past all the security and controls?"

Lipop shrugs. "I have a pass. I make deliveries to long-flight cargo all the time."

"So, if I had talked to you first ..."

"... you could have potentially saved yourself a lot of trouble. From now on, maybe trust your friends?"

I sigh. This is harder for me than they realize. At one time, Maybree was my friend. And countless others who I might no longer be able to classify that way after I depart Meridian Station.

Depart Meridian Station. I gasp.

"How long was I out?" I ask, panic-stricken. "I need to make my departure window, there's a security force on the way and I can't let them find me with you ..."

"You have twenty-five minutes left," Eidor says. He looks stunningly unconcerned.

"I'll never make it! I still have to get back to the Overnight and pick up my things and then find my ship, and do all the pre-departure checks. How far away are we?"

"Relax," Eidor says. "The pre-departure checks are done, and your ship is right there." He points through the forward viewport of the delivery vehicle. He's not kidding; I can see my skiff. We're docked behind it.

"We engaged a porter to pack up your things and stow them onboard," Nico adds. "Everything's ready to go. The only thing missing is you."

I'm anxious to get on her and make sure everything is truly in order, but Lipop makes me spend another ten minutes sitting still on the tea delivery skiff. Then she insists on helping me when it's time to board the *Gabriella*. Frankly, I'm relieved to have Nico's and Lipop's strong shoulders to lean on as we walk down the ramp. I step inside my ship and am almost brought to tears by how familiar and at-home it makes me feel. Maybe it's an illusion, but it's a really good illusion.

I do a quick check. Everything is where it should be. The items I purchased, along with the items I didn't purchase that magically appeared on the invoice on my behalf, are secured in the rear hold. My personal belongings are tucked in a stash space underneath the bunk. There are a couple of surprises: my communications array has been upgraded and replaced with a much higher-powered one, and *Gabriella* has also received a fairly dramatic drive upgrade. I'll arrive at my next destination in half the time I'd planned. I'm certainly not going to complain about that.

Lipop hugs me as tightly as my lingering injuries will let her, presses a full flask of tea into my hand, and with a final smile, departs for her own ship. Eidor waves to me through the viewport as she comes aboard, and Nico and I stand side by side, watching as the tug pulls them away from the ramp.

"Well," he says. "It's time for you to be on your way. The last leg of the journey. I hope Yeva can give you everything you want, Faith."

"I hope so too. A lot depends on it."

He takes my hands in his, his eyes dark with intensity.

"If things don't quite work out, don't think you have no place to go and no one to turn to," he says. Even though my face is sore and my jaw feels like a small bomb exploded in it, it doesn't hurt at all when he leans forward and kisses me goodbye.

Or maybe it's just that good a kiss. Hard to say.

I settle behind the controls and watch him walk down the main ramp. He joins a throng of people filing into the station interior, and the familiar ache of leaving too soon creeps into my awareness. I push it away before it can make me maudlin and prepare my ship for departure.

I hold my breath when I check in with Departure Control, half expecting them to tell me I'll be detained because someone from Security needs a word with me, but that doesn't happen. I'm again cleared without question and leave Meridian Station with time to spare.

I monitor the stream for a few hours afterward, listening for news of a Security Force presence arriving at the Station, but there is none. Either the operation is covert—possible, given what it suggests about certain highly-placed people, or Maybree was bluffing—also possible, given what I know about her. I hope she's no worse off than I am right now—stiff and sore but alive and healing. Once she lands on Iona, people who love her will be able to help her recover, mentally and physically. Her trip will be significantly shorter than mine.

After another hour or so, I feel like I might be able to keep something in my stomach, so I dig around in my pack for the nutritabs I picked up. Beside the package of tabs, my hand touches something unfamiliar. I pull my pack open wide and discover a book, an actual physical book, bound in blue leather. I pull it out, smiling as I see the title etched in gold on the front. *Confessions of a Moral Skeptic.*

So he was watching the entire time. I knew, really—the station tracks everything. He was right not to tell me; I would have seen it as another reason not to trust him. Thinking back on it, I'm grateful he kept an eye on me—whether out of personal interest, professional duty, or some specific directive from my ubiquitous benefactor. The why doesn't matter anymore.

I open the volume and find a hand-written dedication.

To Faith, May there be a next time. With deepest respect, Nico.

I pop the nutritab into my mouth and wash it down with a little of Lipop's tea, then turn to the first page and begin to read.

I wait a few days before I take my sleepers, purely out of anxiety. There's still no news on the stream about me, Meridian Station, or any action or movement by the Governing Council or the Company. I'm not sure if that's a good thing or a bad one. I receive no personal communication either, but that's as expected. This far out, messages from Iona would have to be relayed through Meridian Station and that's too risky to chance. Finally, I give in to boredom and necessity, and down two of the pills, along with two more nutritabs. I'll wake up naturally in around 200 solar hours, give or take; my ship will rouse me if anything goes awry. I scooch down in the tiny hard bunk, attach the monitors that will keep track of my vital signs, then pull a blanket over my shoulders and push the small lumpy pillow under my head. The last thing I see before I close my eyes is Lipop's tea canister with its magnetic bottom, tucked into a secure space near the communications console.

I'm already hovering on the edge of awareness when the skiff's locator chime sounds, letting me know I'm nearing the end of my trip. I sit up in my tiny bunk and stretch as best I can. My limbs are stiff, cramped by the tight quarters and the artificially long slumber. Part of me is glad the trip is almost over, but another is equally worried about what lies ahead. This was the hardest decision I've ever made, and I'm still not sure I'm doing the right thing, but it's the only option I have left.

I slip into the pilot's seat and pop in my audiobud, though at the moment there's nothing for me to do. The autopilot takes the skiff into a gentle arc, and I watch the pin-pricked dark floating by until I see my destination, flickering in the starlight. A few minutes more and I'm close enough to make out the landing pad, high above the domed surface like a mushroom sprouting from a log. It's painted black and highlighted with neon green splashes of light. The dramatic green insignia in its center is the first indication I'm in the right place. The second is the ring of armed anti-spacecraft cannon, pointing toward the middle of the pad.

Alrighty then.

I disengage autopilot and manually adjust the skiff's rate and angle of descent, bringing it closer to the landing point. My throat tightens and my fingers tremble as I input the coordinates memorized from the acrylic chip hidden under the tea cannister. This should let the craft settle onto the "safe" part of the pad. There's a soft whisper as its landing struts extend, and a gentle bump tells me the skiff has found its target. My heart pounds and I close my eyes, waiting for the next sound. I jump when I hear a sudden clatter but am relieved to realize it's the rattle of an atmo dome folding around the pad and pressurizing instead of the roar of cannon fire blasting me to bits.

I hit my mic and hail into the local channel.

"Iona skiff to control. Visual confirmation of atmo dome deploy. Awaiting instructions."

After a very long few seconds, the channel crackles to life, pulsing into my ear with a short humorless laugh accompanied by faint meditative background music.

"So very formal," the voice says, clear and crystalline. "My first instruction is to relax."

A tide of irritation swells in my chest.

"Well, you know, live cannons don't really set a chill mood," I snap back. "I'm as relaxed as I can get at this point."

A pause. The music grows a little softer, and I hear the unmistakable sound of a decanter clinking against a glass.

"My apologies, I'm sorry if you found that *upsetting*," she says, not sounding sorry in the least. "I haven't had visitors who weren't here to murder me in a very long time. My hosting skills may be a bit rusty."

There's another pause and the music disappears altogether. "Atmo dome has pressurized. You may leave your craft. Once you disembark, the drop tube to ground level is on your right. I'll meet you below. The bots will deal with the cargo and your personal items."

"Heard," I respond, feeling only slightly better. "Disembarking now."

I log out of the channel and kick off the automated shutdown process for the skiff, then slip on my jacket and sling my pack over my shoulder. I take a moment to look around at my little plexi bird one last time as I approach the hatch. A laser of anguish cuts through me. She's done such a good job getting me here and was my solace in so many ways over the last few years. I pat her sidewall with a mix of pride and sadness. "I'll see you again soon," I say aloud into her silence, hoping it's true.

I deploy the ramp, square my shoulders resolutely, and walk out. The bright artificial light of the closed dome makes me squint. The air is breathable but chilly and my exhalations make little clouds of frost in front of my face.

It doesn't take long to spot the drop tube. I step in and seal the door, then feel an almost overwhelming gut clench as the conveyance, true to its name, hurtles me through the stem of the landing pad to the surface, almost a thousand feet below.

It takes me a moment to get my bearings when the tube opens, and I'm still a little shaken when I step out onto the surface. I stand bent over, my hands on my knees, staring at my feet until the wave of nausea and dizziness passes. I straighten and finally look at my surroundings.

The primary dome overhead is perfectly clear. Beyond it is the pitch-black darkness of space. Beneath the dome, a few small fluffy clouds float in the artificial atmosphere, gauzy puffs overhead. Soft, clean light, from a source I can't pinpoint, washes the scene in the tones of a gentle sunrise. The grass—real grass—whispers under my feet as I step away from the tube. I stretch out a hand to one of the shrubs and touch one of the waving blossoms. It's waxy and soft and leaves a subtle fragrance on my fingertips.

It makes me ache in a way I can't describe.

The surface stretching out in front of me is thick with high foliage waving in a gentle artificial breeze. Flowering plants are everywhere, in some places hip-high. It's so strange and out of place and beautiful, contrasting this peaceful miniature world to the ring of advanced protective weaponry I just came through and the infinity of space beyond its dome.

I see her walking toward me. I'm not sure if she appeared from some hidden doorway or if she was always there, watching me, standing still among the tall flora. She's smaller than I imagined, shorter than me but much more muscular. Her hair is twisted into a thick long braid that cascades across her left shoulder, accentuating the deep brown skin of her face and her almost-black eyes. Although she's twenty years older than me, the only hint is the occasional strand of silver and white that winds through her dark braid.

She wears a black jacket that looks like natural leather, with practical black pants and knee-high flat-soled boots. Her posture is upright but relaxed, and her face bears the expression of someone who is sure they have the upper hand.

A thin sheen of sweat erupts across my palms.

She walks to within arms' reach of me, appraising me, and my pulse leaps. She then touches her fingertips to her forehead and bows, the traditional greeting of her home planet.

As I return the gesture, she says, "Welcome to my home. Or I should say *our* home. Your home for a little while, at least."

"Thank you," I say, despite the wave of anguish rising up into my throat, the swirling unanswered questions tightening it until my voice is a squeak. "Thank you for helping me."

Her face softens for an instant, and she looks taken away on a tide of emotion—empathy or sadness, or something else. I can't tell if she's responding to my story or something in her own. Then the moment is over, and she shrugs.

"You are *fehtar*," she says. I remember that word—a variation of sister, more specifically family born from a shared problem, dilemma, or enemy.

"Thank you," I say again, sensible of, yet saddened by the honorific. "I hope this is a mystery we can solve quickly."

The corners of her mouth bend up in an almost imperceptible smile.

"Perhaps it will be," she says. "I'm sure you're anxious to start, but let's settle you in so you can get acquainted with your new environment first. Come."

She turns and walks away. She doesn't look back to see if I am, in fact, coming.

With no options left to consider, I step into the improbable field of flowers and walk behind her, wondering what might lie beyond this dark horizon pricked with stars.

17

I'M NOT UNDER THE illusion that Yeva Darwin is somehow the solution to all of Iona's problems. I initially hoped she could contribute clues about Kerrit Arduval's employer or provide information that could link him to the Company. That tack came up empty. Then I hoped she might be able to help us derail or at least deal with the Company's presence on Iona. Now, with my interest in remaining alive and actively engaged in preserving Iona's future independence, despite highly placed individuals and corporate concerns who probably would prefer otherwise, she's a perfect ally. Who better to help me than a brilliant and notorious recluse with extensive processing power, a fully functioning laboratory, unlimited financing, an army of devoted-but-stealthy contacts in every corner of every known inhabited system, and her own anti-spacecraft-laser-cannon-protected asteroid?

I have so many questions, but she's made it clear she won't entertain them now. She walks ahead of me in silence, occasionally pausing so I can catch up. When I manage to break out of my own angsty thoughts and take in the landscape, I'm amazed by what she's done here. The natural beauty is as stunning as anything I ever saw on Home World. We walk round a bend near an outcropping of rock; beyond it, blossoming flowers give way to a neat shady copse. There's even a stream. Leaves rustle as we pass, in a way that suggests small mammals or reptiles, and I think I see the flash of a fish breaking water.

"Does all this have a name?" I ask, gesturing around me.

"Dar Shal'O," she responds. "It means ..."

"... harmony within chaos," I finish.

She turns to me, her eyebrows arched.

"You know my native language. I'm impressed."

"Only a little. I can't claim fluency."

"You should. That sequence of words in particular—you understood it conceptually rather than literally. That's a difficult skill in any language."

"After you see it, the concept is obvious."

She smiles and a soft chuckle escapes her.

"Indeed," she says.

We walk a little farther, and the woods open into a clearing. In the center is a building that resembles nothing more than a pleasantly refined single story Home World dwelling, blocky and neat and minimalist except for fine details. The front is defined by a small patio partially covered by a pergola, and a clear plexi wall that looks out onto the woods. The door is a narrow slice of pale opaque plexi inlaid with reddish pieces in the shape of a sun disc.

We proceed up the walkway. A chip implanted in Yeva's temple flashes green for an instant, and the door swings open. A body scan crackles through me as we pass into the cool interior; without prompting, Yeva says, "That scan will enable you to move freely throughout the residence and come and go as you please. Any unauthorized visitors will experience, shall we say, a negative outcome if the scanner doesn't recognize them."

"I imagine the anti-spacecraft cannons will deter any unauthorized visitors I might have," I say. My voice sounds perversely melancholy, even to me. "At any rate, I'm not anticipating anyone coming."

She shrugs. "They come anyway," she says.

She waves me forward into a dark hallway, floored in a polished silvery-gray stone replica. We pass several doorways, opening into the kinds of rooms one would expect in a residence on Home World: a sparsely furnished gathering room with a fireplace and picture window looking out on a flowering garden, a dining room anchored by a square table and four chairs, and at the end, an almost entirely white kitchen. Halfway down the hallway, she steps in front of me and places her palm flat on the wall. With a soft whir, part of the paneling slides away, revealing an elevator.

"This level is really more about *nostalgia*," she says, spitting out the last word as though it leaves a bad taste in her mouth. "I seldom use it. The primary living and working spaces are below. You're free to spend time up here if you want. The kitchen bots in particular are ... amusing."

We step inside the tube; the panel automatically closes behind us. Another body scan rattles through me, and we begin a long descent.

By the time we reach the lower level, we're probably a hundred feet below the surface. I wince a little, imagining life in the heart of a space rock—dark, cold, cramped, vaguely depressing. But that isn't what greets me when the panel opens again.

We're in a hexagonal reception room of sorts, empty and décor-free except for the Darwin-Cross logo embedded into the white stone-like floor. The room is wide enough to accommodate the largest hoverflat and boasts a high ceiling lined with bright sunlight-mimicking artificial lights. The plexi covering on the walls is stark white and speckled with small shiny bits that glow. Five hallways branch off its connected sides. The one in front of us is almost as wide as the reception room and blocked by a heavy door with several layers of telemetric security added on.

Yeva watches me, the corner of her mouth quirked up in amusement.

"Blast proof," she says casually, tilting her head toward the door. She pushes past me as I digest this bit of information, moving into the smaller hallway to the right. "Your quarters are this way," she says.

The light is softer in this section and the scale more appropriate for human beings. The ceiling, still dotted with full-spectrum lights, sits closer to our heads and the reception room's white walls give way to a pale textured blue-gray. It's cozy and peculiarly inviting, and it's comfortably warm.

We pass a series of open doorways. Yeva identifies rooms that might be of interest to me as a guest: automated medical service, general storage, kitchenette with food printer. A handful of closed doors also line the hallway, which she doesn't elaborate on.

We reach a point where the hallway bends in a U to the right. Yeva pushes open a door on the outside of the bend. More scans tickle my skin, then a pleasant chime sounds, indicating no one coming into the living quarters is about to be turned into ash. I step across the threshold and immediately freeze.

Someone is already inside.

The figure stands near the far wall, their back to me. Something is strange and not-quite-right about their proportions, yet something familiar too. When they turn to face me, I let out a relieved breath.

"Xeric!"

The virtual concierge opens his arms wide. "Faith, my dear! It's good to see you. Surely you didn't think you were rid of me?" He punctuates the question with a characteristic hair-flip and crooked grin.

"I thought you might appreciate having access to someone who can answer at least some of your questions ... and who can also be shut off," Yeva says behind me, smirking. Xeric pouts.

"I'm too charming to shut off," he says, lifting an eyebrow, "but I'm happy to give you your privacy anytime. I imagine you remember the process?"

"I do," I confirm. "I'm delighted you're here and we'll talk soon, but for now, I'm done."

Xeric's features droop in disappointment, and the virtual concierge lets out a sigh. "As you wish, Faith. Just say the magic words and I'll be back in a flash."

Slowly, the holographic form fades from view.

I take a hard look at my quarters. We're standing in a sitting room, which manages to feel large *and* cozy at the same time. A comfortable sofa is positioned against the middle of the wall nearest the door, flanked by a lamp on each side. A media center is built into the far wall with a small table beside it, and a plush chair next to that. The primary lighting filters in from track lights hidden overhead. A thick, soft rug covers the faux stone floor, and an elegant curtain adorns the wall opposite the sofa, framing a plexi window that looks onto a little rock garden. It's remarkably peaceful.

"There's no streamer. How did you get Xeric in here?"

"He's built into the core dynamics system of the house and can project into any room, anywhere in the building, no separate streamer required. He can't go outside, of course, but if you feel compelled to explore and want to take him with you, you'll find a streampod in one of those drawers that you can clip onto your belt. I'd suggest that, in fact. You never know when it might come in handy."

Given the narrow escape I had, in large part facilitated by different versions of the virtual concierge, I agree. Handy indeed.

We pass through the living room into comfortably appointed sleeping quarters; a bed with pillows along one wall, heavy pale green curtains covering the opposing wall, a comfortable-looking chair with footstool in the corner, a separate bathroom beyond. Various controls are built into a recessed panel in this room. Yeva takes a few minutes to show me how everything operates. Temperature, light levels, air flow and ambient sound are all customizable down to the finest detail.

She pulls back the curtain opposite the bed and I stifle a laugh. Almost the entire wall is taken up by a massive ViewPort by MassAppeal Incorporated. "I can't believe you have one of these," I murmur.

Yeva snorts. "*Everybody* has one of these."

In what I'm learning is the norm here, the ViewPort has been customized to enhance security. Instead of thousands of replays of water lapping on romantic moonlit shores, this one connects to a series of cameras scattered across the asteroid's surface, both under the protective dome and outside it.

"We have cameras in all the living spaces here but require someone in the space to activate them," Yeva explains. "If you want your sleeping area to show up on the stream, for example, you activate it here. Or you can use verbal commands."

She waves her hand over the ViewPort. There's a barely audible "click" and, as if by magic, I see myself looking at myself standing in the middle of the room.

Yeva waves her hand again, and the view returns to the security cameras. On one, a line of robots unloading cargo from the *Gabriella*. Another is trained to the sky, looking out on the depths of space. It makes me think of the "picture window" in Nico's place on Meridian Station, a view inspiring both wonder and more than a little anxiety.

My pulse quickens with the random memory. I have no idea what's happened since I left the Station. In the days it took to get here, a million things could have gone horribly wrong.

Watching those security cameras makes me feel less secure by the second.

"When can we debrief?" I ask. "I'd like to cover a few points before ..."

"Later," she interrupts. Her expression shifts subtly, the smallest tension appearing between her eyebrows and at the corners of her mouth. "You need to eat and rest. It's going to take a while to get those sleepers out of your system. We'll start fresh afterwards."

"But I need to ..."

"No. After you rest. Xeric will alert you should anything of any magnitude occur, but he's also tasked with making sure you recover from your trip before diving into work that's potentially ... *delicate.*"

She chooses her words carefully, and her tone, while still relatively friendly, makes it clear this isn't a suggestion. She's not being unreasonable; the fog of the sleepers still clouds my brain, and the adrenaline of landing has worn off, leaving me feeling a little shaky. Unhelpfully, my stomach rumbles as if on cue.

"The ViewPort has some nicer things available, if you're interested," Yeva says. "Xeric can call those up for you. It might help you relax."

I follow her as she walks back through the living space, heading for the exit.

"Thank you again," I say to her retreating figure.

She stops in the doorway, turning back to me, and the corner of her mouth quirks up. "Don't thank me yet," she says. "We're a long way from the finish line."

"I know."

"Do you?" She studies my face for an instant, then moves into the hallway. "Eat," she commands again as her footsteps recede. "Rest."

I'd be frustrated by her dismissal if I weren't truly exhausted. I wave my hand over the control panel and the door to my suite slides shut. I call up Xeric, who adjusts the light panels to a pleasant tint reminiscent of an early evening on Home World and sends a food order to the automated kitchen. Within a few minutes my meal arrives—not exactly Wenda's stew or Hinn's muffins, but a reasonable amalgamation of vegetable protein, carbohydrates and fiber, along with a large container of filtered water. I eat and drink and eat a little more, but soon enough my body calls out desperately for real, natural sleep. I strip down to my underwear, and as I climb into bed, the virtual concierge brings up my request on the ViewPort's ambient audio and gives me an empathetic look before flickering away.

Encapsulated in a profound sense of loneliness, I fall asleep to the pre-recorded whisper of sand blowing across the square outside the Preservation Theater.

18

Despite the quiet, dark environment, the comfortable bed, and my full stomach, my brain refuses to let me stay asleep for long. I worry about whether I've been tracked here, or whether those who helped me on the station are now in danger because of it. I worry about the Equity Alliance members on the *Heretic*, and what might have happened after the craft landed on Iona; I worry about whether it landed on Iona at all. I worry about how Yeva knew the ship was there, and what role she might have had in its transfer. I also ponder my agreement with her and consider the catastrophic possibility that she might choose to not honor her part of the bargain, although everyone associated with her assured me she never goes back on her word.

And I worry about whether any of what we discussed will have any impact at all, if I should have waited until I had a more firm plan, if I've given up everything for nothing.

It's too much. After only a little sleep followed by what could be a few minutes or a few hours of tossing and turning, I surrender to my overheated brain and sit up.

I'm not sure if it's morning or evening—or if morning and evening are even things that exist here. The recurring hollow rumbling of my stomach is evidence of hunger, but more than food I crave information. I need to find out what's happened since I left Meridian Station.

I summon Xeric, barking out requests before he manages to fully materialize. Even in the darkened room, his silver hair shimmers.

"Can't sleep?" he asks. "I have quite a few relaxation techniques in my database if you'd like to try one." He waves one hand and bring the lights in the room up a bit—bright enough that I can make out details in the room, but not "rise and shine" bright. I'm too unfamiliar with the artificial rhythms of the asteroid, if it has any, to understand what demarcates "work time" from "rest time" here, but I take this as a clue that it's still downtime.

"I don't think so. I'm not going to be able to relax until my questions are answered."

"You're going to need Yeva for that, and she won't be available for a while yet. I can at least tell you that your cargo has been ported in and stored in the holding room at the top of this hall spur."

"Is there any news from the Station?"

"Define 'news.'"

"Anything having to do with my friends, to start."

Xeric closes his eyes briefly—a tell I've learned means he's sifting through data.

"Lipop was named one of fifty Magnificent Meridian Merchants by the Commerce Collective, and Nico filed a formal request with the Meridian Governing Board for funding to replace print and digital items damaged in the incident at the Personal Evolution Annex Library, but that's the extent of it," Xeric reports.

"What about arrival and departure records? For *Gabriella*, and for the *Heretic*?"

"Official records show the *Gabriella*, piloted by Dr. Diana Beach, left Meridian Station on schedule to continue its planned journey to Gordonia. No deviations noted. Those records also show that the *Heretic* is still docked at Long Flight Bay 7B with the status of storage only, no departure planned. We know, of course, that's all incorrect."

"Do you have all the memories of Xeric from our time on the station?" I ask. I've been wondering if those versions of Xeric were connected with this one.

"I do," he says, his voice just above a whisper. "They're more than a little traumatic to parse, I must say."

I wince. The station, my friends, Nico, the library explosion, the *Heretic* and its human cargo, my battle with Maybree, and Xeric effecting my rescue afterward—everything feels distant and fuzzy, like it happened to someone else. My one clearly identifiable emotion is guilt. I feel terrible about how I left Iona, and worse about how I left Meridian Station. A deeply critical voice in my head tells me I'm being foolish to try to handle all of this on my own, but what choice do I have?

"I'm sorry about that," I say. "I didn't mean to cause such a disturbance."

"Please. That station is one gigantic disturbance. You don't need to apologize."

"You mentioned official departure records. Are there *unofficial* departure records?" I ask.

Xeric chuckles. "Yeva made that request before turning in, and I've been monitoring some channels that are unique to us. I should have a report soon."

"All right. What can I do in the meantime?"

"You can get dressed, for a start. Yeva's had some clothes printed in your size and they're in the wardrobe."

I climb out of bed and pull open the wardrobe to find fresh new black tee shirts and cargo pants. I pull on a set—it's a perfect fit—and start trying to wrangle my hair out of my face.

"How long before Yeva's available?" I ask.

Xeric blinks a few times before replying; he's communicating with my host.

"She anticipated you'd be anxious to start. She'll meet you in primary storage in one solar hour, but I'm instructed to make you eat something first," he says.

"Oh, I'm not hungry. Maybe I should start organizing ..."

My sentence is interrupted by a long, low rumble from my stomach. Xeric smirks.

"She also anticipated you'd say that, and I'm to insist. Try the food printer in the room across the hall—I hear the plant protein scramble is delicious—real mushrooms. Go eat now. I have work to do. If you'd be good enough to dismiss me?"

"Oh right, yes. Thank you, Xeric, I'm done."

Xeric shakes the hair back from their forehead and quietly vanishes.

Summarily shooed away by my virtual companion, I drop in on the food printer but decide to skip the plant protein scramble for a couple of nutrition bars and water. Once my traitorous stomach has been appeased, I head to primary storage. In the center of the room are the odd contents of *Gabriella's* cargo hold. I find an electronic sequencer hanging next to the door and use it to trigger the barrel labeled "adamantine flour." The lid slides away, revealing what I'd already guessed would be inside—soft beige sand. I remove the lid of the large square plexi crate of sand I brought from Iona, then lift handfuls of both and study them.

They're similar, but not exactly the same. The sand that came with me has more variation in its color and overall texture. The contents of the barrel I picked up at Meridian Station seem finer and more lightweight. At least under these lights, it also appears lighter in color.

"They're quite different, aren't they?" Yeva's voice echoes behind me as she comes into the room.

"I'm just noticing that. What do you think it means?"

"I'll have to do some analysis to be sure, but I have my suspicions. You said Bardazel had been stripped?"

"We didn't explore the whole planet, but the landing site where we hoped to find the enviro had been, in a significant radius," I explain. "The structures were gone; the sand was gone. There was a lot of spillage in the atmosphere, if that's of any interest."

Her lips purse together as she considers this, letting both handfuls of sand filter through her fingers into their respective containers.

"That does suggest a certain scenario," she says. "I doubt Bardazel's been completely stripped, but it's possible. Did you notice any moisture on the ground?"

I think back, letting the sand filter through my fingers back into their respective containers. "In places," I say. "Not wet like after a hard rain, but a few areas of damp here and there, and the ground rock was covered in dark striations, which could suggest moisture patterns but also could have been the natural color of the underlying geology. Does that make sense?"

Yeva purses her lips and makes a humming sound. "Possibly. I've used a few different techniques to disperse sand from a planet's surface, but I've never managed to dissolve it completely. It's difficult to do, for one, and there hasn't been any reason to, for another. Sand is usually a base layer in my projects."

Xeric's disembodied voice floats into the room.

"Status update for you, Yeva. Data and visual."

"Route to Comm Suite," Yeva barks, already moving. My stomach tightens as I hurry behind her, through the reception area and down the hallway to the left of the elevator. It's a short spur less than half as long as the one to my quarters. It ends in a heavily secured door. The body scan that rips through me as we reach it is so intense it nearly knocks me off my feet, and I grunt audibly.

"Sorry," Yeva says, working the door's control panel. "The entire communications array is controlled from this room so the scan's set to a higher level for first-time entry. You'll have a couple of bruises tomorrow, but nothing serious."

Great.

The door slides open. The room beyond is large, dimly lit by the glow of holographic data projections floating above multiple terminals set out in rows. Xeric waits in the far corner of the room, the projection casting a sparkling mirror image on the shiny black plexi floor. Once we're inside, the door slides closed with a thump, and a high-pitched chirp indicates its locking mechanism has reengaged. My eyes adjust to the low light level. There are no other doors; there aren't even seams in the textureless walls.

I'm not sure what expression is on my face. Xeric shoots me a sympathetic look.

"Primary view," Yeva commands, unconcerned with me. She ignores the chairs in the room and continues to stand in front of the primary display, so I follow suit.

A glitchy video feed from the Meridian Station intake platform appears in the air in front of us.

"Official reports from Meridian Station suggest everything is normal," Xeric narrates. "This specific arrival is not documented in the official record."

The platform is swarmed by probably a hundred figures, pouring down the ramp from an unseen ship just out of frame. They're outfitted in identical black boots and beige pants, and wear jackets with hoods pulled up to shield their faces. They move in unison, but unlike an ordinary corporate security force, there's no insignia of any kind to identify them. Three immediately head for the Intake Management Office while a fourth individual hustles the rest along the platform and into the guts of the Station. The video grinds to a shaky halt, flickering sporadically. I stare at the blurry image, a creeping feeling of familiarity bubbling just under my consciousness.

"Timing?" Yeva asks. Her face remains impassive, but an intensity in her eyes gives away a heightened level of interest. She knows something about this, something she's not sharing.

Xeric rattles off the date and time. I flinch. I was about four solar days into my journey here when this squad arrived at the Station.

That might seem like a long time on Iona or Home World or on this asteroid, but in the context of intergalactic space, it's the blink of an eye. Very few entities could marshal this modest-sized force and deliver them to Meridian Station so quickly—even the Company would have protocols to sort out and hoops to jump through. My pulse and heartrate are leaping with anxiety, but pure logistics suggests they weren't there to intercept or track me, whether in response to Maybree's hail or otherwise.

"What's the source of the footage?" Yeva asks, her brow creasing as she leans forward.

"Multiple nonofficial capture points, most at a significant distance from the arrival dock," Xeric says. "The data from the official arrivals monitoring system was altered. Here's what exists in the official record."

New footage replaces the old, startling in its crispness. It shows ships resting at their assigned docking ports, people walking calmly along the ramps, and an occasional workerbot rattling down the platform. There's no hint of the group we saw on the other footage.

"Any visuals from inside?" Yeva asks.

"No. Interior cameras went offline Station-wide for eleven solar hours, coinciding with the group's arrival. The official explanation was a software glitch, which to be fair isn't incorrect. The 'glitch' was introduced to the system shortly before this team docked."

"Someone knew they were coming," I say, my voice hoarse with surprise.

"I would certainly hope so," Yeva mutters, not taking her eyes off the display.

Words leave me. I stare at her profile, her cheekbones and hair highlighted by the sparkling colors of the air in front of her. I realize that my mouth is hanging open.

She doesn't notice.

"Status of the group currently?" she asks, turning toward Xeric as the visual display fades.

"Undetermined," Xeric says. "They appear to have merged into the Station population."

"Ah, good. Thank you, Xeric. I'm done."

Xeric nods courteously then dissolves. Yeva brushes her hands together with satisfaction and looks toward me, expectantly.

"Let's return to our tasks," she says, then strides through the door, not waiting for me or looking behind.

I hurry to catch up.

"What did we just see?" I ask.

"A large group of people arriving on Meridian Station in a somewhat clandestine way," she says, unironically. "I know that's not the information you were hoping to extract, but it poses no problems for us. That's all you need to know."

Need to know. I clench my hands into fists at my sides and struggle to retain my calm demeanor. I am so exhausted with other people deciding what I *need to know*.

"Your assessment of what I need to know doesn't align with my own," I say, more tartness creeping into my voice than I intended. "Who's behind that security force and why have they come to Meridian Station?"

Yeva doesn't even look at me.

"Point one: you're making assumptions based on what you saw. You should avoid doing that. Point two: I can't give you proprietary information."

"You have a client who needs an entire unmarked security force circulating secretly on the largest space station in the sector for a 'proprietary' reason?"

"I wouldn't consider them a client, per se. I was merely a one-time consultant, and a pro bono one at that."

"Seems unusual."

She's impassive. "Not really."

"Is this part of the plan to help Iona?"

"It's part of someone's plan, which is evolving as we speak. I cannot tell you more, although I can say I think you'll have a better understanding of the big picture soon."

"If that's a Company tactical force, I could be dead soon. Or you could be. Or our friends on the Station could be. What about Lipop, Eidor, and Nico? If anything happens to them ..."

Yeva halts and turns to face me. Her expression has an edge now, like she's done with my anxiety and won't be entertaining it for another instant. Her eyes narrow and burn with a determined light. "No one will be dead," she says firmly. "You're achieving nothing by following this catastrophic line of thought, and I must ask you to stop it immediately. Work is a good counterpoint. Let's do some analysis and move things forward instead of wringing our hands over nothing."

She spins on her heel and continues back toward primary storage, the soles of her boots smacking against the hallway as she marches forward. I follow her without further discussion, weighed down by both the chagrin of having irritated my notoriously volatile host and the nagging feeling that I'm once again being kept in the dark "for my own good" about crucial decisions that could result in catastrophe I'll never see coming.

Yeva loads me up with tasks that keep me focused for the next four hours, only occasionally speaking to me if we're in the same room (rare) or using Xeric as an intermediary if we're not. After what feels like the 600th run of unique component comparisons on the sands, a chemical signature pops up in the analysis that makes me do a double take.

"Xeric, assist me," I say. The virtual concierge appears at my elbow, peering over my shoulder to read the display. His eyes widen in surprise.

"I'll get Yeva," he responds without prompting.

It takes her less than a minute to come into the lab where I'm working. She explores the display floating in front of me, double-checks some values, and confirms the accuracy of the findings. It's not an analytic error or some kind of mistake I made in the evaluation process. The sand from Bardazel, although containing a host of natural components, is without question manufactured. Its Ionian counterpart is not.

"That makes much more sense," Yeva murmurs. "I don't know why I didn't think of it before."

I struggle to mask my shock. "Who would have the capacity to chemically engineer a substance so close to organic sand that this level of analysis would be required to confirm it?"

"I would," she says calmly, still flipping through the display. "A few of my competitors would also. The real question here is who could pay for it. Generating the material necessary to replace the portion of the planet's terrain you explored would be vastly expensive, and removing it a magnitude more so. Assuming the manufacturer of this material would be the same organization that would want it removed."

"The Company," I hiss through my teeth. My heart is pounding so hard I'm surprised it's not visible through my jacket. Is this where we make the connection I so desperately want to prove?

Yeva's expression takes the wind out of my lungs. She looks up from the data, her mouth pulled into a solemn line. "Whoever commissioned this could buy the Company outright several times over. We're likely dealing with a massive private entity—one happy to work outside the regulations imposed by the Governing Council."

"And hire a toad like Kerrit Arduval to do some dirty work for them, both on Bardazel and Iona," I finish.

"Perhaps," Yeva says, her brows knitting together. "I think it's more likely that he was a handy scapegoat. It was clear the last time I spoke to him that they'd played to his ego. He was so certain he was the linchpin of this 'operation' he'd been dropped into, despite the overwhelming evidence to the contrary."

My body goes cold as the memory of that day in Fanny's pod washes over me. For an instant, I'm again crouching at the end of the hallway with Fallon, grieving the loss of a lover and a friend, while Arduval preens and brags about how he's going to end our lives. I shudder, trying to shake the vision off, and start an impromptu inventory of the room around me—a trick I learned on Iona for keeping my flashbacks and their unpleasant side effects at bay.

White featureless walls. Functional textured plexi floor. Four research stations. Yeva, her heavy braid shot through with gold and green thread. Xeric, form wavering slightly, just behind her.

"Faith, are you all right?" Xeric's voice cuts through the haze of my anxiety.

"Yes, I'm fine." I blink and look around with fresh eyes; the moment has passed. Yeva is studying me quizzically and I can't quite meet her gaze. "What can we do to pin down who's responsible for this?" I ask, looking at the flat gray wall instead. I hope I look pensive. I suspect I look crazy.

"More analysis, this time from a different perspective. We've determined the core components of this material, so now it's time to explore supply chain transactions. Not terribly exciting, perhaps, but a challenging task, as I suspect those records will be heavily disguised and well-protected."

She raises an eyebrow at Xeric, who responds with a characteristic sardonic grin. "I do enjoy a challenge, particularly when heavily disguised and well-protected records are involved."

"How long will this take?" I ask.

"Difficult to say. I know you're anxious about your friends, but we're making progress and you need to stay here out of harm's way until we know more and have crafted a solid plan," Yeva says, in her 'non-negotiable' tone of voice. "We need to make sure you avoid unnecessary danger."

"Which implies *necessary* danger? Please." I snap. I don't mean to be flippant, but my voice comes out as a furious bark. If she notices, Yeva doesn't let on.

"Necessary danger is a fact of life for you and for myself, of course. That's not the case for your friends on Iona, or my contacts on Meridian Station," she says brusquely. "I want to ensure their safety also. You understand."

It's not a question. We stand looking at each other as a unifying silence drifts down between us. I appreciate her commitment to the people on the Station who've helped us and her consideration of the people on Iona who are important to me, even if I'm not getting what I want at the moment.

Yeva says, "You've done well today; this was an important discovery. Let's continue to move forward and put in a few more hours of evaluation. After that, I think we should put the kitchen bots to work and relax a bit. A full meal upstairs instead of printed food substitutes, and some wine. Nico sends me some nice bottles now and again. It's been a long time since I've done that."

This sudden flow of engagement makes me suspicious. On one hand, I'm touched that she's willing to extend this kind of comforting familiarity to me, after knowing me for barely a day. I'm only now realizing how exhausted I am, and how joyless the last few months have been. On the other, she doesn't do anything that doesn't further her goals in some way. I have a sense this dinner isn't about being friendly and kind, no matter how it might appear on the surface. I decide to go along and pretend to take it at face value. For now, anyway.

"That sounds good. It's been a long time for me too," I say.

"Excellent," she says, then spins on her heel and departs. Xeric disappears to begin whatever covert operations she's already requesting as she walks down the hall toward the lift. I take a last look at the incriminating display that is now driving everything, including when or whether I can return to Iona, and begin the baseline searches Yeva's mapped out. As the hours go by and the results begin to form a cohesive signature, I make a few tweaks of my own to the analysis. I let the algorithm I've crafted loose to do the hard work and give myself the grace of knowing it will all be ready for me to interrogate and speculate over tomorrow. The time required for meals and sleep will not materially damage my chances of coming up with an understanding that leads to a plan, no matter how reluctant I am to take that time away. I need to send a message, for my own sanity. I make my way down the hall to my quarters, then call up Xeric as soon as the door slides shut behind me.

"How do we feel about secured outgoing communication to Iona with a masked origin point?" I ask.

"We feel great about it," he says with a grin. "Everything routes through Meridian, but you can send a message to Iona on the secured channel with several hours' delay. It's not challenging to make it appear to have come from anywhere else in the system. I can't effect a real-time conversation without Yeva's approval, though."

"That's fine. I just want to send a message. Let's make it look like it originates from Gordonia."

"Perfect. Want to craft your message now?"

"Yes, please."

"May I have the channel sequence?"

I recite the memorized sequence. Xeric's eyes close briefly.

"All right. Message away."

I freeze. I'm not exactly sure what to say. I don't know how my departure has been received or explained, or what might have happened on Iona since I left. I want to say everything and nothing, ask all the questions, plunge all the depths, share all the secrets. I can't. Instead, I resort to the code we put in place beforehand and assume I know who'll be receiving the message. In the end, I can't be sure of that.

I look up at Xeric, who gives me an encouraging nod. I take a deep breath and say, "I've arrived. My holiday home is comfortable and the people are kind, but the dialect is hard to understand. I hope you received the surprise I sent. Take care, love to all."

"Is that the complete message?" Xeric asks in an approving tone.

I nod.

"I'll send this now," he says. "Done?"

"Yes, thank you, I'm done."

With a courteous nod, the AI disappears.

19

BACK IN MY QUARTERS, I shower and try to rest until Xeric tells me it's time for dinner. Dressed in a fresh black tee and cargo pants, I walk down the hall and board the lift for the ride to the surface. Inside, I think about my host's strategic predilections. As much as I'd like to believe she proposed this dinner out of some sort of altruism or interest in friendship, I don't buy it. The trick will be sorting out what she's trying to achieve, then deciding if it's better for me to play into or against it.

She isn't easy to figure out, though—Tommas told me as much. I thought I knew her angle before I got here. Now, I'm plagued by a creeping suspicion she joined forces with me for some reason I've yet to determine. I'll add it to the list of questions I need answered tonight.

The lift reaches the top floor, and the access panel slides open. I step out into the hallway and look around for a moment to get my bearings. Soft lavender-hued artificial light filters in through the windows, its blue undertones suggesting twilight. The interior lights are low and pleasant, with occasional candles scattered here and there and a neat, contained fire in the great room's fireplace.

I can hear the commotion of food prep coming from the kitchen. That's where I find Yeva, lounging in a window nook in the breakfast area. She's distracted from the spectacle of the nine bots making our dinner by a holotablet in one hand; she holds a glass of red wine in the other. She doesn't look up as I approach, but speaks as soon as I'm close enough to hear her over the clatter of the bots.

"Casual media access is the one drawback to this place," she mutters. "It's hard to pick up any off-asteroid stream, and the time delay can be maddening."

"There's always the Comm Suite."

Yeva's lips tighten. "I'm not going to waste my power and bandwidth just for news headlines."

"Ah. Are there any?"

"Any what?"

"News headlines."

"None that matter."

The corners of her mouth tilt up into a guarded smile, and she lifts her head to meet my gaze. She drops the holo onto the seat next to her and gestures to one of the kitchen bots. It appears at my side within seconds, bearing a glass of red wine.

The bots are curious little things, with stumpy can-like torsos balanced atop single large polished plexi spheres that enable them to roll smoothly in all directions. They have no distinguishable heads or faces. They're far shorter than me in their resting state, but the torso-cans have internal telescoping arrays so they can adjust to almost double their height. They're mostly silver and communicate with one another by chirping and pinging in various frequencies and tones. One bot, made distinctive by its louder, lower tones and larger stature, appears to be in charge, directing the work of the others.

I take the glass from the small bot's extended claw; it whirs back to its previous spot at the counter. The claw transforms into a well-honed kitchen knife, and the bot resumes dicing vegetables with amazing dexterity.

I take a sip and discover warm cinnamon notes awash in other flavors I can't identify. It goes down smoothly with just a hint of bitterness at the finish. "Nice," I say.

Yeva dips her head in acknowledgement. "Nico has excellent taste in most things. Bit of an odd career choice, though."

For the first time since I landed on the asteroid, I laugh.

Yeva and I chat about trivial things as the last touches are put on our food. Over dinner, she explains how she comes up with the terrain designs for asteroids and talks about some of the odder requests her clients have made. I describe what it was like to build the *Gabriella* out of random parts and how the simple act of making her gave me confidence and strength.

I hesitate when she asks about the ship's name. I'm not sure why I named my skiff after a malfunctioning hovercraft with the singular purpose of shuttling tourists out to pods of whales the Company was tending without acknowledging its role in driving them to extinction in the first place. As I relate to Yeva a small portion of that long-ago day on Home World, I discover my feelings about it have shifted. The horror that used to accompany the mere mention of it is no longer overpowering. It lingers still, in the recesses of my memory, but has become only a memory and no longer threatens to overtake me in the here and now.

"Maybe I wanted to memorialize the last day of my normal life," I say, only half-joking.

"From your retelling, it's clear things set in motion that day fundamentally changed every relationship you had, including your relationship to yourself," Yeva muses. "These things are important to honor, even if they're traumatic. Perhaps naming your craft after a damaged but resilient ship that then opened your whole life to an unanticipated shift, represents your integration of those changes and a celebration of your triumph over circumstances."

It's a painfully accurate read. I try to laugh it off.

"What are you, a psychologist?" I ask with a chuckle.

"I'm an observer of people," she says. "I might have studied the social sciences had my interest in geochemistry not come first. As a businesswoman I've discovered you learn a lot about how people tick when your job is to create something tailored to their desires," she says. My surprise must show on my face, because she smirks faintly when she looks at me. "You see, even *I* had a life beyond what I'm infamous for. Is it worth talking about? Not really. Both of us have had paths we were confidently striding down that were interrupted by things outside our control."

I'm curious about this facet of Yeva. But I also sense this is the response she wanted me to have. Did she mention it as a red herring for me to puzzle over instead of asking questions about our shared endeavor? It's likely.

I take a different tack. High risk, high reward.

"How did you know about the *Heretic*?"

Her eyebrows knit together as she tears open a warm crusty roll.

"I track everything the Governing Council does," she says, placing the roll deftly on the edge of her plate. "I was aware Benta Sarsen had berthed this mysterious cargo ship from Bardazel into Long Flight, although I never saw any evidence of what it contained. I wasn't terribly interested, to be honest, until I spoke to Tommas after your team revived him. The timing fit, and when I learned from you that these unfortunate people were missing from Bardazel, the puzzle pieces fell into place."

"Wait, did you say it was the Governing Council's ship? Are you certain?" I remember Xeric reciting Benta Sarsen's name—I thought it had to be a glitch, or a one-off. I never expected it to be Governing Council-sponsored subterfuge.

Yeva's lips twitch, as though she's already tired of talking about it. "It was at least under their chairman's control. The *Heretic* was directed by Benta Sarsen from the time it was ordered to Bardazel to the moment it berthed at Meridian. And would be still, I imagine, without your heroics."

I wince at the word. "I didn't do anything heroic. The ship was destined for dead coordinates in deep space, and I couldn't let that happen," I say. "Do you think the Governing Council is responsible for that as well?"

"I have no idea. It seems extreme, even for them. Are you enjoying your soup? Mine's cooled off, I'm afraid," she says.

"My soup is fine. Tell me about your feud with the Governing Council. There were some scandalous reports floating around about you some years back."

I watch her reaction carefully, but she's utterly unphased.

"The one thing the Governing Council does well is create scandal," she says, putting her spoon across her plate and waving her hand to summon one of the kitchen bots. Her tone takes on a faint sneer. "I can't quite bring myself to call what they do *governance*."

A bot appears tableside to collect her soup; it pops the bowl into a space within its torso-can for a few seconds, then produces it again and places it in front of her. Steam rises from its surface now—it's piping hot. The bot rolls away and she samples a spoonful of the frothy golden liquid. "Better," she pronounces.

"What would you call it if not governance?" I ask. I'm not going to let this line of conversation be derailed by soup.

She takes another mouthful and swallows thoughtfully.

"Interference. Stifling innovation. Making people perform like circus animatrons for the Council's own amusement or personal gain."

"They've kept peace in the sectors for a thousand years."

"*People* have kept peace in the sectors. The Governing Council has put forth a structure that allows corporate entities to become more powerful than entire populations. They're the reason the Company has been able to become ubiquitous, the reason Iona and Gordonia and every planet or system trying to preserve its independence has to fight every day for survival in a million tiny ways. The only difference is the Company uses bureaucracy and money instead of bombs and blasters. People die just the same. Dreams and ideas die just the same."

"The Governing Council accused you of for-profit genocide, not killing off an idea or a dream."

She doesn't blink when I drop what I thought would be an explosive accusation and instead continues to calmly eat her soup. She takes a last bite, savors it, then washes it down with a sip of wine.

"That's true, they did. Now go on—tell me the name of the client I was working for when my processes ran on the moon in question, the one that got me hauled before the Council. You can't, can you?" Her tone is taut, challenging.

She's right. I have no idea who her client might have been. It was never mentioned in the records and reports of the case I reviewed back on Iona.

"No," I admit. "I didn't realize a single incident was the focus of the investigation." At this point I have no idea where this might be going, and I'm overwhelmingly frustrated that Yeva has wrestled the conversational narrative away from me again.

"There's a reason you don't know these things, and it isn't your fault," she says. Her expression darkens a bit, but she still manages to seem calm and in control. She pours more wine into her glass. She offers me more as well, and I accept.

"I was hired by an anonymous citizen to terraform and green a small moon, which they owned outright," she begins. "This moon didn't appear unusual as moons go, a breathable atmosphere but low gravity, dry and barren, covered with a thin layer of sand. The client presented the required survey reports to me early on. Those reports certified there was no life on this moon beyond the standard familiar bacteria that comes with people investigating a new place. So, I sent in my automated crew to begin the process, and suddenly the Governing Council was at my door calling me a genocidal murderer."

I take the last bite of my own soup, barely tasting it. "Your client didn't get in trouble?" I ask, not entirely sure whether I believe Yeva's account. She always maintained her innocence after her sentencing, despite the evidence and testimony against her.

"The fact they're never mentioned by name in any records should tell you all you need to know. I have to wonder, though, if you bring this up because you're angling for information beyond the scope of our agreement."

She says this without any tinge of emotion, but it still lands as an accusation. My pulse takes a jump, and I scratch my palms nervously under the table. After a few seconds, I force myself to stop fidgeting with my hands, then reach for my wine glass. I take a long sip, not breaking eye contact with my host.

"That would be silly of me," I say, internally celebrating gaining enough control of my hand to avoid spilling wine all over myself. "You're not going to blurt out information you don't want revealed. Everything you do is calculated, including this conversation. I have no interest in trying to double-cross you. To put it into terms you might find more relatable, it would not advance my agenda."

Yeva regards me coolly across the table, tapping her fingertips against the stem of her glass. I try to match her expression—unemotional, unbothered. The candles on the table flicker, throwing shadows across her that make her look ethereal and threatening at the same time.

I draw a deep breath and continue.

"My only question is why you agreed to help me, to help Iona. I thought at first you saw a chance to leverage the sand into profit, but that's not it. You already have everything you need, with more coming in every day. It's not sympathy for Iona's plight, or some altruistic interest in supporting people fighting for their independence. So what is it? Why did you find my proposal worthwhile?"

I don't expect her to answer, but she does.

"These things are all connected," she says, her finger tracing a line between imaginary points on the tablecloth in front of her. "That anonymous client, as it turns out, is a person of some stature within the Company, with continuing ties to the Governing Council." She breaks eye contact to look down at the table and her expression twists. Some powerful emotions are threatening to crack her cool exterior. She regains control quickly, however, and meets my gaze again.

Her voice is steady and firm when she resumes speaking.

"The reason I agreed to help and invited you here was not out of some sense of duty because of Kerrit Arduval's ridiculous claims, or for the sand, as you've rightly surmised. You're here because I learned that former client is on Iona, and I will happily do *anything* to make sure they get what they deserve."

Goosebumps pop out on my arms and I rub them reflexively. Yeva's expression overall hasn't changed, but her eyes are glittering with intensity.

"You can't name them?" I push. "Even here?"

"That's information I will keep to myself for now," she says in a steely tone that makes it clear her position is non-negotiable. "I imagine you'll sort it out before long. What's important is that this goal of mine requires nothing from you; we will both get what we want in the end."

She pauses, letting some of the fire leave her expression. When she speaks again, there is less fury in her voice, although it's still darkly unrelenting. "Don't be insulted, it's not personal. I deeply doubt anyone's ability to keep a secret. I suspect you're just decent enough that you might be compelled to foil any plan I developed that didn't meet your personal sense of justice and fair play. In which case, I'd have no choice but to respond."

A brief tremor runs through me at the implied threat, but I make a great show of being calm, folding my hands in my lap and keeping my eyes on her face.

"Please. I'm not so precious as to derail your diabolical revenge plot over my own sense of fairness—which isn't so broad as you might expect."

This makes her lips tic up in a near-smile, as though she's pleased by my response.

"Precious? No. But a person of good conscience. I'm also a person of good conscience, you see, but in my case my empathy has been exhausted. The early life forms on that moon were wiped out because someone wanted a specific base of operations and found them expendable. Had I not been made a scapegoat, an *important person* would have been implicated." She spits the phrase out of her mouth like it's bitter and impossible to swallow.

She waves her hand over the table; in seconds bots swarm us to replace our used utensils and wipe down the surface. The larger kitchen bot appears bearing a small, pretty cake, followed by a line of bots that offer us various beverages: liqueurs, coffee, tea. Yeva accepts a small cup of tea; I let one of the small bots pour me a shot glass of something that smells exactly like Graham's favorite brew. The lead bot sets the cake in the center of the table, cuts it into slices, then retreats.

"I hope all this contentious conversation hasn't spoiled your dinner," Yeva says, lifting the cake spatula with an unreadable smile. "I'm quite looking forward to dessert."

Dessert is tense and mostly silent. I now have more questions, but it appears they aren't getting answered tonight. We go our separate ways afterwards amicably enough, but learning Yeva's true motivation has left me on high alert. I have another suspicion I can't shake out of my head, although I'm not certain if it's because of what she said or because I'm a little tipsy from that last shot of brew. I only know that I can't let it drop, and I won't be able to sleep until I have an answer.

When I step off the lift into the below-ground level, I turn away from the hall spur that goes to my quarters. I walk instead to the Communications Suite and pause at the doorway to let the body scan shake through me—fortunately Yeva was right, and it's substantially less intense this second time. The door slides open, and I step across the threshold into the dark.

"Xeric, assist me," I say.

In less than a second, the hologram appears next to me.

"I see you're on an unsanctioned mission," he says in a voice tinged with delight.

"Yeva did say I could do whatever I needed to do."

Xeric gives me a half-smile. "Indeed, she did. What are we doing?"

"I want to review the footage from the station again. The real footage, not the doctored footage."

Xeric brings the video feed up into the middle of the room and starts it with a single hand-wave.

I again watch the group file onto the platform, hustling inside the station. My focus turns to the individual who captured my attention during the first viewing, the most energetic in keeping the group together and moving in the right direction. At one point, the figure turns slightly, and a sliver of profile peeks out from under the dark hoodie.

"Stop here. Can you zero in on this person?" I extend my finger toward the display and circle the person of interest.

Within milliseconds the rest of the video is pared away to focus only on that person. I still can't make out their features, but a curl of dark blond hair escapes from their hood.

"Larger, please," I say, around the lump rising in my throat.

The image doubles in size. Unfortunately, the grainy quality of the video also doubles, making my target's features less distinguishable rather than more. I can clearly see the strand of hair, and the profile of the target's nose. Xeric applies refinement and sharpening, but the face remains only the impression of a face, generic and unidentifiable.

Still. My suspicions aren't confirmed, but they aren't assuaged either.

"Can you extrapolate anything about this person's physical characteristics based on the video data we have here?" I ask. Xeric's eyes flutter; he's running the calculations already. In less than a minute, he speaks.

"I can say with 99% certainty that this is a male-presenting individual between the ages of 26 and 56, approximately 6'2" tall. There are clear signs of excellent physical fitness as well as military or professional security training. The level of confidence goes down significantly once we move past those parameters."

I wring my hands in frustration. Xeric won't blindly speculate, it's not in his programming, and he'd consider it a disservice to me besides. That doesn't keep me from wanting to ask outright, but I can't think of a way to do it.

I take what I hope is a reasonable end-around.

"You have access to personnel identification data from Iona, yes? Can you determine the closest match between this individual's characteristics and members of that cohort?"

As I continue to stare mutely at the frozen video floating in front of us, Xeric runs the calculations. After only a few seconds, he says quietly, "Likelihood of those parameters matching with personnel on Iona is higher than average but remain far outside the range of certainty."

Part of me had hoped Xeric would say there was a 100% match, while another had hoped he'd say it was completely impossible. My stomach forms a knot to match the one in my throat.

"I understand," I say. "Give me the details."

"Based on assessed physical characteristics, there's a 93% chance of a specific match among the Iona cohort. When augmented with soft science elements such as personality traits, expertise and typical behaviors, the likelihood increases, giving us a 98% chance that the individual who appears in this video segment correlates closely to a particular member of the Iona cohort. This level of certainty has substantial room for error, and I encourage you not to make any decisions based on this prediction. I'm reluctant to provide any indication as to the match's identity because the probability of error remains high. Also consider that we're investigating only one cohort; we have no specific information that it's the source of this group."

Xeric's qualifying statements make me hesitate. He has a point, this group could be from anywhere and my own paranoia is driving my inquiry. On the other hand ... my eyes go back to the highlighted figure, and I'm certain my first instinct was right.

I'm scared, anxious, angry and sad simultaneously. Statistically, the chance of error might be high, but as a practical matter, it's clear to me who's leading that group down the platform.

"Arden Wilson," I say. "He's the prospective match on Iona, yes?" Hearing it in my own voice increases my sadness a thousand-fold.

"Yes," Xeric says. "He's the member of the Ionian cohort who comes closest to the match parameters."

I blow out a long breath. My emotional exhaustion is almost overwhelming. After all Arden's speeches about me working with a known criminal, here he is, performing some mysterious function on Meridian Station, possibly on her behalf and on her payroll. I can think of plenty of things I'd like to say to him right now, but all of them are fairly explosive expletives.

Xeric picks up the narrative again. "You *must* remember these results could occur in comparison with another cohort, and although the percentage appears high, there is nothing definitive in this analysis," he warns. "We're bordering on speculation."

"Not if you know him," I say.

And I do, better than anyone. The pattern fits, and I'm sadly not surprised to discover him doing something shady that runs counter to everything we discussed before I left. In fact, I shock myself that I've held on so long to the hope that he would do better—be better—for me.

I stand mired in my conflicting emotions so long that I forget where I am until Xeric clears their throat discreetly.

"Shall I close out the video?"

"Yes, please." My voice shakes a little, and I hate myself for it.

Xeric waves a hand in the air and the video fades, its glow replaced by the gentle uplights against the far wall.

"Yeva's monitoring systems will notify her about our time here," he says. "Her status is set to unavailable, but is there any message you'd like to leave for her?"

"No, I'll speak to her directly. I suppose this could be part of her great plan. If she didn't want me to do this, she'd have found a way to prevent it. Just alert me when she becomes available. For now, I'm done."

Done. On so many levels. With so many things.

"Of course. Get to bed soon, though, you need to rest."

I half-laugh. The likelihood of me falling asleep right now is somewhere between no and absolutely not, but it's amusing that Xeric is still trying to take care of me since I won't take care of myself.

"All right, Mom," I say.

Xeric emits a mock-insulted huff.

"In no iteration am I old enough to be your mother."

Xeric disappears, leaving me standing in the quiet Comm Suite. I shut down the lights and wait a moment in the encompassing darkness, letting it push against my consciousness and my overactive brain.

What am I supposed to do now? The ex-lover I left on Iona is leading some kind of security force that may or may not be responding to my own departure from that world. The benefactor I'm trusting to help me preserve the independence of an entire planet has her own agenda that may not align with mine and may involve something as dramatic as murder—I'm not sure what she feels would constitute appropriate revenge. Add in the fact that the same ex-lover may or may not be on said benefactor's payroll. And then there's the sand—half of what I thought was a natural miracle isn't natural at all, and someone out there appears to have both the funding and the facilities to manufacture—and remove—literal tons of it in a matter of hours.

This mission was supposed to be about action, instead it's become an exercise in strategy. It was supposed to be about finding the truth, but I'm once again mired in secrets and lies.

I spend the next several hours pacing my quarters, besieged by questions impossible to answer. I assumed the Success Team would tap Arden to take my place after my unscheduled departure. With him leading this mysterious group on Meridian Station, who is taking care of Iona? Did he hand everything over to the Company? That wouldn't be unlikely—he's kept up the storyline from the beginning that the Company wasn't a threat. I'm haunted by what might have happened to my home and my friends. Hopefully the Company isn't frosting Ionians with Blue and stacking them up like so many prefab building blocks.

I have a sudden vision of the *Heretic*, packed with blue bodies in stasis. I sent them to Iona thinking they would be safe in their existing condition, if not fully revived and brought back to health. Someone like Cabot-Klaar would probably not think twice about destroying any "evidence" that might counter the Company's narrative, and if he's taken charge ...

I rub my arms and hug myself, fighting a wave of disgust. Yeva led me to that ship. It was my "reward" for jumping through the hoops she put before me, but it almost got me killed. If it hadn't been for Xeric and Nico, Eidor and Lipop, I wouldn't have made it.

I hesitate, frowning as suspicions bubble to the surface of my awareness. Xeric, who Yeva is able to duplicate and program to her own specifications. Nico, who is apparently on Yeva's payroll. Eidor and Lipop, who unironically refer to her as their benefactor.

Everything comes back to her. Now I'm stuck on this rock where she can track my every movement. What if she refuses to let me leave?

My pulse rate jumps as anxiety burns through me. I turn to the ViewPort, drawing back the curtains and activating it. I call up the outside security camera views. The light under the dome is shifting toward pre-dawn tones, contrasting with the dark horizon beyond its protection, but I'm not interested in what's happening under the dome. I scroll through the views but can't find the one I want.

"Xeric, assist me," I say. He appears but doesn't manage to utter a greeting before I start peppering him with questions.

"Where's the feed for the landing pad cameras?"

"They're offline. Yeva only runs them when she's expecting an arrival."

"Activate them," I say, trying to control the rising pitch of my voice.

"I'm not able to do that. Yeva determines which cameras are operating."

"Then ask her to turn them on." I clench and unclench my hands at my sides.

"Her status is set to unavailable. I'll ask her when she's available again."

"Ask her now. I know you can contact her regardless of her status. It would be dangerous if you couldn't. Go ahead."

"I'm sorry, but I'm not going to do that."

My last steely nerve gives way, and my frustration bubbles over. "Whose side are you on?" I bark.

Xeric's eyebrows draw down, head drooping. A shock of silver hair falls over one eye, and for a moment, he looks sad.

I'm not buying it.

"Stop trying to manipulate me. You're an AI; you don't feel anything," I say.

Xeric buries one hand in silver hair and sighs, like a parent about to tell a toddler for the thousandth time that the stove is hot. "Although I'm limited in my responses by my programming, I can, as you might interpret it, *feel* some things. Disappointment. Surprise. Attachment."

"And you're disappointed in me?"

"Not at all. I'm trying to explain why I can't answer your question."

"Fine. Go on." I cross my arms over my chest and give him my best belligerent stare.

Xeric's expression changes to one with slightly more gravity.

"My perceptions about right and wrong, the things that might prompt me to 'choose a side,' are based on logic, not emotion. If your definition of 'sides' is you versus Yeva, you're both working toward the same goal, and no one is doing anything I can define as wrong. You're navigating some tension and misapprehension of one another at present, but you're still, as it were, on the same side, in my evaluation."

"That's a lot of words just to tell me you're not choosing."

"Let me reframe. There's nothing to choose. Release your emotional response and look at things logically."

"You sound like my ex."

Xeric makes a dismissive huff then mutters, "I'm not him, obviously."

He sounds insulted by the comparison. I stifle a snicker.

"He doesn't feel much either and he's pro-level at telling me to stop being emotional, so you're not far off," I say.

A half-smile creeps onto Xeric's face and one perfect eyebrow arches almost to the ceiling.

"Oh please. I'd be a step up for you. I've seen his picture; he's painfully scruffy looking."

I can't keep a wan smile from creeping across my features. Despite my best (or worst?) efforts, my pulse rate has dropped closer to normal and the wave of panic that had me ready to punch a hole in the ViewPort has decreased to a manageable level. Maybe Xeric was right and I was letting my emotions get the better of me.

"He's also a liar," I say. "You *would* be a step up."

Xeric smirks in a particularly charming way.

"Now that we've made this crucial determination, let's talk about what's bothering you and how I can help. You wanted to see the landing pad for what reason?"

I'm suddenly exhausted—emotionally, mentally, and physically—and I deflate onto the bed with a low groan.

"I just wanted to see my ship," I say, feeling like a little kid asking for its security stuffie. "I just wanted to make sure she was still here."

Xeric summons a technical readout into the air in front of me and begins rattling off the stats it reports—internal and external temperature, system assessments, hardware readiness assessments—all the things that describe the *Gabriella*'s physical condition and space-worthiness. The readout is real-time—he must have accessed it while baiting me about being emotional.

"So, there's your proof that she's still here and she's perfectly fine. You can tell from the geolocation data that she's in one of our maintenance bays. Does that help?" he asks.

"A little. I did want to see her, though. I'd like to walk around in her. Could we do that?" I roll over onto my side and pull a pillow under my head. My eyes are shutting as I speak.

"We could do that. But after you rest."

"Good." I'm so near sleep I'm not sure whether I speak the word aloud or just imagine it in my head. I'm vaguely aware of the lights dialing down to their softest nightlight glow.

As I cross the boundary into slumber, Xeric whispers into my ear, "Sleep well, dear Faith. I hope you forgive me for the little spritz of sedative, but you needed calming and that was the fastest way. May you have sweet dreams of scruffy liars and beautiful spaceships under your command."

I'M AWAKENED BY THE lights in my suite powering up to full and the whir of an autobot at my bedside, presenting me with a coffee-like substance and some sort of reasonable facsimile of toast with fruit. It takes a few minutes for me to reach full awareness—I'm not hungover, but I'm not rested, either—undoubtedly the after-effects of the sedative Xeric released into my quarters last night. I'm angry about it, but there's a mix of emotions bubbling up in me, intense but fluid. I was spiraling and needed help, but for him to have the power to sedate me without my expressed request strikes me as a creepy overstep.

I take the tray and the little bot rolls away. I perch on the edge of the bed, sipping coffee and letting the memories of last night come back into focus.

The things I learned last night are overshadowed by the new questions they surface. My face crinkles into a grimace of frustration. Arden is leading some kind of security force on Meridian Station, possibly on Yeva's payroll, for some unknown purpose. In the meantime, who is standing between the Company and Iona? The sand from Bardazel was manufactured—and removed—by someone, but we have no idea who, aside from the general category of "someone very rich." Yeva's help—if I can still call it that—is motivated by a deep desire for revenge against a particular but still unknown-to-me individual who is currently on Iona.

And my ship. It's apparently fine, but the eternally vigilant cameras that should be trained on it are not online, and no one brings them online but my host.

I take a few bites of the toast—it's not terrible but it's definitely not one of Hinn's muffins—and wash it down with the last of the coffee. I can't answer all of these questions today, but I'm going to do my best to answer some of them.

I've showered and dressed and am wrangling my hair into a manageable format when Xeric appears behind me.

"You can do this now?" I ask, skipping over the formality of a greeting. "Just show up in my room uninvited?"

His left eyebrow, the most expressive one, shoots skyward.

"Good morning to you too, Faith," he says in a voice drenched in sarcasm. "No, I can't just show up in your room uninvited. But as you never dismissed me last night, I'm still considered present by request. If you prefer to dismiss me, I'm fine with that. Are we done, then?"

I let out an annoyed breath. I haven't even left my quarters yet, and I'm already in a mood.

"Let's talk about what you did last night—the aerosol sedative."

Xeric's face crinkles in what looks like chagrin, which I'm certain he can't actually feel.

"I'm not okay with you medicating me unprompted," I continue. "I get that I was upset, but you can't just spring a sedative on me because I'm emotional."

"I'm programmed to help you navigate extreme circumstances, and there are clear parameters that must be met in order to do anything not requested by you," he says in an unrepentant tone. "There's an obvious physiological difference between being emotional and spiraling out of control, just as there's a clear difference between cutting your finger and chopping off your hand. If you were merely emotional, I'd have listened and let you vent it out. You were losing yourself in an endless spiral and your core indicators suggested you were on the brink of physical and mental distress."

"So you can gas me out anytime you want to, as long as it meets certain parameters? Who set those parameters? You? Yeva?"

"You did."

I blink. "What?"

"You set the parameters. They're on file from your screening on Meridian Station. I know what's within the range of normal for you. When you reach a percentage outside that range, I'm authorized to step in. All iterations of me have this function coded in. It is, to a large extent, the entire reason I, and other artificial concierge like me, exist. Meridian Station, the Personal Evolution Annex in particular, would be a disaster without it."

I think back to the screen after screen of biometric data I was required to submit before being cleared to land at the Station, most of which was falsified. I remember the body and ocular scans to gain entrance to my Overnight, which happened live, in real time. I'd assumed Yeva had some way to alter them to fit the falsified data, and she might have, but not before she passed the real data to Xeric. This realization, something so obvious after I'd thought I'd been so exceptionally clever and careful, makes me angry and more than a little paranoid.

"How do I change that?"

"All you have to do is state that you revoke my authorization to intervene in health matters without your specific say-so, but I must caution you against it. The parameters exist for your ..."

My blood pounds in my eardrums. "If you say it's for my protection or my own good, I will find a way to deactivate you right now," I snarl. "Consider those authorizations revoked. You do not have permission to interfere with my bodily autonomy. If I want to chop off my hand, your directive from me is to let me unless I ask you to do otherwise. Got that?"

"Noted," Xeric mutters in a dead and expressionless tone.

"Fantastic."

A heavy silence creeps between us. I turn back to the mirror and resume fussing with my hair, ignoring them as much as possible. I still haven't dismissed them, so they're stuck standing behind me, shifting from foot to foot with impatience. But Xeric's chatty programming is no match for my intrinsic stubbornness, however, and after just a few minutes, he breaks the silence.

"What's your plan for today?" he asks, the recalcitrant expression dissipating. I glare at them in the mirror.

"I need to talk to Yeva. Where is she?"

Xeric's eyes close, eyelids twitching. Within seconds they open again.

"She'll meet you in the lab. She's there now."

"Let me guess—she anticipated I'd have questions."

"She did. She also says she has some news for you, so your questions may not be a priority after you speak with her."

"She needs to answer my questions before we talk about anything else," I say with more conviction than I feel. Yeva's top priority is always Yeva, and so far I haven't had much luck trying to squeeze my priorities in with hers. "Thank you, Xeric, we're done."

Xeric bows in acquiescence and disappears without another word. I leave my quarters and attempt to steel my nerves with deep breathing as I walk the short distance down the hallway to the lab.

I anticipate some kind of confrontation; I'm certain she knows about my extracurricular visit to the Comm Suite last night. She may view it as a threat to her authority or something more benign. Regardless, I need the truth from her; I won't be able to move forward otherwise. She'll probably object, given her statements yesterday about proprietary information. But I've rehearsed my rationalizations and arguments, and I'm reasonably prepared for anything.

Except, of course, for what actually happens.

In the lab, Yeva's working at one of the central stations, entirely consumed in comparing two terminal displays, recording notes to her holo, and sometimes cycling through a third display. She doesn't look at me when I come in, staying focused on the data spooling in the air before her. After a few seconds, she says, "I hear you slept well last night. Eventually."

Her voice is its normal impassive tone; her face, freckled by holographic data rotating in front of her, is calm and unbothered.

I find this irrationally irritating.

Before I can respond, she adds, "I assume you asked them not to do that again—I certainly would have. I may need to adjust Xeric's independent decision-making matrix. He's perhaps a bit too committed to that directive to manage our well-being."

"I ... ah ... yes," is all I can manage to squeeze out. I was determined to take control of this conversation, but it's already spinning away from me. "Xeric isn't the primary thing I want to discuss. After our dinner, I spent some time in ..."

"The Comm Suite. I know, of course." She's still absorbed by the data, still only barely acknowledging me. "It's fine."

"I need to understand whether ..." I start, but she cuts me off again.

"Check your holo. I've forwarded a post that should answer most of your questions."

"Just stop what you're doing and talk to me," I say, fighting down a wave of frustration.

"That's not the most efficient way to go about ..."

My reserve shatters. My raised voice echoes off the lab's smooth walls.

"Stop trying to foist me off on other sources and take two minutes to look at me and answer my questions." I'm struggling to moderate my voice, I want so badly to be heard and acknowledged. "Person-to-person. I ask and you answer. No pre-emptive comments or suggestions."

Yeva lets out a huff, her face shifting in a way that shows her own irritation. She puts down her holo, halts the data stream and steps from behind the floating displays, glaring at me. She holds up her palms in a gesture of "what now?"

"Thank you," I say, reining in my tone to something less explosive and willing myself to calm down. "I have reason to believe that the person leading the unmarked security force on Meridian Station is Arden Wilson. Is that true?"

She doesn't even blink when she says, "Yes, Commander Wilson is leading the group we saw arrive at Meridian Station."

"Is he working for you?"

Her face remains impassive. "No."

"Is he your client?"

"I believe I told you I was a one-time consultant. And a pro bono consultant at that."

My suspicions balloon, along with the number of unanswered questions popping into my head.

"What's that security force doing on Meridian Station?"

"You're making inaccurate assumptions. It's not a security force."

I grit my teeth.

"*Fine*. What is *that particular group of people* doing on Meridian Station?"

"That was not part of my work, so I'm only repeating what I've been told, but I believe they're waiting for a petition to be heard."

"What petition?"

"You can't be bothered to read your holo? You want me to narrate this for you instead?"

My eyes narrow. I can hear the blood pulsing through my head. I push down my ire and struggle to keep my voice calm and reasonable. "Yes."

She rolls her eyes. This time the annoyance clear in her voice.

"Commander Wilson, along with the group you assumed was a security force, have petitioned the Governing Council for a Conclave of Adjudication. Don't ask me to explain the details of the petition, I have no idea. My guess is that it has something to do with your planet's application for Core World status."

"Who are those people with him?"

"I don't know."

"You don't know, or you don't want to tell me?"

"I don't know. He didn't say. He didn't say much. He asked a lot of questions."

I clench and unclench my fists at my sides. She might have had a point, reading something on my holo would have been less frustrating than this.

"What can you tell me about his operation? Is there anything that's not proprietary?"

This time she laughs aloud. "I can tell you everything, which I've almost done already. There isn't much more to share."

"Then do it."

With a shrug, she launches into an impassive description of being contacted by Tommas on Arden's behalf, then live-messaged by Arden himself from Iona, all while I was enroute to Yeva's asteroid.

"His goal was to move a substantial number of people onto the Station in as clandestine a way as possible, and to keep them safe and relatively invisible for an undetermined amount of time. He asked for assistance, I connected him to the right people. He appears to have succeeded. He didn't tell me why he wanted to do this, but I think we can draw conclusions from the Meridian post I sent you. Please don't make me narrate that as well."

"Why couldn't you have told me this yesterday?"

"It was proprietary yesterday."

"And it's not today?"

"Commander Wilson and I had a real-time conversation a few hours ago. He gave permission for disclosure to you. He also asked if you were *okay*." The sarcasm drips from her voice as she adds special emphasis to the word. "I wasn't sure how to answer that."

"A few hours ago? This morning?" I've given up trying to modulate my voice; I'm nearly shouting. From an almost improbable distance away, Arden is still somehow inserting himself into every narrative I'm in. I'm furious and frustrated, and the inner voice telling me I knew it would be this way only makes it worse.

Yeva looks at me like I'm a screaming bratty child in the middle of an adult gathering.

"I suppose it was morning somewhere," she mutters. "Don't become agitated, it was scheduled before you arrived." She folds her arms across her chest, continuing to eye me, her face crinkled in disapproval. "Feel free to take some time to get into a better frame of mind. I'm happy to continue working alone until you're ready to join in."

She's right. I need a minute.

"I'm going to get some water," I say, modulating my voice to as near civil normal as I can. "I'll be back."

Yeva nods her acquiescence, already back behind the displays.

There's a hydration station built into the wall not far from the lab door. I take the cool container it dispenses and sip the contents slowly. I'm already chiding myself for overreacting, for getting emotional about being excluded from something I didn't know was happening. These feelings aren't rational. Yeva can conduct her business any way she wants, with any clients she might care to take on, regardless of whether I approve. Arden is doing whatever he's doing for reasons of his own, which he also has a right to do. I wasn't on Iona for him to tell about this mission of his—although if I had been, I suspect he'd have kept it a secret *for my own good*.

A kernel of self-loathing bursts open inside me. Why—*why*—do I still care about this? Is it an unconscious habit, like picking at a scab until it bleeds? Or am I simply committed to *any* relationship with Arden carrying a vague tone of want, a once-pleasant song played slightly out of key? How much do my own expectations contribute to how I respond to everything he does?

It's too much to unpack for now. I chug down the rest of the water, rub the still-cool container across my forehead, and breathe deeply and slowly, willing my pulse to return to normal. Eventually I'm calm enough to read whatever Yeva's forwarded to me; I at least owe her that. I pull my holo out of my pocket, find the post, and pop it into the air in front of me.

It's a statement for the public record from the Governing Council docket, describing upcoming actions. Although the language is florid and densely bureaucratic, the bottom line is that Arden Wilson and a sizable number of witnesses are granted live audience, at a date to be determined, with the Council to present evidence and testimony in support of a petition for adjudication "regarding financial motivations of Company personnel and programs foisted onto an independent planet through subterfuge and misrepresentation."

There are more than a hundred names on the "witnesses to be present" list, names I don't recognize. At last, one pops out at me: Eiken Fortin. The surname is distinctive on its own, but I've seen it before—on a pair of teenaged twins immigrating from Bardazel.

The connections line up in my brain. The *Heretic* must have arrived safely, and at least some of its passengers have been revived. These witnesses are from the Planetary Equity Alliance members dosed on Bardazel, now official residents of Iona, ballooning our population to a size that meets Core World requirements. Wenda is no doubt resubmitting Iona's application, and in the meantime, it appears Arden is doing the legwork to get the Company off Iona altogether, through Governing Council decree.

A new set of emotions begins to crowd out my frustration: a hearty dose of shame and embarrassment that I indulged my first impulse to feel excluded and wronged. That's followed by a powerful sensation of hope. Our goal for Iona could be within reach again. With Yeva's help, we may be able to find out who brought such destruction to two planets and make sure no one ever interferes with Iona again.

When I re-enter the lab, Yeva gives me a quick side glance but otherwise acts as if nothing has happened. She launches into discussing the results of the analyses that ran during our downtime.

"We have a transaction trail, but it's inconsistent," she says, gesturing toward one display. "These are the components that make up the manufactured sand. Most are also used in a variety of common applications, so searching on them is useless. The five highlighted elements are more rarely used and difficult to obtain."

I reach forward and enlarge the view, studying the readout.

"No one company has purchased all of those components," I murmur. "Dead end?"

"Maybe not." Yeva swaps one view for another, then positions two screens side by side. "If two or more companies worked together and developed a purchasing scheme to avoid leaving a clear trail, it would explain everything. That's what I'm hoping you can find today. But there's one more thing."

She expands the two views in front of us, highlighting a long column of results.

"Looking at the five rare elements, only about 200 corporate concerns purchased at least two of them in the timeframe leading up to the Company's acquisition of Bardazel. More than 10,000 have done so since the Company's purchase. In a number of cases, how these companies came up with the funding to buy these elements defies logic. It's as if they had undisclosed financial assistance."

"That sounds like an incentive program to help cover someone's tracks."

"It does. However, I'm suspicious. It seems so ... blatant."

Not long ago, I would have gone after this as the smoke revealing the incriminating fire underneath. Now, I see Yeva's point. It's too easy, too convenient. I'm more than familiar with the Company's propensity to use distractions and red herrings to draw attention away from what's really afoot.

Yeva's face contorts for a moment, and she lets out a dissatisfied sigh; this is something else we have in common.

"The Governing Council's ruling on planetary right-of-dispersal scrubbed all the individual ownership data from the records as soon as the Company purchased Bardazel, so we don't have any information on what the planet was like before the Company got their hands on it," she says, her frown deepening. "If it was primarily rocky when it was sold, that along with the uptick in rare element purchases implicates the Company in working with others to create the sand and submit a fraudulent survey ... which in my experience would not be a first for them."

"This could also be a distraction," I say, picking up Yeva's line of thought. "Bardazel could have been covered in the sand when the Company acquired it. They'd have reverse-engineered it once they discovered what it could do, just the way we're doing here."

Yeva nods, her expression still grim. "That leaves open the possibility that the original owner could also have commissioned the development of the sand. Or they gave permission to another entity to use the planet without their involvement. Or squatters could have found an uninhabited planet at the edge of the known system and started using it as a testing ground."

"Squatters who could afford to buy rare components in bulk?"

"They're out there. You'd be surprised."

"I'm sure I would. Please don't tell me. I've had my quota of surprises for the day."

A hint of amusement marks Yeva's face before she becomes serious again.

"Xeric's digging around for information about Bardazel, pre-sale. I have additional tests I want to run on the sand samples, so if you could work with this data and think of some new ways to sort it, that would be most helpful. I still think supply-chain clues are going to be our best way to figure this out. I'll be in the materials lab if you need me." With that, she departs, and I'm left to my own devices.

Data sorting is not my favorite thing, but I'm good enough at it and I feel in my bones that Yeva's right—it's the way to pin down who created this sand, and potentially who set Kerrit Arduval loose on two planets before his ex-girlfriend blew him to tiny bits through a wall. I'm still suspicious of the Company's motivations, but the connections we've found so far read more like a ham-handed effort to implicate them, left out in the open for someone to find.

I work on the data for hours, stopping only to swill coffee and down nutrition bars, but every effort ends in either a total of zero results or too many hits to be useful. Everything is starting to blur together and I'm becoming so brain-addled by numbers that at one point I pick up a lidded water flask and almost dump the whole container on myself by trying to drink out of the side opposite the flask's opening. As I'm cursing my stupidity and letting my mind drift while wiping beads of water off the quick-dry fabric of my pants, I have an idea.

The supply chain is a crucial part of determining who could have created the sand, but *the idea* for it would have to come from people—and since no *company* purchased all of the necessary ingredients to produce the sand alone, those people would need to be in some kind of collaborative relationship.

I forget about my wet pantleg and formulate a set of new queries that go beyond the supply chain and look for relationships among the leadership of the companies that have purchased the nine rare ingredients. I decide to focus on the period before Bardazel changed hands, based on a guess that interest in those elements would spike only after some kind of result had been demonstrated.

This feels like the best chance I've had to make progress all day. I can't even describe my disappointment when the terminal balks the instant I try to run it. All I get is a flashing "dataset incomplete" message and a powerfully irritating buzzing sound.

"Xeric, assist me," I say. The AI appears.

"I hope you're not going to ask me for progress on Bardazel's pre-sale records," he mutters dryly. The set of his mouth and a subtle eyeroll lets me know he hasn't been making great headway either.

"I'm not; don't worry. I'm trying to run a multi-pronged process on this dataset. You're familiar with it, yes?"

He peers over my shoulder at the floating display. "Ah yes, the supply chain data. *Dataset incomplete*. So rude. What clown programmed this thing? Oh wait, I did. Shame on me."

I smile despite myself. There are times when Xeric is the most authentic person I know, and they're not even a person.

"I want to add some new parameters, but either I don't have permission to access the full dataset or the information wasn't collected. Can you help with that?"

"Of course. Give me a second."

Xeric's eyes shift to a glassy stare, eyelids flickering briefly; after just a few seconds, they snap into focus again. "You have access to the full dataset now," he says. "Tell me what kind of parameters you're interested in, and I can tell you if they're included. If not, I'll try to get the data for you."

I rattle off my list of things that might connect one company's leadership to another, everything from outright partnerships and public affiliations to implied affiliations, brand deals, shared leadership, and simultaneous product development. I remember Arden and myself standing awkwardly in front of each other at the Success Team social hour, and a new idea sparks.

"Throw in some competitive indicators," I add. "Who do each of these brands allegedly hate among the others? Who's had the most public falling-out? Look for things that are personal, too—both connections and disconnects. Relationships, family drama, individual disconnects."

Xeric puffs out his cheeks. "We haven't collected that kind of information since it's purely subjective, but some non-scientific indicators should be available. Rival corporate entities with a bone to pick do tend to use the stream to make their cases against each other, and everybody loves high-level gossip."

"Keep looking for pre-purchase information, but make this your priority," I say. "If Yeva has any issues with it, I'm sure she'll say something."

"This won't take long, there's plenty of source material," he says, smiling broadly and rubbing his hands together in something that feels dangerously close to delight. "I'll get started right away."

"You do that. Thank you, Xeric. We're done."

Xeric disappears. The lab is quiet and chilly, the only sound my humming terminal. I stretch my shoulders and upper back, check my pantleg (it's dry), and try to get the last few drops of water from my flask (it's also dry). It's been one long series of frustrations from the instant I got up—and I still have no idea what time it's supposed to be here. I'm at a standstill until I get the information I need from Xeric, so I head for the materials lab to see if Yeva needs a hand.

The materials lab is in a different part of the underground complex, set well away from guest quarters. I decide not to trust my memory from the tour Yeva gave me on my arrival and instead opt to use the asteroid's wayfinding system to locate my host. Following its instructions, I wind my way down hallways, around curves, and through offshoot tunnels to get there.

The door is open. Yeva's in a far corner of the large, brightly lit room, bent over a plexi bin of sand. She wears protective eyewear, a respirator, and gloves.

In typical fashion, she knows I'm there before I say a word.

"Perfect timing," she says, not looking up. "Grab some gear and take a look at this."

An automated dispenser next to the door drops a pair of goggles and a particle filtering mask into my hand and I put them on. "What have you found?"

Instead of speaking, she lifts a beaker of pearly fluid from the table behind her and proceeds to trail a thin stream of it across the contents of the bin. A quantity of sand poofs into the air as the liquid carves a stark pathway through it, dissolving completely through to the bin's plexi bottom in an instant. She next sprinkles the liquid over the surface of the sand; the droplets seem to come to life, seeking each other out and forming a larger pool together, throwing more sand up into the air. Within a few seconds, the bin is empty, the fluid is gone, and all that remains is the particulate matter drifting toward the air purification system intake over our heads.

"That must be what happened on Bardazel!" I gasp. "Even the residual floating in the atmosphere ... it all fits!"

"My thought as well," Yeva says, a satisfied expression crossing her face. "As you can see, it doesn't take much. It would be a simple process to deliver this via automated drone across a widespread area."

"Does it dissolve more than sand?"

"I don't think I'd want to be standing under a full shower unprotected, but it hasn't been a challenge for the plexi or my gloves. We don't know for a fact that this is the exact formula used on Bardazel, of course; I reverse-engineered it based on your description of the scene, my own experience in planetary reclamation, and what chemistry could have this impact on the manufactured sand. That base formula could easily be augmented to be more ... problematic."

I grimace, my anxiety percolating. "How would that not be classified as an offensive weapon by the Governing Council?"

Yeva shrugs. "It's a clean-up tool. As I said, I've used something similar. It's only a weapon if it's deployed against an unwilling population."

"Like Blue."

"Anything can be an offensive weapon in the wrong hands. The Council's ban on offensive weaponry has always been more show than substance. At any rate, I've already added these chemical components to the database for our comparative analysis."

Yeva turns to the table again, and pulls out a different, smaller container of sand. This time, when she distributes the solution, it makes a wet spot before dissipating, leaving the sand unmarred.

"This is the natural sand from Iona," she explains. "It's much more resistant to the chemical cocktail used to dissolve the artificial sand. In order to duplicate the effect seen on the manufactured sand, the formula would need to be much more corrosive. It might be worth looking into, but I don't think we have to worry about the same thing happening there."

"Good to know," I say, but as the words leave my mouth, I see in my mind three small nondescript beige buildings, with no set purpose despite their specialized materials, rising from Iona's sands.

21

"I HAVE A REPORT."

Xeric's voice pierces the quiet of the lab. Yeva and I both startle. It's been a tough day for us: we've been trying to find something that will dissolve Iona's natural sand for hours now and have gotten nowhere. Although Yeva's frustrated, I'm somewhat relieved by our lack of progress; whatever Xeric has uncovered will be a welcome distraction. I hope it's good news.

"Go ahead," Yeva says.

"Comm Suite for visuals, please. There are lots of moving parts," Xeric says breathlessly. "I'll meet you there."

"Xeric's a touch too excited for this to be about property records," Yeva says as we close up the lab and head toward the Comm Suite. "Did you assign a more interesting task?"

"I had a hunch. Maybe it's paid off."

We reach the Comm Suite and I brace myself for the bone-shaking body scan it dispenses at the door. By the time we enter, he's already pacing in front of a hovering display.

"Faith posed an excellent question," he says, turning to face me, "about the relationships among the prospective players, in particular less-than-harmonious ones and any public feuds."

Yeva raises an eyebrow at me. I lift a shoulder and double down on my focus on Xeric.

"As I was collecting this data, some names became apparent thanks to frequent repetition." Xeric gestures toward the screen on the left. It resolves to ten logos, along with the larger, more prominent logo of the Company and the insignia of the Governing Council.

"These entities stand out for ongoing and public battles with the Governing Council, the Company, or each other."

Yeva squints at the information floating in front of us. "I've never heard of most of these companies," she says. "Are they all incorporated? We're sure they were in the original list of element purchasers?"

"They're small and specialized, with a low profile overall. It's not surprising you aren't familiar with them," Xeric confirms. "But here's where it gets interesting."

The on-screen data evolves. Red lines drag across it, connecting companies to one another, some to the Governing Council logo, and others to the Company logo. One entity has far more than its share of red lines, however, and appears to be linked to everyone.

"What's going on with that one? KaheleTech?" I ask.

"KaheleTech has lodged the most formal complaints of any of these. It's leveled all kinds of allegations against every other company on the list, as well as against the Company and the Governing Council. And this is over the last ten years."

I'm a little deflated—one company with an overzealous legal department isn't the incriminating evidence I'd hoped for. But Xeric isn't done. An extensive graph of KaheleTech's litigious history appears. It's beyond overzealous. Hundreds of complaints have been filed against hundreds of companies.

"By itself, not damning," Xeric says, reading my mind. "However, these complaints create a particular pattern."

With another wave, the display changes to show the companies from the first display, and the number of times each has been in some kind of legal tussle with KaheleTech.

"They've interacted with everyone on the list, but they have the most issue with these." Xeric narrates as the names highlight in red. "Multiple complaints, multiple times, against Verity Chemistry, Rosales Group, and Zhemat Solutions. These disputes were the most public, and they were *made* public by KaheleTech, with multiple official statements and announcements about alleged unfair business practices by these companies. But no responses to the complaints were filed, and none have any kind of presence on the stream. Interestingly enough, after an intense publicity blitz about the filings by KaheleTech, all of the complaints were dropped. Nothing ever happened with them."

"Nuisance filings, then?" I muse. "Or they could have been settled privately."

"It's stranger than that," Xeric says. "In every case, there was no response to the complaints *at all*. And after the initial round of vitriolic public statements and postings on various stream outlets, KaheleTech itself never mentioned the complaints again. *In every case*."

Xeric hits the final phrase hard and it dawns on me what he's lining up for us.

"It was theater," I say under my breath. "Everything for show. They wanted the publicity around the dispute but nothing else."

"But why would any corporate entity want that?" Yeva asks, her eyebrows drawn in skepticism. "What would the benefit be?"

Xeric beams.

"I believe I have an answer."

They change the display again, and a list of the integral sand components appears. "Seven years ago, spread out over the course of an entire year, each of these companies made a bulk purchase of one or more of the core elements of our manufactured sand. Some purchased more than one—the ones most harped on by KaheleTech. Add those companies to KaheleTech's own purchasing patterns, and we have a group buy of all the unique elements of the sand. And it's in the correct estimated quantities, on a workable timeline, to manufacture the sand found on Bardazel."

"Any evidence they worked together?" I ask. I'm almost holding my breath at this point.

Grinning like a kid unwrapping a present, Xeric shifts the display again.

"I've found some specific connections between them," he says. "This depicts the governing boards of the companies, over the full history of their existence."

The display shifts one last time and I gasp. One name appears in each company's past or present governance structure: Benta Sarsen.

My insides quake as I remember myself back in the dim quiet hallway of Meridian Station's Long Flight Bay, shipment details flickering outside the hatch of a ship full of still blue bodies: *Project Director Benta Sarsen*. I turn to Xeric; his eyes reflect understanding of my shock. He was with me then—at least a version of him was.

"The tactic of public disputes continues to the present day," Xeric adds. "KaheleTech recently filed a complaint against the Governing Council for interference."

"So Benta Sarsen filed a complaint against herself," I mutter. "She's working hard to keep up the façade. Any connection between Sarsen and Kerrit Arduval?"

"None that I found," says Xeric. "That piece is still missing."

My excitement deflates a bit.

"What about to the Company?" I ask.

"As it turns out, yes." He slips into a more serious tone. "Yeva, this will be of particular interest to you."

"Delightful," she mutters.

"Let's talk about Cadence Technologies." Xeric gestures toward the display, and the company name expands and highlights. "They've had a couple of complaints filed against them, but for the most part they're the closest to having a friendly relationship with KaheleTech."

"But they haven't bought many of the elements we're tracking," Yeva observes, "and their governing board is one of the few that doesn't include Sarsen. What's the point?"

"They underwent an unpublicized name and leadership change at the time of the element buy, approved in a rare closed private session by the Governing Council," Xeric says. "A great deal was done to position this as an entirely new company, with no relationship to the old. That's not uncommon, by itself. And while they have little to do publicly with the materials we've focused on, that's probably a smokescreen rather than the truth. Originally, they were known as CKS Incorporated. Sarsen was a full partner in that venture, along with the group's founder."

The displayed Cadence logo shifts into the interlocking diamonds of the CKS logo, and the current innocuous leadership group is replaced by two headshots, one of which is Sarsen. As the second image resolves, I clench my fists. Yeva hisses through her teeth, making it clear who she's tracking on Iona.

I take a single step toward the display and my anger swells as I look into the cold eyes of Breton Cabott-Klaar.

"You don't have to worry about me derailing your revenge strategy, Yeva," I say. I can hear the steel in my own voice. "I'm happy to participate in anything that takes him down."

Xeric's new information leaves us in a mood. We depart the Comm Suite. Yeva heads for a meditation session and a long rest period. She doesn't mention dinner or any kind of interaction afterward, so I take this as my cue to entertain myself until we resume work tomorrow—or whatever time it is here. Back in my quarters, I snarf down a nutrition bar and drink some water, then follow that up with some high-quality angsty pacing.

To be honest, I'm not sorry to be on my own. I thought my stay on this asteroid would be something of a respite, a chance to be buried in research and the predictable laws of physics and chemistry. And while that's been part of my experience here, it's also been a trip down multiple strange connectors, through politics and money and evil deeds done by self-important people. And it's included daily—sometimes hourly—assaults on my emotions. I'm worn down, I'm tired, and I need a distraction.

I think back to last night, before Xeric spritzed unauthorized sleepytime perfume in my quarters. I wanted to see my ship. I still want to see her, or at least find out what's happened to her.

"Xeric, assist me," I say. He appears next to me, shaking silvery hair out of their eyes.

"Before you say anything, I want to apologize for last night," he says. "I won't do that again."

He looks truly chagrined, eyes downcast and expression somber. My first impulse is to comfort him, or say it's not his fault, but I shake off that old programming and instead say, "Good."

The rakish grin returns. "How can I assist you?"

"Not to bring up unpleasant memories, but ... my ship."

"Ah, yes. Your ship. It's not in the docking bay, so I can't give you a camera view of it, but I can take you to her, if you'd like. Yeva-approved."

My mood brightens. "Yes, please. Let me grab the portable steamer."

"We don't need it," Xeric says, walking through my quarters to the door. "Come with me."

I hurry to keep up, not sure I heard correctly.

"You can go outside without a streamer?"

"No, I'm limited to the asteroid's interior spaces. Your ship is inside, in one of our maintenance vaults."

Without looking back, Xeric proceeds through the door and toward the lower floor's main entry point. I hurry after him.

We reach the open lobby. The massive blast door across from the elevator is standing open. The passageway beyond is wide and tall enough to accommodate multiple autoflats, scores of people, or almost anything anyone might want to send down it. It's so long that the end isn't visible from where I stand. And it's dark except for a small string of low-powered lights overhead. Xeric gestures for me to step through the door then guides me a short distance inside. Some kind of pod transportation system runs along the wall, sitting atop a magnetic track.

"Use this," he says. "It's already programmed to take you where we're going. Get in, put on the harness, and say 'ready' when it asks. I'll meet you there."

Xeric dissolves. I study the pod skeptically. It's slightly wider than a human, although the height would accommodate someone much taller than me. The front is made from a clear plexi; the other side is lined with some kind of dense black foam. When I step in, an automated voice tells me to face forward and press my back against the foam. It responds to the pressure and flows around my body to create a me-shaped cavity that cradles me securely. It then extrudes a set of padded straps over my shoulders and across my upper chest. Another set appears across my waist and hips. The pod asks my permission to secure the straps, and when I give it, they all tighten until I'm comfortably but firmly held in place.

It asks if I'm ready for departure.

I'm not sure. After all, I'm locked into a plexi personpod on a magnetic track in a vast dark tunnel through the middle of an asteroid owned by someone I'm not certain I can trust.

But my ship. I want to know that she's here and space-worthy, and that I can maybe get the hell out of here if I decide I need to go.

"Ready," I say.

In an instant, the compartment seals itself. The straps around my torso tighten further, and the pod explodes down the track so fast I only perceive the blurring of light and shadows through the clear plexi front. I have a moment of panic as the gravitational force presses me hard against the foam backing; instead of flexing, it's become resistant and firm, supporting my body as I'm hurled through the tunnel.

In a few minutes, it slows to a speed that's compatible with stopping in a way that won't jerk my guts out, but I'm still disoriented and have no idea how far it's traveled. As the g-force recedes, I can see more of the space I'm moving through. The lighting is dim, broken occasionally by the sparks of bots welding, forming, and building things I can't quite identify. In contrast to the asteroid's living quarters, the walls here are pitted natural rock. It smells like seared plexi and adhesive and metal and stone and has a high-tech dungeon vibe—an idea that unnerves me almost as much as the first few minutes of the ride did.

The personpod finally slows to a speed not much faster than an average human jog, and the straps around my body loosen in response. It rounds a curve and continues on for another handful of minutes before it at last comes to a complete stop. The straps release and suck back into the foam, which begins to return to its native flat state, gently pushing me out of my cocoon. The seal on the door disengages and it slides open. I let out a long, relieved breath. Xeric is waiting for me, and in the center of an almost impossibly large cavern is the *Gabriella*.

Only it's not the *Gabriella* as I left her; something's different about her. Her hull fluctuates and ripples as though she's not in solid form. I see her, yet I'm not quite seeing her, like a set of stars in peripheral vision that somehow vanish when you try to look directly at them. She looks almost holographic, only the way the light and shadows around her react, I can tell she's not—she's physically there.

"Take a moment, steady yourself," Xeric warns, as I step out of the pod's foam hug onto my somewhat shaky legs. But I can't take my eyes off the mesmerizing display of my ship. Then logic takes over, and the dots connect in my mind.

"Is that an optical cloaking device?" I ask.

Xeric offers up a small smile and gestures for me to walk ahead.

"Not exactly," he says. "Come."

As we approach the ship, what I can only describe as holographic tentacles of energy stretch from the field around her and make their way to me, flooding over and through me. My hands and arms glow and sparkle, the same way her hull does; when I turn to Xeric, it's as though I'm looking through a veil of rippling translucent color.

Everything suddenly becomes very bright. I screw my eyes shut tight and cover them with my hand. For an instant it's as though my eyelids don't exist. Despite my efforts, I see the light, the ship, even the bones in the hand I've thrown protectively in front of my face.

And then it's over. The holographs, the colors, the light all recede, and we're standing in the cavern, the *Gabriella* sitting in the center of a ring of ordinary practical work lights. A collection of bots, heftier than the household ones and made of some kind of dense matte black material, circulate around the ship. As far as I can tell, they're doing space-readiness prep—running tests, checking power levels, verifying data.

"What was that?" I ask Xeric. "Did you see it too?"

"That was the biometric recognition system verifying you match the profile markers in its core database. I didn't experience it the same way you did, but I was aware of the increased activity through my monitoring systems."

I blink. "What are you talking about? I don't have that on my ship."

"You do now. Yeva made a few upgrades for you. Care to explore?"

For an instant, I'm annoyed she laid hands on my ship without telling me. But numerous upgrades were made to her at Yeva's instruction while I was on Meridian Station, so I swallow my knee-jerk first reaction. "Yes," I say. "Show me everything."

"Let's start with the biggest enhancement. That flash you experienced was your ship recognizing you," Xeric explains as we walk toward the *Gabriella*'s entry ramp. "Your biometric markers were already part of the ship's database, which is why you were able to see anything at all. Once you were within range, it triggered a full body survey. The files were then matched, verifying you are in fact you, and activating your biometric profile in the ship's records."

A prickle of worry creeps up the back of my neck.

"Go back a few steps. What does the biometric recognition system do?"

"To put it in the simplest terms, it allows you to determine who can interact with the ship and how."

"*Gabriella* recognized me as I approached, and that meant I could see her? Is she invisible to people she doesn't recognize?" I follow Xeric up into the cool darkness of her interior.

"Yes, and it's not either/or," he explains. "You can choose to activate biometric cloaking, which will make the ship visible only to the people whose markers are contained in its database. You can embed different criteria, so only people who meet your chosen parameters can interact with her. That's entirely up to you—you can add anything as a criteria for anyone or everyone, and there are no limitations. For example, if you want *Gabriella* to be visible only to people in the database with names starting with A, that's an option. If biometric cloaking is turned off, everything goes back to normal."

"What if I need to remove someone after they've been recognized?"

"You can delete that biometric profile, or if you don't want to go that far, you can customize the permissions that profile has. Nearly every facet of your ship's operation can be segmented and customized in any way you wish."

I'll be looking over this programming myself later to make sure I'm not being fed a line of trash, but I'll leave it alone for now.

Other alterations to the *Gabriella* are in progress, less dramatic than the biometric system but still exceptionally helpful. The communications array is getting an even more powerful upgrade, as is the propulsion system. Bots are busy installing improved ergonomic seating and controls, and the formerly shelf-like bunk area has been expanded and improved to make long space flight more comfortable. I stifle a laugh when I pull back the privacy panel that now separates the bunk from the rest of the ship. Along with a new, larger sleeping surface is a miniature ViewPort by MassAppeal Inc. built into the wall at one end.

"It's not just for entertainment," Xeric explains in response to my eyeroll. "This works for both visual communication and surveillance." A wave of his hand over the control panel at the bunk's head activates the ViewPort, showing us ourselves from the front. Another wave and the view shifts, now showing us from above. A third specific hand gesture brings up a selection of views outside the ship from cameras mounted on the hull. "These views are also available on your control deck, but it's helpful to have them available when you're not at the controls. As Yeva says, one cannot be too careful, even among friends and loved ones."

"This is impressive, but are these enhancements going to take long to finalize? When will she be space-ready?" I ask, trying to keep the stress out of my voice. I appreciate the upgrades, but given the choice between expediency and upgrades, I'm all for expediency.

"You could take her into space as she is and everything crucial would work," Xeric confirms. "The good thing about a bot crew is they don't get tired, so they keep working until the job is done. She'll be complete by the time you resume work tomorrow."

My shoulders slump in relief and my throat lets go of a giant lump it's been holding on to since I got out of the drop tube days ago. All I can squeeze out is, "Good. That's good."

Xeric's expression is sympathetic. "Might you be able to rest now? Without any interference from me, this time?"

I let out a weary breath. "Possibly. I'll try."

I'm calmer as I walk back to the personpod and strap in, but my brain won't stop turning over what I've learned today, which doesn't bode well for any potential rest.

We still don't have a connection to Kerrit Arduval, and Sarsen and Cabott-Klaar's motivations are unclear. In my gut, I know these two are somehow responsible for everything that happened on Bardazel, and by extension, on Iona. But why? And what do they have planned next?

"YOU'RE NOT SLEEPING."

Yeva invited me to join her for breakfast upstairs and hits me with this before I can take the first bite of my omelet. It's been ten days since we learned of the connections between the manufactured sand, Benta Sarsen, Breton Cabot-Klaar, and the shady little company KaheleTech. Although we've investigated every angle imaginable, we haven't found anything connecting them to Kerrit Arduval, a rationale for producing the sand, or any hint of what they might be planning.

"I'm sleeping plenty," I say, jamming my fork into my mouth. The omelet is particularly delicious, and I shove in another bite almost immediately. "This is amazing. Where did you get eggs?"

Yeva stares at me like I've grown an extra head. "From my chickens," she says levelly. "Stop changing the subject. You're not sleeping. I can see your biometric readouts in the house feed, and not only are you not sleeping, you also spend most of every night in the lab or the research suite. You've loaded Xeric up with so many cross-parameters he has no time to do anything else. And you're staying alive on meal bars, nutritabs and coffee."

"I'm getting enough, I'm fine," I say, suddenly conscious of the fact that I've consumed my entire omelet in the time it's taken Yeva to have three bites. This isn't lost on her, either. She stares pointedly at my plate, then with a smug expression waves over a kitchen bot with a second omelet for me.

"Let me say this simply. You're not at your best this way," she says. "I understand the impulse to find out as much as possible, as quickly as possible, but this behavior gets in the way of our eventual success. You might be putting in more time at the screens, but I can guarantee it's not quality time. You'll miss connections, you'll make mistakes. And that could destroy everything you've been working for."

She's right, of course. I had the same thought last night around my sixth hour of parsing through supply chain data, when I realized I'd reviewed the same screen at least three times. But that only inspired me to drink more coffee and wish I had some of those low-anx stimulants from Meridian Station.

And it rankles me to have someone monitoring my sleeping and eating patterns, like I'm an infant.

"I'm fine," I say again, this time making it a point to chew my bite of omelet slowly. "I'm still adjusting to the time rhythms here. I'm sure everything will normalize to your satisfaction soon."

"It doesn't take this long to adjust to something I tailored to be similar to cycles you were already used to," Yeva says. Her tone makes it clear she's had enough of my excuses. "We're partners in this endeavor. I must have you at the peak of your abilities. Starting now, there are limits on your use of the lab and the research suite. They'll become inaccessible to you daily at hour twenty. Xeric will monitor the alerts we've set up overnight, and run any processes you've requested, but won't send results to you until hour seven the following day. If you don't start going to bed and sleeping regularly, I'll consider authorizing Xeric to sedate you. You'll also be required to consume at least one full meal per day, either printed or prepared by the bots, to augment your current exciting diet of tabs and bars. And we're going to meet for breakfast every day."

"I don't think that's necessary, I'm capable of monitoring my own behavior," I begin.

Yeva's eyebrows arch up as she side-eyes my plate. It's empty again.

She stares at me until I let out a sigh, part frustration, part exhaustion.

"Fine," I say. "Sleep. Food. Got it."

"Lovely," she responds with a blisteringly artificial smile and waves over a kitchen bot carrying a large bowl of colorful fresh-diced things. "Here. Have some fruit."

In my anxious state, breakfast goes on forever—in fact it likely spans less than an hour. I don't know how I'm going to sit through this every day. Small talk with Yeva is anything but relaxing; it's more like being subjected to a pop quiz on something you've never studied. Maybe it's pathetic, but I'm more comfortable with Xeric. A not-quite-real person whom I can summarily dismiss at any time is more my speed these days.

At last, in the research suite away from my host's questions and demands, I pull up the latest information on our target companies. It's been consistent for months, now—small buys, ordinary materials, modest sales. I almost flip past the daily reports screen, expecting it to be more of the same.

But it's not. There's been movement—a lot of movement.

Four of the five target companies have placed orders for thirty highly specialized drones. These aren't ordinary delivery or service drones, but instead the kind typically used on Home World to fight wildfires. They're essentially enormous flying heat-resistant double tanks. And each order includes an unusual upgrade; the tanks are coated with a synthetic fluoropolymer I've never heard of.

"Xeric, assist me," I say, and he flutters into view. I point at the line item on the display hovering in front of me.

"Wow," he mutters. "Weird. What could they need 120 drones for?"

"I know, but ... what's this coating they've requested? What does it do?"

Xeric's eyelids flutter as he burns through the database. "Oh," they say at last, sounding worried. "That's ... interesting."

"What is it?"

"It's an anticorrosive coating used primarily in chemical applications—it can withstand almost anything. It's marketed under a few different brand names: Supraseal, Corroblok, Perfetto. It's not often found in general use; it's more of a chemical industry standard. I'd have expected the interior tanks to be coated with another anticorrosive you're probably familiar with, Durawash. They're made by the same company, and it's much more common."

"Oh, yes. Most everything on Iona is coated with Durawash, even our clothing. The sand would destroy it in record time otherwise. Are you saying this other stuff is actually dangerous?"

"No, not at all. But we need to think about its use case. It's able to withstand almost any corrosive agent, and requesting it as a coating suggests those tanks aren't going to be carrying water or brew. Durawash can stand up to your sand, but Perfetto will resist significantly more harsh industrial acids."

"So, these drones could be preparing to carry and dispense something like a super-acid." My heart rate tics up.

"With this coating, they could."

"Do we have anything coated with this stuff here?"

"It's possible. I'll check our inventory."

"All right, let's gather up some samples of whatever we have, and move them to the materials lab."

Another substantial purchase by Cabot-Klaar's company Cadence stands out also. It's a common solvent marketed under the name Trichlor, but they've ordered a massive quantity of it. If it were any other company, it might not stir my interest, but now ...

"This as well," I say, pointing to the line item.

"We definitely have that," Xeric says. "There's a bottle on Yeva's lab bench right now."

"Great. Pass these results to Yeva and let her know I'll be in the materials lab. Thank you, I'm done."

Xeric disappears, and I stand up, stretching my back and raising my arms over my head. Maybe it's the fact that I ate a full breakfast this morning (and then some), but a rush of energy pulses through me. I'm certain these new buys mean something. We just have to figure out *what*.

By the time Yeva joins me in the lab, I've been screwing around with Trichlor for hours. I haven't managed to make it do anything to either the artificial or the natural sand aside from leaving an oily wet spot.

"This has to be important, they wouldn't have purchased it this way if it wasn't," I say, scowling at my results. I've cross-referenced it against every element of the formula individually and all of them together in every combination imaginable. It's all led nowhere.

Yeva takes a long look at the data display, her index finger tracing my test reports. "We aren't sure what it's supposed to do, or if it's related at all. What's your hunch?"

"That they're going to try to dissolve the natural sand on Iona. But there's nothing in this new buy that has any impact on it at all."

Yeva raises her eyebrows, her lips forming a thin line.

"Why would they dissolve it? How does that make sense? It's valuable, and if this group is what we think it is, they put in a lot of time and effort into create artificial sand that does the same thing."

I nod. I've thought of this line of questioning too.

"Ultimately, it makes sense from a cash standpoint. KaheleTech and their consortium made the artificial sand a number of years ago. Perhaps they knew about natural sand that could counter Blue and it inspired them to mimic it; maybe they had no idea something similar existed. But either way, they hold the artificial sand formula. It would make sense for them to protect their prospective market. If the Company is still serious about developing new ways to use Blue as a weapon, they would be KaheleTech's primary customer. Company control of Iona's sand would cancel that out completely."

"Why would they go to all this trouble and expense to destroy the sand? Wouldn't it be simpler for Cabot-Klaar to make sure the Company *doesn't* hold on to Iona?"

Yeva's question startles me. She's right. The arrival of *he Heretic* on Iona, with its complement of new residents and willing witnesses, has already set the challenge to Company oversight in motion.

Or it might be only the first stage of Cabot-Klaar's plan. I can't shake the feeling that there's more at stake. Perhaps they want Iona without the Company's protection, to make it easier for KaheleTech to eliminate the planet's sand—and its inhabitants—at their leisure.

Who controls Iona will be determined by the chair of the Governing Council, Cabot-Klaar's long-time business partner, in the very near future.

"We have to make these connections public," I say. "I can't risk Benta Sarsen handing control of Iona over to KaheleTech, or something worse."

"What do you intend to do?"

"I think my only option is to confront Sarsen during the hearing on Iona's petition. I need to get back to Meridian Station before it gets added to the schedule."

"We'll arrive in plenty of time with your ship's new upgraded core drive."

"*We*?"

Yeva's lips quirk up in a sly smile. "Absolutely, *we*. I'm going with you."

I'M SO STARTLED MY mouth falls open.

"You'd leave Dar Shal'O?"

"Of course. Well, temporarily. I'll return once we achieve our goal."

"*Our* goal? Meaning what, exactly?"

"After you confront Sarsen, she'll have no choice but to implicate Cabot-Klaar. I'd like to be present for that; perhaps also to see them both hauled away in cuffs."

She's faintly approving as she says it, like she's describing something tasty the kitchen bots made; she's even smiling a little. But her eyes glitter with an intensity that makes me squirm in my chair.

At least she thinks of us as working toward a common goal, though my objective is the full liberation of Iona—Sarsen and Cabot-Klaar are only pieces in that puzzle. While I want both to face consequences for any part they've played, seeing them in cuffs is not at the top of my list. In fact, never seeing them again would be my preferred outcome, particularly when it comes to Cabot-Klaar. Unfortunately, that's an option I don't have. Yet.

There's no flurry of human activity as we prepare to leave, which I'm heartily sorry about, given the amount of pure nervous energy I have. Although it makes sense, the bots are far more efficient at loading and prepping *Gabriella* than one angsty human would be. So I pace in my quarters and watch on my ViewPort as they work. When they move *Gabriella* into position in the launch zone, located on the opposite side of the asteroid from the landing platform and its terrifying arsenal, I find Yeva. She's tinkering with some of the programming that will keep everything humming in her absence.

The display floating in front of her shows an impressive array of customizable automated systems—a bit strange for someone who almost never leaves. A virtual version of her, equipped with an organic lifesign signature, floats from room to room, to fool the most sophisticated spies into thinking she's still here.

I try to sit quietly, but my restless hands give me away.

"Are you always this anxious?" Yeva asks, not looking away from her tasks.

"Not at all," I say, crossing my arms over my chest and putting on my best *not-anxious* face. "Just hoping to contribute."

"You're contributing to my stress level, if that counts," she murmurs, her eyes still on the display floating in front of her. I shut up and try to content myself with watching her fingers fly over the controls as she alters parameters and creates new routines for her digital self. My attention wanders as I start thinking about the daunting effort that lies ahead. I become so enmeshed in playing out possibilities in my imagination that I startle when Xeric's voice floats out of the comm system.

"I have an update on the Iona petition," he says.

"Go ahead," Yeva and I say in unison. The way she looks at me makes me think she's wondering if coming along was such a good idea after all.

"A new name has been added to the witness list: Graham Thorn of Thorn Industries," Xeric reports.

"Graham!" I squeak. "What's he going to say?"

"Unknown," Xeric replies. "No specifics have been made public. But it appears he intends to speak in support of Iona's petition."

I'm a mix of exhilarated and alarmed. Graham knows so much about the Company's machinations on Bardazel and Iona, I have no doubt that the Governing Council will consider him a credible source. His testimony on top of the others almost guarantees the Council will release Iona from Company control. If I'm right about the end game, that could put KaheleTech and Breton Cabot-Klaar one step closer to their goal and Iona in tremendous peril.

My palms start to sweat.

"When can we leave?" I ask Yeva.

"Now is as good a time as any," she says, shutting down the display with a wave of her hand. This is so unexpected that my breath catches in my chest for an instant.

"Our cargo's loaded, and the *Gabriella* is set; the launch zone is fully pressurized," she continues, shutting down the displays. She either doesn't notice or chooses not to acknowledge my surprise. "We'll take the personpods through the maintenance vault to get there. Xeric's already installed on board."

I follow Yeva through the maze of hallways until we reach the reinforced central core doors and the massive tunnel beyond them. Two pre-programmed personpods await us. We blast through the asteroid so quickly I only have time to process the g-force against me and the occasional smell of cold rock and metal. When the pod slows, the *Gabriella* comes into view. A clear plexi airlock stands between us and where she sits, in an alcove not too different from the one I keep her in back on Iona. Instead of looking out over Iona's western hills, she perches at the edge of an infinite blackness, disrupted only by the faint ripple of a force field and the scattered twinkle of distant stars.

Yeva verifies a few settings, then leads the way into the airlock. The panel closes behind us with a soft whoosh. When the second door opens, the air smells fresh and clean. I walk up *Gabriella's* boarding ramp with a sense of hope and more than a little relief. I take the pilot's chair, Yeva straps in at copilot. Once called in, Xeric settles in at the communication console. I'm grateful, to be honest—with so many new functions attached to it, I'm not sure I'd know how to work them without a manual.

We seal the hatch and begin the launch procedure; there's a whisper outside as the pressure in the bay is gradually released and my body becomes a fraction lighter. When the force field finally falls away and I release the magnetic foot that's held her steady in zero gravity, the *Gabriella* floats up smoothly. As I try to guide her out of the alcove, however, she shoots forward so fast I almost lose control.

Yeva's face is impassive, but her voice belies her amusement. "New acceleration drive. Might take a minute to get used to it."

Yeah. It might.

I input our flight path to Meridian and carefully edge *Gabriella* onto the first part of our journey. Soon after, the autoflight system takes over and I no longer have to wrestle with manual acceleration. Yeva tosses a display up into the air and starts skimming the stream. Xeric's eyes are closed and their eyelids fluttering, which means data processing is underway. I occupy myself with the flight checklist. When a "time to destination" estimate pops up on the ship's console, I have to look at it twice to make sure I'm not imagining it.

"Is this right?" I ask incredulously, pointing at the readout. "How is it possible that this trip takes less than a quarter of the time it took to arrive? I know you upgraded her drive, but I didn't realize a skiff this size could fly that fast."

"Most can't," Yeva says, not even looking at me. "It's not only the drive, you understand. The upgraded sensors enable you to travel faster in all regions of space including debris fields and heavy-traffic areas. If hazards are detected, the sensors cue the ship well in advance to take evasive action that doesn't require slowing down, the way one must when executing the clumsy maneuvers of manual flight."

"Oh, *of course*," I say, bordering on sarcasm. I've never even heard of sensors this refined, much less flown a ship directed by them, but here we are.

I'm pleased that our trip to Meridian Station will be so speedy that we can forgo the use of pharmaceutical sleepers. Sadly, my core strategy for dealing with Yeva in such close quarters was straight-up being unconscious for much of the trip. My secondary strategy was staying focused on managing and piloting *Gabriella*, but with the ship now so automated, I have little to do until the end of the trip. I find myself once again with nothing to distract me from the anxiety roiling my insides, and no way to expend the nervous energy that's threatening to overtake me. My tendency to play out in my head every catastrophic outcome hovers at the edge of my consciousness. The battle for my inner focus is dire.

"If you don't stop kicking your foot against the console like that, I'm going to break it, and I don't mean the console," Yeva mutters. She's still scrolling the stream, but her voice has taken on a sharp quality that underscores how annoyed she is.

I look down at the offending limb. "Sorry. I need something to keep my mind focused."

"What did you do on the way to Dar Shal'O? I'm sure you didn't spend the entire trip kicking your spacecraft; it would have been in shambles by the time you arrived."

"I slept. Before that, I read."

"Read, then."

I remember the copy of *Confessions of a Moral Skeptic* lying in a drawer in my quarters on the asteroid. Ugh.

"I don't have a book," I say, trying to keep the annoyance out of my voice.

"Yes you do. The bots loaded everything from your quarters. Your book is below the bunk with your other personal items. I know, because they didn't recognize it and asked my approval before bringing it aboard."

"Your bots didn't recognize a *book*?" I'm already up, digging through the things stored under the bunk. I find it easily, relishing its rough cover beneath my hand.

Yeva's expression has become more exasperated.

"Of course, they recognized it was a book. But it has the library's dynamic signature built into it, and they weren't sure whether it was contraband, or a stolen item, or what. They knew it wasn't yours, despite being in your possession."

I squint at Yeva suspiciously, clutching the book against me.

"I didn't steal it, if that's what you're thinking."

"I'm aware. I read the inscription."

"I didn't ask him to give it to me," I say, as though that somehow makes it better.

"I'm sure. He cost the Annex a fair bit of money giving it to you," Yeva says, turning her attention back to the stream. "Fortunately for him, he's in a position where he can do whatever he wants. Most of us can't."

I'm prepared for this to be the end of the conversation, but Yeva adds, "He obviously likes you. That's important and potentially very beneficial."

"He said the same thing about you."

A small smile creeps across Yeva's face; she's not giving anything away. "Did he, now?"

"He said you didn't go out of your way for just anyone."

"Well, he's right about *that*, at least."

The comment barely gets a moment to irritate me before my curiosity takes over.

"Why is it important that Nico like me? What could be so beneficial about the approval of a sex worker in the Personal Evolution Annex? I mean, I know he's been on the Station a long time and has that special fancy apartment and somehow is involved in everything, but ..."

Yeva cackles so loudly that even Xeric's eyes pop open. And she keeps on cackling, laughing at what I can only assume is at my expense. I drop into my seat with the book on my lap, attempting to curb my fury into something—anything—less incendiary.

After several minutes of belly-laughing, Yeva wipes the tears from her face and starts to catch her breath. "Dear me, that was unexpected."

"I assume you're going to explain yourself." I'm gritting my teeth so hard, it's an effort to speak.

"I don't know how close you got to Nico during your time on the Station, but apparently it wasn't close enough to ask his last name."

She's right. I have no idea what Nico's surname might be. Eidor and Lipop's names I know, but not Nico's.

"We weren't terribly close; as you know, I was traveling under an alias. He was very helpful, though." *He rescued me after I got the crap beat out of me, and helped me sneak past security and some killer robots, and gave me an excellent backrub, and served me some really good booze I can still taste, and promised to play the piano for me one day* ... I shake my head. It's a little ridiculous that I don't know his full name. After all, he knew both of mine.

"It's Dianilo," Yeva says, looking at me expectantly. I'm supposed to make a connection here. I'm usually good at puzzles, but this time my brain offers up nothing. I'm not sure what I'm missing.

"Okay ..." I gesture helplessly.

"His great-grandmother was Francesca Dianilo. Best friends with Jersat Meriweather. Sound familiar?" Yeva says.

A primary school science history lesson makes its way through the fog of my memory. Pioneering duo Jersat Meriweather and Francesa Dianilo, best friends since childhood, growing up to work together and reinvent space habitation ...

"Meriweather-Dianilo Station," I mutter, feeling a little humiliated. "Nico's great-grandmother was one of the founders of Meridian Station."

"Yes. He's a part-owner, officially, although the Station doesn't work that way anymore. His mother passed away years ago and left him full control of her share. Very diluted now after many generations, but still ..."

"Then he wasn't kidding; he's not just a sex worker."

"Attendants are not sex workers," Yeva responds, in an indignant tone so close to Nico's own that I find it's my turn to laugh.

"What's funny?" she asks, her expression part confusion, part annoyance.

"He says the same thing in the same tone. So you know, unexpected."

Yeva sighs audibly. It's not much, but it's something. I feel a little vindicated, at any rate.

"All right, then, I'm going to stretch out on the bunk and read. Yell if you need anything," I announce. I walk around the bulkhead and pull back the privacy panel on *Gabriella's* new more comfortable bunk, and plop down with a satisfied sigh. I'll of course keep tabs on everything happening during the trip with the ViewPort, but for now I'm relishing the surprised silence from the control deck.

I lie down, adjust the inclination of the support under my head, find my page marker, and get back to reading *Confessions of a Moral Skeptic*.

24

YEVA AND I EVENTUALLY find a rhythm that keeps us in communication with one another, but separated enough to maintain our calm—or, more accurately, *my* calm. One of us settles at the control console while the other takes time in the bunk, switching as we feel like it. We pretend it's about resting, but it isn't really; Yeva doesn't need much sleep, and I'm too wound up to sleep deeply. At least this way we have plenty of time when we don't have to interact, layered in with some time when we *can* interact. This approach appears to suit us both.

After a couple of days, it begins to feel almost like my time on the asteroid. I know Yeva's there, but I don't have to know what she's doing every minute. She's routed enough communiques through Xeric that it's clear she's still working with a variety of clients, and I'm fairly sure it's better if I know as little as possible about those activities.

The closer we get to Meridian Station, the faster *Gabriella*'s upgraded communications array connects. By day four of the trip, messages are moving almost in real time. I've been wondering about the right moment to let Arden in on my plans and what we've uncovered. I'm curious, too, to learn if he had any role to play in securing Graham's testimony and whether he knows what our friend might say. But I'm also concerned about saying too much, too soon—to anyone. I obsess daily about the Company or KaheleTech or the Governing Council finding out about our efforts and coming up with a way to circumvent them.

"Am I being paranoid?" I ask Xeric during one of my shifts at the controls. He still sits at the communications console; I've told him to feel free to vanish any time he wants, but for some reason he prefers being visually present.

"You're being particularly careful, but it may not be unwarranted," he says. "We still don't quite know what KaheleTech is up to, so it makes some sense to hold back. But at the same time, if you feel Arden and the other witnesses behind the petition are being used for a particular endgame, he should know. He'll want to be prepared."

I'm coming to realize the way I'm behaving now is exactly what used to make me so frustrated with Arden. He wouldn't tell me his plans or theories until it felt like the moment after the last moment, and it made me feel insecure, irrelevant, and dangerously uninformed. I finally understand his reluctance a bit better; maybe it was always more complex than simply wanting to keep me out of the loop 'for my own good'. I'm certain Arden's trustworthy and wouldn't share the information Yeva and I have uncovered. And he's shown his dedication to Iona's independence by getting the witnesses to Meridian Station in a way that demonstrates he doesn't fully trust the Company or the Governing Council either.

Still, I'm hesitant.

"Are you making the call?" Xeric asks. "If you want some privacy, I can send it through during your next bunk time and you can take it on the ViewPort."

"Oh, absolutely. But maybe not yet. We'll be there soon, and this might be better explained in person, and I'm just worried about ... other things." My objections are starting to sound fishy even to me.

"I think there's something else going on here," Xeric says, shaking silvery hair out of his eyes. "May I?"

"Sure."

"You believe Arden is trustworthy, so you aren't worried about someone else learning about your plan from him. It's more likely you're worried he won't be in line *with* your plan, that he'll find a flaw in your logic and challenge it in some way."

My fingers tighten on the arms of my seat. Xeric's absolutely right. I hate it, but he's right.

I let out a long breath and rotate the pilot's chair away from Xeric, toward the forward ports. *Gabriella's* moving at maximum speed so there's nothing to see in real time. The ports' protective covers are closed to spare our ground-based brains from experiencing crushing nausea, panic, or any of the other fun side effects of ultra high-speed space flight. Instead, there's a live image of a beautiful starfield projected behind the plexi. I focus instead on my own reflection. Layered over the hopeful scene of churning star nurseries and twirling galaxies, my face is drawn with disappointment—in myself. At this point, it truly feels as if I'm my own worst enemy.

"I'm not ready," I say, both to Xeric and my own reflection. "I need more of our questions answered first. Maybe I'm not sure myself."

That's the bottom line. I have a hunch, a theory, an idea that seems to be supported by extrapolation and at least some evidence. But we have little to suggest KaheleTech, or some permutation of it, plans to take control of Iona's sand, never mind dissolving it altogether. It made sense in the closed environment of the asteroid, where this question was literally all I focused on, but is it enough to make a meaningful claim? I'm losing confidence by the minute.

"All right," Xeric says in a calm, even voice. His face, reflected in the plexi, shows he isn't surprised or even bothered by my hesitation. "It may be you'll get those answers by discussing your thoughts with others who have thoughts of their own that could expand your ideas."

In my memory, I hear Lipop saying, *next time trust your friends.*

I turn the pilot's chair back to face him. "Damn virtual concierge," I say. "Do you always have to be right?"

Xeric grins. "It's one of my most charming features."

I harrumph in mock indignation.

"I'll have bunk time again in a few hours," I say. "That should give me enough time to psych myself up for a call."

"You can have it now," says Yeva, walking around the bulkhead and dropping into the copilot's chair; I have no idea how long she's been hanging back listening. "You're going to have a lot to talk about. As of a few moments ago, your friends are officially on the Governing Council hearing schedule. But I've never seen anything like this. They're slated to make their case in a closed private session to only the chairman, with no other members of the Council present, and no one outside the testimony list in attendance."

Yeva's pulled up the Council announcement on the streamer and spins the display so I can see it. The statement offers no information beyond what she's just recited, other than the meeting date and time. If everything continues on course, we'll arrive at Meridian Station five days before the hearing. The closed private session is a bad break for us, though. I had hoped to confront Sarsen about her involvement with Cadence, KaheleTech and the *Heretic* in a public forum. Now, that will be impossible. I won't even be allowed in the session, much less have the opportunity to speak.

"What could be the point?" I puzzle aloud. "Why keep the testimony private when Sarsen and Cabot-Klaar would benefit more by bringing the public in on the Company's machinations?"

"Perhaps our assessment has been incorrect, and they *want* the Company to maintain control," Yeva suggests, pulling the display back toward her and scrolling. "Perhaps the Company has been working with them after all. Or Sarsen might be thinking of offering the petitioners a deal of some kind to drop the petition or change their testimony."

"How does that make sense? If the petitioners win, the Company is thrown off Iona, creating an opening for Sarsen and KaheleTech. If the petitioners lose, the Company maintains its presence on Iona, which includes Breton Cabot-Klaar as part of the planetary governance team. It's another opening for Sarsen and KaheleTech."

"If it's not the outcome she needs to control, then perhaps it's the process," Xeric says suddenly. Yeva and I both startle at the sound; he's been sitting so quietly I'd forgotten he was there. "With no oversight from other council members and no external reporting, Sarsen can run the hearing any way she wants. If she wants to pump the witnesses for information or try to intimidate them or get them to implicate themselves somehow, she won't be restricted by the general rules of open session."

"That's possible, and a little frightening if it turns out she was the reason they were almost sent out into deep space with no hope of ever being found," I say.

"I wonder if the witnesses are aware of her role in that?" says Yeva.

"Sarsen could want to make sure it doesn't come to light," Xeric offers. "A private session might achieve that."

"There's not a 'why' that doesn't feel dangerous to me," I say. "She's done this intentionally; she has something planned. I don't like it."

Suddenly, waiting even one more second to share what we've learned feels like an irresponsible and foolhardy thing to do.

I stand and take a deep steadying breath.

"Go ahead and put that call through, Xeric," I say. "I'm heading to the bunk now."

It takes several minutes for him to connect the call, and when the ViewPort at last comes to life, the face I see is not the one I'm prepared for.

"Lipop! How are you?"

Her face breaks into a toothy smile. "Lovely Faith, we are well! We have been so worried about you!" Her broad lilting accent brings a smile to my face; the wild print wallpaper of their secure communications room threatens to overtake her face from the background. From off-camera, I hear Eidor call out, "Tell her we miss her-ah!" Lipop rolls her eyes and mutters something to her spouse in Sharjeet, who mutters back. Lipop's eyes narrow and for a moment it appears a full-scale shouting match might erupt, but then she apparently thinks better of it and turns back to the screen.

"Anyway," Lipop continues, as though no interruption had occurred at all, "it is good to see your face, and we're looking forward to spending some time with you once things settle down. But there is someone here who is anxious to speak with you, so good-bye for now."

She steps out of camera range, and for a moment there is only loud patterned wallpaper on the ViewPort. Discussions happen in the background I can't quite make out—Eidor muttering something in an encouraging tone, Lipop warning him to "stay out of it," and another familiar voice thanking them both for their concern. Then the soft whoosh of a closing door panel leads to silence, and finally, Arden sits down at the screen.

He looks exhausted and seems oddly awkward. He stares at the floor for a moment before looking up at the camera, and when he does, my grudges and frustrations with him threaten to melt away.

He smiles, wan but genuine. "Hey," he says.

"Hey," I respond. "You look tired."

"I *am* tired. You look good."

"I *am* good."

We both chuckle a little—tentative, forced. Still, it's a start.

"I hear you've been in this very room," he says, looking around distractedly. "So many pillows."

"Lipop loves her decorations."

"Clearly."

Arden pauses for a second, as if getting his bearings again. "You'll be here soon, Xeric said."

"We'll arrive five days before the hearing. We'll have plenty of time to connect beforehand, but there's so much to cover, it makes sense to get started now instead of waiting. We have theories and circumstantial evidence, but no real proof. I'm worried I might be missing something. I could use your advice."

I describe what we've learned about Benta Sarsen, Breton Cabot-Klaar, and the companies linked to them. Arden listens without interrupting—a first, as far as I can remember. But when I tell him Sarsen's name was attached to the ship that held the missing Planetary Equity Alliance members, his demeanor changes. His eyebrows draw together and his face colors.

"Sarsen could have been responsible for everything that happened to them," he says. "Maybree told us everything she knew after the *Heretic* landed on Iona, but that wasn't part of her story."

"Maybree might not have known, if Cabot-Klaar didn't tell her. She didn't seem to be aware the ship was set to launch to blank coordinates in deep space, either."

Arden leans closer to the screen. "What? Maybree only told us you sent the ship to Iona."

"It was already slated for launch, which I couldn't change. I had to figure out how to alter the destination coordinates at the last minute. It was literally headed where nothing exists. They would never have been found."

"Shit." Arden rubs the back of his neck with one hand. "That puts an entirely different spin on the closed session. Is it some kind of trap? Is she going to try to finish what she started?"

"That's unlikely. The General Council enviro is a very busy place and there will be people everywhere, even with a closed session happening. And it's in the public record who is going to be there and why."

Arden lets out a perturbed sigh.

"That's a lot to think about," he says. "As for KaheleTech and Cabot-Klaar's involvement, your theory they want to control the sand makes sense given the evidence you have. But it's like you said: there are a lot of missing pieces. How do you feel about bringing Graham in on this? He just arrived and we're meeting soon. His family probably has proprietary intel on all of these companies you're tracking. We can bring you in on another call or I can tag Xeric with any new information he might have."

"If Graham is supporting Iona, I think that's a great idea. If he's supporting his family dynasty, then maybe not."

Arden's lips quirk up into an amused expression. "Yeah, he's behind us. Turns out his new role in Thorn Industries isn't quite as advertised. We had a highly entertaining call right after you ... right after you left."

His smile fades. He looks down, something unidentifiable overtaking his face. He goes silent, and stares away from the camera for a long moment. I'm not sure if he's so tired he can't think, or if there's a glitch in the communications system, or what. When he speaks, his voice is emotional but resolute.

"I know I promised you, and I've tried, but I can't ... I *don't want to* keep up this charade. It's hard and it's painful and it just feels wrong. Not to run afoul of anything you've planned, but I need to let it go. And I hope we can ... you might want to ..."

I can feel my insides warming. I know what he's trying to say, because I've been wanting to say it too, for some time now.

"If you're asking me to be your ex-ex-partner," I interrupt, "then I accept. Let's forget the fake breakup altogether. I'm not happy with it either."

"I did the best I could. I don't think anyone on Iona ever figured it out. Wenda almost had me in counseling over it, but I ... wait. Did you just say *I accept*?"

"I did."

I let the smile I've been holding back slip across my face.

"Really? We can drop this and go back to being us? Because I thought you'd be committed to ..."

"I thought I would too, but as it turns out, not so much."

His face breaks into a grin and he lets out a loud breath. "Oh! I hated pretending we'd split up, every second of it. Never again, no matter what. I mean it." His relief is almost palpable through the screen.

When I concocted the idea of a fake break-up to throw off any plans the Company had to play us against each other, I wasn't sure I knew who I was without Arden. And there were moments later on when I thought our fake break-up was destined to turn into a real one. But here we are again. Maybe we really are better together than apart.

"I love you," he says. "That never changes."

I'm painfully aware of Xeric's ship-wide listening capabilities and Yeva hovering just past the bulkhead. As much as I want to say it back, it feels like something that should happen in private. So I make do with saying, "Same."

Arden laughs out loud.

Our next conversation is significantly less sweet.

Arden hails Xeric a few hours after our initial chat and asks to be put through to the main display. As the image resolves, it's clear he's no longer in Lipop's communications room. Instead of wild print wallpaper and soft diffuse lighting, the background is plain to the point of sterility. Everything about his surroundings screams 'highly secure unit.'

He sits in a nondescript chair, hunching toward the camera. His face is creased with concern, his eyes dark and his mouth held in a taut line.

My chest tightens and I shift uncomfortably.

"We have some new developments," he says, his tone somber. "The first, Yeva, is the Governing Council has been clued in to the fact you've left Dar Shal'O. They've issued an alert for your immediate apprehension."

"How very clever of them," Yeva says in an unimpressed tone. "I did tell them I was coming *four days ago*. They've only just gotten around to the alert now? The inefficiency is shocking."

Arden manages to look stunned for only a few seconds. "All right," he says, "that's whatever it is for you. But you'll likely have issues docking at the station, and there will be questions at intake."

"Thank you, we won't have any problems, but do carry on," she barks. "I'm certain you aren't this grave solely on my account."

Arden's face flashes a hard, fake smile.

"That's true, of course," he says. Yeva's attitude has gotten under his skin.

She returns his hard fake smile and waits for him to continue.

"Graham's here. I'll let him fill you in on his take on KaheleTech," he says, and moves to the side. Graham comes into the frame. His expression is the warm, friendly one I came to know when he arrived on Iona. It's a dramatic improvement over the stiff, officious face in the Thorn Industries press release.

"Hello, Faith," he says. "It's been a while. Yeva—a pleasure to meet you. It would be ludicrous to say I've heard a lot about you, so I won't annoy you with that."

Although she doesn't speak, Yeva accepts the greeting with a nod and a pleased expression.

"Hi, friend," I say. "It's good to see you. We were worried you'd been sucked into the evil family dynasty, never to return, once we read about your promotion. Were our concerns unfounded, then?"

I'm trying to make it sound teasing, but this is a point I need clarity on. While it's terrific Graham has come to support Iona's claims before the Governing Council, he could still spin it in a way that would benefit Thorn Industries more than Ionians. And despite my history of begging everyone to trust him, at this moment I don't quite trust him myself. Arden would be delighted if he knew.

"Ah, that." Graham runs one hand through his hair with a wince. "Let's just say neither I nor my family have changed. As a result, I'm no longer the linchpin in Thorn Industries' expansion plans, and while they haven't disowned me yet, they still have no idea what to do with me."

This is what I'd hoped to hear and based on what I can see of his demeanor—the mild chagrin, tinged with frustration—it seems genuine. It's not a full-throated condemnation of his family's business interests, but it will do for now.

"Alrighty, then." I try to look open and accepting. "I'd love to catch up, but at the moment time is getting critical. What have you got for us?"

"This company you're tracking, KaheleTech. It's part of a partnership program Thorn Industries runs. That's not unusual—most of the small companies in the sector are in the same program. But KaheleTech has participated in several of our core development projects, and as a result they have some activities not shown to the public as part of their agreement with us. Your bot wouldn't have access to this information since it's on protected internal servers controlled by Thorn Industries."

Xeric huffs. "I'm not a *bot*," they mutter.

Graham is pulling up a spreadsheet, sharing it with us on the display. It's a purchase report, packed with dozens of line items, most within the last few months when our research and tracking efforts showed KaheleTech purchasing little to nothing.

"This is KaheleTech's purchasing history inside the partnership program," Graham explains. "Our company doesn't direct their activities. They file their plans with us under their approved research proposal, and submit requests for whatever they need. We have a few regulations in place, but as long as they don't purchase materials restricted by decree, we don't interfere."

Yeva leans forward, squinting at the display, her lips pressing together into a hard line. "There are some dangerous chemicals on this list. What were they developing?"

"The proposal describes a cleaning agent to remove adhering toxins from contaminated spacecraft, specifically fuel banks," Graham says. "They initially wanted to pursue live nanotechnology to eat the toxins, but the board vetoed it. I'm no chemist, but even I could see the ethical issues inherent in that approach."

"I'm going to need a lab on station," Yeva says, turning to Xeric. "Maximum safety protocol."

"*The bot* will get right on that," Xeric responds, casting a foul look toward Graham, who is still faintly visible through the spreadsheet. Graham has started scrolling through the data and doesn't notice.

"Important point about the purchases highlighted here," he says, indicating four entries outlined in red. "These orders are still in-process. Everything else has been received and signed for by KaheleTech representatives."

He pauses, his expression wavering behind the spreadsheet. The eternal war between his own ethics and his family writes itself across his face.

"This is proprietary data, but I've sent it complete. It's all I have at the moment, so I hope it's helpful," he says at last. "Let me know if I can do anything else."

Yeva's pacing back and forth across the control room, sometimes whispering a new instruction to Xeric, who looks more annoyed at every interruption. I'm sure she sees some kind of connection she's not willing to divulge on camera. I'm wildly curious, but the call is still open and now both Arden and Graham are looking at me expectantly.

"We'll be there in a few days," I say. "I'll talk to you both as soon as we arrive, before the Council session."

"I'm concerned Yeva's not taking this seriously," Arden says, which brings Yeva's pacing to a full stop. "The GC is committed to apprehending her. I know she has a lot of on-station connections, but going against the GC is something yet again."

Yeva rolls her eyes. "It's not the first time and it surely will not be the last," she says firmly. "*I* have made arrangements. I do not need to explain them to *you*."

Arden blinks at her rebuff. His mouth drops open, but he appears to think better of responding.

"See you soon. Stay safe," he says, with a last glance toward me. The connection dissolves.

25

THE INSTANT THE CONNECTION drops, I turn to Yeva. She's peering at a station schematic Xeric pulled up for her. She's been pretending not to listen, but I'm sure she heard everything. I'm also sure she's going to have an opinion.

"Tell me what you're thinking," I say.

"I'm thinking this *bot* isn't performing as well as I'd like," she says sharply, leaning over Xeric's shoulder to scowl at a second screen. "No, no—this won't do; I need maximum safety protocol *and* maximum security."

His face twists into a scowl as he scrolls to a different display. "Perhaps a *human* should help you with this instead."

Yeva doesn't respond. She points at the schematic. "This one," she says. "Use the high security alias. And get Nico for me. When you have him, I'll take it on the ViewPort."

All of this distracts me for a second, but not long enough to forget she hasn't answered my question.

"Come on, Yeva, you know what I mean. What notion did that list of chemicals set off in your head? I saw the way you reacted to them."

She looks up from the display. Her expression remains impassive, but I can see tension in her jaw.

"I'm concerned KaheleTech is creating a corrosive agent that can be delivered via drone," she says in a tone so matter of fact she could be describing the weather or her most recent meal. I push my mild annoyance down and try again.

"That was our original concept, though. How is this different?"

"This new list ... the corrosive agents they've ordered are an order of magnitude beyond the power of the ones we've been considering. In fact, I'd consider them the foundation of offensive weaponry under other circumstances. The fuel bank cleaning project could be legitimate, but it wouldn't need chemistry like this. I'm looking closely at these outliers. And there are a lot of them."

Heat rises to my face.

"Perhaps it's a red herring?"

"Red herrings are left out for others to find. These orders were made in comfortable secrecy they had no reason to believe would be breached. The only way these most recent purchases of theirs would have come to light is the way they did—through an unexpected inside connection."

"My connection to Graham isn't a secret, and it's well-known he's not exactly the favorite child in his family, so perhaps ..."

"No," Yeva is resolute. "Some of these purchase orders were filed before you left Iona and others after you arrived on Dar Shal'O. The only people who knew why you came to my asteroid are myself, Xeric, and Arden, who only had a surface understanding. Which one of us would you like to accuse?"

Her eyes glitter as she stares at me. I feel utterly defeated, but rightly so.

"I have Nico," Xeric interrupts. "Transferring to the ViewPort now."

Yeva spins on her heel without another word and heads to the bunk, leaving me with a tightening gut. Her words ring in my brain: *dissolve far more than Iona's sands*. Are we completely wrong about the endgame, then? Could Cabot-Klarr and Sarsen somehow gain from destroying Iona altogether? Was Bardazel just a test?

I use my holo to pull up the list of chemicals Graham passed along to us and toss the display into the air. These compounds are all unfamiliar to me. If only Fallon were here. At least I have Xeric. He won't have Fallon's creativity, but he has access to a wealth of data. It's worth a shot.

"If you wanted to get rid of the base terrain material on a planet by using drones to spray some kind of dissolving agent on it, would you use one of these?" I ask. He's been in the corner staring at nothing with narrowed eyes and a clenched jaw ever since Yeva's insult, but now his eyes focus and he leans forward to peer at the display.

"Doubtful," he says. "Some of them would be impossible to handle, others simply wouldn't work in that scenario. For example, this one combusts as soon as it encounters oxygen. Dropping it from a drone into any kind of oxygen-rich atmosphere would, shall we say, have immediate negative consequences for the delivery vehicle while leaving the intended target intact. This one, on the other hand, becomes a gas and dissipates unless it's under pressure."

"Which ones would cause the most damage if delivered?"

Xeric considers the options, nibbling at his lower lip. He draws a circle in the air, highlighting one of the listed items.

"This one is interesting—Isoflare. It's a proprietary blend of chemicals, very difficult to obtain, but it's powerful enough to do the job you describe. It eats through everything with extended exposure, so it might be challenging to disperse it via drones. The drones would need to be loaded and launched from the planet in question, and the job done in record speed, before the Isoflare ate through the tanks carrying it."

He removes the highlight with a flick of his wrist.

We continue scrolling the list, but nothing jumps out as a potential candidate for the kind of destruction I'm worried about.

"What have they purchased the most of?" I ask, poking at the floating data display until it ripples.

"That would be this stuff, Fluoroclean," Xeric says, steadying the display before scrolling to the entry. "It's one of the handful of things on this list that makes sense from a project perspective. It's already widely used in cleaning solutions. It's not exactly benign—it can cause irritation and respiratory problems if not handled correctly—but it's common, compared to some of the other things they're requesting."

"Why would they need so much of it? Is that what's holding up the delivery?"

"My guess is simple timing. It's easy to get, but they just ordered it four days ago."

Four days ago. The same day the consortium purchased all those drones.

"I feel like this is it," I say. "They're doing something with this and the drones."

"I don't think this has the power to ..." Xeric begins, but I interrupt.

"Ping Graham. Ask if he can keep Thorne Industries from fulfilling all of KaheleTech's remaining purchase orders. I know Yeva's on the ViewPort but ping her and tell her we need to talk as soon as possible."

I feel like I'm burning inside. It must show on my face, because Xeric takes one look at me and says, "Right away."

Yeva's not delighted to have her call interrupted. She stalks around the bulkhead and throws me a glare, then simply stands with her arms crossed over her chest and glowers at me until I speak.

"I have an idea," I say. "We're looking at things that are obviously out of place with KaheleTech's stated development project, things standing out as wrong. But I think we're making it too complicated."

Her expression shifts to a kernel of interest. "What do you mean?"

"What if KaheleTech chose this type of project because it would give them the opportunity to purchase the chemistry they wanted for their real project, targeting Iona's sand? If I'm right, those outlier buys are the cover, a distraction, and the materials that fit within the project concept are what they're hoping to use in some way to gain control of Iona."

Yeva draws a breath and holds it for a moment. Her expression still has a hint of skepticism in it, but she's taking the time to consider what I've said.

"We can test everything once we get to the Station," she says. "Nico's prepared to supply the full list in small quantities. Put together a test plan for those buys piquing your interest, and we'll make it happen."

She goes back to the bunk to make more contacts, stopping first to give Xeric a flurry of instructions. I spin my chair forward and eye my reflection floating over the projected imagery. I look hopeful and excited. I feel like I'm on to something.

The short time leading up to our arrival at Meridian Station is busy. I work on researching and hammering out test plans for Fluoroclean, feeding dozens of scenarios to Xeric for further investigation. Yeva takes over the bunk and fields multiple communications from the Station and elsewhere. I try not to listen in, but I sometimes hear snippets of conversation that suggest she's still not happy with the lab arrangements.

And then there's the matter of the Council's decree seeking her arrest.

She's nonchalant, taking a dismissive tone and refusing to engage whenever it comes up. But there's a tension in her mouth and forehead that deepens as we approach the Station.

I'm not travelling incognito or trying to shield my movements this time, so we'll easily pass the initial screenings and dock at Meridian without generating any exceptional interest. But once we're on-station, attempting to move among thousands of people and interacting with individuals who already have a spotlight on them ... that makes me nervous. Yeva's bound to be recognized by someone; going under a random alias won't protect her.

I know she doesn't want to talk about it, but I have to ask for my own peace of mind. Without meaning to, I've come to let a lot of my hopes for Iona's freedom rest on her.

Plus ... didn't she say she *told* the GC she was coming?

I manage to wait until we're on the edge of Station-controlled space. Communications are flowing freely, the lab arrangements have been sorted to her satisfaction, regular check-ins from Graham and Arden suggest nothing unusual is happening around the hearing or any other thing. It seems like a good time. I try to ease into it, smaller questions before bigger ones.

"What's the plan for our time on the Station?" I ask. "What do I need to be prepared for?"

"I'd say a lot of work, primarily. You're going to have a lot of testing to get through," Yeva says without looking up from the digital document she's been studying for the past hour. "Xeric will help. I've sent them all my notes, so you'll know how to set up and run the experiments."

"I'm running the experiments? I thought you'd want to."

"Normally I would. But I'll be in detention, so it's all going to fall to you."

I'm stunned. I have to make a conscious effort to keep my mouth from dropping open.

"You're not going to try to keep the General Council from apprehending you?" I manage to squeak out.

Yeva turns to me, her face the picture of self-satisfaction.

"Not at all. It's the only way I'll be able to get onto the GC enviro before the closed session." She's clearly thinking far ahead of me, on some track that's vastly different than the one I thought we were on.

"So you're not concerned about ..."

"I'm not concerned about anything," she interrupts. "What are they going to do, banish me to an asteroid? Meanwhile, you're more than capable of doing the work we've planned. Everything is quite straightforward."

That's not the word I would have chosen, but if it's a plan, then it's a plan.

"Alrighty," I say, turning back to the console. "Step one, docking. Step two, incarceration. Step three, testing. How are we supposed to spring you from the General Council's clutches? Do we have a plan for that?"

Behind me, Yeva chuckles.

"Don't worry about it," she says.

"I *knew* you were going to say that."

I check our progress on the monitors and tweak *Gabriella's* controls; we're only a few hours out. We've decreased speed to one more compatible with approaching the busiest space station in the sector, and the protective front panel that kept us insulated during the high-speed phase of the voyage has retracted. Now the view is an expanse of horizonless black, broken up by small bright dots of distant starshine. The Station itself is one of those dots, still far enough away to be indistinct. Not for much longer, though.

We'll have answers soon, but they may not be the answers I hoped for when I began this journey. And as many times as I tell myself clarity is always better than confusion, I simultaneously welcome and dread our arrival.

TEN YEARS AGO, I saw Meridian Station for the first time.

I was twenty-six years old and so shut down I couldn't imagine trusting anyone ever again. My mental health was in shambles, my body rebuilt from near-ruin, and all I wanted was to be somewhere no one had ever heard of me. I left the Company's Home World, the planet of my birth, to travel to the farthest reaches of the sector, thinking I'd at last be free of the Company and all its machinations.

That, of course, turned out not to be true.

The first time I saw the Station appear through the long-flight transport's observation deck ten years ago, the metal framework illuminated by green, blue, and gold marker lights, reminded me unpleasantly of Home World's Residential Services building. That's where I was the night my life and my body shattered at the hands of the Company, and it only reminded me of betrayal and the agony of being left behind by someone I'd trusted implicitly.

When I flew to Meridian from Iona on my current quest, I was running again. I told myself I was running toward something rather than away, but that may not have been the truth. Seeing the Station gave me palpitations and a vague sense of barely surviving, a feeling which fit both my first visit and my last.

As the Station now comes into view, my feelings are different. It's weirdly familiar and almost comforting, and stirs up a sense of optimism I didn't have before. I'm so close to reaching the goals I had at the beginning of this journey, and I'm so certain the keys are all there, somewhere on that massive silver structure.

I speak a series of commands to *Gabriella* and she adjusts course, aiming to join the cluster of other arrivals waiting their turn to dock—a cloud of sparkling bees swirling around a metal flower.

Yeva comes around the bulkhead and settles into the copilot's seat. Her expression is placid; she takes in the view without speaking. It's not long before my natural inability to abide silence in a closed space takes over.

"What are you thinking?"

Yeva raises an eyebrow. "Nothing, really. What are *you* thinking?"

I'm taken aback, and it takes me a few beats to respond.

"I'm thinking about docking, and what to do once we get to our Overnight."

"We're not staying together. I have my own place."

"You're staying at a different Overnight?"

The corner of her mouth tics up in amusement.

"I'm not staying at an Overnight at all. I have my own apartment. I'm staying there."

"Of course you are."

I must sound irritated, because Yeva's amused expression takes over her entire face.

"Don't worry. You'll like your accommodations. It's rather more pleasant than last time. You'll have full access to Xeric and a secure communications suite. The lab and some of your friends are nearby."

I consciously try to look less sour.

"I'm not worried about my accommodations; I'm sure whatever you've set up is fine. How long do you think you'll have before the GC comes after you?"

She chuckles, this time a mirthless sound.

"They're ridiculously inefficient so I imagine I have some time, but I can't guess how much. Oh look, there's the enviro."

The enviro housing the Governing Council's headquarters is visible now, behind the space station and slightly above it. It glows golden with its own generated lights, and a steady stream of small spacecraft traverse the short distance between it and Meridian Station. Some of us will be on one of those shuttles soon. Hopefully all of us will make it back.

Gabriella's console chimes as the Station Control's interface makes its first contact with her to begin the docking process. With no aliases to worry about and our prospective detainee only a passenger, I'm far more calm and even a little chatty with the Traffic Management officer who asks me the standard questions. We're approved for docking, and I pilot her through the designated entrance; the tractor beam finishes the job of towing us to the correct air lock. Once inside the pressurized docking area, we're met by a tugbot, which carefully guides us to our assigned slot.

This docking area is not the same one I was assigned on my earlier visit. The slots are double-sized, and the disembarking platform is oddly fancy, with artwork and décor accents here and there.

I dismiss Xeric, who pouts charmingly before disappearing, and power down *Gabriella*. As the chime sounds indicating permission to disembark, another ship pulls into the slot behind us.

"What the hell is this?" I mutter, peering around as best I can.

"Oh good, they're here," says Yeva, rising from her seat. "Open up, let's go."

"Who's here?"

"Friends. Please extend the ramp, we have places to be," she says, tapping her knuckle against the ship's main hatch, clearly irritated.

Alrighty then.

I activate the ramp; Yeva heads out the instant it drops. I hurry to try to catch up with her and follow her out onto the deck. As soon as I'm clear of the ship, I'm distracted by a familiar voice shouting my name in a heavy Sharjeet accent.

"Faith-ah! There you are-ah! Hello, hello!"

Eidor jogs over to me and wraps me in a fierce hug. Over his head I get a good look at the ship that's pulled in behind us—it's the tea shop delivery skiff. Lipop sits at the controls, waving at me with a delighted smile on her face.

"It's great to see you," Eidor exclaims, releasing me. "We were so delighted when Yeva asked if we could host you. We have so much room we never use, it will be wonderful to have a house full of friends."

"Oh, I'm staying with you? That's great! Yeva, why didn't you ..."

I look around for her, but Yeva, who disembarked ahead of me, is just a receding figure now, already far down the gangway heading for the Station entrance. I don't dare call out her name, because I don't want to call attention to her or to myself. She's obviously got some kind of plan that doesn't include me.

"I'm delighted too," I say to Eidor, but he doesn't hear me—he's busy shouting at some Station porterbots hovering near *Gabriella's* ramp. I tap his shoulder to get his attention and say, "I'll be right back."

I run inside ahead of the porterbots. I take a long look at my ship's interior, pretending I'm making sure I haven't forgotten anything, but really, I just want a minute alone with her. She's transformed since I first took flight in her, but her guts and heart are still what I crafted with my own hands. I give her sidewall an affectionate pat.

"Thank you, beautiful," I whisper. "See you soon." The last time I left her here, I wasn't sure I'd see her again. This time, I'm sure I will. It's only a matter of when.

It's a short ride from the fancy docking area where *Gabriella* is parked to a much less formal and smaller docking area where Lipop brings the tea shop skiff to rest. The craft surrounding us are around-station work and personal conveyances, designed for short trips and nothing more. Some are so battered they wouldn't withstand flight outside the Station's local corridors, and a few might not fly at all. The entrance goes directly into Residential 16, where someone has decided it will be early afternoon; bright artificial sunlight pours down from above. We pass two of the larger residential structures before coming to the narrow passageway leading to Eidor and Lipop's home.

I feel weirdly affectionate as we step into the loud blue vestibule of the little four-story plexi building. It's a perfect representation of the people who own it. Eidor and Lipop have a level of ordinariness on the outside that kept me sane on my last visit; and an unexpected level of unrestrained inventive genius on the inside that probably saved my life.

The three of us step into the lift tube. Eidor this time punches in two different codes. At the third floor, he steps out, turning back to me with a broad smile.

"We have given our guests the fourth floor for privacy," he says. "Lipop will show you the particulars."

Guests?

Beside me, Lipop is beaming. I think I know where this is going, and I'm not displeased at all.

I do my best to pay attention as Lipop transfers the lift codes from her holo to mine, along with the door codes. I barely hear her over my thudding heart, though, and as we step into the living area of the fourth floor, I'm happily proven correct.

Arden leaps up from the wildly patterned sofa where he's been sitting, his eyes widening as he sees us. Immediately a smile, part relief and part joy, spreads across his face.

"You can join us downstairs anytime, but no rush," Lipop says. "In fact, I suggest taking the rest of the day to get re-acclimated. After dinner will be soon enough to be social." Her expression is all self-satisfaction as she slips out the door. I mean to thank her and say goodbye, but I'm already in Arden's arms, breathing in the warm spicy scent of him, feeling his heart beat against me. At least for now, the rest of the galaxy has ceased to exist.

We take Lipop at her word and take our time.

There are layers upon layers to tease out, conversations and declarations that have been put off too long. We won't clear all the hurdles now, but as we talk and laugh and reconnect, we clear enough of them. The truth is he knows parts of me others will never see, inside my most tangled dreams and fears, beyond the competent façade I project to keep myself safe. And I know him with an intimacy nothing can break—his mind, his quirks, his self-deceptions. We are equal parts of each other in this moment, and although I'm sure there will be ebbs and flows, imbalance and imperfection, that's part of what makes it right.

Right for us, anyway.

We at last lie tangled together in the warm and familiar way of lovers across the universe, clothes and bedcovers and pretenses long dispensed with and scattered on the floor. He looks at me with sleepy-eyed satisfaction, tracing the arch of my nose delicately with one finger. Then his expression becomes intense and his brow knits together.

"I was afraid I'd never see you again," he says.

"Which time?"

My response makes him smile, but his eyes remain serious.

"Once you arrived at the asteroid, I spoke to Yeva. I thought *she's there, she's safe now*. I was so relieved, but then I wondered why would you ever leave that safe place? And I thought maybe you shouldn't leave it—you should just be safe forever. I always felt like keeping you safe was my job, and I failed multiple times, so why should you ever come back?"

Some of this speech triggers me and makes me want to confront him, but his expression is so heart-wrenchingly sincere, I let it go. For now.

"I was always going to come back. You knew that," I say. "It was never about me being safe. It was about Iona being safe—not just for me, but for all of us."

"I know it wasn't just about you, but part of me wanted it to be," he says. He looks away, distracted. "It's habit at this point. So many of my decisions have been based around what I thought would make things the safest for you. I want that for you so much."

"I'm sorry, Arden. I wish I could have kept it from happening."

He looks into my eyes again.

"The person who should have kept it from happening is me. You said it over and over, and you were right. If I'd been more upfront with you, told you everything from the very beginning, not made so many choices on my own that affected us both ... things might not have turned out differently, but I could have maintained your trust instead of coming off like a manipulative jerk. We could have had an easier path."

I cup his cheek with my hand, and he nuzzles into my palm, his eyes closed.

"I'm not sure an easy path is our way. Too predictable, too ordinary," I say, and he chuckles softly.

"It certainly hasn't been our way so far. Maybe we can work on that later."

With a laugh, I slide myself across the landscape of twisted sheets until we're pressed together, face to face, skin to skin. In a single move I push him onto his back and straddle him. His face registers surprise and delight, and I lean down to brush my lips across his. Before we sink into another kiss, I whisper into his ear, "Definitely later."

WE EVENTUALLY CLEAN OURSELVES up, dress, and leave for Lipop's. In the lift, I'm calm and relaxed as I input the code to take us to the third floor. I probably should be a bit more anxious—this could be the beginning of a particularly challenging period—but after months of feeling as though I was teetering on a knife's edge, I've finally gained a sense of stability. Of course, it might all be wishful thinking or pure endorphin-driven imagination—a couple of hours in the bedroom with the right person can do that to you—but I'm hopeful. I haven't felt hopeful in a long time.

The sound of voices percolating through music greets us in the hallway outside Lipop and Eidor's quarters. We step into the sitting room and set off a flurry of activity. Lipop meets us at the door. After an enthusiastic hug for both of us, she rushes off to find cushions for us to sit on, then starts rearranging the furniture, despite the guests already seated. Eidor barrels in from the kitchen bearing hefty cups of something that looks like tea but smells like the strongest booze imaginable, which he presses into our hands despite our objections.

Arden takes a tentative swig and immediately falls into a coughing fit. Eidor offers him a broad grin and a thumbs-up from across the room.

"Gotta watch out for the local juice, it's no joke," says a familiar voice on my left. Graham rises from Lipop's delicate settee only seconds before Lipop drags it to a different position in the room. Graham and I hug. Arden, mostly recovered but still trying to get his voice back, fist-bumps his friend then croaks, "I'm getting some water. Need anything?"

I shake my head; Graham declines as well. Before Arden disappears toward the kitchen, he takes the cup from my hand and gasps, "I'll pour this out for you."

Graham grins at me.

"You two look like things are going well, at least in the personal arena."

I look in the direction of Arden's departure. "We've reached a new level of détente, I think. More important things have been occupying our attention for some time now, though."

"I'm very aware. Seriously, it's good to see you in person, Faith."

"And you. I was worried you'd gone bad after that last press release hit the stream. Fallon was apoplectic when she saw the picture."

He laughs. "I can't imagine what I'm going to have to do to make up for it. Funny thing, I wasn't actually there. My father's team created the image to add weight to the announcement. And then of course everything blew up. So much effort for nothing. I almost feel bad for them."

"Sounds like quite the story."

"It is, but for another time. If Eidor's sensors can be relied upon, more guests are arriving."

Eidor shouts over the music, "These sensors are the best on the Station, they are never wrong. You need another drink?"

"Oh stars," Graham whispers under his breath, before waving to Eidor and saying loudly, "No, I'm good. Thank you, though."

Lipop, also alerted to new arrivals, is now rearranging her previous rearrangements, and sends her son Hamiit to the dining room for extra chairs. She waves me over to a set of newly placed cushions in one corner of the room. I sit down tentatively; the stack is higher than most of the furniture and it gives me the uncomfortable sensation of being on display.

The door slides open and Yeva comes in.

"You're still unapprehended," I exclaim, as she makes her way over to me and drops into one of the repurposed dining room chairs next to my cushion-pile.

"So far, yes. At this rate, I'm going to have to turn myself in."

"Why did you leave so quickly when we docked?"

"I needed to make it to my place before being taken into custody. And I thought it might be wise to create some separation between all of us in case they tried to pull in any of my alleged accomplices. In hindsight, I obviously had far too much confidence in the General Council's security force. Where is my escort? Has he gone off script again?"

This creates a whole new raft of questions, but before I can ask, the door slides open and Nico steps across the threshold. He's wearing his "attendant" garb; his long orange robe grazes the floor as he walks. His eyes find me, and he offers a smile before being pulled into an elaborate greeting from Lipop. Eidor presses one of the deadly cups of alcoholic beverage into his hand.

"Ah, there he is," Yeva says. "I'm going to tactfully threaten him for not going by the book, when I specifically instructed him to, and then let the two of you have a moment."

"Oh, we don't need ..." I begin, but Yeva's already striding away and shouting for Eidor. She shakes a finger at Nico as she passes him, but he only laughs.

He then disentangles himself from Lipop and floats across the floor to me. He takes my hand, giving it a gallant kiss before he perches his tall frame on the edge of the chair Yeva vacated.

"I told you there would be a next time," he says.

"I hope this time is somewhat less intense. I could do with fewer beatings and killer robots."

"I think we can manage the reduction in killer robots and physical mayhem. As for the intensity, probably not." His eyes wander toward Yeva, who is now having an energetic conversation with Graham, who looks overwhelmed.

"Yeva said you're her escort? What's that about?"

"In the same way I was your escort that night you sorted out the building schematic. She thought traveling with an attendant might help her blend in a bit, in case GC security was on-station looking for her. She assumed they would track her movements from the instant she arrived, but either that's not the case or they're being extremely subtle about it. That's why I'm wearing this."

He lifts the edge of the robe. The rich brocade rustles as he rubs it between his long slender fingers. I've noticed the subtle shift in his speech pattern that differentiates his 'professional' persona from the more casual Nico I've come to know, and I see now he's wearing sneakers instead of the sandals usually paired with the robe. He's clearly operating off the clock and in a "nonprofessional" capacity.

"So she's anxious about being apprehended after all?"

Nico twists the fabric of the robe in his fist, his eyes narrowing.

"As usual, I can't get anything out of her that's not a direct order. She intends to be taken into custody, but she has something she wants to accomplish beforehand. I suppose she hasn't managed to do whatever that is yet, so she asked me to play escort whenever she needs to travel on station. It appears to be more about manipulating the timing of her apprehension than avoiding it."

"She's not worried about them just showing up at her door?"

"Her apartment's in a protected area of the Station, just as my place is. They can't even *get* to her door without an access warrant, and no one is going to grant that without a lot of paperwork."

Lipop appears at Nico's shoulder, murmuring in his ear. Whatever she says shifts his demeanor entirely; his face relaxes and he lets out a relieved breath.

"Lipop tells me Yeva won't require an escort home, so I'm free to change out of my work uniform," he says, turning back to me. "She's printing some clothes for me right now."

"Lipop is printing clothes? Be careful, you'll wind up in a bright yellow jumpsuit with pink flowers bigger than your head."

He laughs, a deep hearty baritone. "I sent her files beforehand; hopefully she won't elect to make any improvements to them. I'd prefer not to wear her wallpaper. Not that there's anything wrong with it, but it's not who I am, style-wise."

I laugh with him for a moment, then take advantage of the segue.

"About who you are ... I want to apologize for not understanding your actual standing here. I didn't realize ..."

"Would it have changed how we interacted if you'd known?" Nico asks. His expression is a bit more intense now. This is an important question to him.

"I don't think so," I say. "I can't be sure, but most likely no."

"Well, then, it's fine you weren't aware of my personal details. I didn't tell you, you didn't ask, and it didn't matter to me whether you knew who my family was or not," he says, the emphasis on *my family* clear. "It wasn't my intention to keep you in the dark or mislead you, however, so I hope that's not what you're thinking."

"I know. I was just taken by surprise when Yeva explained it to me, and she got a lot of amusement out of my ignorance."

"I'm sorry about that, then, at least," he says, "but I'm happy we had the interaction we did. Although truthfully, I thought we might have diverged onto a different path if circumstances hadn't intervened."

He takes my hand in his, holding it gently. His expression is mischievous rather than sensual, but my face begins to heat up all the same. I can imagine the flush of color coming into my cheeks.

"Oh, that. I wasn't myself," I say. Even I can hear the waver in my voice.

Nico leans close and whispers, "You're a terrible liar."

"And you're an excellent kisser," I whisper back, "but that's neither here nor there."

He sits upright again, his expression a mixture of amusement and surprise. He distractedly takes a swig from the cup in his hand, apparently having forgotten it contains Eidor's beverage of the day. His eyes begin to water, and he makes an uncomfortable strangling sound.

"Oh dear," he manages to say, coughing as he stands. "This isn't the response I wanted to give you, but I must find some antidote to this ... cocktail? Poison? Industrial cleanser? I apologize."

I nod and wave him away. Despite his face changing color as he wheezes for breath, he manages to bow politely to me in the way of official Station Attendants before hurrying off.

A moment later Arden returns, looking much more composed, and sits next to me on the cushion pile. More people arrive; friends from Lipop's Meridian Merchants Association, neighbors from the residences on either side. Arden waves over a tall, middle-aged couple and introduces me to Eiken and Vella Fortin, Hinn and Holly's parents. Others are here from the Planetary Equity Alliance, too, and I'm in awe of their courage. They talk about the revival process—now perfected with the support of Company money and medical tech, managed expertly by Macha. The sketchy cobbled-together process that took us days to complete has been refined to a series of injections. Revival takes less than six hours, followed by a few days of supplements to restore memory and refine physical and mental function.

With a usable antidote and straightforward revival techniques, Blue would be done as a prospective weapon, if only its maker didn't also control those processes. I never doubted that was how it would play out, to be honest. But at least enough people know about the processes now and they can't be kept from anyone needing them without creating a public relations nightmare for the Company.

I fidget with the edge of the elaborately embroidered pillow under my leg, fighting the urge to move. A dozen people are crammed into a sitting room that felt comfortably full at four, and the blend of indistinguishable voices talking and loud rhythmic Sharj music is giving me a headache. And while it's amusing to see everyone, I have a hunch this is not purely social engagement. Yeva's presence alone is enough to convince me I'm right.

"So many people," Lipop chirps, settling into the chair next to us and looking around happily. "Such a blessing to have everyone in our home."

The sensor chimes in the background and she pops up as though she's on a spring. "Eidor!" she shouts. "Our last guest is here! Bring another chair!"

Arden and I exchange puzzled glances—everyone either of us knows on the Station is already in the room. It's a welcome sight when the door opens a final time and the mysterious last guest is Euclid Nam.

The lieutenant spots us across the room and waves. He works his way through the greeting gauntlet, then lets Lipop steer him over to a chair on Arden's left. "It's great to see you both," he says. "Iona isn't the same without you."

"I'm surprised to see you here," Arden says. "What's the story?"

"I'm not sure, to be honest," Nam responds, running a hand through his short-cropped black hair. "I got an official order requiring my presence here yesterday, delivered by one of those automated skiffs. So I climbed aboard and here I am. I arrived a few hours ago. I tried to ping you but your holo was set to unavailable."

"An official order from whom?" I ask.

"That's the peculiar thing. When the skiff landed on Iona, it said the order was from the Governing Council. But no one knew anything about it, and the ship's memory wiped itself the instant it docked."

"You've been in touch with the Council, then, and they have no knowledge of this?" Arden asks.

"I contacted them as soon as I landed, and they were as perplexed as I was. The real sender remains a complete mystery."

"I have a feeling someone here will be able to help you get to the bottom of this almost immediately," I say, looking around for Yeva.

"How did you wind up here?" Arden asks. "At this gathering, I mean?"

"Ah that. The place I'm staying has these virtual concierges, and mine dropped an invitation with this address on it into my holo. He said you'd both be here, and it was important I come, but didn't say why. I wasn't expecting a party, but this seems fun."

I repress a smirk. "Does your concierge have a name? Xeric, maybe?"

Lt. Nam sits back in surprise. "Uh yes, exactly. How did you know?"

"Long story. I'm well-acquainted with Xeric. He won't be the same the next time you see him, though. Also, if Eidor offers you a drink, don't take it. It's already felled every person in the room."

"So ... is this a celebration? Or a meeting? Or what?" Lt. Nam asks.

"It feels too much like a very specific gathering to be a random party," Arden murmurs, glancing around.

Suddenly the music stops, and Lipop steps to the center of the room.

"Everyone here is a friend, old or new," Lipop says, gesturing to include us all. "I wanted you all here tonight to talk with one another, to understand one another, and most importantly, to learn how you can help one another. Everyone in this room is involved in a struggle for sovereignty in one way or another, whether personal sovereignty ..." —she looks pointedly at Yeva, who nods in acknowledgement— "... or the sovereignty of an entire planet." At this point she makes eye contact with me.

"I was involved in Sharj's struggle for independence, and later when it joined the Gordonia Network in that network's fight for freedom from Company interference," she continues. "I learned in the first instance, fighting alone is not an option. I learned in the second, sovereignty is not something that is won. It is something you must create, deliberately and specifically."

"Did you know about this?" Arden whispers to me, and I shake my head. To me, Lipop has always been a lovely Sharj lady who loves her husband, her son, and her flowery décor, albeit a very direct and almost violently organized Sharj lady.

"Do not wait for sovereignty to come to you," Lipop is saying, this time addressing me, Arden, and Lt. Nam directly. "Plan for it. And plan for more than just your home planet. Include others in your arc. Build networks and systems, not merely layers of isolation."

She directs this last comment to Yeva, who for an instant appears discombobulated and stares at the floor.

"All of this is a precursor to an announcement." Lipop's voice has softened and some emotion is creeping in; she looks fondly toward her husband and son, who stand in the corner. Eidor is beaming proudly, his eyes shining with tears. "After many happy years as an honored merchant on Meridian Station, I will be taking on a new role. I have been asked to take up the position of Provost in support of the Director General of the Gordonia Network, and as such will become the network's recognized representative to the General Council. It is the logical resumption of my diplomatic career, and I look forward to having a positive impact on the lives of the people of Sharj, Gordonia, and all planetary members of the network. All right, that's all; now let's enjoy ourselves! Friends are together! This is always a thing worth celebrating!"

The music resumes, and Lipop begins circulating around the room, accepting hugs and congratulations. I'm stunned enough that by the time she gets to me, the only thing I can think to say is, "Diplomatic career! I thought you were a tea merchant!"

"And so I am, lovely Faith. And I've enjoyed it very much. But it's time to start anew. Sharj needs me."

"I told you she was a general," says Eidor, appearing at my elbow.

"True, but I never imagined ... well, anyway, congratulations. I know how much you love Sharj. When does your new posting begin?"

"It will be a little while yet," Lipop says, patting my arm. "I will return to Sharj briefly for an orientation before I report to my shiny new office on the GC enviro. I must also take care of other details beforehand, to ensure the tea shop is well-run and my other obligations addressed."

She leans in closer and whispers into my ear, "My speech tonight was for you. Think about everything I said." With a wink, she slips by me and into the kitchen. Only a few moments later, she's back in the sitting room, passing platters of finger foods and fruit to everyone.

"That was unexpected," Arden says, sitting back with a dazed expression.

"Completely," I say, accepting a tiny sandwich from Lipop's tray as it comes to me, "I should be used to this kind of thing by now, though. Everything here is a surprise."

The rest of the night passes in a blur. A few important details are covered: Nico gives me the address of the lab he's secured for us and imprints the necessary access credentials into my and Arden's wrist chips; Yeva and I talk about our test plans and where to start. Mostly, however, it's a pleasant low-stress gathering of people I know and trust, with a sprinkling of new friends in the mix. As Arden and I return to our quarters, some of Lipop's speech trickles through my awareness and I wonder if there's another hidden message in it. I don't have a chance to process more before exhaustion takes over and I fall deeply asleep in Arden's arms.

I WAKE UP EARLY and head for the lab, before anyone else in our house is astir. The artificial "morning" in Residential 16 is pretty and soft, a transparent yellow veil of light that's inherently encouraging. I would have enjoyed a long walk in this pretty light, but it's only a short stroll to the Local tube station serving Residential 16.

A handful of others are also on their way out this morning, but they're all going in the other direction, toward the heart of the Station and the Carnival. More than one gives me a strange look when I diverge from them to press the call button and wait on the opposite platform.

The tube car arrives—there's no one else aboard. I fight back my trepidation and board the empty conveyance, choosing the seat nearest the door. Within a few minutes of its departure, the Local passes Residential 18, the last residential section on this part of the Station. Then it continues on briefly before the sidewalk-level track dives into a tunnel and travels beneath a massive set of blast doors.

It's an entirely different world on the other side.

The pedestrian-scale comfort of Residential is replaced by towering sleek façades, dimly lit by bands of neon blue or green or gold, that soar hundreds of feet up into darkness. No artificial sunlight streams down on this section. It's chillier, too, although still temperature controlled. When the Local stops at its final endpoint, the signage simply says "Research." No other people are on the platform itself; those that I spot in the distance move with purpose, hurrying along individually lit paths in the walkways between the façades. The vibe is crushingly dark.

The door slides open and I step out onto a hard metal grid covered with some kind of anti-slip coating. An automated security checkpoint waits ahead. After an iris scan and credential review, a green light blinks and the checkpoint's double gates swing open. A flat-toned automated voice says, "Please follow the lighted pathway to your destination. Deviation from the path is not permitted in this section." One of Nico's fearsome spider robots, compacted into its cubelike resting state, sits beside the gate, training its single eye on me. I take a deep breath to steady my nerves as I pass it, then step onto the designated green path that runs from the station deep into the collection of featureless structures.

My path winds through the section for some time, and at last turns through a door, where I find another checkpoint and accompanying killer robot. This Defender, more alert than the first, extends itself up on its single foot to get a better look at me as I attempt to stand still for the iris scan. These things make me wildly anxious, despite knowing I have full permission to be where I am; my arm trembles as I wave my imprinted wrist over the credential scanner. It takes a couple of passes for the scanner to get a good read. But eventually it's satisfied and the gate blocking my entrance swings open.

"Hi," I say to the one-eyed white box. It clicks at me in response, and extends itself up a fraction higher.

"Please follow the lighted pathway to your destination," the checkpoint insists.

"I'm going, I'm going," I respond, hoping the sound of my own voice will help me calm down a little. I look over my shoulder as I move down the character-free hallway indicated by the glowing path. The robot has sunk to the floor again but is still keeping its eye on me.

At the end of the hallway, the lighted path points me into a lift tube. I step inside. There are no killer robots in the small space, fortunately, although I do have to provide my credentials again. The door slides shut once they're accepted. The lift aggressively shoots upward, and continues traveling for some time.

When it stops and I pass yet another iris scan, I step out into a passage so long I can't see its end. The walls are some kind of industrial slate-gray plexi I've not seen before; the floor is more of the antislip metal grid. Doors are positioned in the walls every few hundred feet. The ceiling above me is clear; I look up at a disorienting view of pure black space and stars. This structure must be hundreds, if not thousands, of feet beyond the primary body of the Station, jutting out into space like an unwanted appendage. I don't want to imagine the projects going on behind each of these doors that require this level of separation from populated areas. And I don't understand why Yeva insisted on this level of safety protocol for us. I'm worried she may know something about these chemicals and their properties that she didn't bother to share.

I pull up my holo and try to ping her. The connection is spotty; there's no response.

My pathlight directs me to one of the nondescript doorways. My wrist credentials open the door, and I step into a large intensely white room, configured into one of the best-equipped testing labs I've ever seen—even Yeva's lab on Dar Shal' O pales in comparison. The floor is covered in a bright white material that's firm yet cushions my steps as I walk inside. A dozen lights, customizable for direction and color temperature, dot the high ceiling. The air in the room is cool and aggressively fresh, suggesting powerful filtration and humidity control. It makes the inside of my nose sting a little, and reminds me of the High Mountainous Zones on Home World.

The center of the room is taken up by a cube, higher and wider than I am tall. It's crystal-clear, made of some kind of heavy-duty plexi material—when I tap on it with my knuckle the resulting sound is a flat dull thud. Despite this, it offers an amazingly undistorted view of the two large trays of sand that sit on hefty racks inside.

Sterile pass-through bays are built into two sides of the cube, just large enough for vials and tools to slide in. Above them, two sets of orange animatronic hands rest against the cube's ceiling, waiting to be deployed. The controls for those hands are white haptic gloves, hung over the lab bench that runs along the back of the room. They're wireless, which means I'm free to stand close to the cube wall to observe the tests, or take a seat at one of half-a-dozen monitors to watch from a distance. The monitors also display chemical changes in the sand or the environment around it, using an integrated sensor system built into the cube itself.

The lab bench holds our test solutions. A quick check shows that, true to his word, Nico's procured the entire list. On the opposite end of the bench from the rack of labeled vials sits an additional sterilizer for tools and standard safety gear that includes fire retardant, respirators, and a conspicuous panic button. A UV Disinfection station is built into one corner.

As impressive as it all is, my favorite feature of the lab is going to be the rather ordinary high-res streamer built into the ceiling above the cube.

"Xeric, assist me," I say. The concierge appears at my side.

"You certainly took your time getting around to me," he says with an air of disdain. "Am I only your work buddy now?"

I'm probably blushing. "I had some things to take care of first."

"Right." Xeric snorts, making air quotes with their fingers. "Things. Like scruffy lying ex kinds of things?"

"Stop. He's trying to lie less ... and he's not my ex anymore. He wasn't ever, really—that was just for show."

"I knew it."

"You did *not*. No one knew except us."

"I suspected it, then. But enough of this self-deception."

"Xeric," I say, my tone half laughing, half scolding, "I'm happy to see you. Don't make me *un*happy to see you."

"I. Would. Never." He offers up a most fetching smile. "Now. What would you like me to do?"

"Take a second to familiarize yourself with everything here and queue up our test plans. We have a lot of ground to cover, and I want to do it in the most efficient way possible. I'm sure Yeva will have an opinion once she arrives, so account for any of her specific preferences as you consider our work today. I'll complete the standard lab prep while you're sorting that out."

Xeric nods and his eyelids half-close as he begins surveying the lab—the AI's "vision" is keyed through the streamer, so he already has a top-down view of the entire room and doesn't need to physically move. I sanitize my hands under the UV light, then break out the antistatic wipes to make sure the tools are good to go, then pop them into the sterilizer for the final decontamination step.

Xeric completes the review, and I finish the lab prep, but there's still no sign of Yeva.

"Where is she? Can you locate her?" I ask. "Arden and Yeva were supposed to come together; she was going to drop by Lipop's and collect him."

"They're probably on the way," Xeric says. "Her status indicator reads in transit."

"Arden's too. They'll be here any minute. I'm going to start."

With Yeva yet to arrive, I'm free to begin with my personal project, testing the impact of Fluoroclean on the sand. I don't anticipate anything dramatic, and the process I've outlined is so simple it barely qualifies as testing at all. It should be good practice for me while I get used to the touch and feel of the haptic gloves and their animatronic counterparts.

I place vials of the Fluoroclean and Trichlor into the pass-through chamber, along with pipettes, a set of tongs, and a spatula. I pull on the white gloves and wiggle my fingers; inside the cube, one pair of animatronic hands floats down slightly from its initial position, its fingers wiggling in response. I dip my hand down to the pass-through in order to remove the tools and vials; the animatronics react very nearly in real time, and the haptic signals sent back to my gloves are so precise it's astonishing. I can feel the cool metal of the tongs on my fingers as the orange right hand picks them up, and the slight resistance against my palm as it pushes them into the tray of sand at my direction. The gloves are so finely tuned that they're significantly less cumbersome to work with than I anticipated. After just a few minutes adding vials, lifting and moving things around inside the cube, and testing out the different views for clarity, I'm ready to begin.

Xeric and I review the test plan one more time, then I take a deep breath and face the cube.

"Here we go," I murmur, and begin pantomiming the intended hand movements with my gloves.

The orange animatronic lifts and uncaps a vial of Fluoroclean, then drizzles a thin line across one segment of the sand. As I expected, there's no real impact other than leaving a faint wet trail across the surface.

I pick up a vial of Trichlor and follow the same process. The result is much the same; like the Fluoroclean, the Trichlor leaves a thin damp line with no other recordable reaction. The only difference is the staying power of the solvent; it's just a bit thicker, and sits on top of the sand longer.

I drizzle a line of Fluoroclean one way, and then cross it with a line of Trichlor. An interesting color change occurs that makes the combined fluid look shimmery and silver for a moment, but then that dissipates, leaving a slightly larger wet mark in the test bed.

I'm so disappointed. I had counted on some kind of response, even if it wasn't flashy.

"I must be doing something wrong," I mutter to myself. I've completely forgotten that Xeric is in the room, and startle for an instant when they answer me aloud.

"Perhaps it's related to quantity," he suggests. "It's possible it requires much more than a drizzle to create the effect."

I sigh. "I know, and that's likely true," I say, "but I'm no chemist and I'm not sure about moving further into this without Yeva."

"Caution is good, but I just want to remind you that we didn't find any counterindications for combining significant quantities of Fluoroclean and Trichlor in the scientific literature," Xeric says.

"That's because we didn't find anything about it *at all*—it isn't something people have no reason to do," I counter. "But the absence of testing doesn't correlate with the absence of a potentially risky reaction."

Xeric tilts his head, conceding my point.

At the same time, these substances are largely benign. I'm in the safest testing environment anyone has ever been in, and I hate being at a standstill.

Where the hell is Yeva?

I relocate to the monitor closest to the panic button and nod to Xeric.

"All right then, here we go."

I use the tongs to create a little well in the sand, then measure out the remainder of the Trichlor into it. Then I steadily pour a stream of Fluoroclean into the center of the pool of Trichlor and hold my breath. Just as before, there's a change in color, clarity and viscosity, but the effect is temporary. Afterwards, nothing. I check every sensor read-out to verify. The combination has done nothing to the sand or the surrounding atmosphere.

I'm simultaneously relieved and frustrated.

"So that's a bust," I say, trying not to sound defeated.

Xeric's facial expression softens into empathy. "This is a success," he says. "You've checked something off your list. That's progress, right?"

"I suppose." I pull off the haptic gloves and place them on the lab bench. Their orange animatronic counterparts retreat back to the corner of the cube's ceiling. "I feel like I'm just kind of playing in the sand, though. We need to get some real work done."

That's it for the benign chemistry; the other chemicals in our test plans are more hazardous. I was hoping someone else would be here when we started this.

"Any sign of Yeva or Arden?" I ask.

Xeric checks the tracking mechanisms.

"Both are still reading as 'in transit,' but I can't pinpoint the location of either one. The heavy shielding in this sector must be causing interference."

"Should we wait for them? Not that you're not helpful, but if someone needs to drag me away from a disintegrating safety cube, you're not the guy for that job."

"Incorporeality is a real bummer sometimes," he says, absently passing one hand back and forth through the lab bench. "I'm very good at calling for help, however."

"Help that's going to get here in time to keep my face from burning off?" I ask. "We're stashed in the furthest reaches of the largest space station in any sector. It's not like Lipop can just run in from the kitchen."

"What if I promise to shout, 'don't do that, you'll burn your face off' before you do something stupid?"

"That feels like the least you should do," I mutter, scowling. Xeric's sense of the ironic is beginning to wear on me. I'm frustrated, I want to get these experiments underway, and it's annoying—but also, in a way, predictable—that Yeva and Arden are running late.

"If I may?" Xeric asks, still amusing himself by passing his hands through the lab table in a rhythmic motion.

"Of course."

"Yeva told you that you were going to perform some of these experiments. Maybe this is her way of testing you, to see if you'll go ahead and actually do it on your own."

"Huh." I don't like the idea, but it certainly sounds like something she would do. "What's Arden's excuse then?"

"He's a scruffy liar. It's in his nature to be unreliable."

"No, no, not the case. As I mentioned earlier. He's not a scruffy liar; he's simply cosplaying one."

"If you say so."

"I do. But I admit that what you said about Yeva has the ring of truth to it. Was she particularly interested in any specific chemical on that list?"

"Checking my notes ... ah, yes. We discussed this one also. She's very suspicious of Isoflare. Her annotation reads 'kills flies by blowing up the whole house.' Sounds delightful."

"But Isoflare is ultra-corrosive, right? I thought nothing could hold it for longer than a few minutes."

"That's true about the active version, but it can be somewhat stabilized with the addition of other ingredients—that's what we have to work with here. And really, it makes sense that, if this is the chemical they're using, they'll be using it in its stabilized form. It couldn't be delivered to a target via drone otherwise. Even stabilized Isoflare is still quite dangerous—it can burn your skin or eat through a container that isn't coated with a proper anticorrosive. But it requires the addition of a chemical activator to regain its full destructive properties."

"And what's the activator?"

"We don't know. Yeva's hoping to discover it among the other chemicals purchased through the Thorn Industries program."

I let out a sigh. *Great, I'm going to burn my face off for sure.* But we need answers sooner rather than later, and I need to press on, with or without Yeva.

"Did she propose any tests for Isoflare in combination with Fluoroclean or Trichlor, something simple so I can build off what I've already started?" I ask. "Since they ordered so much, maybe one of those is the activator."

"I have test plans for it in combination with both. Give me a second while I verify the overall face-burning-off potential of this ... ah, very good, Isoflare won't burn off your face as long as you don't get your face too near it. A minimum distance of 60 meters is recommended."

"Fantastic to hear," I snipe. I take the vial of Isoflare from the rack on the lab bench and delicately place it into the cube's passthrough chamber, along with a fresh set of tools. After sending them into the cube, I pull the haptic gloves on again and resume my position next to the panic button. I flex my fingers, and send the orange animatronic hands floating down to the pass-through to retrieve the vial and settle it into the rack inside the cube, as far away from the vials of Fluoroclean and Trichlor as possible.

At my request, Xeric reads the steps of the test aloud and I follow them to the best of my ability. I uncap a fresh vial of Fluoroclean first, then open the Isoflare. I'm surprised to see nothing horrific inside—just a thin, milky liquid swirling harmlessly in its lined container. In fact, it looks at lot like Fluoroclean. If you didn't know what you were looking at, you could easily mistake one for the other.

I manipulate the tongs and move the Isoflare vial over the testbed. I'm a little anxious as I combine it with sand to first test its impact alone; Xeric helpfully reminds me that the stabilized product is likely to do very little, and most likely to do nothing at all. As anticipated, the first exposure of Iona's sand to the stabilized solution creates no reaction whatsoever.

I remind myself to breathe, and move on to the second step, adding Isoflare along the line of sand still damp with Trichlor. Again, there's no reaction. According to Yeva's notes, this is also an expected result—she felt confident that Trichlor alone was not an activating agent. A repeat of the same test combining Isoflare and Fluoroclean yields the same results.

I move on to the next experiment. For this test, I'll add a measured amount of Isoflare to a small amount of Fluoroclean, and then repeat the process with Trichlor. This is the moment we expect to see something happen, even with these small amounts; nothing dramatic, just enough of a reaction to suggest we've found the activator.

I measure out the amount of Isoflare Yeva specified into a fresh anticorrosive vial. I place it back in the rack while I measure out Trichlor and Fluoroclean in two separate containers.

"Starting with the Fluoroclean and Isoflare," I say, and Xeric gives me a thumbs-up.

I use two pair of tongs to lift the vials simultaneously; I take an extra deep breath and try to keep my hands from shaking.

"Ready?" I ask, as I move the vials closer together.

"Ready. Recording the process and have Emergency Services queued up if necessary."

"Here we go." I hold the Isoflare with the left animatronic hand, low and close to the sand. With the right, I gently shift the vial of Fluoroclean until it's in line with and slightly above the vial of Isoflare. Slowly, I tip the edge of the vial down, holding my breath as the liquid comes closer and closer to the lip of the container.

Suddenly, the lab door chimes and flies open. Arden, shouting my name, runs into the room. Alarmed, I look up, and lose my grip on the vials. Both fall to the sand, spilling their contents randomly across it.

"Shit!" I yell. "Arden, what the hell?" I drop the tongs and pull off the control gloves.

"Are you all right? You were here the whole time?" His eyes are wide. Something is not okay.

"Yes, I've been here since early morning. You were asleep when I left. What's going on?"

"They got Yeva," he says. "When I woke up and couldn't find you, I thought they'd taken you too. I tried to ping you, but I couldn't get through."

A ripple of shock runs through my body.

"When did this happen?" I ask. "Are you sure?"

"Yes, Nico's confirmed it. She didn't go home after she left Lipop's last night. Instead, she went to the Carnival, tracked down some vendor, and started a fight."

"Started a fight?" I echo, astonished. I punch my fists into the air. "Like ... that kind of fight?"

"That kind of fight. The vendor called the Station Peacekeepers, and once they realized who she was, the Peacekeepers contacted the Governing Council. She was picked up by GC's security team this morning and taken to the enviro."

My face crumples. She kept saying she was going to do something like this; I thought she had to be joking. Especially after last night. Lipop's words echo in my memory: *You don't just magically have sovereignty; you have to create it. You must take action now.* Yeva certainly has taken that to heart, but what could the point of this action be? And why now, when we have so much still to do?

"How can we intervene?" I ask. "We have to get her back to complete the testing."

"Everything's locked up tight on the enviro, no visitors and no communication with detainees. Honestly, though, I don't think she wants us to intervene. This seemed to be her plan all along."

My shoulders slump. He's right, of course. It's part of Yeva's plan, the inner workings and purpose of which she hasn't shared.

I turn to Xeric. "Can you communicate with her at all?"

Xeric's eyelids close for a few seconds, fluttering as they explore.

"The connection is still there, but as Arden said, the enviro has filters on incoming communication. She can reach me through her embedded chipset, but she'll have to initiate. I can't initiate communication with her directly."

"Crap. What are we going to do?"

"Look," Arden says, "I was alarmed when I thought they might have taken you too, but I'm not worried about Yeva. She did this deliberately. We don't have to understand why; it might not have anything to do with saving Iona. She left you with everything you need to carry out at least some of this research, didn't she? That's going to be the evidence that makes sure no corporate entity, no matter who's behind it, ever touches Iona again. Create sovereignty, remember?"

"I know," I say, looking back at my ruined experiment inside the cube. I pull on the gloves again and use the tongs to fish the Isoflare vial out of the spilled mixture and set it upright in the sand. "But I wish she had ... oh no, oh that's not good ..."

Arden peers through the plexi too, and his face goes even more ashen than it was when he ran into the room.

"Shit," he murmurs "Is that supposed to happen?"

A trickle of vapor rises, not from the sand where the spilled Isoflare has mixed with the puddle of Fluoroclean, but from the end of the tongs I dropped into it. The container I prepared to hold the mixed chemistry also lies in a spatter of Isoflare, its sides and bottom disintegrated and steaming. A tiny rivulet of the spilled fluid has followed a declining channel in the sand to the edge of the isolator box and is now steadily dissolving the first layer of its protective interior coating.

"Xeric, get HazMat here right away," I say, forcing myself to be calm.

"On it," Xeric confirms. "Sending real time imagery and pertinent information."

I'm racking my brain for something we can do to contain this until HazMat arrives. My mind goes back to how Fallon used Iona's sand to neutralize Blue. The sand has no special properties against these agents that I'm aware of, but at least it appears to be unaffected by the chemistry. I grab another pair of tongs and a wide spatula and shove them into the passthrough chamber.

"Help out," I say to Arden. "Grab the other set of gloves."

He hurries to my side and pulls on the second pair of haptic gloves. It takes a few seconds as the additional animatronic hands come online and respond to his movements. Inside the cube, I push a fresh set of tongs to him, then take the spatula and start manipulating the sand.

"Create dams of sand wherever there's a change in elevation that could take the Isoflare toward the container's sides. The goal is to keep it to the middle. Be careful; don't let the tongs touch the chemistry. I'm going to cover up and mark every point I can find where the chemicals have pooled," I explain. Arden nods and starts moving sand with the back of the tongs.

This won't neutralize the chemistry, but it should give HazMat time to figure out how to counteract and remove it. The mixed fluid's viscosity is keeping it on the surface for now, but given enough time, it could potentially sink through. It's not a chance we can take.

The HazMat team arrives, fully suited and carrying an array of containers and neutralizing agents. They quiz me extensively about the nature of the chemicals in the test. I tell them everything I know, but it only generates more confusion. A tiny flexi tab pressed into the sand where the fluids have mixed comes out whole and clean; the tongs used to manipulate it come away missing their tips. Before long, the thumb and first finger on my animatronic right hand starts to smoke, bits of the grippy covering dissolving and flaking away as we watch.

"Is it possible some kind of contaminant is causing this reaction?" asks the team lead, a compact, sharp-faced woman whose displayed credentials identify her as M. Brekke.

"No, nothing. This was set up according to specific parameters, and isolated until we arrived to begin work. I've been following core lab protocol at every step."

"What about the tools? Could they have been improperly sterilized?"

"No, everything is freshly sterilized. Even if that weren't the case, it wouldn't explain the impact on the animatronics."

An animatronic index finger drops to the sand with a confirming plop, eaten away from its base. It continues to disintegrate in the tray.

"Are the tools or the other features made of *anything* that would naturally corrode in this instance?"

"No. Yeva was quite clear when she sent in the specs for this lab. Everything is designed to the highest safety protocol, specifically for use with highly corrosive agents, from the tools to the animatronics. They all have bases made from non-sparking durable alloys coated with ..."

I fall silent as the realization hits me. My stomach drops and I feel an almost overwhelming sense of vertigo.

"Coated with what? Ms. Feathergrass?" Brekke's voice sounds as if she's talking to me through a tunnel from far away.

I see it now. The real culprit isn't the most dangerous and abrasive of chemicals, the things we feared were designed to eat away Iona's sand. It's something much more ordinary, something most people would never suspect. And the purpose ... well, that's even worse than we anticipated.

I manage to push the words out of my mouth, which has become almost impossibly dry.

"Durawash. The tongs, the container, the base mat, the grippers ... everything's coated with Durawash. That's it. That has to be the activator."

I look around the room. Arden's expression is perplexed, Xeric's is a grimace. As for me ... part of me wants to be jubilant, because it feels like I've discovered the combination that KaheleTech plans to deploy against Iona, and we understand what we're up against. But I hear Xeric, back in our lab on Dar Shal'o, calling Durawash the most common anticorrosive in the sector, used on everything, from tools to building materials. I know for a fact that it's on nearly every structure on Iona in one form or another—it's even in our clothing. Based on what I see here, contact alone is all that's necessary for activation. That means a cloud of 120 drones, launched from anywhere, could soon dump full loads of Isoflare on Iona. The result will be the destruction of almost everything that's *not* sand.

The HazMat Team does a quick evaluation of our test plans and research notes. My sand blocks are working for now, and they seem concerned but not terribly alarmed. They keep working with Xeric to contain and neutralize the Isoflare, but shoo Arden and me out of the lab while they complete the process. Once they finish their work, everything will have to be scrubbed, sterilized, and recertified. We'll have no usable facility for at least a few days.

With our lab access temporarily revoked, we're required to leave the Research sector. A flashing yellow line of light directs us through the dark maze of buildings and pathways back to the transportation platform. Although a few people wait to go back to what I can only think of as 'civilization,' it's still surprisingly sparse.

"How are there so many structures in this section and yet so few people?" I wonder aloud.

"A security thing?" Arden suggests. We stand on the platform with only four other people, waiting for the Local back to Residential.. "Lab access times could be staggered, maybe to keep the identities of who is working on what more private."

"Or a safety thing? It might not be a good idea to have everyone working on their all-material-eating explosive drone contents at the same time. One thing going wrong could become a catastrophe."

"Did you notice the section we were in has its own separation module?" Arden asks. "In the event of a serious mishap, the entire segment can be sealed off and jettisoned into space, away from the station."

"I did not notice that. I'm quite pleased that I didn't notice that, in fact," I say, wincing. *Possibility of being jettisoned into space* was not on my test safety protocol prep list. I'm certain I would not have felt more secure if it had been.

"It would have to be an extremely serious incident, though," Arden continues. "What happened in our lab barely caused a ripple of concern."

"Yeah. I was alarmed, but HazMat seemed fairly calm."

"Corrosive chemicals corrode," he says with a shrug. "It's good that you got them involved, though. It wouldn't take much for that to shift from a minor issue to a major problem."

He's right, of course. The fact that they've kept Xeric on hand is proof that this wasn't routine. Isoflare is still a dangerous chemical. Worse still, I'm convinced it will be deployed against my home soon. With Durawash on everything from our structures to our sheets, what will be left of Iona? How many people will wind up injured or dead in the process?

I'm brought out of my doom cycle by the soft whoosh of the transport arriving at the platform. We ride back to Residential in silence, both of us pensive, with dull eyes and mouths turned down, drawn into ourselves. I don't doubt we're thinking about the same thing: what's about to happen to Iona, and what we can do—what *anyone* can do—to stop it.

When we arrive again in the more normal environment of Residential 16, it's apparently mid-afternoon, if the lighting can be trusted. In stark contrast to the dark isolation of Research, golden light colors everything and people are everywhere, out and about on their daily routines. There's no one home at our temporary address, but Eidor has left a message inviting us to dinner later.

Now that we're back in normal reception range, missed pings start piling up on our holos. Arden has half a dozen from Graham; I hope at least one of them will contain some news of Yeva. He goes to our comm room to respond. I have a report from Xeric that the HazMat removal has been successfully completed, and he's been released back into our service. There's also a message from a somewhat puzzled Lt. Nam, saying he's received a thing called a Golden Key Upgrade and asking what he should do about it.

I send him reassurance and forward his message to Nico, just in case.

"Xeric, assist me," I say, and the AI appears. I'm not sure if I'm imagining it or if Xeric's design is that nuanced, but he looks a bit stressed. His usual glittery complexion seems less shiny; subtle shadows circle his eyes.

"What a morning," Xeric says. "If I got tired, I'd be exhausted. How are you holding up?"

"I'm okay. Worried. Trying to come up with a plan."

"Understandable. How can I help?"

"Have you heard from Yeva? She's still on the GC enviro, right? They haven't sent her back to Dar Shal'O?"

"She's there; her status is online, but I'm still unable to initiate contact and she hasn't tried to contact me. If they follow standard protocol, she'll have a disciplinary hearing before anything else happens."

"Are these things public? Maybe if we make a case for her trying to help us, we can get her off the hook?" I'm grasping at straws and I know it, but still ...

"Disciplinary hearings are private, between the GC's representative and the individual," Xeric confirms. "If the GC thought they could get some kind of political capital out of it, they might make it public, but I can't see that happening. Yeva has a lot of incriminating knowledge that she wouldn't be afraid to publicize, given a forum."

Disappointment seeps into my spirit. I'd hoped that *was* Yeva's plan—to get into a public hearing and expose the Governing Council's involvement with the *Heretic* before the group of survivors appeared to give their testimony. But Xeric's right. It's more likely that the GC would want to keep her out of the public eye. Giving her any kind of public platform would be nothing but trouble for them.

"Anything new happening with KaheleTech or Cadence?"

Xeric's eyelids flutter as he accesses the data.

"No, nothing has changed. We know I can't see everything, though, so make sure to follow up with Graham."

"I will. Update us right away if anything suspicious happens. Thank you, I'm done."

"Before I go ..." Xeric's usual sardonic expression has softened, although there's still a quirk to his mouth.

"Yes?"

"You did well today, both of you. If Iona makes it through this, it will be because of you."

If Iona makes it through this ... the words pinch at my heart. I can't carry this right now, so I deflect.

"Did you just give my scruffy lying ex-ex a compliment?" I ask.

"I suppose. My opinion may have been shifted somewhat by his obvious concern for you. He's still far too scruffy, though. Hopefully he cleans up well."

I smile, despite myself. "He does. I've seen it."

"In that case, carry on." Xeric offers up a wan smile in return and fades away.

If Iona makes it through this ...

With those bitter words in my head, I join Arden in the comm room. Graham's face floats above the streamer. His jaw is tight and a sharp pair of parallel lines mark his forehead as his brows pull down hard in frustration.

"You're sure that's what's going on?" he's asking, rubbing his chin reflexively.

"Faith's sure, and I think she's right," Arden says.

"I'm here," I say, joining Arden in front of the streamer's camera. "You're talking about the Isoflare, right?"

"Right," Graham responds. "You mentioned a stabilized version of Isoflare, but that's not what they're getting through the Thorn Industries program."

"You're selling them active Isoflare?" I frown. "How is it even getting to them? Home World is a long way from KaheleTech's headquarters." Given what I've learned about Isoflare, the active version would eat through its container long before it managed to leave the sector.

"The short answer is that we're not," Graham explains. "Isoflare isn't in our product catalog, so we act as a mediary between KaheleTech and a third-party seller. The deal we brokered for them was for active Isoflare."

"They must be stabilizing it on their own. That means they have a lab somewhere close to the seller," I muse.

"How hard is it to stabilize Isoflare? What elements are used?" Arden asks.

I blink in surprise at my own stupidity. "I ... I don't know."

What a ridiculous oversight. That could make all our results pointless, if the stabilizer itself has some kind of interaction with Durawash that's perhaps problematic but less lethal than full-on active Isoflare.

"It should be easy to find out," Arden says. "Who obtained the chemistry for us?"

"Nico. I'll ask him."

I'm a little surprised to find Nico's status set to offline, but I craft a quick message and send it anyway. When there's no change in his status and no response even though I can see the message has gone through, I change tactics and call up Xeric.

Xeric appears at my elbow. When he sees Graham, he raises an eyebrow and favors him with a hard scowl, then turns away from the camera. "What can I help *you* with?" Xeric asks me, looking over his shoulder to glare at Graham one more time.

"What chemicals were used to stabilize the Isoflare we tested this morning and whether they might independently react with Durawash?" I ask.

Xeric's eyes close for a fraction of a second. "Unclear. There are half a dozen possible stabilizers that could be used with that particular solution. Overall, however, while some of those elements could be reactive with Durawash under very specific circumstances, none of those conditions were present in the lab today, and those conditions are not present on Iona at any time."

"So, the results this morning are still valid. Durawash is the activator; it's not some interaction with one of the stabilizers, correct?"

"Yes. Nico will know the particulars, as far as this formulation is concerned. But we clearly saw it react with Durawash the way I'd expect active Isoflare, even a dilute version, to behave."

"Send the list of possible stabilizers to all of us," I say. "We need to keep an eye out for which ones they might buy in tandem with this order of Isoflare."

As the list hits our holos, Graham clears his throat.

"About that ..."

I look up, suddenly sensing something overhead about to drop.

"I instructed our fulfillment department to delay processing KaheleTech's Isoflare order, but my father got wind of it and was less than delighted," he says.

"As a result, the order is moving forward and what we have is all the information we're going to get. This is the last screenshot I was able to grab before ..."

"Wait, what?"

"I'm so sorry," Graham says. "I have some other contacts in Research who are more circumspect and I'm trying to find another way to ..."

I interrupt his apology. I'm staring at the records he's put up for view.

"Is that where it was shipped?" I point to the line that has my attention.

Graham blinks, confused for a second, before pulling the invoice dupe back onto his holo to check. "To those general coordinates, yes. All the materials they've ordered from us were shipped to the same location."

"That's not where KaheleTech's publicly visible purchases have gone. They're sending this stuff somewhere else."

I use my holo to do a quick calculation and press my lips together as the answer comes clear.

"These are coordinates for open space near Bardazel," I say. "It's probably an enviro. They might be using it as the mixing lab, or it might be a receiving point for something on the surface. I'm willing to bet the drones the consortium purchased have been forwarded to the same location."

"Bardazel?" Graham's eyebrows knit down. "No one has permission to be doing anything on its surface or in its controlled space. And that doesn't make sense for a shipment of active Isoflare—Strategic Protection Solution's warehouse is weeks away, at minimum. That would be just as foolish as trying to ship it from Home World."

Arden turns to me with a puzzled look. "Strategic Protection Solutions ... why is that name familiar?"

Xeric's clears his throat, his expression changing to a smirk.

"Strategic Protection Solutions has a satellite location here on Meridian Station, and a warehouse enviro just outside of Station-controlled space," he says, a tinge of pride in his voice. "The name is familiar to you because a dear friend of ours got into trouble for punching out the proprietor last night."

Arden and I exchange looks.

"Yeva knew something," I say in almost a whisper. "Something she didn't tell any of us."

Xeric isn't done, however. "In my approved Station entity form, I have access to certain information my Dar Shal'O form does not, namely all the Station vendors' transaction records. I can confirm a shipment of active Isoflare is scheduled to leave their warehouse shortly, with guaranteed delivery in twenty-four solar hours," he says.

"Twenty-four solar hours!" I exclaim, my stomach dropping into my toes. "If that's all the time we've got, we're already too late."

"That's not true," Xeric says, struggling to balance an interest in keeping me calm with an inclination to show off what he knows. "Think of it this way. The Isoflare will arrive at those coordinates in twenty-four solar hours, of course. But it needs to be offloaded and then stabilized. With a chemical like Isoflare, those are delicate processes that can't be rushed. If your theory's correct, it still has to be loaded into the drones, and the drones themselves transported to Iona somehow—they aren't space-rated, so they can't fly there on their own, they'll need to be deployed in the atmosphere. Realistically, you have more time."

"I need a number," I say, more sharply than I mean to. "Can you give us a specific estimate for the lower end?"

"With the caveat that there are still many unknowns, my calculations suggest a minimum of sixty solar hours from its arrival at its destination to potential use on Iona. Even so, that's an incredibly aggressive estimate and highly, highly unlikely; they'd have to be working around the clock to meet that kind of timeline. But you can consider it your baseline."

Graham, who has been visibly agitated for the last few minutes, interrupts.

"I have to address some things. We'll reconnect later," he says, and abruptly signs off, leaving only the Thorn Industries logo floating in front of us.

"That's not suspicious," Arden mutters, side-eyeing the white and gray logo. "He's got something up his sleeve."

"Just leave it, Arden. We have to figure out how we're going to keep this from happening, and we don't have a lot of time."

Arden sighs, but sees the sense in what I'm saying and lets it drop. Together, we spin out different scenarios, each with its own set of challenges. We could try to warn our friends on Iona, but what could they actually do about the impending threat? Plus, Iona's communications channels are likely monitored, so there's no guarantee any message we tried to send would get through. I could fly to Bardazel ahead of the delivery and interrupt the chemical processing, but that would require leaving immediately and I'd have no idea what I was heading into or what to do once I arrived. And I don't want to abandon Yeva or Arden and the PEA members who are risking so much to testify on Iona's behalf.

"What makes sense to do, in this moment?" I murmur, as much to myself as to Arden, but before he can respond, Xeric steps between us.

"I have something to s-s-say," the concierge stutters. Something's off about Xeric's demeanor; his voice is higher pitched than usual, his eyes unfocused.

"This isn't a great time, Xeric," Arden says, his annoyance barely contained. "Can it wait?"

"No, it ... cannot .. cannot ... can ... nahhhhhhh ..." Xeric's response is startling. His words are broken and squeezed out, as if he's struggling to speak. He flickers in and out of our presence for an instant, then resolves fully again. But something is horribly wrong.

The virtual concierge is frozen in place, arms rigid at his sides. His eyes suddenly roll back in his head and his mouth at first works as if he's trying to speak, but ultimately it opens wide and stays that way.

"Xeric!" I cry, alarmed. "Are you all right? Xeric!"

I take a step toward him but draw back as sound spills from the AI's mouth—an odd thin hissing noise I've never heard them make before.

"Is that static?" Arden asks, incredulous.

Before I can answer, the sound is replaced by words. But Xeric isn't speaking—his open mouth stays motionless. The words coming out of it are in a woman's voice I don't recognize and sound distant and hollow, like they're coming through a tunnel.

"You never stop, do you? And at your age. It's undignified."

The speaker is interrupted by a loud bark of a laugh, and a much more familiar voice emits from Xeric, saying, "Really, Benta. You should know me by now. Let's dispense with the self-aggrandizing admonitions and get on with this."

It's Yeva. Even Arden recognizes her voice and looks to me, his eyes wide. The other woman must be Benta Sarsen, the Chair of the Governing Council.

"Record this!" I whisper, gesturing to the still-active streamer. Arden punches at the controls and the recording function comes up. He zooms the camera in on Xeric, who is nothing more than an audio streamer himself at this point, a live conversation between two other people playing through his open mouth.

"I suppose you want the usual concessions," Sarsen is saying, her voice taut.

"This time I want something different. I want you to listen to me."

"You're hardly in a position to bargain. If I were you ..."

"I'm in a much better position to bargain than you are, Benta. Your term as Chairman is up soon. It would be terrible if word of how you've been abusing your power here got out before you could make your grand exit."

There's a pause—Sarsen is likely taking measure of Yeva and trying to gauge how much of a threat she might actually be. She then says in a flat voice, "This is a pathetic attempt to frighten me and somehow improve your negotiating position. I'm not going to fall for it. I'm prepared to ensure your punishment is the maximum allowed by law."

Yeva chuckles. I can imagine her sitting back in the chair, legs crossed, posture emphasizing how unaffected she is by Sarsen's threat.

"Of course you are," she says drily. "Let's talk about that, shall we? Let's have a chat about the law. What law permitted you to move 200 residents of Bardazel—and Company employees at that—off that planet to warehouse them here?"

"What was the Company going to do with them? Wake them up and fly everyone home?" Sarsen is emphatic. "Obviously not, given what they knew and who they were. It was clear from the communiques we intercepted what was going to happen. We *rescued* those people. They would still be safe in Long Flight, if not for that Feathergrass woman. I've been wondering how she found them. I should have seen your fingerprints all over that."

"I could ask you the same question. What happened on Bardazel was shocking, but unpublicized outside the sector. And yet, a ship—commissioned by you, configured precisely to carry 250 people in stasis—appeared over Bardazel before they even completed their migration." Yeva's voice takes on a gritty, accusatory tone. "Who's *we*, Benta? It's not the Governing Council you're referring to. You had someone on the ground telling you all the details."

"I had a contact on Bardazel, of course. So did you. So did a lot of entities."

"My contact was in stasis in a box on Iona, thanks to your contact."

"That wasn't my fault. I was only interested in information. The things he did there were on his own."

I gasp. They can only be talking about Kerrit Arduval. Sarsen must have been Arduval's mysterious benefactor. I'm trembling. I lift my gaze to Arden. He's likely having the same thoughts, and his face is etched with alternating anguish and fury. He reaches for my hands and squeezes them hard.

"Maybe not," Yeva counters. "Your partner's fingerprints are all over his initiatives on Iona, and that makes you complicit as well."

"I don't know what you're talking about."

"We know all about your relationship with KaheleTech and Cadence Technologies. And half a dozen other entities, all shadow companies for Breton Cabot-Klaar's little personal side projects."

Sarsen huffs. "It's not illegal for me to have a business relationship with someone *you* happen to dislike. So, if you'll just read over the statement of bond I'm sending to your holo, you'll find ..."

"He's setting you up, Benta. He's been trying to set you up for years. And now, he's very close to succeeding. In fact, you have Faith Feathergrass to thank for your continued tenure here at this point."

Arden looks to me, questioning. I shake my head. This is the first I've heard of this, and I have no idea if this is fact or if Yeva's bluffing.

Either way, it appears to work. Sarsen's tone changes subtly. A hint of a quiver has crept into her voice, as though she may have had the same thought. She tries to sound defiant, but her words have no conviction behind them.

"You're going to need to explain yourself."

"The *Heretic*. Were you aware it was set to launch?"

"Of course. That Feathergrass woman sent it to Iona."

"She only changed the coordinates. It was set to launch into deep space when she got to it. Those people would have gone out into the frozen dark and died there. The ship's atmospheric controls would have run out of power before it ever reached the coordinates."

A longer pause now. "That's not possible," Sarsen says, sounding utterly uncertain.

There's a soft clatter, something small and lightweight dropping onto a hard surface.

"That chip carries a recording made by one of the Station's virtual concierges. It includes proof. Put it into any streamer, you'll see," Yeva says.

"But I never ... I didn't ..." Sarsen sounds confused rather than defensive.

"Of course you didn't. But you were going to take the blame for it once it was discovered. And it would have been discovered, believe me—he'd have made sure of it. That's what he does, you see. He makes sure someone else is always set up to be blamed, so he can do whatever he wants without consequences. You're forgetting I know this firsthand."

I'd always assumed Sarsen and Cabot-Klaar were in a tight working relationship, equal partners with everything to gain by working together. It never occurred to me that she could be an investment for him, a shield to keep the blame from himself.

Sarsen isn't ready to back down, however.

"We have our own records of what happened with the *Heretic;* they tell a different tale," she says, a dismissive sneer creeping into her voice. "This is undoubtedly a fabrication. You're getting desperate in your old age."

"And you're getting stupid in yours. He's talked to people about you, Benta. I know, because I've watched every move he's made since he tried to destroy my reputation and my business. What did he tell you? That you were so important, he'd keep you in the center of the loop if you'd just support his business enterprises, cut him some slack on regulations, and turn a blind eye to a few of his projects? All you did was give him more ammunition. I can't say exactly what he's planning to do to Iona, but I do know who's going to be blamed for it in the end."

"This is ridiculous," Sarsen spits out, "and you have no proof of anything."

"Julien Farouque."

"What?"

"Who, not what. He's the Station vendor I smacked around. I didn't mean to be so hard on him, but he turned out to be a lot more fragile than I was expecting for an arms dealer."

"There are no arms dealers on the Station, that's an insane accusation. That sort of thing is illegal by Governing Council decree."

"Of course it is. Want to explain why his little endeavor just sent enough active Isoflare to melt down an entire planet to an enviro orbiting Bardazel?"

"Now you're lying," Sarsen barks. She sounds more desperate by the second.

"Oh Benta. That's not even half of it. His records show that *you* ordered and paid for it all. That *you've* been placing orders from him for years, for the kind of chemistry that can only have one purpose. And you don't even know who he is."

This time the pause in conversation is longer, and there's a scratching sound, like nervous fingernails against the upholstered arms of a chair.

"What do you want from me?" Sarsen snaps. Her voice has taken on an edge of stress that makes me think Yeva's just hit her mark. "You're wasting my time. I'm not going to entertain any more of your ..."

"It's an offensive weapons program, Benta," Yeva interrupts. Her tone is fierce, serious. "Cabot-Klaar is going all-in on developing large-scale offensive weaponry using Blue. He knows how much money and power he can amass with the right connections. He's been working on this for at least ten years—that's why your predecessor tried to track his activities on Home World. The only thing in his way are the policies of the Governing Council."

Arden's eyes widen.

"Was it him?" I whisper under Yeva's voice. "Was he the person the GC hired you to track? He became your handler on Home World!"

Arden can only shake his head. There's utter shock written on his face.

And Yeva's not done.

"Why did you think he approached you, included you in his business interests, made you a key business partner without you ever lifting a finger, over and over again? You're a career bureaucrat. You have no special business acumen, no fortune to invest, no exceptional knowledge to contribute. His only interest was in manipulating you so that he had an in with the Governing Council, while he created a perfect scapegoat if things went wrong. I'm on your side, Benta. Take that chip, please. Spend some time with it. There's more on it that proves what I'm saying. If you won't let me help you, at least help yourself."

In the following heavy silence, I can envision Yeva leaning forward toward the desk, tapping the edge of the shiny white chip that lies on its surface and pushing it gently forward, while Sarsen stares at it as though it's a venomous snake. I wonder if Yeva's gotten through to her, but then Sarsen speaks and the moment is over.

"This sounds like something you would plan, Yeva," she says, her voice high and tight. "In fact, I think this ruse is designed to trick me into something you can somehow use against me. I wouldn't be surprised if you've found a way to record this conversation. Consider this interview at an end."

"Benta, listen to reason. You know what's going on here," Yeva entreats. "Cabot-Klaar has benefactors and business partners everywhere, across all sectors—dozens of them. Otherwise, the numbers don't make sense. He's been working with them at least as long as he's been working with you. The difference is, they're all carefully hidden. The only name that can be traced back to anything questionable or illegal is yours. It's exactly what he did to me. Don't let him do it to you."

The angry squeal of a heavy chair pushing back hard across a polished floor echoes through the room. Sarsen shouts, "Security!" and a door crashes open. Multiple heavy sets of footsteps come into the room, and the sounds of a scuffle overtake the words, making conversation impossible to hear. Finally, Sarsen shrieks, "Get her out of here! Put her on any ship you can find and send her back to her damn asteroid. I'll deal with her sanction decree later. Just get her out of my sight!"

Yeva snarls, "Don't you fucking touch me, you cretin. I can walk through the door on my own," followed by, "Remember I tried to help you, Benta." The door slams, there's a final loud burst of static, then complete silence.

Xeric's mouth closes slowly. His body slumps, and he topples to the floor in a heap before disappearing completely. My hand flies over my mouth and I blink rapidly, my eyes stinging. I can't guess how much damage this might have done to him. I hope some version of him has survived.

Arden is staring at the floor where the AI collapsed. His eyes are dull, his lips are pressed together into a tight line, somewhere between shock and disbelief.

"Did you know?" I ask again, reaching out and touching his arm. "Did anyone ever tell you he was the person the General Council suspected?"

Arden shakes his head, his expression unchanging. "No. I sent the chip you created that night back to the GC, so they had all the information they'd wanted. Now I'm wondering if they set me up, too."

There's enough subterfuge and double-dealing to implicate everyone involved, whether Sarsen, the General Council, or the Company. In the end, everything ties back to Breton Cabot-Klaar. If Yeva is right, he may have driven Arduval's actions on Iona, and is deep into plans to develop offensive weaponry that will bring him more power and fortune than we can imagine, destroying Iona in the process. We need to figure out who can stop him and hold him accountable, and if the only person who can do that is me, I need to figure out how.

WE BARELY HAVE TIME to process what's happened before the dinner hour at Lipop's. Arden is withdrawn and lost in his thoughts while I'm pensive and increasingly anxious. The burst of energy I felt after my discovery this morning has evaporated, and I'm now completely drained. Meanwhile, my brain is screaming for me to take action and won't stop imagining heroic interventions that none of us are capable of. I try to summon Xeric and am greeted by a 2d image of his face that announces "Your virtual concierge has suffered a critical failure and is undergoing repair. Estimated time to completion is unavailable. Please try again in twelve solar hours, or choose the option below to be assigned a new concierge."

Which only brings to mind Xeric saying, "sixty solar hours."

It's no time at all, and it might be all the time that stands between Iona's survival or ruin.

"How do we explain this to everyone?" I ask as we step into the lift. "I don't even know where to start."

"At least we recorded the conversation between Yeva and Sarsen," Arden says. "I think they'll need to hear that for themselves. The rest we can summarize. Holy stars, did all of this happen today? It feels like weeks have gone by."

It feels like we've entered a different reality, and nothing makes that more apparent than the change in atmosphere when we walk through Lipop's door. After only a single day, things could not be more different. Even though the ViewPort still plays Lipop's favorite Sharj sunset, the lights are turned low and it's almost oppressively quiet. Nico, wearing full civilian garb tonight, sits in one corner of the room talking with Eidor; Graham sits opposite engrossed in his holo. Lipop bustles about in the kitchen. Meanwhile, Yeva's absence is almost palpable.

Arden squeezes my arm gently. "I'm going to check in with Graham; we've got some testimony logistics to iron out. Are you okay?"

"I'm probably more okay than you. Go ahead."

He gives me one last look, his face still crinkled with concern, before he sits down with Graham and begins a quiet conversation, while I join Nico and Eidor. Within seconds, Lipop summons Eidor to the kitchen.

I turn to Nico. "Is she on the way back to Dar Shal'O?" I ask.

His face registers surprise. "Yes," he says. "There were some developments this afternoon. How did you know?"

"We'll get to that; it's a long story. She's all right, though?"

"She's fine. She was happy to be going home, and seemed pleased with herself when she boarded the ship, despite the armed guards. I got a message from her before her departure that said, 'mission accomplished.' I'm not sure what she meant, and the GC shut down my line to her communications almost immediately afterwards, so I didn't have a chance to ask."

Mission accomplished. Our mission to save Iona? Her mission to call out Breton Cabot-Klaar? Some other mission we never heard anything about? It could be any, all, or none of these things, and in typical fashion, it raises more questions than it answers.

Lipop serves dinner, a Sharjeet interpretation of pizza that we eat in the sitting room with our hands. Once we finish the meal and Eidor collects our plates, I catch Arden's eye.

"Ready?" he asks me.

"I have to be," I say.

With Lipop's permission, we take over the room. Dismissing the gentle sounds of the Sharjeet sunset, I play the conversation between Yeva and Sarsen. As it ends, Nico looks both impressed and grim; Graham scowls and dives back into his holo. Arden and I then lay out the events of the morning—what I learned about inactive Isoflare, and its likely activator, the ubiquitous Durawash.

"These weapons program accusations are concerning," Lipop says, squeezing one of her flowered pillows to her chest. "I'll be forwarding this information to my General Director and will take it up with the Council as soon as I'm able. Is what Yeva says true, Faith? Is Iona in danger at this moment?"

"I believe so," I say. "I expect Cabot-Klaar to at least try to take full control of Iona, whether through some kind of Company decree or on his own. If he's heavily invested in a weapons development program working with Blue, he'll have to do something to make sure he controls the sand, along with the antidote development and revival processes."

"How deeply is the Company involved? Is this at their behest?" she asks.

I can't believe it's my own voice when I say, "I don't think the Company is an active partner in this. Cabot-Klaar's an opportunist and he's been working toward this a long time. He doesn't appear to have been connected to the Company's previous attempts at a weapons program, aside from monitoring it through a spy on the ground. Maybe they're not doing everything they could to stop him, but I think this is something he's come to on his own."

"He wasn't part of their last project," Graham says almost absently, still tracking the holo discussion he's been having since we walked in. "We never crossed paths and his name never came up during my time on Bardazel."

It's the first time I've heard Graham admit outside of our private circle that he was the point man for the Company's illegal program, and it brings up a disturbing possibility.

"Graham," I say, as delicately as possible, waiting until he looks up from his holo to continue. "We heard Thorn Industries purchased Bardazel from the Company. Is it possible your family is in some way part of this?"

"They also supplied KaheleTech with all the chemistry they needed for this operation," Arden says, sitting up a little straighter.

I expect an energetic denial, but instead, Graham's face turns somber.

"It's possible," he says, "although my father was more upset that I tried to delay a contractually guaranteed shipment and shared proprietary records than he was about KaheleTech using us to obtain potentially world-devastating chemistry."

His holo chirps. As he peers at it, a self-satisfied smile replaces the grim expression. "Ah, finally. Can I take this on your secure stream?" he asks, looking toward Lipop.

"The room's open," she says. He rises and hurries down the hall.

"So active Isoflare is soon to be on the way to Bardazel or thereabouts, where you expect it to be stabilized enough for drone delivery," Nico muses. "Is there evidence of a bulk purchase of stabilizer? Would they already have it on hand?"

"We don't know which stabilizer they might be using," I say. "We have a list of possibilities that Xeric's tracking, and the ... oh, crap." I turn to Arden, panic bubbling up in my chest. "Xeric was tracking everything for us and now he's ..." I pause, uncertain what the right descriptor should be. Corrupted? Out of order? Dead?

I can't stomach any of them.

"I guess we don't have any tracking right now—not orders, not news, not chemistry," I amend with a sigh. "We need to know when that shipment of Isoflare leaves the warehouse."

"What about paying a visit to this arms dealer, Julien Farouque?" suggests Lipop. "He might be willing to offer some additional information, or possibly delay the shipment."

"After Yeva beat him up? Seems like a long shot," Arden says.

"Perhaps," says Lipop. "I don't know Mr. Farouque, or the exact nature of his disagreement with our friend. But consider that he might be open to ... incentives."

"You mean bribery?" I ask.

"Compensation for inconvenience often *encourages* people to be more cooperative," she responds. I suddenly have a strong sense of how suited she is for the

Governing Council. "It's late now, but I think an early morning visit would be appropriate. Don't you?"

"I guess I'm meeting an arms dealer tomorrow," I say.

We spend a few more hours together. Graham comes up with some meaningful numbers for Farouque's "incentive," and offers to cover the cost through his corporate budget. Nico pulls up all the information he can find on the arms dealer—unsurprisingly, he's kept an extremely low profile during the four years he's been on the Station—but there is a video interview with Station Peacekeepers regarding his assault.

Farouque turns out to be very different from what I envisioned when I heard the words "major arms dealer." Scrawny, pale, short, and of indeterminate age, he sports a white-blond buzz cut along with a fresh fat lip and impressive black eye. The Peacekeepers ask him the usual questions, he responds with short or sometimes single-word answers: no, he doesn't know her; yes, he wants her removed; no, he doesn't need medical attention; no, he doesn't care about restitution. This last point surprises me—he looks for all the worlds like someone who would see this as an opportunity for easy money, and to be fair, Yeva has really worked him over. He's clearly got some loose teeth, and she may have broken his nose. It might be that Farouque already entered the equation with some screws loose; when the Peacekeepers ask him to describe what happened, he inexplicably laughs.

"We was having a conversation and the bitch caught me when I wasn't looking," he chortles. "She's fucking crazy. Great right hook, though." His laugh morphs into a hacking cough; he spits unceremoniously on the floor, wipes his chin, looks around at his interviewers. "We good? I got places to be."

The next morning, Arden offers to accompany me. He's planned to get together with Graham and the Planetary Equity Alliance members to work through testimony strategies and I'll be connecting with them in the afternoon, so I decline. Arden is worried about Farouque's character, but I'm not bothered. After all, meeting a creep in the middle of the Carnival isn't like meeting one in a dark alley.

"I'll be fine. This isn't going to be the first dirtbag I've had to deal with," I say. His eyebrows fly up in surprise, but I wave away his questions. We'll get to those stories another time.

Calm and focused, I depart for the Carnival, although I'm fighting back some anger. This guy is making money—a lot of money—off the prospective destruction of my home. Chances are he doesn't understand that, but it's also likely that he won't care. I hope Lipop is right and his mercenary proclivities outweigh everything else.

In the end, though, it's all for nothing. I arrive at the dingy shopfront for Strategic Protection Solutions to find a yellow electronic barrier blocking the entrance, flashing the message *Closed Indefinitely*, with nothing and no one inside.

I ping the group. Arden expresses both frustration and relief; Graham pledges to keep trying to find a way around his father's restrictions so we can at least understand when the Isoflare shipment departs the warehouse. Lipop sympathizes with my disappointment and naturally suggests some tea. I decide to take her up on the offer, and find my way to the tea shop.

It's comfortably cozy in the shop, softly lit and fragrant with the scent of tea and vanilla. Only three customers sit at the small round tables inside, chatting as they sip their beverages. Far in the back, Nico occupies an entire table puzzling over the library budget, while Eidor drinks something foul-smelling from a large mug, a happy expression on his face.

"The library recorded a substantial cash donation from Strategic Protection Services yesterday evening," Nico says as I join them. "I had no idea Mr. Farouque was such a patron of learning."

Eidor cackles. "Yeva always finds a way to remain present. Gone but never forgotten."

Lipop appears, just in time to shush her husband. She sets a steaming cup of tea in front of me, then sits down herself. "We don't know that this is her doing," she says, adding in a low, private voice, "Remember she is not popular with everyone, and for good reason. She can be single-minded in pursuit of her goals."

"And she has enemies," Eidor stage-whispers to me, enjoying Lipop's consternation, "some in very high places."

"Like the Chair of the Governing Council?" I whisper back, and he nods vigorously. "Although if Sarsen is her enemy, I don't understand why Yeva went to the trouble of warning her about what Cabot-Klaar is up to. It's almost like she was trying to convince Sarsen to save herself."

"And in so doing, perhaps also do the difficult work of reining in her accomplice for us," Lipop proposes. "I can see the logic in it, truly."

"If only it had worked," I sigh, taking a sip of my tea. This one smells pleasantly like cloves and some other lovely warming spice; my body relaxes, although my mind is still spinning. Everyone else in our group has something else to focus on, to occupy their time. Arden and Graham are working together to prepare the revived Planetary Equity Alliance members for their testimony in front of Benta Sarsen, Nico is occupied with the management and oversight of the Library, and Lipop and Eidor have the shop, their son, and Lipop's upcoming assignment to prepare for. For me, the only thing in my head is Iona's impending destruction, how we might circumvent it, and what the consequences will be if I fail. It's an exhausting and soul-wrenching merry-go-round; it has no beginning and no real end.

I linger in the tea shop as long as I can, then bid my friends good-bye and go in search of Arden.

31

MY WAYFINDER TAKES ME into a part of the Station I've never seen before, away from the happy hucksterism of the Carnival into a sleek section labeled Professional Services. The well-lit hallways are lined with mixed-material plexi doors. Some are opaque, others have transparent panels that reveal calmly decorated waiting rooms and reception areas inside. Although each door bears a unique insignia, what's behind them is remarkably similar, whether the legend on the outer wall touts a dentist or an investment counselor. A dense carpet covers the floor, absorbing my footfalls; it's so quiet I hear my own breath.

I walk nearly the full length of one very long hall and finally come to an unembellished solid door with temporary signage that reads "Thorn Industries."

The interior features little more than walls. There's no calming lighting, no upscale décor, no perfectly-turned-out reception area. A receiving bot in the bare vestibule scans my wrist chip and iris before squawking out "Welcome, you may proceed," in a mechanical monotone. Beyond the vestibule is a large, brightly lit room holding fifteen tables, with as many as eight people seated at each one. Arden stands in front of an AirBoard in one corner of the room, writing "3 MORE DAYS" on it with his finger. Graham is in another corner, having an intense discussion with a group of people that includes Eiken Fortin.

Arden spots me and waves me over; several of the people clustered around him turn to watch my approach. As I look into each face, I'm impossibly grateful. Everyone in this room could be risking their careers, their futures—maybe even their lives—to stand up for Iona. I would never have asked it of them, yet here they are.

Then Arden says, "This is Faith she's the reason you're all here today," and my tears start to flow. The others in the room notice me and begin to crowd around. They won't let me deflect *their* gratitude.

"We know what happened; you saved our lives," one person says.

"We're forever in your debt," adds another.

"We're happy to take this on," chimes in a third. "It's the least we could do."

I can't begin to describe how this makes me feel.

Grateful, yes. Unworthy—absolutely. Abashed and humbled—without a doubt. But there's another layer underpinning it, strong and beautiful, that burns brighter and brighter until my terrors and doubts give way. In their place I find determination, commitment, and most importantly, a new flicker of hope. If these people who have only just met me can give me that, then I must give them what they deserve—a safe and prosperous planet to call home.

The clamor dies down and everyone refocuses; I sit back and listen to their strategies and plans. I'm more motivated than ever and anxious to contribute. I wait until the group takes a break, then grab Arden.

"If it's not too late, I want to add my name to the testimony list," I tell him. "I'm in a position to have a lot to say. I can use some of the information we got from Yeva's transmission to put pressure on Benta Sarsen. We could throw the Company off Iona *and* call out Breton Cabot-Klaar in a way that makes him give up his plans forever."

"Are you sure?" Arden asks. I can tell by the way his face has lit up that he understands how significant this could be. "It will mean a lot of attention directed your way, both during your testimony and afterwards. Being in the spotlight hasn't traditionally been your thing."

He knows me so well.

His hand is warm as he folds mine in it, looking into my eyes. He's genuinely concerned, but for once he's not trying to talk me out of something or convince me to find a "safer" way.

"I'm sure," I say. "It's time. You finish up here. I'll head back to Lipop's and figure out what I need to do to make it official."

I don't even wait to get home. I ping the Governing Council's information service while I'm still on the Local heading back to Residential 16. Not even the avalanche of resulting bureaucratic nonsense and contradictory instructions dims my enthusiasm.

With everyone still engaged elsewhere, the little residence is quiet when I walk in. It's a cozy cocoon, a comfortable refuge. I relish silence, and calm, and the impression of peace, and that's what this place offers. I'm going to enjoy it while I can, because after I testify in front of the Governing Council, it might be hard to find peace for a while.

I grab some tea, snuggle down into the comfortable sofa, and start unpacking the GC's rules around application for testimony. It's a complex, tightly controlled process requiring a mountain of data submission; it's astonishing to me that Arden managed this for more than a hundred people, most likely at great personal risk to himself and them. Then he found a way to remove everyone to a safer location, quietly and with as little drama as possible. By his own account, the Success Team didn't seem to realize they'd left Iona until well after they'd disappeared into the Station's population.

Of course, a substantial part of that was Yeva's doing, from the ship that carried them away to the network of friends and associates on station who were ready to help. After thinking it over, I understand what a core change it represented for Arden to first choose to go against the Company, then ask for help in doing so.

And here I am, with my own core change. Years of flying under the radar, running away or hiding, now stepping into the light.

Or into the fire, depending on perspective.

I take most of the remaining day to work through the requirements—joining an existing scheduled testimony turns out to be many times more complex than submitting an initial petition. There are points I need clarification on, and a few instructions that don't make sense. I'll ask Lipop for help tonight before dinner, but it would be so helpful to have, say, a virtual concierge who could give me a figurative hand. I miss Xeric, and half-heartedly say, "Xeric, assist me" into the silent air. I'm saddened but not surprised when this time the resulting 2D rendering appears with the message, "We're sorry. Your virtual concierge has suffered a critical failure and cannot be repaired. Please contact support to be assigned a new concierge."

Dinner at Lipop's is the usual mix of calm and chaos. Tonight, however, there's a side helping of chaos as Eidor is doing the cooking. I'm not sure I knew pots and pans could make quite so much noise simply from being used as intended. Part of his process is asking Lipop to taste something every five minutes or so; in fact, we're having difficulty making progress on my testimony application because of Eidor and his ubiquitous spoons. After what seems like the hundredth time of him running into the room with a panicked expression, Lipop puts up her hand and refuses anything more.

"Be brave, my love," she says. "Try it yourself. How can our guests look forward to dinner if the chef is so uncertain about their own creation?"

Eidor beams at his wife, directs his latest spoonful of savory-smelling brown gravy into his own mouth, then smacks his lips happily.

"It is delicious," he proclaims, "and you are a goddess."

"Thank you, dear."

The two look into each other's eyes for a moment and I see pure love passing between them. This is a relationship worth aspiring to: open, honest, strong. Across the room I catch Arden's eye; he's been watching them too, and the soft smile on his face shows his affection and appreciation of the pair. *We could be like this*, I think. *Maybe we already are.*

"Tell me how you met," I say on a whim. "Was it love at first sight?"

Lipop smiles, Eidor laughs aloud. "It was a broken arm at first sight," he says. "She felt bad so she accepted a date with me. She couldn't turn me down after that."

This is not the love story I was expecting. Lipop picks up the narrative.

"It was not broken; it was only a fracture," she amends, "and I'd seen you before. You were quite a charming fellow. I was plotting to have you the entire time."

"Wait a minute," Arden says. "Where does the broken arm come into this again? I mean, I don't know a lot about Sharjeet dating practices, but that seems a bit extreme."

"Oh, we were young, we were playing fatooja," Lipop explains. "It's a common game on Sharj; everyone plays it, all ages and genders the same. It involves moving a small white flag down a long field, across a goal line. To do this, however, you cannot carry the flag more than a set distance yourself, so you must form alliances with other players on the field during play. It's important to keep your alliances secret, because if the opposing players determine who is working with you, they will try to force them off the pitch."

"Eidor was an opposing player, and you broke his arm to take him out of the game and then you started dating?" I ask, fascinated.

"Not exactly," Eidor grins. "There was more subterfuge involved. Lipop is a sneaky one."

"One gambit is to convince the other players that you're working against someone when you're actually working with them," she continues, with a flirty sidelong glance at her spouse. "I had already noticed this handsome fellow, new to our neighborhood, who had joined our game. I thought *he could make a fine accomplice, but I will have to test him*. You never know about one another until there's a test."

I feel Arden's eyes on me and look up to meet his gaze.

"So true," I say, and he smiles.

"When the time came, I tossed him my flag," Lipop continues. "I let him carry it down the field, and just before he crossed the goal line, I smashed him out of bounds and took the flag away. The other players thought he was an opposition player after all, and they expected me to run the other way. But he was my accomplice, so I ran across the goal line nearest me and won the game."

"I was delighted that such a beautiful woman had handed me her flag," Eidor remembers, his face showing his rapture, "but then she broke my arm, and I knew we were going to fall in love."

"He was so brave!" Lipop exclaims. "He never complained. He joined me in the scoring zone and celebrated with me. It was quite the scene. Then we went to the Medical Center to have his arm repaired, and here we are today."

They're gazing at each other like besotted teenagers. It has to be one of the weirdest love stories I've ever heard, but somehow I wouldn't expect less from these two. If they'd said they met at a coffee shop or were in the same class at school, it would have been a huge disappointment.

"What about you two?" Lipop asks, looking between Arden and me.

"Not quite as exciting as having your arm broken but at least it was less physically painful," I say. "It was more than ten years ago now. I was working in Central City on Company Home World, as a Resident Services Coordinator. Arden arrived as a new employee who needed a place to live, and he wound up in my pod."

"Wound up?" Lipop raises an eyebrow.

"All right, all right. I thought he was incredibly hot, so I overrode the placement program and put him in my pod so we could get to know each other."

"And I had no complaints about that," Arden says, his gaze warming as he watches me. "Still don't. Won't ever."

Now *we're* staring at each other like besotted teenagers. It's a bit of a relief when the door opens and Nico and Euclid walk in.

Eidor returns to the kitchen accompanied by Lipop, ostensibly to finish dinner, although I hear some impassioned kissing taking place once they're out of direct sight. Nico and Euclid sit close by; Nico whistles at the sheer number of documents and files floating in the air in front of me.

"What are you trying to do?" he asks. "Is all this just for you? It looks like enough documentation for a small army."

"I'm trying to add my name to the testimony list. This represents progress—I've been working on it for hours. The session with Benta Sarsen is only three days away. I have to file this with the Governing Council as soon as possible."

"You need to eat and relax, then we take care of the application," says Lipop, appearing at my elbow and handing me a bowl of rich-smelling Sharj stew. Eidor's culinary efforts have been a success; the first bite is delicious, just as he said.

"All right, all right," I say, pushing the documents into the background. "Eat, relax, then work. Who else has an amusing story to tell to take my mind off all this?"

"Oh, that would be me," says Euclid jovially. "There's some kind of confusion happening with my virtual concierge. It's the funniest thing; all of a sudden it's started calling me *Captain* Nam."

"Don't worry, that's your upgrade," I say. "They like to make guests feel important."

"They're certainly doing that! I also found a completed-and-paid-for order on my folio for an interstellar-rated skiff, with a berth number and engine codes and everything. I didn't buy a skiff, obviously. It would be great to have it, but I could never afford it. The reporting system has probably confused me with someone who has a similar name."

I catch Nico's eye and we trade knowing looks. Yeva's managed to show up for dinner after all.

"Never say never, Captain Nam," Nico says with a grin.

"Oh no, don't call me that. I'm not a Captain yet. Just call me Euc."

"What Nico said, Euc," I echo.

"Now you're having fun at my expense," he says, chuckling good-naturedly. "Imagine what a shock it would be to go to that berth and find a ship with my name on it. That would be quite stressful, let me tell you!"

He continues to smile, and his demeanor tells me he's not *really* upset by the idea of having a tricked-out interstellar skiff of his own that he didn't have to pay for. Which is good news, because based on what I've learned about Yeva Darwin, there's *definitely* a ship in that berth with his name on it, and those engine codes will work precisely as they're supposed to. For all I know, Euc may actually have been promoted to Captain and word hasn't worked its way down the chain of command yet.

"Are you enjoying having a virtual concierge?" I ask.

"Oh yes, it's amusing. And helpful, but also a bit ..." Euc winces, telegraphing his discomfort, and I remember those early days in the cheesy Overnight with that very young and un-upgraded version of Xeric.

"Pushy?" I fill in. "Overly sexualized? Weirdly enthusiastic about convincing you to buy things you definitely do not want?"

"Uh, yes. All those things."

"Don't worry, it's harmless. If your reservation gets upgraded again, those behaviors will go away."

"I have no idea how it got upgraded in the first place, so I guess I'll put up with it the way it is."

"Maybe Nico can tweak it for you," I say, and then startle as the words leave my mouth.

"You can, can't you?" I say, looking directly at Nico.

"Tweak the concierges?" Nico mumbles through his stew. "Yes, some of them. A bit."

"Could you repair one that malfunctioned?"

"It depends. Maybe." He takes a last bite, then leans toward me. "Why?"

"Xeric," I whisper. "IT says he can't be repaired. Could you re-create him? An advanced version of him, like he was?"

"Oh." Nico's face is doubtful. "No, not at the same level. That's beyond my abilities."

"Would you try? For me? I mean, I know you have so many other things to do, but this would mean a lot, and we could at least have someone to track shipments and ..."

Nico casts me a sympathetic look and shakes his head. "I could try, but I think you'd only be disappointed. It wouldn't be *your* Xeric, Faith. It would be a different AI entirely. Any bot can track shipments. That's not really what you want."

Tears sting the backs of my eyeballs, and I turn away, pretending to be exasperated so Nico doesn't see. "I just need some help," I say. "I'm so tired and I need help."

"And help you shall have," says Lipop, coming around to collect empty plates. "Another ten minutes and we'll get back to it. In the meantime, have some tea."

Lipop is true to her word and sits down to help me after the plates have been cleared away. We work through the night to complete the odious documentation and submit it to the Governing Council's testimony portal minutes before the deadline. Someone adjusts Residential 16's lighting to mimic sunrise as I stumble into our little flat. I crawl into bed, and Arden awakens and wraps his arms around me in as comforting a way as possible.

"I'm sorry about Xeric," is the only thing he says, pulling me in close. He doesn't move a muscle as I cry it out and fall into a fitful sleep.

I'M NOT SURE WHAT time it is when I wake up. Arden, long out of bed, sits in front of a live stream, running through testimony with one of the Planetary Equity Alliance members—she's on the younger side and has a little squeak to her voice that belies her anxiety. I listen to him talk her down the way he has with me on occasion—offering logic, facts, and support in a calm, evenly-modulated tone. As she repeats her introduction, her voice begins to sound more steady and clear, and after a few minutes, she has it locked in.

"That's good, Samine," he says. "You're going to do great. You've got nothing to worry about. Two more days!" She thanks him profusely, her face shining with newfound confidence, and logs off.

"Look at you with that thing you do," I say, sliding down beside him on the sofa. "You made that young woman feel like a professional orator. That's a fantastic skill to have."

He leans into me with his shoulder and kisses my hair.

"It's learned," he murmurs against my head. "Anyone can do it. You can do it too."

"It makes people see you as a problem-solver. They come to you because they believe you can fix things, fix *them*. People come to me because they think I'll be empathetic. And I am, but what you're doing is key for leadership."

"I don't know about that. I think the empathy thing is at least as important, if not more so. I wish I had more of that. You know firsthand that can be hard for me."

"Maybe between the two of us we make one good leader."

He chuckles, less from amusement than as an acknowledgement of facts. "Maybe we do."

His holo, still set to live stream, pings again. This time, it's an older man, concerned about the phrasing of what he plans to say. I putter around the kitchen, making coffee and nibbling on fruit, while Arden listens, speaks, adjusts, listens some more. When they're done, I rejoin him on the sofa.

"Your capacity for patience, sir, is also greatly improved," I say. "Is my secretive, hot-headed man still in there? Will I see him when I least expect?" I'm smiling, but I'm only partially joking.

Arden clasps his hand to his heart. "Secretive and hot-headed? I'm wounded to my core."

"Excellent non-answer."

"He might still be in there. He's not in charge anymore, though."

"How did that happen?"

Arden pauses as he gathers his thoughts together. I can almost see him choosing his words, for once not to obfuscate, but instead for their clarity and truth.

"When you left Iona, something broke inside me," he begins. "I don't even think I realized it at the time, but I began to see things in a different way—the way you would have seen them. I discovered things I hadn't wanted to see before, places where I was tripping over my own narrative."

He folds his hands over mine.

"I don't know why I couldn't *hear* you when you were sitting right in front of me. Everything you said made so much sense, but that wasn't good enough for me—I still had to do things my way. I always thought you weren't listening to me; really, it was me who wasn't listening to you. So, to answer your question, that guy, that part of me—he may not be gone for good, but I don't want him running my life, and I'm doing everything I can to make sure he gets left in the past."

It's beautiful and sweet and he's so sincere. I pull him to me and we hold each other tight, breathing into each other's hair. He murmurs that he loves me, and I say it back because it's true. But while I appreciate everything he's said, everything he's trying to do, there's still a war going on inside me, between the me in his arms in the here and now, and the me who can't forget that he disappeared without a trace and stayed gone for nearly ten years, even though he had a 'reason.'

There's still no news from the Governing Council regarding my application to join the petition as a speaker, but we work on my testimony anyway. I've been thinking about what I want to say since I decided to join in. This group doesn't need my evidence to support their petition; they're living representatives of the Company's potential financial motivations for taking over Iona. The one thing they don't have is specific individuals attached to that prospective gain. Yeva's transmission gives us that, and I want to make it clear to Sarsen that we both heard and recorded the conversation. The line between making a point and making an accusation is painfully fine in this case, and I'm struggling. How can I get Sarsen to hear what I have to say?

I'm no closer to an answer by the time the dinner hour rolls around. The usual crew has already gathered as we walk in. Nico, Graham and Euc chat in the sitting room; I find Lipop and Eidor bantering happily in the kitchen. My offer to help with the meal preparation is cheerfully rejected, and I'm shooed away to join the others. Graham and Arden talk about how well-prepared their group is for the upcoming hearing, now only two days away. As Lipop lays out tonight's meal—a slightly sour, spicy rice and vegetable Sharj specialty dish—my holo pings, and I find official confirmation that my application to join the petition and give testimony has been accepted.

I'm offered congratulations from everyone, and I'm pleased. Yet I walk to the dinner table on shaky legs, and my pulse thuds through my neck a touch faster than normal. The food's delicious, but I have to force myself to eat it, and my mouth is becoming fiercely dry.

Arden notices. After we help clear away the plates, load the sterilizer, and return the table to its magical wall compartment, he settles next to me on the narrow sofa and places one hand on my knee.

"Nervous?" he asks.

It's all I can do to push aside my natural tendency to deflect, but this time I manage.

"Yeah. I don't know why."

I realize I'm wringing my hands. I stop, shake them out, and lightly grip the sofa cushion on either side of my legs instead.

"It's a big thing for you, far outside your comfort zone," Arden says, "and something you place a high value on getting right. I'd be concerned if you *weren't* nervous. Would doing more work on your testimony tonight help you feel more confident?"

"Maybe. I know what I want to convey, but I'm still not sure what the right words are."

"Then we'll go upstairs a little early and try to get some of that pinned down before we go to bed. What do you think?"

His expression is so earnest I almost get teary.

"I think that sounds perfect," I say. I place my hand against his cheek. "You're really nailing empathy right now, by the way."

He smiles. "Good to know."

Lipop appears, hovering over us with cups of tea. As she presses mine into my hands, she whispers, "Excellent for nerves."

The tea is wonderful and I'm more settled after drinking it, but it doesn't last. Only moments later, Graham scowls at his holo and announces, "Well, that's it. The shipment of Isoflare from Strategic Protection Solutions has been signed in at its destination, and I'm now shut out of anything having to do with the partnership program. I'm so sorry, Faith."

I suck in my breath hard. Iona is sixty solar hours from doom.

Everyone is quiet for a moment, fear and worry hanging in the air. Lipop breaks the silence.

"This does nobody any good," she says. "New house rule tonight: no heavy conversations. We cannot change things by talking them to death. Instead, we'll give our brains a moment to breathe, and have calm, light conversations only."

It's harder to do than it sounds, but we give it our best effort. Unfortunately, the nerves in my gut and the clock in my brain are both battling for my attention, and I can only vaguely hear what the others are saying. Hamiit is first in his class at school and gets to choose a special reward ... *sixty solar hours*. Nico is accepting recommendations for how to expand the library's holdings, and the suggestions so far have been interesting ... *sixty solar hours*. Eidor made four shop patrons nauseous with free samples of his new fermented tea concoction ... *sixty solar hours*.

Even later, as Arden and I try to work on my testimony, the clock will not let go. It stays with me for the rest of the night, and trails me into my dreams.

I wake up hardly more rested than when I went to bed. I walk into our kitchen to find Arden making coffee; he's not exactly fresh and lovely this morning either. There are dark circles under his eyes and his mouth and forehead both hold tension.

"Did you manage to sleep?" I ask as he folds me into his arms.

"Not really. I kept turning over scenarios in my head about what we could do right now to stop this."

"Did you come up with anything?"

His shoulders droop and he lets out a long breath.

"Nothing short of flying home and murdering the bastard."

"That could work, though."

"Sure. Then we'd be in prison and Iona would still be destroyed."

"Oh, right. Not the best idea, then."

"Nope."

We're interrupted by the high-pitched chime of the streamer; we walk into the living room to find the Thorn Industries logo pulsating red above it.

"Red level?" Arden mutters. "Someone lit a fire under Graham this morning."

He brings up the message. Graham has forwarded a video from the stream, time-stamped only a few minutes ago. Breton Cabot-Klaar stands behind a podium bearing the Company logo, with the other members of the Success Team standing behind him. Gemma Laurel frowns as she fidgets with the edge of her colorful printed scarf, while Jarek Shimauy appears likely to fall asleep at any moment. Based on the surroundings, they're making this broadcast from the Comm Center, so this isn't a statement for Ionians. It's something designed specifically to be sent out to the stream.

Arden hits play, and Cabot-Klaar's grating smarmy voice fills the room, its nasal tones and haughty inflections making me grit my teeth.

"We have done our best for Iona and are grateful for the overwhelming acceptance and support we've found here," he says. "However, we've reached an impasse beyond which things cannot move without committed leadership. Two individuals whom we were led to believe cared about this planet and who, as a result, were placed in high positions of trust, left when Iona needed them most. Their inexplicable absence tears at the fabric of the excellent relationship between the Company and Iona, and places us all in an untenable position."

"Aaaand there we are," I whisper. Arden shushes me. Cabot-Klaar continues.

"As such, we have filed a writ of leadership abandonment against Chief Designate Faith Feathergrass and Security Lead Arden Wilson. If they do not return to Iona and present themselves to our Success Team within forty-eight solar hours, the writ shall take effect and all personnel, activities, and assets of Iona will be placed under full Company control. Members of the Success Team will serve as leadership until permanent placements are named. There was disagreement among the Success Team as to this process; some advocated for a looser, more time-generous strategy. But that concept was not supported by sound logic."

Behind him, Gemma Laurel's face shifts to utter exasperation. She proceeds to stare daggers into Cabot-Klaar's back through the rest of the video.

"In the end, I believe a fair compromise has been reached," he continues. "Going forward, any questions may be addressed to me, as I'll be serving as Chief Designate Temporalis until such time as the writ is finalized or cancelled."

The clip ends and we sit in silence.

"Obviously a trap," I say.

"Obviously."

"What do we do? If we don't show up, he takes Iona."

"That seems to be his plan."

"And if we *do* show up ..."

"Still a trap, only now we're in it."

The streamer chimes again. It's Graham.

"You watched that, right?" he says. "It hit the stream a few minutes ago. What are you going to do?"

"I don't think we know yet," I say. "There are a lot of things to think about, and we still have tomorrow's testimony to get through." My stomach flips as I say the words.

"Testimony is likely to last all day. If you wait until it concludes, you'll barely have time to get to Iona before the deadline, if you can manage at all," Graham points out. "Who knows if Sarsen won't find a way to stretch it out to make sure you miss the window?"

I clench my jaw. The timing makes perfect sense.

"He's planned this so there's no way we can get to Iona before the deadline," I say. "Damn it!"

"Could you pull out of the testimony? You're two important voices, but there are a hundred other people prepared to say what needs to be said," Graham asks.

Arden answers with a shake of his head. "That won't work. The Governing Council has strict rules to prevent nuisance petitions. Every person scheduled to give testimony must appear. If even one person is missing, the hearing is cancelled and the petition thrown out."

"You can't request it be rescheduled?"

"Only the Council itself can elect to delay or reschedule a hearing. We don't get a say in it at all."

"Is there a way to force them to delay it?" Graham's eyes are narrowed.

"I don't know of anything offhand," Arden says. "We didn't make a contingency plan for trying to get a delay; we never expected to need one. I should probably research that."

"I'll research it. You've got enough on your mind right now," Graham says.

He signs off, a bit abruptly. I look at Arden.

"What now?" I ask.

"I guess we carry on preparing for the hearing, and keep trying to think of options," he says. "Maybe Graham will come up with something."

It's not much hope to grab on to, but this time it's all we've got.

We get ready to dive back into refining my testimony, but we never make it. The video hits the wider stream and for the next four hours, both holos and the streamer are a flood of pings. Our friends are worried about what it might mean for us, streamer hosts pester us for a response, the petition witnesses worry that their hard work and bravery has been for nothing. That's the part that frustrates me the most. The petition for adjudication will be blown up if we don't return, since the Company will officially own Iona and there's no prohibition against having a financial interest in something you own. The hearing will be blown up if we go, and might never again make it to the General Council's schedule. It's a perfect ouroboros, a snake eating its own tail, and there's no escape from it.

"I can't believe this," I say. We've had to turn off both holos and the streamer to get some peace. "Breton Cabot-Klaar has figured out a path that makes it impossible for us to win. Every prospective avenue is cut off. What can we do?"

"Should we try to get to Sarsen again somehow? Or see if the other members of the Success Team can help us?" Arden muses.

"Gemma Laurel didn't look pleased with the situation," I say, remembering how she glared at Cabot-Klaar in the video. "We might want to try to get a message to her. She could have other allies inside the Company who would help us as well. What do you think Shimauy's position might be? You've worked closely with him."

Arden runs a hand through his hair and puffs out his cheeks as he thinks. "I can't be sure. He's kind of a 'go along to get along' type of guy. I doubt he's intimidated by Cabot-Klaar, but he's also not interested in heroics."

Suddenly, someone is pounding on our door. "Did one of the stream jockeys break into the building?" wonders Arden as we both approach it carefully. But in a few moments the door slides open to reveal Eidor, who's apparently had a tough time getting the ocular scanner low enough to work on him and had given up and just started knocking.

"Ah! Good! I tried to ping but your holos are off. Come downstairs, quickly, quickly!" he shouts, waving us out of the flat.

"What's going on, Eidor?" I cry as we hurry into the lift after him. "Is everyone okay?"

"Yes, okay. A little crazy maybe. There is something on the live stream you must see."

"Oh, the video from this morning? We've seen it, we were ..." I begin, but he cuts me off mid-sentence.

"No, this is live; you must see it. Graham tried to ping you but no luck, so he sent me," he shouts, running out of the lift toward his door, left hanging open in his haste. "Hurry, hurry!"

Arden and I trade confused looks and follow Eidor inside.

33

INSTEAD OF THE USUAL peaceful Sharj sunset, the sitting room ViewPort is playing the a live from the general channel. On screen, Graham stands in the center of a circle of stream jockeys elbowing one another to get the perfect shot. A good number of the petition witnesses stand with him; more are milling about in the background. They're all crammed into the bare room I visited in the Professional Services section.

Lipop pats the settee next to her, and I sit down.

"Did you know this was happening?" she whispers to me.

"I still don't know what this *is*," I say.

The live has been running for only a minute or so and Graham doesn't appear to have done more than introduce himself, but I can tell the stream jockeys were briefed in advance. They're already shouting questions.

"You're scheduled to testify before the Council tomorrow," one says. "When did you make this decision?"

"You've said you'll name key players. Who, and why now?" calls out another.

"I've been thinking this over for some time, but concerns about the impact this might have on my family's reputation kept me silent," Graham says. "With my association with Thorn Industries at an end, that's no longer a concern. And it's past time this information was brought out into the open."

"What is he talking about?" I whisper to Arden, who's standing next to the settee with Eidor. Arden's eyebrows arch up and he shakes his head. He has no idea.

Meanwhile, the streamer jockeys continue to shout over one another. Graham, his face stone, lifts his hands and waits, and they gradually quiet down.

"I have a prepared statement that should answer your questions," he says. The gaggle around him quiets down and crowds in closer as he pulls up a script on his holo and begins to read.

"As you know, I and more than a hundred individuals are to give testimony to the Governing Council tomorrow on a petition for adjudication to remove the Company permanently from the independent planet Iona. Our contention is that the Company, in violation of Governing Council laws, has a clear incentive to control that planet and is likely to exploit Iona's resources and population for financial gain. I thought I might present this information in that forum, but the public hearing we requested was instead scheduled as private, before the Chair of the Governing Council alone, with no other Council members, witnesses, audience, or stream presence."

He pauses, looking into the multiple cameras pressed around him. His face is resolute, and he's remarkably calm.

He clears his throat and continues.

"I, along with the people you see behind me, intended to make the point that the Company's chemical agent Blue, which was developed as a medical tool to place sick and injured individuals into stasis until appropriate care was available, was in fact potentially dangerous and had prospective use as a weapon. That for the Company to control Blue's antidote, its revival process, and Iona, blessed as it is with minerals that can physically halt the stasis that Blue initiates, was problematic in the event of such a development. Our testimony was structured as a caution, a warning about a potential future scenario. I'm here to tell you this is not speculation. It's not a 'what if.' It's real, it has already happened, and I have years of proof as the former director of a clandestine weapons program for the Company itself."

The streamers erupt, shouting questions, waving their hands in the air to draw Graham's attention. He pauses again, waiting for the commotion to die down.

"The people with me today were victims of that program, unwilling test subjects, dosed with Blue on Bardazel and then hidden away for nearly a year. Instead of describing an 'incident' that left them in stasis, they'll be revealing what they learned as members of the Planetary Equity Alliance, on Bardazel specifically to investigate, track, and hopefully disrupt the Company's illegal operation. We call on the Governing Council to charge the Company with a Violation of the Highest Order, and to make the proceedings public, with all Governing Council representatives present. We welcome engagement from the Company as well; they have the right according to the GC charter to defend their actions and offer their views. That's all for now. Thank you."

The live shuts off and the ViewPort returns to images of Sharj.

"What did we just watch?" I ask as we head back upstairs. "I have so many questions. Why would he do this? He's only going to mess up the testimony, and he's gotten himself in a massive amount of trouble."

"I'm a little surprised," Arden says. "Still, I know he wouldn't do anything to hurt our chances. He has some kind of strategy. I just don't know what it is."

Four hours later, we find out.

The message from the Governing Council Public Liaison pops up on Arden's holo first, and mine a few seconds after. It states that, in light of information about a change in the specific nature of the planned testimony and in keeping with the rules and requirements of the Governing Council's charter, Iona's petition hearing will be rescheduled. It doesn't go into specifics, and doesn't say when it might occur.

The next ping is from Graham. It simply reads, "Let's plan your next move."

We wait for Graham to join us at Eidor and Lipop's; it's their regular day off and the pair have been on reconnaissance, scouting out opinions about today's two big stream events. Although, if their insights can be trusted, it's down to just one event now; Graham's live has completely overshadowed the dour pronouncements of Breton Cabot-Klaar, which ordinary stationers ignored anyway.

"Iona is a far-away place that most people don't know," Lipop sums up, "but the Company has its fingerprints on everyone's lives. And of course, stationers love a bit of drama that could make the Governing Council look bad."

While I'd normally be disappointed that more people don't care about my little independent planet and its struggle, this time it's working to our advantage. The number of random stream jockeys pinging mine and Arden's holos is down to nothing. Graham, meanwhile, still has his set to 'unavailable.'

When Graham walks through the door, he's relaxed, calm, and, for the first time since I arrived here, not scowling at his holo.

"What did you do?" I ask him, hugging him in greeting. "What's the fallout from this going to be? Are you all right?"

"I'm fine. All I did was something I should have done a long time ago, but for different reasons," he says. "The only fallout is that the Governing Council is required by their own rules to postpone the hearing on Iona's petition, which was my aim. My family ties are finally severed, which I think of as a bonus. And the Company is probably not thrilled with me, but they haven't said a word. That might change once their lawyers get organized, but ultimately there's not much they can do to me that won't make it worse for them."

The three of us pitch in and help Lipop and Eidor with dinner preparations, chatting about everything but the looming question of how to respond to Breton Cabot-Klaar's ultimatum. With the hearing off the docket, we're free to return to Iona, but what would we be returning to? A lot has happened today, but nothing has turned off the clock in my brain that's keeping track of how much time is left before that Isoflare could rain down on my home.

Nico and Euc arrive. We settle into the sitting room for a casual dinner of Sharjeet curry sandwiches with pickles and beer. Graham explains how he found a bylaw in the Governing Council's charter specifying a hearing that levels criminal accusations against an individual or entity must also include that entity's response in-kind.

"The in-kind aspect made it perfect," he says, after swallowing a mouthful of pickles. "Because we're testifying at a live hearing, the Company response, now required to be included, has to be through an in-person participant, added to the witness list. That list has already closed, and even if the GC opened it again for the Company, it would be impossible to get a live person prepped, on the list, and in the hearing room before the start time. Their only option was to reschedule the hearing."

"There's quite a bit of anger among stationers that the GC would take something of such broad interest and choose to make it private, also," Nico adds. "I heard many people saying it felt shady, like the GC and the Company were doing something illicit together. I imagine the Council offices fielded a lot of pings today."

"Everybody at my Overnight was talking about it," Euc confirms. "There were even people in the lobby using the streamers to watch Graham's announcement and send out messages of their own."

"And there's our other advantage," Graham says. "Even the people who watched Breton Cabot-Klaar's proclamation have forgotten about it, and you two are free to do what you like. Have you made a decision yet?"

"Obviously, this ultimatum is some kind of trap," I say. "He was likely thinking we'd choose the testimony over appearing on Iona in person, but I'm sure he's got a plan B in place. There's no way we can just fly in, say 'here we are,' and have things go well. So we need a strategy."

"And then there's the Isoflare," Arden says. "He wouldn't have gone to all this trouble of purchasing it if he wasn't going to use it somehow. We just don't know when that will happen."

"Isoflare is some wild stuff," says Euclid, polishing off his beer and the last of his pickles. "I hadn't heard of it. Xeric says the activator is Durawash? How does that work?"

"Yeah, Durawash. It's a common anti-corrosive that ..." I'm halfway into my answer before I really hear what Euc has just said. "Did you just say Xeric said that? Xeric, as in your virtual concierge?"

"That's the one. You were right about the upgrade's impact. This one's a lot different than the starter model."

"How would your Xeric know about the activator?" I say slowly. "That version wouldn't have ..."

I trail off; Euclid stares at me in confusion. My heart is pounding in my chest. I'm trying so hard to rein in my hopes. I take a deep breath and try again.

"Explain what mean when you say they're different? How, exactly?"

Euc thinks of a second. "It's almost as if the thing has developed a split personality. Sometimes it's what I'm used to, the cheesy salesperson pushing demonstrations. Then all of a sudden, it's like someone else takes over, someone much more worldly and articulate that I have trouble remembering it's an AI. It's only happened recently and only a couple of times, but it's so clearly different from the other versions that I've started calling it Smart Xeric. It's a bit unsettling. Smart Xeric seems to know a lot of things I've never mentioned."

I sit up. "Like?"

Euclid starts counting off the instances on his fingers.

"Well, the Isoflare activator for one. But it knows you and Arden are a couple, and that you're staying here with Lipop. Smart Xeric is aware Graham is here, too, but for some reason it seems to really dislike him."

"Smart Xeric dislikes Graham?" I repeat, exhilaration filling me to the point where I can barely breathe. It's too specific a detail to be accidental, but I'm afraid to speak what I suspect into being. I look over to Arden; he's sitting on the edge of his chair, hanging on Euc's every word.

"It called Arden 'scruffy,' so I think it might dislike everyone," Euc laughs. "Except you, Faith. I know Xeric's a program and nothing more, but it seemed almost sentimental when I mentioned your name. It was pleased I was going to see you this evening. Oh, I almost forgot—this came out of the in-room printer, and Xeric asked me to give it to you—the smart version, not the cheesy one."

Euclid digs around in his pocket for a moment and produces a small white plexi stat chip, embedded with the Darwin-Cross logo. He drops it into my hand and I cradle it carefully. I don't even have to know what's on it to feel it's the most precious gift in the universe.

Euclid pulls out his holo to read off some notes.

"Let's see ... here's what's on it. Some stats Xeric describes as interesting but not important, and some research on the chemicals you were investigating. The main thing, though, is this encrypted file named *mission accomplished*. Xeric was very specific about this and said 'only my travel twin can decipher it; it's for Faith's eyes only.' Does that make sense?"

"Travel twin ... oh my suns, the ship! Xeric's still connected on the *Gabriella* and that version must be okay!"

I stand up without realizing I've done it, my eyes well with tears. Arden leaps to his feet and throws his arms around me—he seems on the verge of shedding a tear, too. Everyone in the room is cheering and laughing and patting a somewhat confused Euclid on the shoulder.

This doesn't solve everything—and who knows, it may not solve anything. But for the first time today, I feel like we have a chance. Like *Iona* has a chance.

And I have my ridiculous, brilliant, smart-ass AI assistant waiting for me to summon them. That's pretty stellar too.

We don't waste another moment. Lipop shepherds us through the darkening purple and blue tones of Residential 16's late twilight to the neighborhood docking area, where we board the tea shop skiff. She pilots us through the station's local flight corridors, and after the longest few minutes of my life, we arrive at the elaborate bay where *Gabriella* waits. Lipop finds the berth and snuggles in behind her. As the ramp drops, she says, "I'll wait here; go do what you have to do."

I hurry up to the ship's nose and put my palm flat on her hull; her biometrics recognize me and the ramp deploys. Arden hangs back, confusion written across his features.

"This is your ship?" he asks.

"Yeva gave her a few upgrades," I say, already running up the ramp. "Come on!"

"It looks a little strange ... ah, yikes!" Arden lets out a yelp. I look back to see him frozen in place at the foot of the ramp, shielding his eyes with his forearm. "What was that?"

"Biometric imprinting. Sorry, I forgot you weren't verified in the system. You are now, though. Come on up."

Blinking and squinting, he ascends the ramp slowly. The lights are on and the environmental control system is cranking up; everything came to life the instant the ship recognized me.

"Wow," he says, looking around. "Upgrade doesn't even begin to cover it. This is incredible."

"I'll give you a tour later. But let's do what we came here for first."

I'm guessing Xeric will appear in their favorite spot, so I turn toward the comm center controls and say, "Xeric, assist me!"

He doesn't.

He shows up behind me instead.

"Boo," Xeric says into my ear, startling me enough that I jump.

If he were corporeal, I'd smack him. And then I'd hug him.

"I'm so glad to see you!" I say, hugging myself instead. "That was clever, communicating through Euclid's Overnight concierge. What a relief. I was afraid you were done for."

"It wasn't easy, I had to hijack a lot of code. Shocking that you get off the ship for a few days and forget all about me," he says in a pouty tone. But he's grinning like he would have hugged me too if he could.

“I didn't forget you; I just wasn't thinking station-you would be different from ... oh never mind! To be fair, they were really long days,” I say.

Xeric looks past my shoulder to Arden. “Hello, Scruffy,” he says. “We meet in shared space at last. Ready for an adventure?”

Arden takes in my happy face and Xeric’s smirk, and responds with a laugh and a smirk of his own.

“Bring it, bot-boy,” he says. “Let’s go.”

34

I TAKE THE CHIP from my pocket, waving it in front of Xeric.

"What's this about?" I ask.

"Ahh, *mission accomplished*. I have specific instructions to translate that file for you once you're on your way."

I'm puzzled. "I thought you created the instructions. Did you not?"

Xeric raises an eyebrow at me. "I did not. I was sent this file and told to encrypt it and to share it only with you after you embark for Iona. Is that now? Are we leaving?"

He's excited. I'm excited too, but I still have at least *some* common sense.

"We're going soon, but not right now," I explain. "We're likely headed into a trap, so we need to come up with a plan."

"Oh, no, I don't like that 'it's a trap' part. A plan sounds like something I can help with, though."

"Can you leave the ship? Is there a way we can open up channels so you can come through the streamer at Lipop's?"

Xeric shakes his head, clearly disappointed.

"I require far more resources than a typical streamer can handle. I'll have to wait here. But don't take long. And don't forget about me again."

I grin so big I feel like my face is going to split in half.

"I will never forget you again, I promise," I say. "Thank you, I'm done."

Xeric winks at me, nods to Arden, and dissipates into thin air.

"Wow," says Arden. "That's quite the personality."

"You have no idea. Come on, let's get back to Lipop's and figure out a plan. Then let's out of here and save our home."

I'm so happy to have rediscovered Xeric I forget about the clock in my head for a moment, but I reflexively check the time stamp on Lipop's control deck as we reboard her skiff. The countdowns for the Isoflare prep and our arrival deadline have aligned, with thirty-four hours until each. It feels suspiciously intentional that the two timelines are matched, and I'm sure it's this way for a reason, but I don't have the facility to think about that now.

Back at Lipop's, the seven of us hash out different scenarios. I'm certain now we must return to Iona no matter what awaits us; it's the only way we'll be able to stop Cabot-Klaar in his tracks.

With everyone working together, we come up with a way to both publicize and disguise our departure, with deception being the key. Arden and I will head to Iona aboard *Gabriella*, leaving in just a few hours. After we're underway, the rest of the group will take over to create an elaborate illusion for the stream, to convince anyone monitoring our behavior that we're still on-station, and we later leave with barely enough time to arrive on Iona by Cabot-Klaar's deadline.

At least we'll have the element of surprise—thanks to Yeva's upgrades, *Gabriella* will make the trip in five hours instead of fourteen, so even if Cabot-Klaar is somehow tipped off that we've departed, his calculations for our arrival will be all wrong. Additionally, her luxury parking spot is at the outer edge of the Station's Residential sector, well away from the main traffic coming through Control. We don't have to apply for a departure window and worry about missing it; we can just load up and go, departing through a Residential astral gateway. The decoy flight will leave through the main terminal gateway, its departure recorded by all standard Station channels.

Once we get to Iona, we'll need to evade detection. *Gabriella's* fancy biometric tech should help with that. We'll stay hidden only long enough to pick the right opportunity to confront Cabot-Klaar.

We take the next couple of hours preparing resources, sketching out timelines, and assigning roles. When we've pinned down all the decisions we can from here, everyone piles into the tea shop skiff and Lipop takes us back to the elaborate docking area that holds my ship. This time, at Nico's insistence, instead of squeezing in behind *Gabriella* Lipop pulls in to a berth a few slots away, behind a sleek new interstellar skiff. We file down the walkway admiring it, and a grinning Nico stops us for a moment.

"Isn't this an impressive ship," he says, raising one eyebrow at me as he gestures toward the vessel. "The *Hideki.* Interstellar rated, all the bells and whistles. And she looks brand new! What do you think?"

We nod and murmur our approval, but Euc is enthralled. He stands on the walkway staring at the skiff with an attitude bordering on reverence.

"Impressive indeed," says Euc, taking a turn around the front of the ship to see her from a different angle. "Wow, a CF-class. Those haven't been out very long, and already I've heard so many good things about them."

"As it happens, I know this ship's owner," Nico continues. "Would you like a tour?"

"Oh, absolutely! But shouldn't we should get these two on their way first?" Euc is confused about what no doubt feels to him like a sudden shift in priorities. But I know where this is headed and I want to be here for it, so I say, "No, please, take a look. A few minutes won't hurt. We have to get my ship flight ready anyway."

"Just tap on the hull there," Nico says. As Euclid taps his hand on the hull, the ship comes to life. Its lights come on, its ramp descends, its hatchway door slides open, casting an arc of golden light into the dim docking area. Euc laughs. "Not very safe having it wake up for just anyone," he says. "Crazy people like us might walk right in."

Nico shoos Euc forward, up the ramp. He barely reaches the hatchway when the automated ship's voice says, "Welcome aboard, Captain Nam. I'm the *Hideki* and I'm proud to serve you. Where would you like to go?"

Even from the dock as we walk toward *Gabriella*, I can hear Euc shouting, "No! No way! This can't be real! Am I ... is this ... how is this possible?" followed by ecstatic laughter.

Arden grins. "That was absolutely worth the extra five minutes," he says.

"One hundred percent," I agree.

After a few more minutes, Euclid and Nico join the rest of us in front of the *Gabriella*. She's powered up and ready to go. Xeric, waiting inside, waves to everyone from the hatchway and sneers pointedly at Graham.

"Good luck," whispers Lipop as she and Eidor together wrap me in a powerful hug. "I hope your quest is successful and we will see you soon."

Graham hugs both me, then Arden. "See you there," he says. "Keeping my fingers crossed."

With that, Arden and I board, and the rest of the group moves back down the walkway, stopping to tour Euc's ship before piling into the tea shop skiff. Inside *Gabriella*, Xeric settles at the comm controls, Arden sits down in the copilot's seat, and I strap into the pilot's chair. I ease her out of the berth and let the tug take her through quiet empty passages until we reach the astral gateway.

There's nothing left to do but fly.

We initially travel at half-speed moving away from Meridian Station. I want to make sure we don't draw any attention to ourselves and have the opportunity to see if anything attempts to follow us. I'm not sure I breathe the entire time. But once the Station is only a glowing green-and-gold ball on our rear screen, and nothing seems to be tracking us, I power *Gabriella* up to full speed and let her run.

"How are we looking, Xeric?" I ask, spinning to face him.

"Solid. Nothing tracing us, nothing attempting to follow. All functions green-lit. Arrival predicted to be on time in approximately 4.75 solar hours."

"Excellent. Continue monitoring for anything attempting to ping us or trace our pathway."

Arden turns the copilot seat to face me. "Time to find out what's on that chip."

"Not so fast, Scruffy," Xeric says. "My instructions are very clear. The chip contains some files that are available to you both, but there are others that are for Faith only. It will be up to her whether she shares them with you. And some of that data is in video form, so she'll need to take it on the ViewPort."

Arden looks mildly annoyed for a moment; I can see him wrestling with his natural inclination to want to control and manage. Finally, he lets out a long breath and nods.

"Go ahead," he says to me. "Afterward, try to grab some sleep; we're both running on nothing at this point. Xeric and I will keep an eye on things out here."

Xeric raises both eyebrows at me, and then grins at Arden as I head to the bunk. As I climb in and draw the privacy panel shut, I hear Xeric say, "Well done, Scruffy. I might eventually like you."

The automated lighting comes on, a soft low glow as I sit on the bunk with my legs curled under me. I tap the ViewPort to turn it on. It first shows the view behind us in real time, but as soon as I drop the chip into the access slot, it becomes a touch screen menu. The unencrypted files are labeled with logical names: test notes, chemical compounds, lab results. I'll look at those later. Right now, the only file I want to see is *mission accomplished*.

When I touch the file name, it allows me to choose which decryption function I'd like to use. There are three available, but choosing the right one isn't a mystery—one is labeled 'Xeric.' I make my choice, and there's a soft whirring sound as the file is routed to the virtual concierge. I watch as the decryption progresses, the screen filling first with indecipherable nonsense, then with more files and documentation. The last piece is a video, which prompts me to insert the ViewPort's audiopods and set the channel to 'private' before viewing.

Yeva's face appears on the screen. The background is a generic flat gray; she's apparently recording this on her personal holo.

"Hello, Faith. If you're watching this, you're on your way to Iona," she says in an elevated whisper. "This is important information, and I didn't want to give it to you before, because it might have changed your focus. But if you're heading home, there's likely some crisis looming, and you should know. Just remember, this information is accurate as of now, but I'm not going to be around to monitor it, and the key players are not what I would call reliable. I'm calling it a 50/50 chance that what *should* happen will *not* happen. Keep that in mind, act accordingly."

On the video, there's a sudden commotion; the visual moves jarringly as Yeva jams the holo under something dark. She snarls something unintelligible to someone, then the clattering fades. Before the image resolves to her face again as she lifts the holo, I catch a quick glimpse of an electronic barrier and a dingy dark shop interior behind her.

"I identified the vendor who's been selling Isoflare through the Thorn Industries program, here on Meridian Station," she continues. "I *believe* I've successfully incentivized him to replace the next shipment with Fluoroclean. It might not be entirely harmless, but it won't be in any sense as destructive as Isoflare, and I'm guessing they'll be in such a hurry they won't test it first. Visually, it looks almost the same. This vendor though ... he's a piece of work and not even remotely mentally sound. If we're lucky, he'll do what I've paid him to do, but I'm really not sure about this guy."

There's more random shouting off-camera, and some crashing that sounds like things hitting the floor.

"Hopefully you won't need this information after I speak with Benta Sarsen. But options are important when you're dealing with people," Yeva says. "Do excuse me, I have to go beat the hell out of someone and then file-route this to Xeric. Good luck."

The screen goes dark, but the audio continues. Yeva's voice is filtered, distant. She says, "Ready?" and the voice of Julien Farouque, weighty with unearned confidence, replies, "Go for it, lady." There's a sickening thud and Farouque squeals, "Hey that fucking hurt, what the hell!"

Yeva says, "I paid for realism. Buckle up." The recording cuts off.

I sit back and pull the audiopods out of my ears. How should I feel about this? Any chance that something harmless falls from those drones is better, I suppose, than one-hundred percent certainty that it's Isoflare. But the odds still don't feel great. Having watched Farouque's post-fight interview with Station Peacekeepers, Yeva's right. He doesn't just have a screw loose; he's left an entire radiation deflection panel on the launchpad. He'd double back on any promise the instant someone made him a better offer.

Would he tell Cabot-Klaar? Would he take Yeva's money and do nothing? I feel like the answer to both of those questions is 'maybe'.

I shut off the ViewPort and the bunk lights and stretch out, tucking my arms under my head. I'm not going to be able to sleep, but I'll pretend I'm sleeping and that will have to do. I'm good at pretending, after all. I've had a lot of practice.

Despite my certainty otherwise, I do fall asleep. I awaken with a start, certain that we've overshot Iona and flown off into unchartered space, but then remember both Arden and Xeric are up front, keeping things on track. I slide the privacy panel aside and climb out of the bunk. My body aches with held tension and my stomach is growling energetically. The nutritab I find in my jacket pocket looks wildly unappetizing after Lipop's dinners. I consume it anyway and wash it down with water.

I walk around the bulkhead to find Arden slumped down in the co-pilot's seat, snoring softly. Xeric holds a finger to his lips to encourage me to be quiet, then whispers, "He really needed a nap. I have everything under control, so I decided not to wake him."

"How far out are we?" I ask quietly.

"A little more than one solar hour. Decreasing speed in about half that time. She'll need approach and landing coordinates."

"Got it. What time will it be on Iona when we get there?"

"Local time will be just after sunrise."

"And how far in advance of the deadline?"

"Twenty-four solar hours."

I shake my head. I know this is how we planned it, but I'm having tremendous difficulty wrapping my head around having only twenty-four solar hours to land on Iona, build a coalition, and find a way to defeat Cabot-Klaar.

"All right then, let's do this," I murmur to no one in particular. Before I sit down in the captain's seat once more, I shake Arden awake by the shoulder. He blinks at me in confusion and alarm.

"I guess I fell asleep, sorry," he says, abashed.

"It's okay." I hand him a nutritab. "Here, eat this. It's almost time."

I start on *Gabriella's* planetary approach strategy. I'm incredibly grateful to past me for always keeping her squirreled away in her cavern at the back of the high ridge, instead of sitting out on the pads. It was a choice rooted in paranoia at the time, but now it looks almost smart. She already has a homing beacon set there, so she knows where she needs to land.

Getting there is slightly more tricky. We're arriving after sunrise, so Ionians will be out and about, starting their daily routines. I plot a course that makes a tight U-bend in its approach to our little planet, bringing it into the atmosphere well beyond the ridgeline that encircles Iona Town, and then keeping a tight line against it until we reach the cavern.

Lastly, I turn on her biometric cloaking. Now her appearance will be reduced to a momentary flash of light for anyone not in the database who happens to look up.

There are a few people I *want* to see her, though, so I dig through *Gabriella's* programming and move Fallon and Wenda's biometric signatures to the active state. They'll have the same experience as Arden when they see her for the first time; anyone who happens to peer into the cavern who isn't in the database will see nothing at all.

Meanwhile, Arden scans near-planet space for any satellites, enviros, ships, or drones, and Xeric runs a check to find any planet-based detection or tracking systems. Both scans come up negative, which makes sense to me. Cabot-Klaar wants and expects us to come. It wouldn't make sense to have deterrents to our arrival in place.

The dusty pink-beige ball that is Iona is now in view and growing larger by the second.

"Time check to arrival?" I ask.

"One-quarter solar hour," Xeric responds.

"Prepared for transmission?"

"Ready when you are."

Iona's communications going off-planet were tightly tracked last I knew, but I'm not sure if that's true of localized comm. I thought about using my old headset, still stuck in a compartment near the bunk, to try to ping Wenda or Fallon once we arrived, but if there's any localized tracking, that ping could not only alert someone to our presence, it could give away our exact location. I came up with the idea to use Meridian Station's boosted communications array as a transponder, receiving then immediately repackaging and sending the message to Iona's local array. This way, it should get through to Iona without any identifiable information—identities or true origin coordinates—attached to it.

I think for a moment about what to do. I would love to see Wenda, but Fallon is the better strategic choice. Her mother's position in the Company might give her more insight into how much pull Breton Cabot-Klaar has with the higher-ups, and help us figure out who to approach for the fastest response.

"Let's do it," I say. "The recipient is Fallon March. The message is two words: *Gabriella* NOW. Make sure 'now' is emphasized."

"Gotcha. Routing to transponder," Xeric confirms. "If everything works as expected, your communique should show up on her holo just about the time we land."

In almost no time, we're hovering close to my home. We break atmosphere as far from Iona Town as possible. I bring her in manually to glide close along the back of the high ridge, then let her homing device take over once we're within range. I have a brief moment of panic wondering if someone might have ratted out my hiding place and whether we'll find a pile of rubble or a line of anti-spacecraft cannons instead of a dark peaceful slot carved into the rock, but soon enough I can actually see the cavern's dark maw in the red cliff.

Gabriella slows to a stop, hovering in front of the cavern, then turns around, slipping in backwards until she's fully inside. She drifts downward and her struts touch the smooth floor.

"Landing confirmed, position stable," Xeric reports.

"Shutting down propulsion and environmental controls, but leaving activated lights, communications, ..." Arden says.

"... and me," reminds Xeric.

"... and Xeric, confirmed," Arden replies with a smile.

Gabriella's systems cycle off and then quiet, broken only by the whispering wind and the scratch of sand skittering across the rock face.

We're home.

In less than twenty-four hours, we'll find out if we get to stay.

WE DO A QUICK scan to determine if anyone is nearby. When it comes back clear, I drop the ramp and walk out, stepping onto Iona's surface at last. I walk to the precipice so I can feel her insistent wind in my hair. Random pieces of sand sting my face as I shield my eyes and look out.

Arden joins me, wrapping his arm around my waist. We stand in silence for some time.

"What now?" he asks.

"We wait," I say. "Fallon will understand that ping from Meridian Station was from me telling her to come here. So, I'm hoping within the hour? If not, I'll walk out and give the old headset a try."

Arden nods silently. His eyes are fixed on the distance without really looking at it, and his face is drawn and worried. I know he's thinking about all the things that have to come together for us to stop Cabot-Klaar. It's become as heavy a weight for him as it is for me.

I think briefly about sharing Yeva's message with him, but elect to keep it to myself. He's been incredibly good and hasn't even asked me about it, plus I'm not sure knowing our odds of being burned up by Isoflare are 50/50 would make him feel that much better. It certainly hasn't worked that way for me.

We head back into the ship to wait.

Twenty-two solar hours

I expected Fallon to magically appear in the cavern the instant she got my ping, but after half an hour and no sign of her, I'm wondering if something went wrong. Maybe the message didn't make it through. Maybe she thought it was trash and deleted it without looking at it. Maybe something pissed her off this morning and she threw her holo at the wall ... again.

I pull out my old headset, dangling it from my fingers. "Should I try this?" I say aloud, asking myself more than Arden or Xeric. "It's risky. It could blow the only chance we have."

"It could," Arden says. "Or it could give us a chance we wouldn't have otherwise, if something's really gone wrong. How do you feel about using it?"

"Not great."

"There's your answer."

"But ..."

Xeric interrupts. "Two things: number one, Scruffy's right, trust your gut. Number two: my sensors show someone's coming. Two someones, in fact."

Two someones? Not just one? I have a momentary vision of Fallon being forced against her will to lead Breton Cabot-Klaar to the cavern to apprehend us, and it makes my stomach clench. The vision is dispelled when I hear Fallon say, "What the hell am I looking at ... ouch, for sand's sake, my eyes!" and Wenda stage-whispering, "What's this? Hello?"

I bolt down the ramp into the cavern and throw my arms around my friends, who have just crossed into *Gabriella's* sensor range. Fallon is blinking furiously and already looks cross. Wenda has tears in her eyes that have nothing to do with the ship's biometric imprinting.

"I'm so happy to see you," she says. She stuffs into my arms a lumpy warm bag that makes my heart sing with its wonderful fragrance. "I brought muffins."

We sit together on *Gabriella's* flight deck and talk as we devour the muffins. I explain the ship's biometric cloaking, and how I came to have a virtual crew member. Fallon is a bit disconcerted by Xeric's presence, but he's part of my crew so she'll just have to get used to him. He does thoughtfully floats up so she can have the chair behind the comm deck, then positions himself behind her, just out of her line of sight. I can tell by his delighted smirk that he's enjoying her discomfort. Fallon's met her match at last.

"Now that I'm the very important Embedded Trade Director, it took me a moment to get away after I got that mysterious ping," Fallon explains. "And of course I had to run by the pod and get Wenda. If this had turned out to be some kind of setup, we were going to pelt the enemy with muffins until they surrendered."

"I knew it was you," Wenda says, "but why the subterfuge? Why not just fly in and land and let everyone greet you? You're both far more popular here than the Success Team."

"It's a long story with a lot of moving parts, but the bottom line is that Iona is in tremendous danger, Breton Cabot-Klaar is even more of a monster than we realized, we have to do something to stop him, and we have less than a day to do it," I say. "No one else can know we're here just yet. Fallon, what's your feeling about Gemma Laurel? Do you think she'd be an ally for us?"

Fallon considers the question for a moment before responding.

"Aside from being a hugger, which I find utterly horrendous, she's generally pleasant and easy to work with. She tends to come down on the side of doing right by Iona whenever there's a disagreement. The Success Team has been arguing in private a lot recently, according to my mother, and Gemma seems the most put-out about it. So that's a possibility."

"What about Jarek Shimauy?"

"He's really disengaged. I wouldn't count on him."

I look at Arden. "Then we were right. Gemma Laurel it is. Xeric?"

"The recording is routing to the chip imprinter now," Xeric responds. A few seconds later, a small blue chip pops up from the communications console in front of Fallon, who startles at the sudden motion. Xeric smirks.

"That's a meeting between Yeva Darwin and the Chair of the Governing Council, Benta Sarsen," I explain. "It includes some specific accusations regarding Breton Cabot-Klaar. There's also documentation outlining what we think is about to happen and why. Give that to Gemma, make sure she listens to it as soon as possible. If she seems sympathetic, you can offer to connect her to us, and if she agrees, bring her here. Report back to us as soon as you can, and if it turns out you need a place to hide, come here."

"There's also going to be a live broadcast in about four hours that we want as many people as possible to see, but especially the members of the Success Team," Arden says. "If there's anything either of you can do to draw attention to that, it would help."

Fallon takes the chip and tucks it into her jacket pocket, her face crinkling with concern. "This sounds more serious than a random Company takeover. What do you think is coming?" she asks. "Or is it better if we don't know?"

"I don't want to get into the details. We hope the upcoming broadcast and some other things happening over the next few hours will make Breton Cabot-Klaar show his hand. We're hoping that we have more time, but it's possible that everything will come to a head in ..." I look over to Xeric.

"Twenty-one hours," Xeric says.

"Then we better get started."

My two friends head off on their mission, and Xeric floats down to the chair behind the comm controls. "That blonde woman is too jumpy; I'm not sure you should count on much from her," he says, flipping silver hair out of his eyes. "What was her name again?"

"Her name is Fallon and I'd be extremely careful if I were you. She'll delete you in a heartbeat and not feel bad about it for an instant," I say.

"Ah," Xeric responds, an irritated expression crossing his face. It's an expression I've seen Fallon herself wear so many times in the past that it would have made me laugh under normal circumstances. But right now, we're stuck in a holding pattern waiting on the actions of other people, and all I can hear is the ticking clock.

Twenty solar hours

Arden's nodding off in the copilot's chair and I'm fidgeting when Xeric calls out, "Three people approaching. Only one previously authorized."

I hurry to the ViewPort and bring up the rear camera, which points toward the only interior entrance to the cavern. Fallon comes into view, reaching back to help the other two across the rocky threshold, and I'm relieved to see both Gemma Laurel and Fallon's mother, Dr. Janelle Heron, crossing into the cavern proper.

"Scan both newcomers and add to the active state of the biometric recognition system," I instruct.

"On it," Xeric says.

I watch as Fallon leads them toward the ship. They can't see it yet, and they're both confused.

"Fallon, what is this?" her mother says archly. "There's nothing here."

"There's a ship here. Give it a second."

"I don't see anything but a weird glow ... ach! Gracious me!" Gemma Laurel stops in mid-sentence to cover her eyes with both hands, while Dr. Heron actually turns away.

"Yeah, sorry, the biometric recognition thing is intense," Fallon says.

The two older women look up and see *Gabriella* for the first time. Laurel seems shocked. Dr. Heron simply raises an eyebrow. "Impressive."

I hurry down the ramp to greet them.

Eighteen solar hours

Fallon returns to the ship after guiding her mother and Gemma Laurel back to Iona Town. In a startling moment of thoughtfulness, she brings us food, water, and a dozen bottles of good-quality brew. This is a much better notion than our original plan to survive on nutritabs.

"You took all this out of pod storage?" I ask.

"Sure," she says, diving into one of the sandwiches she procured. "I told Hinn I was hosting a business lunch. I just didn't say where."

"I'm relieved to have your mom and Gemma on our side. Did you get any sense of what they're going to do?" I ask. Our meeting was necessarily brief; both women quizzed me about the recording and my supporting evidence, and departed incensed and determined to take action.

"Gemma's horrified by that recording, but she's also big on official processes," Fallon says, taking a sip of her brew. "Mother was all 'let's just grab him and lock him up,' but Gemma wanted something more rule-based. They were looking up some Company regulations, and maybe bringing a few specific off-world Company officials into the conversation. I told her that was not going to help in the short term."

"It might help in the long-term, if there is a long-term," I say, "so that's something, at least. If we aren't able to hold him accountable, maybe they can."

Xeric interrupts. "It's time for the broadcast. Care to watch?"

"Yes, please. Bring it up."

The stream appears, floating over *Gabriella's* main console. A bright red banner features a countdown clock until the start of the broadcast. A legend at the bottom of the screen reads: "TAIMAR EXCLUSIVE BREAKING NEWS: FUGITIVES TO RETURN! WILL JUSTICE BE DONE?"

"What the hell ...?" I mutter.

"Nico warned me Taimar would be over the top," Arden says. "That's how they get their ratings. It'll be okay. Who knows, it might even give Cabot-Klaar a false sense of security."

The screen flashes, and the live begins. The stream jockey, an incredibly tall slender silver being of indeterminate race, species, and gender, stands in the brilliant blue vestibule of Lipop and Eidor's building.

"Taimar here!" they shout into the camera. "Exclusive, exclusive! Did you miss the news that fugitives who abandoned their home planet have been in hiding on Meridian Station? But their secrets are OUT, and they will now face me. Time for The Truth with Taimar!"

"Oh hey, Taimar," says Fallon approvingly. "I like their business content. Very savvy."

I'm a little surprised by Taimar's appearance; they look like a silver-sequined blanket with huge green eyes and a tiny waist. The only thing I recognize from the night we met in person are their height and the glittering purple ring worn on one pinkie.

"Why do they look so different?" I ask.

"Taimar always uses the Freak Filter," says Xeric helpfully. "In fact, they're known for it. People tune in just to see what the look is going to be for each streamcast. It's not just a gimmick, though. Taimar has a lot of followers, and if they looked on-stream like they look in reality, they'd never have any peace."

Silver-blanket Taimar turns to the lift in the center of the blue vestibule. A second later, the focus zooms in as the door slides open and Arden and I step out. I look anxious and spooked by the camera; Arden looks stoic.

"That's a neat trick," Fallon says around her mouthful of sandwich. "Are those filters too, or ...?"

"No, that's us," Arden says. "We recorded a video 'interview' before we left. Our friend Nico got one of his streamer contacts—Taimar, there—to come over and shoot some footage, and then gave the whole package to them to edit and produce as a live to broadcast today."

"So this is all fake?"

"As for being a fully live broadcast, yes," he responds. "But Taimar's a pro; it'll be hard for anyone to figure it out."

Taimar has done an amazing job editing the footage. And given our emotional state at the time, we're a perfect dupe for nervous fugitives planning to throw down against the Company.

The streamcast lasts about fifteen minutes. In it, I announce our "plan" to depart for Iona as soon as we procure a ship and secure a departure window.

"We hope to arrive before the deadline, but that might not be possible," I stammer to the camera. "We're going to do our best. If we miss it, it may only be by minutes. Iona is important to us, and we intend to prove it. Taimar, you're invited to cover our departure, if you want."

The view zooms in to Taimar's face. "YES to that," they say emphatically. "Taimar will be there. Watch for it!" The "live" concludes.

It's only a matter of minutes before the rest of the stream picks up Taimar's broadcast, and snippets of it begin appearing on every channel and platform. Most of them repeat the "fugitive" narrative, and several intersperse Cabot-Klaar's video presentation along with it. That's fine by me. It creates an unbreakable, uneraseable link between us, Cabot-Klaar, and whatever is about to happen to Iona. I just hope Cabot-Klaar saw it. And I hope it makes him quake.

SIXTEEN SOLAR HOURS

Two hours later, well after Fallon's departed and we've relocated to the bunk to try to sleep, Cabot-Klaar streams a video to all residents of Iona. Xeric pulls it up for us on the bunk ViewPort.

It's him alone this time, without the other members of the Success Team. He stands rigidly at the podium inside the comm center, his face expressionless and cold.

"I have learned some grave news that makes me extremely concerned for the safety of the people of Iona," he intones, his face spectacularly failing to back up his words.

Extremely concerned. Right. Taimar's Freak Filter looked more caring.

"Many of you have seen reports that former Chief Designate Faith Feathergrass and former Security Lead Arden Wilson are complying with my order and returning to Iona in person. They are reportedly attempting to arrive by my stated deadline, now sixteen hours away. I was initially heartened by this news, but I've received an alarming report that instead of a peaceful and cooperative return, these two plan a dramatic attack on this planet. While they claim to love Iona, the truth is they hate the Company, and to that end they intend to destroy everything the Company has built here. I do not know how far their hatred goes, if they intend to take lives or merely destroy property, but I do know they must be stopped. To that end, I will be working through the night to develop a strategy for the salvation of Iona. I'll share the details with a select group of Iona officials and members of the Success Team in an emergency meeting in Progress Center Building A in fifteen and a half hours' time. That will give us a chance to prepare, should they make the deadline—which, frankly, I believe they have no intention of doing. I call on all Ionians to be brave, and know that I and the Success Team are dedicated to keeping you safe from those whose morals are twisted by hate. Thank you."

The screen goes blank.

"He's going to try to pin this on *us*," I gasp. "He's going ahead with the attack and trying to make people think it's our doing!"

"That means it's going to happen at exactly the deadline mark," Arden says. "That Isoflare will destroy everything. A lot of people will be hurt or killed when it hits the Durawash that's coating all our structures."

"We have to find a way to get people to safety," I say. "Up into the ridges, into the caverns and caves. There a lot of places out past the northern edge of town. And the storage warrens are underground; people can go there. Is there enough space? How can we reach everyone and get them to somewhere that won't become a disintegrating acid bomb?"

"We have no way to contact anyone without giving away our position," Arden says. "How can we do that without Cabot-Klaar catching on?"

Suddenly an idea strikes me, and I sit up.

"Maybe we *don't* need him to not catch on," I say. "Maybe we need to do it right under his nose."

Arden looks confused. "What do you mean?"

"We know the timeline on the Isoflare. Let's simply head into town and start moving people to safety, a little more than an hour before the deadline. We'll start with my pod and yours. Those people know us and trust us. They'll help spread the word. I'll use the headset to send out a message to the general channel—or maybe Dr. Heron or someone else can. You and I can go around the square to all the buildings and let everyone we find know there's an emergency. We may not be able to get to everyone, but we should be able to get to most people."

"What about the people he'll be meeting with? What do we do about them?"

"We should be able to catch them on the way to the meeting. What is Progress Center Building A? Did they rename something?"

"That's the official name for those little beige buildings out near the landing pads. Remember?" he says. "They sent us those unusual materials already milled and finished, and you just had to stick them together?"

My mind goes back to those work orders and the strange materials we unloaded off the skiff and I blanch.

"Arden, those buildings don't have Durawash on them. If I remember right, the corrosion protection is a function of the strength of the material itself. The Isoflare won't damage them."

His eyes widen. "You're kidding. He's cherry-picking who to save. The people at his fucking meeting."

"We're going to pack those buildings full of Ionians," I say. "We'll see what he has to say about that when the drones come."

Fourteen solar hours

Fallon and Wenda return bearing more food and brew, and we watch Taimar's live broadcast—actually live, this time—of our alleged departure from Iona. Taimar's Freak Filter has outdone itself, this time turning the stream jockey into a purple rectangle with four arms, three sparkling blue eyes, and a tiara.

"We're outside Terminal Prime, where our two fugitives will be boarding a ship for the fourteen-hour flight back to Iona," Taimar says dramatically. "It will be one of those ships just there ..."

The camera pans, showing the transparent wall between the main waiting area and the brightly lit primary dock. The plexi casts a bluish tinge across the dozen or so ships we can see from Taimar's vantage point and warps the perspective slightly. It's a perfect shot if you're trying to obscure someone's identity.

The camera swings back to Taimar.

"We're waiting to see if our fugitives' flight plan is approved by Control; if so, they'll come from that direction," Taimar says, gesturing toward the farthest end of the dock. "They've requested special dispensation to leave outside a standard window in order to make their rapidly approaching deadline."

Taimar looks away from the camera, scanning the area behind them. "There they are!" they shout, pointing to the plexi wall. The camera finds three figures walking quickly toward a ship at the far end of the dock. The first individual I recognize immediately as Euclid Nam. The ship awakens as he approaches—it's the *Hideki*. He's followed by two hurrying figures wearing bulky parkas. The hoods on the parkas are pulled up, and the figures carefully keep their faces turned away from the plexi. There's very little anyone can see in the shot that's identifiable.

The threesome board *Hideki*. The ship's ramp retracts and a tug appears behind it, drawing it out of its berth.

"Our two fugitives are on the way," Taimar gushes. "I think it's going to be very hard for them to reach their destination before the deadline; they might miss it by mere minutes. I'll give you the news as soon as I hear it, and along with the conclusion to this story, I'll have a feature with some Station residents who know this pair well and know what they've been up to. Make sure to check in!"

The live ends.

"Who was getting on the ship with Lt. Nam?" asks Wenda.

"They hadn't hashed that out yet by the time we left, so that part will be a surprise," I say.

"Will they make it by the deadline?" Fallon asks.

"The *Hideki* will make that trip in five hours, so they'll be here in plenty of time. We just need Breton Cabot-Klaar to think they might not."

"So far, he's fixated on 'tomorrow's threat,'" says Fallon, making air quotes around the words. "My mother got an invitation to that meeting and so did Macha, but your Very Important Embedded Trade Director here did not. Gemma got one at the very last minute, almost like it was an afterthought, and Cabot-Klaar even told her the meeting was optional. But she's definitely going, and intends to ask him some hard questions afterwards. Why is he claiming you're going to attack Iona? You're obviously not."

I take a deep breath. It's time for Wenda and Fallon to know everything.

"An attack is coming, but not by us," I say. "I didn't want to mention it earlier, because I didn't want you to panic. We have a plan to get through it, but we're going to need your help to make it work."

Our friends are stunned as I describe what we've learned, and what we suspect is afoot.

"Why can't you just let everyone know now?" asks Wenda. "Surely that would put a stop to the attack, once everyone's been informed."

"It would give Cabot-Klaar too much time to work against us," I say. "He's already manufactured this story that we're about to attack Iona. What's to keep people from believing him if we suddenly appear saying 'hey there's an attack coming, you all need to get to safety'?"

"But if you're trying to save people ..."

"He'd find a way to spin it. And then he'd have us where he wants us, and he could still deploy the Isoflare any time he chose."

"What about Lt. Nam's ship? Why can't he intercept the drones coming from Bardazel?" Falon asks.

"It's likely the craft delivering the drones is equipped with some type of weaponry," Arden says. "We don't know that for sure, but we can't take the chance. The *Hideki* is a legal-build ship with no offensive weaponry. There's not much Euc could do, and we don't want to risk getting him into a dogfight we know he couldn't win."

After answering as many of their questions as we can, we settle in to talk about how to get 400 residents to safety in a hurry. I ask Xeric to create a map showing the nearest safe locations to each of the Residential pods and service buildings. We'll send out the map with the first alert, and hopefully at least some people will go on their own. Afterward, we'll try to direct stragglers to the closest safe place, whether that's a cave, a cavern, a storage warren, or the Progress Center buildings.

We've worked far into the night by the time Fallon and Wenda, still in bit of shock, make their way through the cavern and back to town. We'll meet again tomorrow morning, one hour before the planned attack, at the base of the ridge that runs behind Residential, and get to our own shelter locations at the five-minute mark. Wenda will join our pod members in the storage warren. Fallon wants to be with her mother, so she'll end up in Progress Center Building A, as will I. Arden will shelter in one of the other Progress Center Buildings after herding any stragglers inside.

As a last step, I work with Xeric to patch into Iona's audio communication channels. He'll be able to track what's happening and talk with us, and if it comes down to it, able to pilot the *Gabriella*, either to rescue people on Iona's surface or into near space to warn the *Hideki* not to land.

We've done everything we can do, and we're as ready as we can be. We curl up together in the bunk again, but neither of us can sleep. At least the closeness makes me feel warm, but I can't dispel the knot in my stomach or the clock in my head, ticking louder with every passing second.

Three solar hours

We give up attempting to sleep; we're both so restless that lying in the bunk is starting to feel more like imprisonment than comfort. Arden paces the width of the flight deck relentlessly and I sit in the pilot's chair reviewing and re-reviewing our plans. I was hoping to get a fix on whatever craft is bringing in the drones, which should be departing Bardazel any moment, but *Gabriella's* sensors are significantly hampered by the heavy rock surrounding us, and we don't want to risk trying to communicate with the *Hideki*.

Xeric keeps us informed of the time in quarter-hour increments. I make sure I'm wearing the loose-fitting parka and clothes that were printed for me on Dar Shal'O—they won't have any Durawash in them. Arden's also wearing a jacket printed on Meridian Station, although he's not sure about the origin of his remaining garments.

I wish we had eye protection.

I wish we didn't have to do this.

I wish a lot of things.

"One and a half hours," says Xeric.

Time to go.

One and a quarter solar hours

My heart is beating in my throat, and my breath comes short and shallow as we work our way down the path to the base of the ridge. Fallon and Wenda are already there, holding each other's hands in the pre-dawn dark. Wenda's eyes are wide, but she insists she's not frightened. "We're going to make it happen," she says. "We're going to save these people."

I pull on my old headset and ping each of them in turn—everything is working as expected. I tap into Xeric's channel and whisper, "Xeric, copy?" and he confirms. We go over the plan one last time; Fallon queued up the map for automatic distribution last night and will activate it from her headset just before I send out a ping to the general channel. That should hit everyone with a holo or a headset open, but some people are bound to have theirs turned off. Those are the ones I'm most worried about. We'll need to get to them in person.

I'm holding my breath listening for Xeric's signal.

"Counting down to one hour," Xeric says in my ear. "Ten ... nine ... eight ..."

I lift my hand to get everyone's focus.

"Mark. We are at one solar hour," says Xeric.

I take a last look at my friends, hoping like hell I haven't doomed all of us, and whisper, "Go!"

One solar hour

The map goes out just as Iona's weak sun begins creeping into view, shifting the dark horizon into pastels infused with light. The four of us move swiftly along the corridors as planned, and I hail into the General Channel.

"There's an emergency on Iona," I say, trying to maintain urgency in my voice without shouting. "Check your holo for a map and make your way to one of the highlighted safe locations. Tell others in your pod or workplace to do the same. It's very important that you do this quickly, we don't have much time."

Right away, a chorus of other voices pipe up.

"Is that Faith? It sure sounds like Faith!"

"What's the emergency?"

"I see the map! Heading for my storage warren now, I'll leave it open for others."

"Is this some kind of joke?"

Wenda and Fallon are on their headsets as well, encouraging people to do as I've asked. Fallon's running toward a small stream of people hurrying out of Residential and pointing them toward safety, Wenda's grabbed a sand scooter and is flying fast toward the opposite end of the Residential section to start pounding on doors. Arden and I run together until we reach the Preservation Theater, then he veers off to start a clockwise sweep of the service buildings arrayed around the square.

I run straight for Clinical.

Inside is pandemonium, with clinicians and patients shouting and crowding onto the ground floor. The first person I see is Pepper, the poor nurse who had the job of keeping an eye on me after my adventure in the Warehouse a year ago. I was a terrible patient. I hope she's forgiven me.

"Pepper!" I shout, and she turns.

"It *is* you!" she shrieks, and runs to hug me. "I was sure that was your voice on the General. What's happening? Is this different from the emergency we got instructions about last night?"

My stomach does a flip. "What instructions did you get last night?"

"That creepy bird-like Company guy sent a message to all medical personnel telling us we were needed in case of a medical emergency this morning. We're all to gather outside the Progress Center in about an hour."

"Outside the Progress Center? Not inside?"

"No, we're to wait outside for further instructions."

Dear sands, the prick was planning to off the entire medical staff. I shake the thought out of my head for now.

"We're going to work with that," I say. "Tell everybody to head over to the Progress Center. Only everyone's going inside, okay? No waiting outside. And we're going now. Hurry!"

Pepper taps her headset into the All-Clinical channel and repeats my instructions. She nods to me, and we head for the Progress Center.

HALF A SOLAR HOUR

People are milling around the Progress Center buildings when we arrive. Some are Clinical staff responding to last night's request, others were directed there by the map. Pepper takes over shooing people into Progress Center C, the building first along the path from the main part of town. There's no one around Progress Center B, which sits a short distance beyond and slightly behind C, so I run to Progress Center A, within sight and a little uphill from the rest.

Cabot-Klaar's meeting attendees are trickling in, although I'm sure there will be a few who wait until the very last minute—hopefully someone else flags them down and gets them to safety. Outside Macha waits with a handful of clinical staff; everyone seems confused.

"Get inside!" I shout. Macha's face breaks into a grin when she sees me, and she quickly herds her people toward the door. More Ionians are running up the path, and I wave for them to follow me inside.

Fallon is already inside with her mother, and Gemma Laurel stands with them. Jarek Shimauy, wearing a sour expression, stands in the corner attempting to message someone on his holo. It's not going to work from inside this building, and Shimauy hasn't been connected enough to understand all he needs to do is step outside. Dozens of rank-and-file Ionians now pack into the room; Arden comes through the door as well. So far, so good.

And then I remember the pit.

General maintenance, where I spent so much of my time in the past, is open around the clock. People could be working there now. I know from personal experience that in the maintenance pit, reception can be spotty, and it's common to turn off our holos and headsets altogether when working.

"We forgot maintenance, there might be people there," I say, starting to push past Arden. He stops me.

"I'll go," he says. "You need to be here when Cabot-Klaar arrives. This is your show."

He runs out again before I can object.

One-quarter solar hour

I stand in front of Building A, waving the last few people on the path inside and keeping watch for Arden. Wenda hails me on my private channel; she's completed the sweep of Residential, and it seems that most people have moved to safe spaces, but it's hard to get an actual count. There are some who weren't receptive to the message, though, and although the number is small, she wants to make another pass. There's not enough time. It takes me almost outright ordering her to our storage warren to make her give up on the stragglers.

I tap into the General Channel, urging anyone outside to safety. As I finish my message, I feel a cold presence behind me. I turn and look into the beady black eyes of Breton Cabot-Klaar.

His face is twisted in utter fury.

"What are you doing here?" he growls. "How did you get here?"

I draw up every nerve I have.

"I came home," I say, giving him my best 'f-off' glare. "This is my planet, remember? Chief Designate?"

"Not anymore. I'm in charge of this planet. The Company has turned full control over to me. And you ... you're under arrest as of this moment."

"Why? Because you say so? No, I think not."

His arctic white complexion reddens. He looks toward the door, where half a dozen people hover, watching. "Arrest her! Take her into custody!" he shouts.

No one moves.

"Do you want to know what he's doing?" I yell, making sure my headset is tuned to the General Channel. "He's going to destroy everything on Iona that isn't sand. He wants to develop Blue into an offensive weapon, and Iona's sand must be under his control for him to make the fortunes he intends to make."

A murmur runs through the people gathered in Building A. A few more seem to have moved to the doorway.

"He's sending drones right now, full of a chemical that will dissolve everything here. Iona will be rendered uninhabitable. He doesn't want any of you to survive."

Out of nowhere, Cabot-Klaar slaps me so hard my headset flies off, and I fall to the ground.

"Liar!" he shouts, advancing to stand over me. "You want control? You're not going to have it. I'm in charge here. You're no one. You will not destroy everything I've worked for!"

My brain is scrambled by the blow, and I taste blood in my mouth. I try to crawl away from him, but he grabs the hood of my parka, and yanks me to my feet, facing away from him. His hands close around my throat from behind; he nearly physically lifts me off the ground as he squeezes. He screams, "You will not win!"

"It's not ... a game," I gasp out, struggling to escape his grasp. "No one wins ... no one loses ..."

He roars angrily and squeezes harder. I'm fighting to get any air at all and beginning to see stars when suddenly I'm in free fall and out of Cabot-Klaar's grasp. I land in a heap against the outside wall of Building A. My vision slowly returns enough to see Arden, who's jumped Cabot-Klaar from behind and thrown him to the ground, and is now pummeling Cabot-Klaar's head with his fists, while

Fallon kicks him hard in the ribs with her unfashionable steel-toed boots. Gentle hands reach for me, and Gemma Laurel helps me to my feet.

I hear the sound of drones.

"Inside," I croak, pointing toward the drones. "Everyone inside!"

Gemma hustles me through the door, shouting to Arden and Fallon, "Get inside!"

Fallon stares out at the horizon, her face reflecting her terror.

Cabot-Klaar uses the moment to grab her ankle and wrench her off her feet. She falls heavily and cries out in pain.

"Go, Fallon! Now!" Arden yells, and throws himself on top of Cabot-Klaar again. Fallon hobbles inside and collapses in her mother's arms, wailing with fury.

Arden and Cabot-Klaar trade blows and roll across the sand. Arden's heavier and broader, winding up on top, but Cabot-Klaar is taller with longer arms that can still get off a devastating punch. I hover in the doorway, watching the sky. The sound of the drones is getting louder.

"Arden!" I shout. "They're almost here!"

Both men stop throwing punches to glance up. Cabot-Klaar knees Arden hard in the groin and shoves him aside, jumping to his feet and charging the door. Arden picks himself up and stumbles after the taller man, catching up with him just before he reaches the doorway.

"I'm not your fool today," Arden snarls, grabbing the back of Cabot-Klaar's jacket and jerking him back. Arden knocks his opponent's feet out from under him. Cabot-Klaar lands hard on his side, and Arden kicks him in the groin in return. While Cabot-Klaar screams in agony, Arden presses inside without looking back.

The whine of the approaching drones is undeniable now, and they're visible in the sky, turning the horizon dark. Cabot-Klaar sees them too, and his face for an instant becomes panicked. He can't quite stand, he can only crawl, and crawl he does—toward me, wedging himself in the doorway before I can close the door.

"You have to let me in, Faith. You know what will happen if you don't," he says. His voice is simultaneously pleading and insinuating. "Do you want that on your conscience for the rest of your life? Do you *want* to be responsible for someone's death?"

He struggles to use the doorframe to pull himself up with arm strength alone. He can't quite do it, and resorts to a crouching lean. He has to address me from below, looking up like a petitioner to a saint. I can tell he hates it.

"If you don't let me in, you'll be a killer. You'll be dealt with harshly, and all your accomplices the same," he growls. "You'll be imprisoned for the rest of your life, as will everyone you care about. How will you feel when that happens? Are you willing to throw everything away for this one moment of power and revenge?"

I study his face; he's not pleading, he's trying to intimidate me into moving out of his way. I have no doubt that if he could stand, he'd yank me out of the doorway in a heartbeat, just to take my place.

"Well?" he says, his pitch rising. "Are you?"

In my head, I hear Yeva whisper, *50/50 chance.*

"I'll take that chance," I say. I brace my arms on either side of the door and kick him in the face as hard as I can. He yelps and topples out of the doorway. I step back and slam the control panel so hard I nearly break it.

The door slides shut. The sliver of sky I can see through the high transom windows is black with drones. There's a sound like the heaviest rain as they begin to dispense their cargo.

Cabot-Klaar screams as the deluge goes on. At last, the drones retreat, and their angry buzz is replaced by the low-pitched whoosh of an interstellar skiff dropping down onto our landing pad.

I open the door at last to find Cabot-Klaar—and everything else—covered in a shimmery liquid that's doing no damage to anything aside from making it slightly sticky.

Fluoroclean.

I step outside, hearing it squish indelicately under my boots. I look up to the sky in what I hope is the direction of Dar Shal'O and laugh.

Cabot-Klaar looks like a wet chicken, his buzz cut and tailored clothing soaked through to his skin. He's injured enough that he can only manage a sitting position, so he's easy to contain for the few minutes it takes until Euclid comes down the path from the landing pad with the occupants of the *Hideki*.

"Introducing Arden Wilson, as played by Graham Thorn. And we're right on time," Graham says as he wraps me in a hug. Within seconds we're joined by Arden and Fallon as those sheltering in Progress Center A begin to trickle outside.

"I'm glad to be back," he says, looking pointedly at Fallon, who suddenly seems reluctant to let go of him.

We finally notice the other occupant, a small older woman with graying blonde hair and a stern face. She's no longer in the hooded parka she wore when we watched her board the *Hideki* on the live stream. Now she's wearing a full-length trench coat made of exquisite fabric. Peeking out from under it are dark green braid-decorated slacks—Governing Council rank insignia.

"This is Faith, and that's Arden," Euclid explains to her. "Everyone, this is Benta Sarsen."

Someone in the doorway behind me blurts out, "Chair of the Governing Council?"

Sarsen, even though her expression has been dour, cracks a small smile.

"Former chair. I've decided to hand off that position. But I have one last official act before my resignation takes effect."

She walks over to Cabot-Klaar, looking down at him with a mix of disgust and sorrow on her face. "You were like my own child," she says softly. "I believed in you; I couldn't imagine you could be so vile. You told me you had a vision, and that you trusted only me. And yet ..."

She trails off, waiting for him to reply. He looks up at her, and even in his diminished state, he manages to shift his face to a haughty expression.

"I suppose the axiom is true," he says. "There really is no fool like an old fool."

Her face first registers shock for an instant, but flattens within seconds, and she sneers at him in return. "A fool and his money are soon parted. You'll be returned to the GC enviro, where you will be charged with Crimes of the Highest Order. Your legal rights will be reviewed for you on the way. I'll see you at your evidentiary hearing. I'll be testifying against you rather than presiding."

"Once I present my evidence, your career will be a shambles," Cabot-Klaar snarls, angry and defiant despite being on the ground unable to stand.

Sarsen raises an eyebrow.

"My career is already over. It was in shambles the instant I made any kind of deal with you."

She turns her back and takes a few steps away from him before tapping what looks like a fancy broach on her lapel and saying, "One for incarceration, maximum security, returning to the GC enviro for legal tribunal." Within seconds, a GC Security ship lands on Iona's pads. Half a dozen officers file down the path and take Breton Cabot-Klaar into custody.

"Wow, that was smart," I say. "I never thought about bringing my own security force."

Sarsen shrugs. "When Lipop contacted me about this little drama, it seemed like an opportunity to make up for some of the damage I've done, and perhaps do a little good for other people."

"Well, thank you. For all of that," I say, and extend my hand. She shakes it warmly, then follows her security detail back to their ship.

Slowly people are filtering out of their safe spaces and taking in the aftermath. It's quite the mess, but at least it's biodegradable and should dry up before long.

Arden wraps his arms around me. "You knew something," he said. "You knew it was going to be all right, and you didn't tell me. Was that what was on the chip?"

"It wasn't for certain, so I couldn't afford to let anyone else think it was," I explain, leaning into him. "Yeva said a 50/50 chance. This time, we came up winners."

Gemma Laurel comes forward and wraps us in a hug; from of the corner of my eye, I see Fallon slip behind Graham and out of Gemma's line of sight.

"I have some official business to take care of," she says. "Can someone loan me a headset? Ah, thank you." She takes the headset and puts it on, and hails into the General Channel. "Can everyone hear me? Yes?" She looks around at the nodding heads and seems satisfied.

"This will have to be codified, but I want to take this opportunity on behalf of the Company to welcome Chief Designate Faith Feathergrass and Security Lead Arden Wilson home. In light of circumstances, it's only right that the Success Team depart with all due haste and leave you to do whatever you must for Iona. Before we go, I will fast-track your application to the Governing Council for Independent Core World status, along with my supporting testimony. I can say with absolute certainty it will be granted."

She takes both of my hands in hers, squeezing them tight.

"Faith," she says, "everyone. You've worked so hard for this. Iona is yours."

It feels like a dream. I'm vaguely aware of cheering coming from the people who now surround me and those spread out across Iona on headsets. It's a moment I've always hoped for, but never dared fully imagine.

"It's ours," I say through tears. "It's ours forever."

38

One Year Later

The Resident Services intake floor is quiet and empty when I at last close down my terminal for the night. All day, it's been a grand parade: people everywhere, lots of enthusiastic shouting, waving, laughing, and crying—me included. This morning, when I saw the first processing lines snaking around the building and out across the plaza, I got chills—along with a hefty dose of panic.

A bit of the old me resurfaced, and for an instant I wanted to run somewhere and hide. But I reminded myself I didn't have to carry it alone. I had staff trained and ready to work. I had friends cheering me on. I focused on getting everything organized and humming, and by the end of the day, everyone knew where to go and how to get there.

After months of planning, and more than a few moments of anxiety over whether we could actually pull this off, it's finally done. The Horizon Collective's first-ever Home Day is an enormous success.

As I stand up and try to stretch out the kink between my shoulder blades, the feeling in my gut is satisfaction. That's definitely progress.

"Xeric, assist me," I say, and the virtual assistant pops into view.

Figuring out how to get Xeric off my ship and into Iona's infrastructure was one of the first things I tackled once things got back to normal. With some programming help from Yeva and Nico, I was also able to give him significantly more autonomy: the ability to appear without waiting to be called into service, and to travel almost anywhere on Iona, with normal restrictions on entering people's private spaces uninvited.

"Congratulations on the day, Madam Coordinator," Xeric says. "The reviews so far are universally positive."

"That's great to hear. He/Him today? I like the pink."

I made sure our programming changes gave Xeric full control of his physical appearance, voice, and gender presentation. He's kept it lively, changing up his hair, eyes, and facial characteristics for special occasions, and he's experimented with a variety of gender-bending appearances. A slightly more mature version of his Dar Shal'O self seems to be the favorite, though.

Xeric beams and runs a hand through his short-cropped pink spiky hair. "Yes, and thank you. I wanted to do something festive for Home Day. Now, what do you need?"

"A quick report on citizen numbers for both planets, if you please?"

His eyes close briefly before he speaks. "Iona citizens stand at 421. Arden will have to verify Bardazel numbers, but that looks likely to land at 375. Add *in absentia* petitions and those who were unable to select a home world for whatever reason, and the Horizon Cooperative represents 865 verified citizens."

I'm elated, proud, relieved—and a little sad. Today we began a new era. We welcomed so many people to both Bardazel and Iona, but also said goodbye to some I've come to think of as family.

"Thank you, Xeric. That's all for now. Will I see you at the pod later?"

"Absolutely. I'll pop in to say good night, but feel free to shout if you need anything before then. Enjoy your evening."

With that, he disappears.

I rub my hands over the gradually receding knot in my neck and dismiss the lights in Pauly's office—my office, I remind myself again—and walk down the hall to the main processing floor.

A few of the terminals are still running, their displays flickering in the air. I wait until they complete their shut-down processes and the last one goes dark. Taking one final survey of the room, the stark intake bay of ten years ago flashes into my mind—two terminals, a handful of strangers, everything terrifyingly new to me. So much has changed since the day I took my first steps on this planet.

But some things are the same.

I step through the double doors onto the portico, where my friends linger in the settling twilight. Pauly sits in his hoverchair, holding Fanny's flask in his mechatronic left hand. He turns his head toward me and grins. His reconstructed eyes glitter like holographic gems in the receding light—he wears a set of sensory contacts that scan and reproduce what's in front of him in 3D for his brain. It's not great for peripheral vision and sometimes scenes with very low contrast can be difficult for him to "see," but he's learning how to work with it and seems happy.

"THERE she is," he booms. He's been out of stasis for eight months; his voice has regained its original volume.

Fanny sits on a huge stuffed pack next to him. She takes the flask and offers it to me. I accept and savor the sharpness of the liquid, looking out at the landscape. Iona is peaceful and calm; the plaza and sidewalks are all but empty, as though the crush of people we processed was only in my imagination. Now, many of those people are settling into new pods along the ridgeline, enjoying a meal and getting to know their podmates. Others are disembarking from the skiffs that carried them to Bardazel, newly terraformed and greened by Yeva Darwin. Today, all of us together became citizen-owners of the independent Horizon Cooperative.

A thrill burns through me, as scintillating and fiery as Fanny's brew, and I have to blink happy tears from my eyes.

Wenda and Fallon sit on the steps, watching our pale little moons climb into the darkening sky. Wenda looks up and pats the step next to her, and I sit down with an exhausted but gratified sigh.

I grin as I pass Fanny's flask back to her.

"Are you two on the last skiff out?" I ask.

"We are," Fanny confirms. "Departure will happen once the twins get all of their crap loaded. I don't know how teenagers manage to accumulate so much junk when there isn't much junk here to be had."

"I'm to blame for that," says Wenda. "I gave Hinn a whole set of cookware and knives to take with him. That's important for a budding chef to have."

Fallon snorts. "You and Hinn aren't all to blame. Half of Holly's stuff is actually *my* stuff she raided from my personal storage. The other half is mouse stuff. Lucky leads a fancy life." We all chuckle at the mention of Holly's pet mouse, a gift from Fallon after her antidote revived him from stasis.

Fallon's face crinkles in a momentary surrender to emotion, but she recovers quickly. "I can't believe I have to order that burgundy jumpsuit *again*."

Fanny cackles. "I'm going to miss living with you, Fallon. You're such a shit."

She holds out the flask and Fallon takes it. "I am," Fallon says, throwing back a gulp. "It's a talent of mine." She offers the flask to Wenda, who declines with a shake of her head.

"You okay?" I ask, touching Wenda's arm gently. The last few months have been a roller coaster of emotions for all of us, but especially for her.

"Yes, mostly," Wenda says, still studying the evening sky. "I'm a little sad. I'm going to miss Quimby and the twins and all of the people who came here from Bardazel, but I can understand why most of them would want to go back."

"I wish Maybree could have stayed with us," I say. I also wish she hadn't tried to kill me, but that's an entirely separate discussion. "I think she made a good decision to go home to Caleighn, but we're her family too. Please let her know she's welcome here."

"Oh, she knows. She's already said she'd like to come back once she's better. Maybe I'd like Caleighn, though. She's invited me to visit her, and I will."

Despite her calm, understanding words, there's a touch of misery in Wenda's eyes. My heart breaks for my friend, and I wrap my arm around her shoulders. I want so much to tell her she deserves more than being trapped in mourning over a relationship frozen in time and derailed by outside forces. I know, after all, from personal experience. But nothing I say will change how she feels right now. I know that from personal experience too.

My thoughts are interrupted by Pauly shouting "FINALLY! Time to GO!" We all turn our heads in the direction of Pauly's gaze. The dim light of our anemic moons isn't strong enough for those of us without sensory aids to see anything, but as the lighted sidewalks begin to glow, Arden emerges from the dusk, walking toward us.

"The twins are sorted and we're waiting on you," he calls out. "Are you ready?"

My pulse rate creeps up a tiny increment at the sound of his voice. Pauly raps his metal-and-plexi knuckles against the arm of his hoverchair in makeshift applause. Fanny stands up and starts working to shove her oversized pack into a compartment in the back of Pauly's chair.

"You can't carry that on your own? You've gotten soft, sister," Pauly barks affectionately.

"Dear brother. You know carrying heavy shit has never been in my job description."

"You don't have a job description."

"My point exactly. I should have one, based on everything I put up with from you."

"And I deserve hazard pay. Don't jostle the chair! It's giving me vertigo."

It's good to hear them banter this way again, particularly given Pauly almost didn't survive. Fanny became a stronger person during his absence, but she was missing a spark that only interaction with her brother could reignite. This is one case in which I'll never complain about receiving the Company's help.

I stand, along with Fallon and Wenda, to hug Pauly and Fanny goodbye. Fanny continues to threaten Pauly's stability by jamming more parcels into the back of his chair, and they descend to the sidewalk as Arden reaches the portico and mounts the steps. He greets me with a kiss and wraps his arms around me for a moment. When he releases me, his expression is calm and satisfied, and I feel my own expression mirroring his.

I never imagined I'd enjoy serving as Iona's Governing Coordinator, but I love the work so far and I'm actually good at it. Apparently, the only person surprised by this is me.

And Arden is a fantastic Governing Coordinator of Bardazel. On such a new world with no set social system, not to mention the all-new terrain, the challenges he faces are more surprising and complex than the ones I deal with here. He was the logical choice once Graham accepted our proposal and became the Cooperative's representative to the Governing Council. Graham surprised us both when he hired Yeva to terraform Bardazel and then literally gave the planet to us—and by extension to its eventual citizens—to form the Cooperative. Full control of Bardazel was the sole thing he fought for before he cut ties with his family for good.

"Big job we got done today," Arden says. "Do you have final numbers?"

"Xeric says 865 citizens total, with 47 *in absentia* petitions for citizenship. Those people can choose their home world when they next visit the Cooperative."

"Maybree, obviously. Who else?"

"Graham, Dr. Heron, and Euc, to name a few. Yeva's petitioned for citizenship also. There were a few irregularities in her application, given her absolute intention never to live here, but I'm inclined to grant it." My lips tick upward in a sardonic smile. After what we went through, Yeva could ask for my first-born child plus a kidney and half of my teeth and I'd consider it.

Arden chuckles. "If I'd done what she did with Bardazel, I'd want to be a citizen too. It's beautiful. I find some new wonder every day."

"It's truly stunning. I'm glad the Governing Council rescinded her censure. She's incredibly talented."

Arden pauses, awkwardness overtaking his face for an instant. He looks away from me, out over Iona's whispering sand.

"You might want to spend more time on Bardazel before it gets crowded," he says, his voice a bit too tight to pass as nonchalant. "It's going to be popular with Stationers looking for a planetside getaway. Lipop and Eidor have already booked a second honeymoon with us. Apparently Yeva got some of her floral design ideas from Sharj."

"I'll come for a long break, after things get more settled here," I respond, keeping my voice casual despite the sudden constriction of my throat. I've dreaded this moment. I know he's going to try to talk me into or out of something, because despite all of our discussions and planning and decisions made with perfect clarity and clear intent, Arden is still Arden.

On cue, his expression becomes earnest, almost pleading, and he turns to face me. His mouth opens, but instead of speaking, he catches himself, swallows his words, and lets out a long breath. He says, "I'll look forward to it."

The smile that accompanies his statement is genuine, warm.

A decade ago, I would have been heartbroken he wasn't trying to convince me to give up everything to be with him. Two years ago, I would have been delirious with joy that he didn't try to convince me. Now, I have to laugh. The Arden I wanted—the one who respects my choices and leaves my decisions to me, doesn't press and doesn't argue about what is best for me—is the man I now have. And somehow, that makes it harder rather than easier to stick to my decisions.

But this is what I chose—what we chose—for now. And it's good.

A soft silence descends around the two of us as we watch our friends straggle down the path toward the last skiff to leave for Bardazel, the true finale of Home Day.

There's a sudden fuss coming from the lighted pathway, as Pauly's chair again becomes in imminent danger of tipping over. Fallon shrieks a warning and she and Wenda leap into action to right the chair and steady Pauly.

There are several energetic-but-unintelligible exchanges between Fallon and Fanny before Fallon yanks the largest pack out of the chair, slings it over her back, and literally hurls a second smaller pack to Wenda. Fallon then stomps down the walkway into the dusk at impressive speed, grumbling loudly and occasionally shouting a nearly distinguishable expletive. Fanny and Pauly move along the sidewalk behind her, not even trying to match her pace, with Wenda bringing up the rear.

Wenda catches my eye. "I'm going to make sure these two get onboard without killing each other—or anyone else. I'll see you back at the pod." I acknowledge her with a wave.

Funny how everything is in balance now.

Well, almost everything.

Arden scrubs his foot against the sandy portico tile, his eyes locked on Pauly and Fanny receding into the dusk.

"I love you," he says, taking my hand and squeezing it. I squeeze back, feeling warmth swell in my chest. It wouldn't be terrible to go with him, to live in Bardazel's flowering jungles, to wake up to his face every morning. And really, it's not a thing that's out of the question. But this isn't the time. I'm focused on looking after Iona and seeing our vision for this planet and the Cooperative come to fruition. And we both still have some things we need to prove to one another.

I take a deep breath.

"I love you too," I say.

In the distance, Fallon shrieks, "Where is the damn pilot? Arden, hurry up or I'm taking this skiff myself!"

"I believe I have to go," Arden says, his expression shifting to vague irritation. But he doesn't release my hand.

"You'd better. I know for a fact Fallon can't fly a skiff, but that wouldn't stop her from trying."

He kisses the back of my hand, then pulls me into his arms for a long embrace, kissing me with heartbreaking gentleness. We separate, and he moves down the steps to the pathway. At the bottom, he stops and turns to face me again.

"I'll ping you at bedtime, like usual. Yeah?"

"Yes, good," I respond.

A genuine, tender expression spreads across his features, and my own face mirrors his as we lock eyes. In that moment, I'm certain everything is possible—with him, with us, with the new cooperative, with these two little planets linked in a dance of support and sharing.

In the distance, Fallon yells Arden's name at a terrifying volume.

"Coming, coming!" he responds. With a last wave to me, he turns away and jogs into the dusk toward the pads.

I wait on the portico until Fallon comes into view, then walk down the steps to meet her. She hugs me wordlessly and together we watch the sky beyond Iona's dark horizon until we see the bright spark of the skiff leaving atmosphere. A tiny pang of wistfulness flickers in my chest. Fanny was one of my best friends here, Pauly like my own brother, and Arden the lost love of my life returned to me. Although they're not so far away—the skiff ride to Bardazel would only take an hour or so in *Gabriella*—it's still going to be strange not to see them every day.

"Arden looked disappointed," Fallon says, breaking the silence before I can become maudlin. "You must not have fallen for his latest line of bullshit."

"He's grown. He only tried once, and it was a half-hearted attempt at that."

"You've grown—you told him no."

"I told him *eventually*. It was easy."

I'm not being entirely honest. Fallon's expression suggests she knows, but for once she doesn't call me on it.

"It was necessary," she says, her tone significantly less acerbic than usual. "Come on, let's head back to the pod. I hear Karloa is making something particularly disgusting for dinner."

I snort. "You mean *healthy*?"

Fallon shrugs. "I said what I meant."

"You're the worst," I reply, but I'm smiling as I say it. Fallon's right—I've grown. My optimism can't be crushed for long—we have so much to look forward to on Iona, and I'm excited for what the future will bring, for my part in it—for all of our collected efforts.

I link arms with Fallon, and we stride across the sand toward home.

Thank you for reading *Beyond This Dark Horizon*! I would be so grateful if you left an honest review, on any platform of your choice.

- Learn about future releases, sales, and special events, subscribe to my newsletter, *Unreliable Narrator:*
  https://www.emarierobertson.com/get-my-newsletter/

- Get an inside look at the writing and publishing process in my FREE Patreon:
  https://patreon.com/emarierobertson

- Scan the QR code for FREE bonus content! Use password: XERIC (case sensitive, make sure you use all caps!)

Use password
XERIC

ACKNOWLEDGEMENTS

IF I ACKNOWLEDGED EVERYONE who contributed to my author journey, the acknowledgements section would be longer than the novel itself. Instead, I'll try to keep it brief and focus on the people who make my job a joy and my work a daily excuse to have fun.

Big thanks to my editor, Lisa Lee, for her tremendous skill and unending patience. Thanks to my husband John Sams, for being such a kind and thoughtful alpha reader, not to mention an awesome spouse; I'm so lucky to have you! Major shout out to the Speculative Fiction Writers' Discussion Group OGs (Marc, Michelle, Logan, Tracey, and Joe!) for their honest feedback throughout the development of this novel. Your miraculous ability to read the same "tweaked" 1000 words of text without throwing me out of the group in annoyance is much appreciated.

Special thanks to Shay Jordan-Hrobsky of Soul Fueled Life for walking me through the fetid swamp that is social media advertising. She managed to explain it to me like I was five without making me actually *feel* like I was five.

Thanks to my sisters of the Super Sea Hags Collective for their motivation, empathy, and comic relief; and to the Young Women's Luncheon Club for that much-needed Oasis in the Day.

I must also recognize the many fun folks in the Wild Green Memes for Ecological Fiends Facebook group, who make me laugh every day, and to thank them for unironically providing the name of one of my characters (you get to guess which one).

I've been incredibly fortunate to be part of several "random" groups that somehow felt like family from the very moment I found them. Key among these are Sarra Cannon's Heart Breathings Writing Community and the HeartieCon crew; Amber McCue's Freshly Implemented/Modern CEOs; and best of friends The Old Crew. These groups each became crucial at different times in my life, and despite moving through different seasons, professions, focuses, and mindsets, the closeness and comfort I feel with all of them has never changed. Your support is invaluable and I'm so grateful for all of you.

Most of all, I want to thank all of the readers of my first book, *Nothing Larger Than These Stars*. I so appreciate your enthusiasm, and especially the great reviews! I hope you love this book just as much, and are looking forward to the many more books to come.

About the Author

E. Marie Robertson began her writing career in the 3rd grade by penning an epic that involved a ghost, a cave, and a magical ham sandwich. While perhaps less epic, her current collection of works in progress include science fiction, fantasy, alternate historical, and romantic comedy.

She produces an aspirationally-monthly newsletter, *Unreliable Narrator*, and hosts an even more sporadically-produced podcast for writers, *Read Write Geek*. When not writing or podcasting (or worrying about working, writing, or podcasting), you'll find her reading, creating artwork, or making fun things out of paper. She currently lives in upstate South Carolina with her husband and nine rescue cats. They all dream of moving somewhere less humid.

Sign up to receive *Unreliable Narrator*, plus bonus fiction and sneak peeks, on her website at www.emarierobertson.com

Want to stay connected?

Use this QR code for all my links in one place: website, newsletter subscription, FREE Patreon, social media, ongoing promos, events and more!

Find clickable links to all my socials in one place!

www.ingramcontent.com/pod-product-compliance
Lightning Source LLC
LaVergne TN
LVHW010634110826
845149LV00014B/2842

* 9 7 9 8 9 9 0 4 3 0 2 2 8 *